The Winter Gathering

The
Winter Gathering

DEIRDRE
PURCELL

HACHETTE
BOOKS
IRELAND

First published in Ireland in 2013 by
HACHETTE BOOKS IRELAND

3

Cataloguing in Publication Data is available from the British Library.

ISBN 978 0 75533 233 5

Typeset in Sabon and Book Antiqua by Bookends Publishing Services
Printed and bound by CPI Group (UK) Ltd, Croydon, CR0 4YY

Cover photographs: snow scene © Mitchell Funk/Getty Images; figures
(left to right) © plain picture/Image Source, colinspics/Alamy, Dougal
Waters/Getty Images, Dmitry Elagin/Shutterstock, plain picture/Johner;
dog © YAY Media AS/Alamy; pine branches © mythja/Shutterstock
Author photograph © Colm Henry
Cover design www.cabinlondon.co.uk

Hachette Books Ireland policy is to use papers that are natural, renewable
and recyclable products and made from wood grown in sustainable forests.
The logging and manufacturing processes are expected to conform to the
environmental regulations of the country of origin.

Hachette Books Ireland
8 Castlecourt Centre, Castleknock, Dublin 15, Ireland

A division of Hachette UK Ltd
338 Euston Road, London NW1 3BH

www.hachette.ie

For Breda Purdue and Ciara Considine,
who kept the faith

ONE

My four friends first came to my house for Christmas dinner following my husband's desertion on 18 December 2002, over ten years' ago. They included my best friend, Mary Guerin.

Derek's departure came as a major shock, despite the difficulties he and I had been having for a few months, and I had worried that Christmas Day might not pass off without drama or tensions between the three of us: him, my sister Chloë and myself. Things had quietened down, however, and we were getting on well. Or so I'd thought. In fact, he'd been really nice to me, had even given me that year's Christmas present in advance some days previously. In a heavy black frame, it was a small, glorious oil painting of a magnificent red rose drooping over a wedding ring. 'You can hang it now so that you can enjoy it over the whole of Christmas, Dumpy.' (Dumpy, short for Dumpling, was his pet name for me; he was – is – a professional chef.)

1

I was over the moon. It was a genuine original, signed by the artist, Thomas Ryan, the first real work of art I had ever had. 'Derek! Can we afford this?'

'We can, we can. I had a better year than I'd thought I'd have, and the signs are that next year is going to be better still. It's this Celtic Tiger thing. We can't keep up with the bookings in the restaurant. Yer man is even thinking of opening a second. All going well, you might be looking at its head chef!'

'Oh, Derek, that's fantastic.' I hugged and kissed him. It wasn't only the status he'd enjoy, although I knew that was important to him: I'd been made redundant recently and a few bob more in the kitty would be wonderful.

I immediately took down the old print of a lakeside scene that had come from my parents' house and had hung over the mantelpiece in the sitting room for yonks, replacing it with the rose painting. I was looking forward to boasting about it to my friends as, happy out, I continued to go about ticking off the tasks I most enjoyed each year, conquering the Big Christmas Lead-in. By the eighteenth, I was optimistic that this Christmas might be the best ever.

How thick and unperceptive can one woman be?

I love Christmas, always have. I'm known for it and make no apologies for my devotion to the gleam and glitter of the season, despite the good-natured teasing of my friends. ('It's getting near the end of October, Maggie. Tree up in your house, I suppose.')

That morning, 18 December 2002, I had left home when it was still dark and Derek was in the bathroom, getting ready to go to work. Because of the manic nature of the traffic at this time of year, I had taken a bus and all morning had zipped merrily around the city centre doing bits and bobs of shopping, thoroughly enjoying myself. I'm always sent on a high by the Christmas atmosphere in Dublin city, where at the bus stops in O'Connell Street, with mountains of shopping bags impeding the queues, even the loud complaining is good-natured; with cries of the Henry Street vendors of tinselly tat, toys and chocolates almost drowned out by competing buskers and carol singers.

And although, when shopping, I'm a woman most at home on that northside street, at this time of year I present my passport at the Liffey Crossing and venture into the southside. There, I'm enchanted by the insouciance of the girls who totter on six-inch heels into the posh shops in Grafton Street to finger the spangled confections on the rails. I'm the audience for the same girls who, singly or in pairs, drop the pretence of sophistication as they ogle displays of solitaire diamond rings in jewellers' windows. I'm the fond smiler when I see young men half concealing bouquets of red roses under their oxters as they hug the walls on the way home. And so, despite what happened later that day ten years ago, I remain faithful to the shimmer and dash of December.

At around twelve thirty, I met a photographer friend for a lunch at which we exchanged gift-wrapped book vouchers of identical value and then, throwing caution to the wind – after all, Derek was now a Tiger Cub and on his way to greater things – I took a taxi home.

It was mid-afternoon when I opened our front door, dumped my parcels and, first thing, switched on all my Christmas lights. I was thirsty and decided not to deal with the packages right away but to put on the kettle for a cup of tea.

Then, out of the corner of my eye, I spotted a piece of jotter paper, folded over like a little peaked roof, propped against the lamp on the hall table. He'd marked it 'Urgent'. No doubt, I thought, he'd written it asking me to get something else for the Christmas dinner: he was forever experimenting and we never seemed to have some ingredient he absolutely definitely needed. I didn't really mind another trip to those crowded shops. I was tired, though; I hoped he wanted something I could find locally, rather than having to go all the way back to some speciality place, like the Italian deli in Smithfield.

I picked it up and unfolded it:

Sorry, Dumpling, but you must have known this was coming, I guess. These things happen. It's for the best. You'll see that eventuly and you'll be glad to be rid of me. Sorry. I'll ring you. Try not to worry too much. I won't leave you short. By the way I've left the stuffing recipe on the stove. I know how much you and Chloë loved that stuffing. Sorry, Dumpy. I really am. D.

Strobing from the Christmas tree, the lights winked and blinked. On. Off. On. Off. Incongruously, those TV warnings to us viewers, 'This broadcast contains flash photography', puttered through my mind.

On. Off. On. Off. I registered the little crescents of paper at the top of the page, ripped so forcefully from their retaining wires that they were untidy and uneven, bent every which way. Poor little bits of paper. Derek had big hands.

This didn't make sense. What did he mean, 'These things happen'? What things? Why was he apologising so much? I read it again.

On. Off. On. Off. I noticed the misspelling of 'eventually'. Spelling had never been Derek's strong suit.

On. Off. He had used the past tense, 'loved' – as in Chloë and I had 'loved' his stuffing. That brought it home. Sort of. Not fully. Not yet.

Whatever he had thought as he sat down to write this, I had not seen it coming. His irritability with me during those weeks in October and November – I could do or say nothing right – had been mystifying but I'd thought we had put it behind us, as I said. So, no, I had not seen this coming. At my feet was the lump of spiced beef I had just bought for our Christmas dinner. Spiced beef is a Cork speciality. Derek was originally from Cork. He had asked me to buy it, as he had every year of our marriage. It was very expensive. It wasn't that easy to find in Dublin. You had to order it from specific butchers. You had to travel. You had to earn spiced beef.

These days, I don't know if all that pertains – I have never bought it since. And while I customarily ate only a token slice or two, I had always loved the way its cooking on Christmas Eve filled the house with aromatic complexity. Thanks to Derek, at that time I associated spiced beef with Christmas. And Christmas with spiced beef.

Would I have bought spiced beef if I'd seen this coming?

Derek had left me?

On. Off. I looked down at the packages. At the top of my shopping bag, the Tesco luxury crackers still showed their silvery crowns through their cellophane window. The blackish, powdery spices continued to stain the double layer of white plastic in which the beef was sheathed. But Derek had left me?

From behind the closed door of the sitting room I could hear canned laughter: Chloë was ensconced in front of the TV. What was I going to tell her? She doesn't react well to change.

My brain rose from its sickbed, took a breath and logged on. Performed a search through its archives.

The improved atmosphere between us during the last couple of weeks.

The calmness.

The red rose—

My husband had been planning this murder. Buying that painting had been his blood money. Giving it to me marked a decision made after weeks of indecision and irritability. He had chosen his time well, had known I'd be busy all through December. I could see it all now. I'd read enough novels: I should have recognised the warning signs. Why hadn't I?

Nausea rising, I sat at the foot of the stairs, lowered my head and swallowed, forcing bile back into my stomach. The shopping bag, propped against my shins, keeled over, rattling against the tiles.

On. Off. The fairy lights were relentless. Who was going to cook the Christmas dinner for Chloë and me? I had never cooked a Christmas dinner. Ever. It was only one week from Christmas Day and, to judge by the fuss Derek always made about producing the food, with the kitchen a no-go area and I as his acolyte taking orders, it seemed incredibly complicated. It was too close to the day for me to learn how to do it.

Abruptly, I realised I was taking this seriously. I was already thinking of him in the past tense. Maybe I had seen this coming after all.

I got up again and switched on the overhead hall light; the colours from those on the tree instantly paled, losing their power over the piece of paper still in my left hand.

Well, at least he had left me the recipe for his famous stuffing.

Funny how the details blur the big picture, isn't it? My husband had left me but he hadn't forgotten that I loved his potato stuffing.

I can't find a word for how I felt as I picked up my shopping and went into the kitchen to put everything away. Dazed? Stunned? Neither even remotely describes it.

Panicked? No, panic would come later. It was still too soon.

Shattered? No. Not quite yet. Acceptance of abandonment, I discovered in the weeks and months to come, is a slow burn.

Stupefied? Closer, but it doesn't quite summarise the essence of being so unexpectedly and unpleasantly snookered.

There must be some adjective in the space between 'bewildered' and 'disbelieving'. Something that could adequately convey the winding effect of Derek's note. I was suffocating in the small kitchen where the air seemed to have thinned. Its pale yellows and greys, chosen so recently after weeks of poring over paint samples, now seemed not cheerful but gaudy; they pressed in all around me, dancing in my peripheral vision, while, like an automaton, I opened kitchen presses and closed them again without adding to their contents.

As for the dining alcove where Derek and I – and then Derek, Chloë and I – had eaten so many meals together, that now looked ridiculous. I had copied its window treatment of café curtains and swagged pelmets from an article in a magazine about beautiful homes in New England; had even bought myself a small sewing machine in Argos so I could make them. Now all I could think of was how stupid I'd been to have spent so much time on such a frivolous conceit.

My refurbishing efforts had been meant to surprise Derek: I had painted the kitchen and made the curtains while he was in Tuscany, taking a course in Italian peasant cooking, and on the night before his arrival home, I had worked on the finishing touches until after eleven to have it ready. That was only – what? – eight, nine weeks ago? I calculated. Nine and a half weeks – I pulled out a drawer, then found I had nothing to put into it.

'Hi, Dumpy!' he had said, having come through the door on his return, not even glancing towards where I sat, dizzy with anticipation. 'What's new?' He pulled open the fridge door to check on stocks. 'Hmm – no crème fraîche. Did you forget it? Remember I asked you?'

'Crème fraîche? Is that all you've noticed?'

'For God's sake, Maggie, I asked you to get me one thing when you were out shopping. Just that one thing. Could you not remember just that one thing? It's not as though you're overwhelmed with work, is it?' And he'd slammed shut the door of the fridge and stomped up the stairs. Our bedroom is above the kitchen and I heard him moving heavily back and forth, opening and shutting dresser drawers and the door of the wardrobe. After a few minutes of this he came crashing down the stairs again and called from the hall, 'I'm going out.'

'You just got home. Where are you going?'

'To get bloody crème fraîche,' he yelled back. 'And I'll probably go into town to check in at the restaurant. I need to see if I've been given additional shifts.'

'Could you not do that on the pho—' But the closing of the front door cut me off. I felt let down, furious that he hadn't said anything about my efforts, but also hurt. The gibe about work had been below the belt.

That particular spat happened around the middle of October 2002 and, although I didn't cop it at the time, looking back at this scene with the advantage of ten years' hindsight, I can see now that every thump of his size-nine feet that evening represented a nail into the crucifix of our marriage. Because, you see, much later, during one of the so-called settlement meetings about maintenance and so on, he finally admitted that he had met someone during his course in Italy. She had been a fellow student. I saw her only once, at a distance, about four years after he'd left me. The two of them were coming out of the Savoy cinema as, directly opposite, I was crossing O'Connell Street. She's tiny. A little dancing doll, pretty as a picture, the living antithesis of me. I didn't approach them.

On that jotter evening, shopping tidied away, I sat at my alcove table, staring at bottles of vinegar and ketchup, already placed in anticipation of the takeaway for Chloë and me. The lead-in to Christmas was always busiest for Derek, when his normal lunchtime shift was lengthened to encompass dinner. I hadn't expected him home until after midnight.

Now what should I expect? He'd said in his note that he'd ring. Should I ring him?

Maybe not. He hated it when I rang him at work.

But we hadn't discussed any of this. We had to discuss it.

Maybe this was just a whim. He could be a bit impulsive. A treacherous skein of hope showed itself. Maybe it had all been a mistake. Maybe Derek would come home with his tail between his legs and I'd have created a storm for nothing.

Of course I didn't know about the popsy that day.

But that little sliver of hope sent me to the hall phone. We had just got one of those handsets you can carry around with you. Thank God, I thought, picked it up and punched in Mary's number as I walked back into my kitchen. I didn't want Chloë to hear me. Ring him or not? Mary will know what I should do.

She answered at once. 'Hi there, kiddo. All set for the big day?'

'You knew it was me?' My voice sounded shaky. Maybe I wasn't all that calm.

'Just got one of those phones you have.' She sounded delighted. 'They're great, aren't they? That little panel on it where I can see the number of the caller. Christmas present to myself.' Then: 'You sound a bit odd. Coming down with a cold or something?'

'No. Not really.' I looked at my own handset, showing her number. Derek had got it for us about six months previously: 'Must keep up with the technology, Dumpy!'

'Cold? Maybe. Do I sound a bit snuffly? I don't know … ' I'd called to cry on her shoulder but, oddly, when put to it, I couldn't summon the words.

'Something wrong, Mags?' She'd caught my tone. 'Is Chloë all right?'

'Grand. Same ol' same ol'.' If I aired what had happened, it would be real. But it *was* real, wasn't it? The piece of jotter paper was right there on the kitchen counter beside the sink. 'Derek's gone.'

'Gone? Gone where?'

'Gone. He left me a note.'

'What do you mean, "He left me a note"? What did it say?'

'Are you just being dense, Mary? He couldn't even have the decency to use proper writing paper. He tore a page from a jotter—' Alarmingly, I could feel my throat constricting. I was not going to cry. I was not going to be one of those women who thought she couldn't live without a husband. 'Hold on. I'll read it to you.' I picked it up and, having swallowed hard, relayed in a steady voice the words my husband had thought apt to end a marriage. I did leave out the 'Dumpy' bit. I had grown rather fond of being called that because it was cheffy: lean and tall as I am, Derek's pet name for me had been ironic and, in present circumstances,

I didn't think I could say it without getting emotional. Anyway, 'dumpling' in others' ears, particularly Mary's – she would have leaped on it – meant I was doughy and compliant enough to float aimlessly in whatever liquid my husband had placed me.

She wasn't reacting. She was silent. I thought I could hear her thoughts crackle.

'What'll I do, Mary? He said he'd ring me. Do you think I should ring him? He's at work. At least, I think he is … ' I faltered. I knew nothing now, did I?

'Read it to me again.'

I did.

This time, she didn't wait. 'Stay there. Put the kettle on. I'm coming over.' Mary lived less than a mile away. We shared a bus route.

'Chloë – I don't know what to tell her—'

'I said, "Stay there", Maggie. We'll deal with that later – and anyway, if he is actually gone for good, what's the problem with Chloë? It's her dream come true, isn't it?' She hung up.

Stay here? Where did she think I might go? But that 'we', as in 'We'll deal with that', had been good. As I hung up at my end, however, the import of what had happened finally made a serious hit, causing actual physical pain in my solar plexus as I put on the kettle.

She'd probably been right about Chloë. Between herself and Derek competing for my attention, I sometimes felt like a little cat, standing on my hind paws with the front ones outspread, trying to hold off one of two dogs hell bent on eating each other. If they couldn't get at each other, they would both turn on me as the source of a snack.

Maybe Derek just couldn't take Chloë's presence in our house any more. He'd said that time after time but words were just words and he hadn't bolted. Up to now.

I picked up the potato-stuffing recipe that my husband had, indeed, left for me on our cooker – *my* cooker now. How thoughtful of him. How very nice. My first instinct was to ball it up and put it into the bin but, for some reason, I couldn't. Maybe this was all I'd have left of him. This and the jotter note.

I raced up the stairs to our bedroom. Hangers strewn on the bed. Drawers half open and empty. His nightstand, empty; the clock radio he liked so much – missing. All that was left on his side of the wardrobe were two pairs of old training shoes and the jokey Christmas tie I'd given him last year. I picked it up, sat on the end of our bed with it clutched in both hands and, for the first time, wept. Huge, hot tears of distress, but of anger too.

I was spent and still lying on the bed, that stupid tie clutched in both hands when, some time later, the doorbell rang. As I went down the stairs I heard Chloë raise the volume on the TV. She hated to be disturbed by visitors when she was in the middle of watching something.

Maybe he had just had one of his temper tantrums: had I forced Mary to race over here for nothing but hysteria?

'Thanks for coming,' I said, as I opened the door. 'I really …' but then I saw her, standing there in the bucketing rain, wearing a dowdy black coat, woolly hat pulled down over her hair. Mary has gorgeous hair, the colour of postcard sunsets. My voice wobbled and I could say no more.

She threw her arms around me, her strong signature scent, Shalimar, laced through with that of damp wool. 'Sorry I took so long,' she said, into my shoulder. 'I missed a bus.'

'You're not late – come in. I really appreciate this. You must be busy with Christmas and all.'

'For God's sake, what else would I do? I'm your friend, Maggie – I was the fucking bridesmaid at your wedding. It's what friends do, you clot!'

I was taken aback. Mary very rarely swore. She was definitely taking this seriously, I thought, the tendril of hope beginning to recede.

'Anyway, you're the Mrs Christmas here.' Mary let me go. 'Dear God!' When we were both inside under the light, she stood back to gaze at me. 'You look desperate. And you've been crying. Don't cry for that man. He's a snake. That's how you've got to see him now. A reptile. How dare he treat you this way and at this time of year too? He knows what it means to you.

'And on that score, one of the reasons I missed the bus is that I was making a few quick calls. No arguments, now, Maggie, we're all going to come here for Christmas dinner. Each of the others offered to host us and I would have too, but then I remembered Chloë would be uncomfortable anywhere but here.'

'Who are "the others"?' This was quite frightening.

'Me, Dina, Lorna and Jean,' naming the three who at the time were in the process of becoming friends with Mary and me. We're a clackety bunch but we seem to get on. 'I know you like them.' Mary began to unbutton her coat. 'I do too and we'll have a good time together. I promise. Who needs a man? They're just bad news, sweetie! They clutter up the place.'

'But … ' I had to smile, wanly, at her furious expression.

'No arguments. It's all arranged.'

'Who'll cook, Mary? Derek always—'

'Pish, tosh, Derek's loss. It's organised. We're all bringing a dish. You can do the drinks.' She glanced into the kitchen. 'Kettle on, I see. Good.'

'You'll need to boil it again.'

The relentless fairy lights blinked on and off as, still in the hall, we argued about provisions, particularly since I'd put deposits on all the Christmas meat and had already paid a fortune for the spiced beef. It felt good to have something concrete to fight about. I was still standing on the cliff with the abyss beneath, but with her presence, Mary had put up a fence. 'Anyway, Mary,' I said to her now, 'I'd feel better if I had a go at the cooking. It's about time I learned, isn't it? And if it turns out to be a disaster, well, we can fall back on the smoked salmon. I already have a whole side of that and tons of prawns in the freezer, shelled and ready. Derek likes to—' I stopped.

'Let's not bicker.' Briskly, she removed her hat and shook out her red hair. 'We'll reverse. You do the food, but we'll bring the drink. I'll ring them when I get home again – OK?' Then she noticed the ketchup and vinegar on the alcove table. 'Great. We're having fish and chips this evening, yeah? Ages since I had any. I'll go and get them in a few minutes – you have one of the best chippers in Dublin just around the corner, that right?'

'He got me a red rose, Mary.'

'Fucker! Where is it?' she yelled, looking around.

'Not a real one. A painting. It's over the mantelpiece.'

Instantly, she wheeled around. 'Don't, Mary,' I called, alarmed. 'Chloë's in there. She doesn't know any of this.'

'So what?' She sped into the sitting room, heels tapping on the tiles.

I went into the kitchen alcove and sat at the little table as though I was a guest. She had not even taken her coat off, but already I felt a small bit better. It was good to yield control to a paramedic, or a First Responder, as they're called now. She had cut me out of the crashed car and was going to take care of me.

It was late when she left that night with the painting under her arm. I never saw it again. One of Mary's jobs is as a part-time counsellor in a women's refuge and, with my permission, six months later, she put it up for auction at a fundraiser in aid of this and refused to tell me how much it had made. 'No need for you to know. But that bloody husband of yours has paid for repairs to the roof of the conservatory. No more buckets, thank God.'

TWO

That promise to cook for six people, my four friends, Chloë and myself, had not been my brightest. Because of it, I'd had a late night on Christmas Eve because, starting at just about midnight, I had stripped the Christmas tree of its lights, baubles and tinsel, ripping them off willy-nilly, not caring that in the process I was skinning the tips of my fingers and scattering pine needles everywhere.

All during that day I had struggled with preparations, mucking around in the kitchen, boiling potatoes, mashing them with fresh thyme, tarragon, butter, salt and 'freshly ground black pepper' – hate that phrase – as outlined in Derek's recipe for turkey stuffing. I'd done it all, I thought, when by chance I turned over the page and found that I also had to use chopped walnuts and 'a pinch of cumin'. A rummage through our store cupboard – my store cupboard – failed to yield such exotica and I had to dash again to the local shops in a (failed) search. Well, I thought, as I drove home, getting more agitated by the minute, we'd just have to do without the bloody walnuts and shagging cumin in the stuffing. I was usually slow to anger but fury, building gradually since the moment I had lugged home the bird and the ham, had possibly been liberated by the tranquilliser I had taken, prescribed by my kind GP while Derek and I had been having problems earlier: 'Just for two weeks, Maggie, to tide you over … '

When I was parking the car in front of the house, something caught my eye. A very large, Christmas-wrapped parcel at the front door.

It proved to be extremely heavy, and when I got it in and examined it, I found it was a wicker hamper, stuffed with champagne, three bottles of wine, red, white and dessert, a half-bottle of port and posh chocolates in a small, ribboned box. There was a chocolate log, chocolate fingers, a net of chocolate sovereigns, a box of After Eights, a bag of espresso coffee, six crackers, a big red Christmas candle in a porcelain holder, and a tea-towel illustrated with a picture of angels gambolling around a tree. There were several jars of those aspirational condiments you get for presents and never use – the organic 'natural' ones with the lumps, created in west Cork or somewhere like that; there were teabags, would you believe?, and a small sad poinsettia, bracts squashed under the hamper's crystalline covering, looking as though it wished it were already dead.

The hamper was from Derek, who had attached a Christmas card, a nativity scene, in which he had written: 'Hope this helps. D.'

Yeah, right. Very helpful. No sentence could contain what I felt about Derek and his mangy, mingy hamper. The coward, I raged, the effing, bloody, yellow, spineless coward. I wouldn't have been surprised if he'd been lurking around the neighbourhood waiting until the coast was clear before making his lily-livered bag drop and scarpering. It was the first contact since he had walked out. Obviously, he couldn't face me.

My first instinct was to bin the lot, but then I remembered my guests. I was glad of the chocolate, to tell you the truth. Dina, in particular, was a chocoholic; somehow I hadn't taken that enough into account, and although I had a couple of Terry's chocolate oranges, the larder was light on the stuff. She'd be delighted. Yes, we would all chew and drink our way through as much of this as we could and then the rest of them could take home what was left so I wouldn't have to be looking at it and getting annoyed. I gazed at the array: it had clearly cost a fortune. And, strangely enough, having up to that moment given no thought to my financial situation, I decided there and then to take my husband to the cleaners.

Revenge is not in my nature, though: it had been temper talking. And as my rage abated I found myself making excuses for him, even as I rescued the poor little poinsettia from its crackling tomb and gave it a drink. Life in this house had not been easy since Chloë had moved in.

On the other hand – I had put it down to the Christmas spirit – for the first time ever, in the second week of December, my sister, uncharacteristically happy, had helped me decorate our tree. She had made a real offer: 'I'd like to, Margaret. Are these the lights?' She'd picked up the garden-sized rubbish bag in which, the previous year, they had been so carelessly stored.

'Yeah. But they're all tangled up. It's a big job.'

'Not a problem. I'm not busy right now, Margaret.' She had

set about disinterring them, pulling them out in one great messy ball, looking not unlike that massive round sculpture thing, criss-crossed with road markings that some council or other had thought fit to put at the end of the Naas dual carriageway some years previously. 'Uh-ooooh,' she'd drawn it out dramatically, 'this is going to be harder than I thought.'

'Will I help you?'

'I said I'd do it, Margaret!' Flashing.

'Fine, fine,' I said hastily. The last thing I wanted was to ignite a row. 'Thanks so much. That's really great.' I rooted around in the second bag, pulling out tinsel and – 'Oh, good! There are three full packets of icicles.'

'Great!' She was kneeling on the floor in front of the mess of lights. It might seem slight, and ridiculous to make much of it, but this was an uncommon moment of togetherness between the two of us.

Ten minutes later, with all my baubles now marshalled in rows, I looked at her. She had successfully found the plug on one of the strings and, head bent, was patiently following its cable through the snarled wires and bulbs. I didn't remark on it because the key to dealing with Chloë, for me anyway, was to enjoy these small moments as they occurred. They were rare, and so fragile that the smallest comment, any intervention at all from me, could wreck them.

If only it could be like this every day. Unexpectedly, I felt tears fill the spaces behind my eyes. We were at odds most of the time, but I was all she had and I really did love her.

Christmas Eve, with the tree at full blinking pelt in the hall, I gazed around my kitchen at about half past eleven. It looked as though a battalion of small children had stampeded through it – and my mood was not improved by my mental survey of the culinary news. The smell of spiced beef throughout the house could not compensate for the fact that I had cooked it for too long. The ham glaze was nearly black when I took the joint out of the oven, and the vegetables in the giblet soup had turned to mush. When I checked in the fridge, the jelly in the trifle had not set: I had probably used too much of the juice from the fruit cocktail.

I had to work hard not to dump the lot. I was not only bushed, I was nauseous. I had given Chloë a pizza for her dinner in front of the TV, but for mine I had eaten most of Derek's chocolate log, followed by several handfuls of cheese sticks, washed down with half a can of Guinness. I don't drink Guinness, but the only single can I could buy in my local shop in which to cook the spiced beef had been one of those large 'draught' ones; I had needed only half for the cooking, and had left the rest to languish on top of the microwave. 'Waste not, want not' was my new motto and so, flat and all as it was, I had slugged it. Now I couldn't figure out whether I was feeling sick from it, from tiredness, from too much junk or because I needed real food. With Christmas dinner in prospect next day, it was too late to eat now, anyway.

And as if all that weren't enough, I discovered that while I would need at least twelve potatoes for roasting with the bird, I had only five left: I had used too many for the famous stuffing. Grimly, I peeled them, cut them into thirds and dropped the pieces, now officially called 'roasties', into a saucepan filled with cold water. By osmosis, I had absorbed a few cooking rules from Derek and knew that to soak naked potatoes in water prior to cooking was a complete no-no, but it wasn't Chef Derek with his spotless whites, starched weekly by yours truly, who still had a pile of unpeeled Brussels sprouts to deal with, was it? The pyramid of hard little greenery and I stared at each other. 'Tomorrow? OK with ye, lads?'

Jesus. Talking to sprouts now.

I seized the paring knife and started in on the little buggers. Halfway through, the knife slipped, slicing into the index finger of my left hand. I searched through a number of my 'everything' drawers for a large enough plaster to wind around it but had to settle for two small ones, butting one alongside the other.

I stared at them. At the blood seeping into the split between the two. At the offending knife beside the piles of sprouts, peeled, unpeeled, and peelings.

At the spuds winking at me through their water.

At the famous stuffing, smug in its bowl.

Despite nearly fourteen hours of slavery, this dinner was going to be an absolute pile of shite, the culmination of everything that was wrong in my life.

Feeling as though I had a propeller whirring painfully in my chest, I swept all three sprout piles into the bin, then kicked my way with both feet through the mélange of plastic wrappings, fallen vegetables and unspecified debris littering the floor. Then – for some reason I have never been able to find – I set out, through what seemed like a red haze in front of my eyes, to attack the Christmas tree.

As I yanked at the first branch, I relished the sharp sting in the injured hand. Enjoyed that.

It felt great to tear at the tinsel, to rip off the light cords, then to throw handfuls of baubles into the air and over my shoulder, listening with great satisfaction to them popping, bouncing and rolling all over the tiled floor.

As it happened, thank God for their plastic cheapness. A

few minutes later, with the red mist clearing and noise abated, I surveyed the multicoloured chaos I had created, the few remaining strands of tinsel hanging forlornly from the listing tree, the coils of lights and cords strewn and tangled at the base, all six twisted strands of them. It would take me ages just to separate them again, never mind reinstate them. And now both my hands were throbbing and sore.

Dismayed, I sat on the stairs, dislodging a few baubles. And as the last one rolled to rest against the door of the sitting room, a revving engine some distance away accentuated the profound hush outside. Inside, all was quiet too, except for the gentle, rhythmic purr from upstairs where Chloë slept. Guilt rushed in to replace temper. It wasn't fair to her that I had destroyed all that patient, uncomplaining work. I had no option. Tired or not, I had to put the whole thing back together again before I went to bed. With leaden legs and fingers burning like sods of turf, I did penance for losing my rag and started on the long haul of making repairs.

The guilt was confined to Chloë. Pushed to the limit, as I had been, after a lifetime of restraint and being a Good Girl, the tantrum had felt righteous, even energising. For the first time in my life, I had some understanding of how adolescent rock stars feel having trashed their hotel rooms: a combination of ruefulness – all that financial compensation due – and peace. All I wanted now was bed and dreamless sleep. But it was well after two o'clock by the time I had finished the job and got there. Belligerently, I changed my alarm setting to nine a.m. My guests would just have to understand. Anyway, they weren't due until four.

When my alarm shrilled next morning, my first reaction, as always, was to listen for movement in Chloë's room but all I could hear, still, was her medication-induced snoring.

Grand.

Then I heard how unusually silent the house was, eerily so.

Outside too – no traffic. Well, that was to be expected, with the neighbours, no doubt, involved in their own family matters or maybe at early Mass. There was some extra dimension to the hush, though: even the ticking of the old-fashioned alarm clock on my nightstand seemed thick and muffled – and the humming of the fridge downstairs was so loud that the appliance could have been in the room.

What was going on? I stumbled out of bed, parted the heavy curtains at the window – and had to squint against the light. Snow: real, foot-deep, 'white Christmas' snow had transformed the world in the six and a half hours since I had retired. Snow glistened under a huge, red-orange sun hovering over the roof of the house at the end of our cul-de-sac. Snow covered the roofs of all the houses, garden walls, hedges and lawns, making lace of trampoline safety nets, adding pretty lids to wheelie-bins and creating Swiss chalets from backyard sheds. That morning, our crowded little Dublin estate could have been a swish ski resort. I've never been to a Swiss ski resort but I'm an avid consumer of travel supplements.

A blackbird, feet buried in a little pillow of white, perched on a branch of the solitary apple tree in my back garden, so still I fancied he was as stunned as I was by this unexpected tableau. Perhaps his was one of the sunken trails I could see here and there through the whiteness on the ground. The indentations were so deep, however, it was not possible to know whether they had been made by something as small as he was, or a cat, rat, fox or even something really exotic to suburbia. People keep all sorts now as pets, don't they? I opened the window, gently, so as not to startle the creature but he flew off, the whirr of his wings startling in the white, singing silence.

The air felt ultra clean in my mouth and nose and I stayed there for as long as I could, until the cold hurt my throat and I was forced back into the fuggy warmth of my bedroom. White Christmases were so rare in Ireland – had this one been sent by the universe as compensation for Derek's perfidy? That was probably what Dina would think.

Dina! I looked at my watch. They'd all be here in less than seven hours and thank God for them. If they hadn't been coming, I would probably have spent the entire day pretending to Chloë that I wasn't upset. The image of the two of us sitting opposite one another over all that food was so dismal I could barely entertain it. Funny, I thought now, she hadn't once questioned Derek's disappearance.

No time for analysis or introspection – I could hear her moving about in her own room. She'd be down, clumping around in the kitchen, boiling her breakfast egg and making toast soon. I needed to get a head start on her. Less than seven hours to make right everything I had done wrong yesterday. I threw on my dressing gown and, as I clattered downstairs, was already composing my excuses for the shoddy meal my guests would have today. Chloë wouldn't notice, probably, I thought, and nobody liked sprouts all that much anyway, did they?

Maybe I could make amends with a brilliantly moist turkey. Butter, I thought. Butter seemed to be the answer to everything, both for Rachel Allen and that TV-cook guy from Cavan, Neven Maguire, with their smiles and their silvery clean gas rings. Does Derek—

Stop it, Maggie. No Derek today. I'd tell everyone his champagne had been on special at Marks. 'You're all worth it,' I'd say.

They were, too. When they came, all together, which led me to believe they had met somewhere in advance, it's not an exaggeration to say that they love-bombed me, so much so that I found it hard not to become emotional.

I was still a little teary when, at the end of the main course, they raised their glasses to me. I was particularly proud of Chloë, who had behaved very well throughout the afternoon. In fact it was she, right at the moment the others were toasting me, who christened us as a group: holding up her glass of Fanta, she had stood up, dwarfing Mary, Dina, Lorna and Jean, and beamed around at us all. 'Isn't this a very excellent winter gathering?' she said, and sat down again. Even I had to laugh, but then, looking around automatically to gauge Derek's reaction to such a positive action from her, I was hit by the pile-driver. No Derek. His absence was corporeal, a black, Derek-shaped hole cut out of the overheated air. Turning back, I forced myself again to laugh with the others, who, rustling it around on their tongues, were now trying out the sound of our new communal identity.

Despite later events that day, the idea, if not the name as Chloë had exactly articulated it, stuck as a handy shortcut to describe ourselves. 'Gathering' is a lovely word but it was easier on the tongue, and quicker, just to call ourselves a club.

One year, when we were at the dessert stage of our quarterly meeting for lunch, Dina brought it up and not for the first time. 'I hate this business of being in a 'club'. Our local butcher ran a Christmas Club. My mother put a half-crown into it every Friday to pay a bit towards the Christmas meat. So depressing.'

'Depressing for you, you mean,' Jean retorted. 'My mother did it, too, and I'm grateful she did. We always had nice Christmases.'

'So did mine.' This was Lorna; she and Jean usually support each other. 'We're a democratic group, Dina. The rest of us like it, it's a small thing. Trivial. Don't make a big deal of it.' She had looked around for affirmation.

Club, gathering, assembly, troop – even jamboree would have been fine for me. (In fact I would have quite liked that: the winter Jamboree. Trips nicely, eh?) Specification didn't matter as long as the concept was accepted because it was Chloë who had designated us a group, and I felt that this was something positive she had brought to that first event, which had ended so terribly …

Names are important.

Anyhow, on our first Christmas together in 2002, following Chloë's declaration I held up my wine glass to make my own speech, a rather emotional one, I fear. As I spoke, it struck me, looking at them all, that around that table sat a perfect snapshot of the season's culmination: my sister and my circle of friends happy together over the ruins of a turkey, candlelight glinting on jewellery, Waterford glassware and softened faces as snow patted the outside of the alcove window. It was as though we had all stepped into a Christmas card.

But then I experienced, somewhere under my breastbone, the sensation of being pricked with what I can only describe as a sweet-sour dart, inviting me to heed this moment: you may never see its like again.

And although we have had many Christmases together, my four friends and I, I do preserve that one in my most private gallery of imagery. The difference nowadays is that my sister is no longer part of the picture.

THREE

As it happened, that evocative, Dickensian depiction of Christmas dissipated within minutes of my experiencing it. Chloë's expression had changed and she was drumming rapidly on the floor with one foot. I wasn't the only one who had noticed. While Lorna, Jean and Dina had known only peripherally about her afflictions, Mary was totally familiar with tales of my sister's mood swings and stubborn disinclination to do anything other than watch TV. Now, as she gazed at Chloë, she was frowning a little.

During the meal, I had already recognised Mary's puzzlement at my sister's display of sang-froid and, once or twice, I had caught a lift of an eyebrow in my direction. She had clearly expected something very different and, in acting so positively, Chloë had made a drama queen of me. Although I knew how quickly life in the house could darken, I was unprepared for what happened next.

At about seven o'clock, I decreed a shift of the entire proceedings into the sitting room. 'Bring your drinks. I don't know about you lot but I'm so full I'm not able to wag! Time for a break. We'll do presents now and have dessert later. OK? Now go!' Despite persistent offers to help with clearing up – 'It's my party and I'll be a slattern if I want to!' – I managed to shepherd all five of them through the hall and into the other room. Six crowded into a space where there was formal seating for only five. I'd thought of that earlier and had brought in the stool I use when cleaning the tops of the kitchen presses. Jean, who was the smallest of us, was directed again to take that, as she had when we'd had our pre-dinner drinks.

'And we're off!' Dina cried, as we started digging into the piles of presents.

We don't go overboard for each other: the thought is always there, but every one of my friends had, most kindly, included my sister in the bonanza – small offerings, a hair ornament from Lorna, a pair of knitted bedsocks (what else?) from Jean, lottery scratch cards from Mary and a jokey rubber duck from Dina. 'For the bath, Chloë.' She chuckled. 'Be careful, though – he bites, sometimes in the wrong places!' We all laughed, including the recipient.

As we continued ripping and tearing, bantering with each other and in general high good humour, I was so absorbed in the ceremonial I didn't notice Chloë's absence until Mary, looking up from her own stash, asked suddenly, 'Where's Chloë? She's been gone for a while.' I cocked an ear and from upstairs, sure enough, I could hear the growl of the pump in the hot press on the landing as it pushed water through the system. It was probably refilling one of the two toilets in the house, I figured, most likely the one in the main bathroom: Chloë had always complained of claustrophobia when using the one under the stairs. 'It's OK,' I said to Mary, 'no big deal, she'll be back in a minute.'

But a little later, I was gathering up the discarded wrappings from all over the room when, from her perch on the stool, Jean shushed us: 'Quiet a minute!' Then, when the rest of us looked at her in surprise: 'Can anyone hear water?'

'I can!' cried Dina, a second later. 'Do you hear it, Maggie?'

I certainly could now: a drip-drip-drip, fast and getting faster. Drip-drip-drip-drip-drip onto the tiles in the hall just outside the door. Upstairs, the pump continued to push. 'What the—' I dropped the papers and rushed out.

It's odd what you notice at a time like that: the first thing I saw in the hall was that the baubles on the Christmas tree were agitating and bouncing. It took a second to realise they were reacting to small but multiple streams of water spilling on them from above. I looked up. The water was pouring, as through an opening canal lock, from the gaps between some of the balusters along the landing above. Thank God the presents aren't there, I thought inappropriately, but even during that second or two, the streams had widened and the flow fell faster. 'Mary!' I yelled, racing for the stairs, barely avoiding a skid in the puddle that was steadily spreading over the tiles. 'Pull out the fairy lights, will you?' Again oddly, I had remembered my father's admonitions about electricity and water not mixing. 'All the lights! Pull all the plugs out of the sockets!'

I took the stairs two at a time. The area of cream carpet under my feet on the landing was now dark and spongy and I saw the source of the flood: water, a lot of it, was oozing from under the bathroom door as the pump in the hot press continued to growl. 'Chloë! Are you all right?' Two steps to the hot press. I wrenched the door open and turned off the pump. In the ensuing quiet I could hear the taps running. Two steps back, and I was hammering on the locked bathroom door. 'Chloë! Chloë!'

There was no answer.

'Is she all right?' Mary was behind me now.

'I don't know – the door's locked. Chloë!' I hammered harder.

'Have you a screwdriver?' Mary was examining the lock.

'I don't know – no. I don't. Yes!' I remembered I had changed the plug on my bedside lamp. 'Hold on, I'll get it.'

As I ran towards my bedroom I could hear Mary resuming where I'd left off: 'Chloë! It's Mary. Will you open the door, please? Chloë?'

When I came back with the screwdriver, Lorna, Dina and Jean had crowded together at the top of the stairs. Mary grabbed the screwdriver out of my hand. 'Shit. It's a Phillips,' she said. 'It won't work on this.'

'Wait!' Absurdly, Jean remembered that she had received a tiny screwdriver set in the cracker she had pulled during dinner and ran down the stairs.

Mary and I continued to call Chloë and bang on the door. 'This is no use.' Mary turned to me. 'Could we break it down, the two of us together?'

'Worth a try.' Panicked, I would have wrecked every door and wall in the house. We stood back. Then: 'One, two three—' We ran at the door. All we achieved, however, was pain in our shoulders – but by then Jean, breathless, was back with her cracker toy, tiny but recognisable as a screwdriver.

'I brought a knife too,' she panted. 'It has gravy on it, I'm afraid.'

Mary snatched both from her. The knife blade was too thick

and kept slipping out of the slots. She threw it onto the sodden carpet. 'Stand back, Maggie, you're in my light.' I gave her the space and, for the next few interminable seconds, watched as she carefully manipulated the miniature tool into the first of the four screws holding the steel handle plate to the door. The wait was interminable, the taps continued to run but finally, finally, the screw came out.

The stress of waiting intensified then, but there was nothing any of us could do as she worked. I was super-conscious of the sounds from inside the room where the taps were still pouring but not as fast as before. The water that continued to come through the door was at a slower pace too. 'Mary, hurry, please!' I knelt beside her.

'Shut up!' she snapped. 'I'm going as fast as I can. I'm afraid this fucking toy will break if I push too hard. There's only one more,' she added more quietly, using her fingers to rotate the last few threads of the third screw, then starting work on the fourth. The taps continued to run. The water continued to seep. Under our knees, the carpet was now a swamp.

'Help me here!' She dropped the last of the screws and pulled the handle off the door, which, locked from the inside, still held. She pushed the little screwdriver right into the empty socket and rattled it around. Nothing happened. 'Have you a hammer? Where is it?'

'Toolkit under the sink.' Why hadn't I thought of it before? Panic is a dreadful thing. 'I'll get it.'

'I'll get it.' That was Lorna.

'Bring up the whole box,' Mary shouted after her, as she ran down the drenched stairs.

An eternity later, Lorna was back beside us. I took the kit from her and tipped everything onto the carpet. The hammer made a little splash. Mary picked it up, along with a piece of metal pipe I use for mixing paint. She inserted this into the hole where the handle used to be and hammered at the end of it, slowly first, then harder and harder until, at last, the plate inside gave way and we heard the handle fall. She pushed at the door but still it didn't give. 'There's one of those little bolts too – the little gold ones?' In my panic I had forgotten.

'All of you,' Mary commanded, 'all together!'

Lorna was right there, and Dina got to us before Jean. Along with the other two, Mary and I pushed and heaved at the door until finally it gave, so suddenly it almost toppled us all, crashing so hard against the wall inside it broke four of the tiles and liberated a gush of water that poured, tide-like, around our legs.

Mary and I ran inside. We didn't need to go far. The bathroom is small, the bath taking up one whole wall. Fully clothed, Chloë was in it, her dress floating like a downed sail above her stomach, her hair spread like seaweed around her head, propped between the taps. The water was patched and streaked reddish-brown.

The scissors with which she had cut her wrists gleamed in the dirty flood on the floor. She had hacked herself with them: ragged edges of skin floated slightly above the wounds while the head of the rubber duck bobbed quietly beside her as though trying to escape. Its torso, half in, half out of the water, had lodged in the hem of her dress.

'Let me through.' Lorna is a retired nurse and, within seconds, her instincts and training kicked in. 'Is she breathing?' Quickly, she turned off the taps and raised my sister's head, cradling it in one hand while feeling for a pulse in the neck with the fingers of the other. 'She has a pulse. Someone take the plug out of the bath, please! Have you a first-aid kit, Maggie?'

'No,' I whispered, as Mary leaned in and pulled at the plug chain. 'I always meant to but—'

'Don't worry. Jean, hand me a towel, then pick up the scissors and cut that other towel into strips. Maggie, get me two of your belts. Run! Dina, ring 999 right now – tell them it's life or death. All of you. Move!'

As I dashed towards the bedroom, I could hear the drains gurgle and Dina running down the stairs to the phone. By the time I got back to the bathroom with a handful of belts, the level of bathwater had lowered so that Chloë's dress was clinging to her stomach and Lorna was using one of Jean's towelling strips to staunch the ooze of blood from the first of her wrists.

'Is she going to be all right?' I waited until Lorna had finished with the towel and gave her the belts.

'I don't know,' Lorna said. 'Now, hold up that arm, high,' she indicated the bandaged one, 'and give me one of those belts.' As, mutely, I obeyed, I heard Dina talking on the phone below but could not make out what she was saying.

Quickly, Lorna threaded the end of the belt I'd given her through the buckle and pulled it very tightly around one of Chloë's forearms. 'Hold that up as high as you can now, Maggie.' She passed me the loose end. 'Keep it tight. Another one, please.' She held out a hand.

Jean picked up one of the other belts from where I had dropped them all and handed it to her.

'Have you another strip of towel ready, Jean?'

'Yes.' Moving efficiently and quickly, Lorna took it from her, bandaged the wrist, tied the second belt similarly around Chloë's second forearm and handed the end to me. 'Keep both arms tight and up.' She checked my sister's neck again for a pulse.

'Is she OK?' I couldn't keep the terror from showing. The pain in my own arms from holding both of Chloë's so high with the two belts was excruciating.

'The pulse is there and we've managed to stop the blood flow. That's something. Now, someone help me with this.' Lorna delved into the water and, with Mary's help, managed to insert a towel under Chloë's nearest hip, creating a gap through which the water could escape to the drain. Quite quickly its level reduced to just a few inches around her and her dress clung to the outline of her body. I couldn't bear to look at her for long, at her still, pale face and straggling hair, her heavy stomach and thighs. So, with eyes averted and my arm muscles trembling under the strain, I heard, rather than saw, Lorna stand up and squelch out onto the landing to call down to Dina, 'How long until the ambulance gets here?'

'They say five to seven minutes.' Dina was coming up the stairs. 'They were on a call in Glasnevin, but from what I told them, it isn't as urgent as this and they've diverted. They say to keep her legs elevated, if possible.'

'Shouldn't we try to get her out of the bath, Lorna? There are four of us.' This was Jean.

'No. Better where she is. And we're not going to be able to raise her legs. We just have to wait now. Try not to worry, Maggie,' she added kindly. 'I think we got to her in time.'

The next minutes were the longest of my life as we all waited, straining for the sound of the siren. When finally we heard its approach, my instinct was to drop Chloë's arms and run into the street to direct them to the house. 'I'll go.' Mary gently touched my shoulder and left the room. The siren screamed louder for an instant as she opened the front door, and then there was just the sound of its diesel engine ticking over, and of two men powering up the stairs and into the bathroom. Quickly, they scanned the scene and took charge. One left to run down and fetch some equipment.

The next quarter-hour is a blur. I can't tell you what happened between the time those big, blessedly strong saviours arrived and when I found myself sitting on a seat in the ambulance beside my comatose sister. She was hooked up to various wires and had an oxygen mask over her face as the vehicle, sirens blaring again, tore out of the estate.

You can never predict or prepare reactions, your own or anyone else's, to situations like this, certainly not when the need is to stay on top of every minute. I have just five clear memories of that screaming departure for the hospital.

I remember the calm, deft movements and encouraging language of those wonderful men as they connected Chloë to wires and oxygen.

I remember that some of Chloë's hair had got caught under her oxygen mask and how, without permission, I raised the mask to take it out, then recoiled because her skin felt so cold and wet and lifeless. Like that of a dead salmon.

I remember how dark the streets were through the back window of the ambulance and how incompatible the garish, fairy-lit sleighs, Santas and reindeer seemed, cruelly winking and blinking at us from gardens as we raced by.

I remember how the culture of my childhood rose from somewhere mysterious to give me comfort and to lead me into making a fervent but rash promise, to whom or what I had no clue, that if my sister recovered, I would go as a pilgrim to Lourdes.

Most particularly, I remember my last sight of my four friends standing in my driveway. They were making no effort to save themselves from the rain that was turning the snow to slush under their ruined shoes, flattening their hair and streaming off Christmas outfits.

I could to this day re-create their exact positions. Behind Lorna and Dina, who were standing just in front of the open doorway, the baubles on my tree flashed dimly, while my dearest Mary, with one of Jean's arms wound tightly around her waist, was standing a little to the side. I could see she was crying. Mary, stalwart Mary, never cries.

And just before the doors of the vehicle closed, I saw her half raise one arm, bidding us farewell.

FOUR

There is some justification for Chloë's frequent accusations these days that I think of her as an infant instead of a woman who is now in her fifties. Since her suicide attempt I don't often have the nerve robustly to challenge her in case she does it again. Yes, it happened ten years ago but that night is a permanent implant in a part of my brain to which I have no access in order to excise it. Hers had not been a cry for help, but a sudden serious attempt to kill herself.

I have to believe that those who do this have no idea of the crippling effect it has on those around them. If you had not witnessed it, it would be virtually impossible to understand the destabilising effect. And when there's just one to take responsibility, no matter how deep the friendships, it's a burden carried alone.

And, yes, in some respects I accept that I do treat her

inappropriately as a child, not just because she regularly behaves like a child but because of that night. Every day, almost every hour of every day, a bubble of fear rises to cloud whatever routine or work I'm performing. It is not becoming easier as time passes. The horror is that it has become normal. Suicide-watch is for life.

Reactions vary, of course. In the immediate aftermath of the episode, demonstrating the impulsivity of which I accuse my sister, I had that bath taken out to be replaced by a shower enclosure with a curtain, not glass doors. I had to wait, of course, until after the tradesmen's lengthy Christmas break, and because the work had to be done on a shoestring, I spent hours on the Internet, trying to find someone who was not only cheap but honest.

When the plumber I eventually chose came to assess the work, I told him, unnecessarily, that we were having it out because we were worried about legionnaire's disease: 'I hear there's a lot of it about these days.'

He looked at me as though I'd lost the plot, which, of course, I had. 'Yeah. You'd have to be careful of that, pet,' he said, and we made arrangements.

I didn't tell him why I couldn't bear to be in the house when the work was going on, and when he arrived with his helper on the day we'd agreed, I was all dressed up, pretending I had to go to work. I gave him his money and the spare keys of the house – 'Pull the door out after you when you're finished and drop those keys through the letterbox' – then took myself off on an outing in my car.

Not Wicklow. Everyone goes to Wicklow. The other direction – Clogher Head, I thought. Monasterboice. Maybe Newgrange. I'd never been there even though I'd heard so much about it from Mary. Or Annagassan? That's lovely altogether, according to Jean.

Maybe I'd take in the whole lot. I had all day. The plumber had told me the main difficulty would be physically getting the bath down the stairs. 'We might have to take off that doorway.'

Not my problem, had been my attitude. 'If you have to, you have to. I'll leave it to you and your mate,' I said, and fled.

I might even be adventurous and cross the border into Northern Ireland, I thought, as I drove off, refusing to give the plumber, the bath, the doorway, the stairs, or anything in that region any more airtime. The last time I'd been in the North had been on a school trip to Belfast. Their chips were definitely nicer than ours. Other than that, there are only two other things I remember. In every shop we went into we had to show the inside of our handbags, and in the shops themselves, there was very little you could buy that wasn't available down south. It was a bit of a novelty, however, paying for things with different notes and coins that flashed the Queen's head.

In the event, by the end of my mini-trip that day, I had explored a wide swathe of north Louth and a small slice of south Armagh.

I got out of the car at Clogher Head and took a brief walk along the headland. For once it was not raining; the view across the pier and the open sea with the Mourne mountains as background would have done justice to a John Hinde postcard. Despite the blue sky and sunshine, however, it was windy, and chilly enough to drive me off the heights back down to sea level and the port. There, for a peaceful few minutes, I watched the biggest seal I had ever seen trail a slow, V-shaped wake in the murky brown ripples as it nosed in and around the trawlers. Seeing its leisurely patrol, I wondered, not for the first time, why we humans think our way of life is superior to that of the so-called lower species. All that this big guy had to worry about, it seemed, was where to find the next discarded fish head. And he didn't look at all concerned.

For the next few hours, I drove into dead-end coastal roads around Omeath, Greenore and various other places, including Annagassan. I even found a gem of a place I'd never heard of before: Gyles Quay, a quiet harbour settlement. Not a sinner in the place at the time, the only sign of human life that afternoon was the rusting metal frame of an old-fashioned baby go-car upturned on the small beach. I was an explorer in Louth. That felt good.

I got back on the Dublin Road then, heading for Warrenpoint, expecting a hint of danger when crossing the border. Totally anticlimactic, as it happened. I actually missed the moment in both directions, coming to only when I saw, well into each territory, the difference in speed-limit signs, miles versus kilometres and vice versa.

At about four o'clock, with the light fading, I stopped at a phone box to ring home. No answer. The plumber was done. Fleetingly, I hoped my house hadn't been, but as soon as that little daisy poked its head above the parapet, I stamped on it. Nothing I could do about it now, eh? I trusted the guy. He had a nice Dublin accent, the old version I associate with my father and his pals, many of them tradesmen, who came to the house to play Solo on Wednesday nights. Yes, I had liked him.

But when I called in to see Mary on the way home she was scandalised. 'He could have robbed you blind, Maggie! You could have come home to find your whole house empty. And you gave him keys?'

'I told him to put them through the letterbox when he left and he said he'd do that.'

'"He said"? Jesus, Mary and Joseph, Maggie Quinn, you can't

be let out on your own. Anyway, even if he does give them back, who's to say he didn't have them copied? You were gone long enough. You'll have to change your locks. If you don't, you won't be insured when and if you're out some day and that man comes back with a couple of his mates and a pantechnicon to clean you out. Don't say I didn't warn you, you daft mare! Where'd you find this plumber?'

'Where everyone does these days. On the Internet. Get with the programme, Mary!'

'I give up. Did you at least haggle with him about the price?'

'Of course I did,' I said, injured. That eyebrow of hers shot up. She knows me.

I don't know enough about psychology to explain how I felt in the days following Chloë's actions. All I can tell you is that I couldn't have cared a sausage about anything material. Day to day, those first weeks, with her being properly cared for and expected to make a full recovery, at least physically, I was upset when I was with her, but when I was not, I existed in a weirdly lightsome bubble. And as I drove north on Saturday, 4 January 2003, just sixteen days after Derek had left me and nine after that Christmas Day nightmare, as far as I was concerned the plumber could have his pick of any or all of my possessions. With me, I had my car, my wallet, the clothes on my back. I had my sister in a hospital where, for quite a while, she was going to be other people's responsibility, the kind of people who gravely gave me permission to resist her piteous calls for me to take her home. I had some money set aside for her care and hopefully would have more when I had sorted things out with Derek. I had my circle of friends. What else could anyone want? (Isn't it funny, though, how quickly priorities and even crises can swap positions in the order of business? Derek, absent just a wet week, was, on that day at least, a very poor second to Chloë.) I felt positively airy. However long that would last.

Not long, of course.

There was the small matter of my daily visits to Chloë, being passed from harassed social workers to psychiatrists and back again while the mental-health services tried to decide how to proceed. This day was the first on which I would not be seeing her since she had been admitted. I had warned her not to expect me and, before I left home, had telephoned her ward to ask the nurse who answered the phone to remind her. 'And tell her I'll see her tomorrow.'

'I will.'

'How is she this morning?'

'Still asleep. We'll be getting her up shortly.'

'Don't forget to tell her, please. I'm not sure she remembers this kind of thing from day to day.'

'We'll tell her, don't worry, Mrs Jackman. Enjoy your day.' At the time I was still known by Derek's name but as I hung up, I wondered if it had been a barb: 'We're in here looking after your sister and you're off on a skite?'

This was paranoia – it was clear I needed my day away.

After treatment for her wounds, sedation and a period of observation while locked in by cot sides on an A & E hospital trolley too short for her long frame, Chloë had been transferred to a psychiatric hospital. I can still barely imagine what it must have meant to her to be brought in and left there by me. Because no thoughtful décor – skylights, garden seats, pastel wall art or blond, comfortable furniture – could disguise the fact that the patients, for their own safety, were not free to walk out even if, like Chloë, on paper they had been admitted voluntarily for assessment. No printed and framed notices outlining a Charter of Patients' Rights – the right to dignity and participation in decisions about them – could obliterate the unpleasant truth that, whatever the intention and assumed ethos, the reality was that, for now at least, power over their fate and lives lay not with themselves.

I could have insisted on taking responsibility for her there and then, signed her out and brought her home. I was told I had a right to do that by every single person I encountered, but I was afraid to. That image of the seaweed hair quietly floating in the water around her face would not let me. So, in effect, I had become her gaoler.

The screaming was the worst. A woman in Chloë's ward screamed and sobbed all day as though her heart was breaking, which it probably was. From long experience, the staff behaved as though this was white noise, but I can tell you that for other patients and visitors, including my sister and me, it was not only heartrending, it was frightening. That first time I went into the ward on that St Stephen's Day and had to run the gauntlet of locks and security bolts felt surreal, as though I was acting in a movie. On the plus side, every member of staff was kind to me, concerned about Chloë. It was somewhat consoling, too, to notice that a brave effort had been made to inject some kind of celebratory ambience into the place. A Christmas tree, a small one, colourfully decorated, dominated an area beside the nurses' station and there were displays of Christmas cards taped to the panels of the desk. The wall-hung TV in the open area was showing *The Sound of Music.*

It was humiliating for Chloë to have her phone charger, the belt of her dress, the shoelaces of her trainers and even her Ladyshave, a present from Derek the previous year, taken away from her and put in storage. They were nice about it: 'Don't worry, we'll keep it all safe for you. If you need your phone charged, we'll put it on. All you have to do is ask any one of us. OK, Chloë?'

It defined what was happening here and I think I was more upset about it than she was.

Leaving her there, hearing those locks clicking shut behind me as I left, was one of the more difficult things I have ever had to do. Every nerve in my body told me to get back in there, rescue her and take her home, although I knew full well that could not happen. She needed to be there.

It did not get easier as her treatment progressed and it was very difficult to act positively and upbeat each time I went into her room, uttering inanities such as 'Just a few days in here, Chlo, and when they get your medication sorted out we'll be grand. You'll be back home with me and it'll seem like you were here for just a jiffy. All this will be just a bad dream.'

Every visit tortured both of us as she wept and begged, 'Take me home. Please, Margaret. Let me come home, I want to come now. I'm going to die in here,' while I rationalised and coaxed and was forced into outright refusal. The woman beside her in the other bed was disgusted by all of this. On one occasion, when she got up to go out for a cigarette, her tone was heavy with accusation as, on passing, she glared at me: 'She's cryin' non-stop since she came in here. It's doin' me bleedin' head in.'

'They can be manipulative, you know,' I was told sternly, by a jaded-looking nurse in whom I had confided how worried I was about my sister's distress. 'You'll be gone ten minutes and there'll not be a bother on her.' That made me feel worse. How did I know she was telling the truth? There would be no one there to speak on her behalf.

There is a curious space occupied by relatives in this situation. While common sense – and all advice – is to be assertive, even demanding if necessary, in the interests of your patient, you're afraid to alienate the people who wield power over him or her when you're not there. I suppose the easiest way to explain it is that it's akin to being a parent in a school situation. I do know it's somewhat different, these days (though not all that much, I submit), but on the one occasion my lovely dad, having learned how miserable I was in my school, confronted the teacher – the woman claimed to be astonished to learn that I was upset. Couldn't understand it. Of course it would be sorted out.

Twenty seconds after he'd left the classroom she had me standing up in front of the class, making disparaging remarks about me and my family. I suffered in silence from then on.

For me, this is what it feels like to deal with mental-health professionals. You want to protect the person you love and show her you're on her side. Equally, however, you feel the need to be pleasant and agreeable with those who have the power to make her life even more difficult than it is, whether intentionally or subconsciously. Throughout Chloë's illness, I have found that psychiatrists, in particular, 'know best' and resent being challenged. So for Chloë's sake I don't. At the back of my mind is always the risk that if I shout too loudly I will be marked as a troublemaker, that the consultant will get fed up with me, my sister and the whole situation, and will simply tell me that nothing more can be done for her. I emphasise that this has never happened, but it's always at the back of my mind, rendering me compliant and giving Chloë a legitimate excuse to accuse me of being on 'their' side.

I don't mean to be so negative about the mental-health services, really I don't. There are good people out there who, against all the odds and really horrible behaviour by their ungrateful clients, don't give up. I do accept that dealing with mental illness has to be about the most testing of all the disciplines facing health professionals. Patients tend not to believe that their doctors and nurses are trying their best to help them. Chloë is not appreciative; neither were many other patients I encountered in the hospitals she attended until we found Merrow House.

Thank God we did.

There are various theories among my Club friends, to whom I will be eternally grateful, about why Chloë did not die that night. Not one of them ever took credit for helping, brushing off all my attempts to thank them.

One theory, Jean's, is that my sister's unusual height saved her; her body was longer than the bath, so her head did not slip under the water.

She had hacked at herself with scissors rather than the (more usual, I gather) razor blade. This was Dina.

Di-dah-di-dah-di-dah. Who cared what or how? She was safe now. As for the 'why', that was a different story. It lurked, like a conger eel, huge and predatory, at the back of my consciousness, but in those first few days, weeks, even months afterwards, I refused to try to hook it.

Right this minute I bet you're thinking, Chloë, Chloë, Chloë! This woman is obsessed. Does she ever talk about anything else?

Ten years have elapsed. You have a point. Firm purpose of amendment. Chloë out – Maggie in.

FIVE

Since that magical awakening on the most difficult Christmas Day of my life a decade ago, I've always trusted that the snow could happen again and, in anticipation, always left my curtains open on Christmas Eve. The telly forecast last night had been promising enough, with its 'precipitation on higher ground'. No joy, though: not only is there no snow here in the city this year, it's so un-Christmassy outside you could spit. Grey, grey, bloody grey. Grey inside and out, rain running down the window, howling wind, clouds so heavy you'd hardly know whether or not it was morning. I venture out of bed to check: puddles on my lawn (so-called) and that twig on the apple tree, the blackbird's, is drooping under its own wet weight. I go back to bed, pull the covers over my shoulders and, in the half-light, cast an eye around the room. Just as depressing: same décor for years, same dreary old wardrobe, same sheepskin rug at the side of my bed—

But it's Christmas. Get a grip, woman! Mary and the other three are coming to dinner in a few hours' time.

I promise I'll get up when I hear the central-heating boiler kicking in downstairs.

Everything is grand anyway. I'm ahead of myself. I have it down to a fine art now. The turkey won't go into the oven for at least an hour and the girls' (yes, we're aware of the irony every time we say it!) presents are wrapped and waiting under the tree along with others to be given or collected later in the week. Stretching my arms and legs, I yawn so hard my jaw cracks.

I'm amazed that, after such an extraordinary start to our decade of Christmas dinners together, my four guests continue to come. They should all be waking up around now, I think lazily, from the comfort of my bed. I can picture them: Jean throwing back her hand-sewn quilt, Lorna surveying the rain through her bedroom window while hoping her grandchildren will appreciate the presents she sent, Dina turning over in her pillowy boudoir to take one last snooze. As for Mary, in her little Cabra flat, she's no doubt planning all her moves. She's a great planner.

I have to admit she wasn't in the best of humour when we did our thing a week ago. We have our own little tradition now. On 18 December every year, exactly one week before the Big Day, and on the anniversary of Derek's desertion (in its weird, silver-lining way, the spark that ignited our Club), we meet for afternoon tea. Going Dutch, we rotate this annual treat around the more salubrious of the Dublin hotels that offer it: the Gresham, the Westbury, the Shelbourne and this year it was the turn of the Merrion.

'Isn't this lovely?' As we took our seats in front of the fire, I scanned the plush, hushed drawing room with its polished wood, draped windows, beautifully upholstered seating and, glowing from the walls, the paintings that even I, philistine that I am, could see were the real deal. 'No recession here, eh, Mary?' The place, with its calm, unhurried waiting staff, whispered opulence. In a corner, half hidden by the wings of his chair, some bloke with a beard, probably a writer, by the intense look of him, was being interviewed by a journalist, who looked to me to be about fourteen years old. Nearby, a blonde, dressed in black, stared at her iPad, but was quite obviously listening closely to what was going on. The bearded one's minder. Sent, probably, by a publisher. I've done a lot of that kind of interviewing myself and can spot the type a mile off.

'Far from it we were reared, eh?' Mary unwound her woolly scarf and unbuttoned her new Christmas coat. She buys one every year. This one was dark green. It suited her colouring. 'Nice decorations. Tasteful.'

'Yeah.' I ignored the implied criticism of my own excesses: 'Will we order?' I picked up the classy menu.

'I can't wait for the whole thing to be over.' Her tone remained tart.

'Ah, you say that every year. Deep down you love it, like all of us. Why are we here, for God's sake?'

'Sometimes I wonder. Look at it. Everyone's behaving as though nothing's happened to this country. As though people aren't suffering.'

I was determined to remain upbeat. 'C'mon, Mary, we won't sort out the sorrows of the country by not having one little celebratory afternoon tea. Let's order, eh? The hell with the outside world!'

'The eleventh Christmas! Ten whole years since the five of us first got together – can you believe it?' Sighing, she picked up the menu. 'Can you believe it?'

'Barely. I really don't want to go back to that awful night in 2002 – but you're right to mention it. Ten years? That's worth marking. We should have real champagne with our dinner this year instead of the pretend stuff! Hey! Will we have a glass now?' I peered around to catch the eye of a waiter, but Mary was horrified.

'Get a grip! Did you see the price of a single glass?'

'All right, keep your hair on!'

'And, by the way,' she added, 'I was thinking of a Kris Kringle this year. We're all affected by that disastrous budget – immoral, if you ask me.'

My turn to sigh. All the talk in Ireland, on the radio, on TV, in shops, in buses, effing everywhere, is of nothing but austerity, austerity, austerity. Thank God I don't have a mortgage. But I will be hit with the new bloody property tax; at least Mary, as a renter, won't have that to endure. But I certainly don't want to descend to a Kris Kringle. 'Kris Kringle? Oh, Mary, I don't know. It's just once a year ... and none of us goes overboard.' I hate the idea of that foreign import. I know it makes sense in the current climate of penury but one of the best parts of Christmas for me is the choosing and wrapping of presents with specific people in mind, picturing their faces when they open them. In my house, wrapping goes on for days, deliberately so because I want to enjoy it as much as possible. 'It's too late for me, Mary. Maybe next year. I have everything wrapped and ready.'

'Why am I not surprised?'

'Don't be such a wet blanket.' I still refused to engage. 'Look around you, Mary. Relax. Enjoy! Can we just order?'

'You order for me. I'll have the standard. Camomile tea, OK?'
She heaved herself out from among her cushions. 'I need to go to
the loo.'

'Then tea it is.'

I gazed after her retreating figure. What had got into her today?
She could be acid-tongued at the best of times but she wasn't
often so negative. There's something more going on underneath,
I thought. I'd probably never know what it was. We do swap
intimacies but, in truth, I'm the one usually offering.

Some of the harshness she deals with in the women's shelter
understandably leaches into her own life; her stories about the
upsurge in the flight from violence during this season are deeply
upsetting – and maybe the budget has affected the funding of the
place. Better not to rile her anyhow, I thought, so while I'd have
loved champagne, when the waitress came I ordered identically for
both of us.

This Christmas morning, I snuggle further under my duvet. I
hope she's going to be in better form today. I'm not giving out
about her, honestly. She is who she is. And anyone who knows
me would tell you that, despite my Christmas addiction, I'm
not impervious to what goes on at this time of year. I accept the
sadnesses and, as I know only too well, the absences. If you read
newspapers, you can't miss the 'Do They Know It's Christmas'
articles, the bringing into high relief of homelessness, house-
fire tragedies, drunkenness. I accept that much of the cheeriness
is forced or assumed but, stubbornly, maintain that a lot of it is
not. It offers a bridge to the people we love and if a little scarf, a
candle, a book, cufflinks, or a box of Dairy Milk can buttress that
emotional bravery, well, hooray!

More good things happen around Christmas than at any other

time. You meet friends you haven't seen all year. You let animosities die, however temporarily. You go the extra mile for your favourite charity or your elderly neighbour. You max out your credit card for a dear friend when you see something sparkling under the lights in a jeweller's window. And when in daylight you see why the trifle you bought for someone who did you a favour cost only €14.99, you show your gratitude by using particularly heavy wrapping paper and a bigger than usual bow.

At Christmas, I can even drum up semi-kind feelings for my ex-husband and, if pushed, keep my trap shut about his popsy. This year, I figured ten years was long enough to be angry and sent them a card. Almost by return I got one back, an innocuous robin chirping from a tree. Inside, I was wished a happy Christmas by Derek, Fiona, Crystal, Marjorie and Sunniva. Three little girls. I've never met them, of course, but it hurt to see the names in writing for the first time. I'm unable to have children.

But, what the hell, it's not the kids' fault. I do wish them all well.

What time is it? The better to see the face of the bedside clock, I turn on my lamp, with its cheery yellow shade, and immediately the whole room looks better. Simultaneously, from downstairs, I hear the whoosh of the boiler. Flora hears it too, or senses that I'm about to move – she's amazing that way – and puts her head around the door, a polite, but enquiring look on her brown and white face. Excuse me, I wonder if you wouldn't mind letting me out?

In this three-bedroomed house, one is mine. The second belongs to Chloë, who now spends weekends with me but who, at present, is away for a week, as she has been every Christmas since the notorious one. Flora enjoys the third, a tiny box room, as her own. It is nominally the spare room, but the only overnight guest I entertain these days – and only now and then – is Mary. Neither minds sharing with the other. Flora, who likes her privacy, is happy to crawl under an intruder's bed.

She comes over now to me, ears cocked, tail wagging. She has quite a repertoire of wags, from a full-on thrilled body wag to greet me as I come through the front door, right down to this one, tentative, with just the white tip of her tail moving. This one, I've learned, means 'I don't like to disturb you but I'm making an application … '

'All right, all right.' I give in and she prances in front of me, checking over her shoulder that I'm really, really coming. I clamber down the stairs, being careful because my Florence and Fred slippers from Tesco (with the memory-foam insoles) are floppy on my feet. Don't want to fall. Not today.

Lights, sound, action! When I get down to my handkerchief of a hall, the first thing I do is press the button on the CD player so the air is filled with Nat King Cole. Then, while Flora waits patiently, I switch on the nets of fairy lights on the wall alongside the staircase, then the ones around the windows on each side of the front door, then the six sets of lights on the tree. Yes, the same six sets I nearly wrecked ten years ago. They were worth the money: they're survivors.

Like me. When I think about the shambles I was ten years ago – I was a completely different woman.

Derek? Go away, Derek. Stay away, Derek (not that he's shown any inclination to return!).

At least we can be civil now. He's done well, head chef in a famous restaurant, and I don't begrudge it to him. He's now Mr Moneybags, happy with his lot and so am I. It makes a difference.

I stand back to admire my tree – getting better every year, in my opinion. This year's addition, plugged into one of the extension cords, is a three-feet-tall IKEA Santa-in-outline, a continuous LED coil in violet, that I've placed beside it. And, yes, my bristling skirting boards do look as complicated as that ESB power plant thingy just beyond the big roundabout in Finglas. I don't care. I'm singing along with Nat about chestnuts roasting. I'm the Christmas fairy and my hand is a wand as, one by one, the lights begin to flash under my direction.

I'm never happier than when I'm ticking off lists, wrapping, writing labels. Unless I spot something extra-special, 'Cheap Presents, Great Wrapping' is now my motto. Finding a scarf, a pair of gloves, handbag or wallet in TK Maxx and nestling it into tissue from Tesco, then expensive goldy paper from Eason makes me happy as I picture what this scarf will look like on that friend, or hesitate while trying to decide if this book would really lift the spirits of that acquaintance's hard-faced husband. Chloë's little pile is off to the side. I'll take them to her tomorrow.

We go into the kitchen, Flora and I, and there too turn on all the lights. There's disorder in here, but it's organised, with 90 per cent of the work done and the air spicy with ham fragrance. I cooked that last night, with cloves, honey, the whole works. Christmas in my childhood was nothing like this; neither was Christmas in this home when it was marital, with Derek fussing and issuing orders and losing his temper, as though he was already Chefgod. I did go through hell when he left, but at some stage not too long afterwards, I decided that happiness was a decision I was going to make.

To be honest, if this doesn't sound too weird, I became a little bored with grief and all the solicitous enquiries about my feelings. I have my own house. I have a guaranteed income: monthly maintenance, indexed annually as a percentage of Derek's salary, so far continuing to rise satisfactorily. Part of my settlement with him was a lump sum, invested wisely as a pension and augmented annually as his wealth increases. And so, physically, except for my obligations to Chloë, I'm on my own and I'll do what I like. And what I like is celebration, which was in short supply in my early life, even in my life with Derek.

I know exactly when I decided to be happy. It was one year and one day after Derek's note informed me he didn't love me any more when he walked out of this house to be with the popsy. And so, that day, on 19 December 2003, I went to a pound shop and bought so much shiny tat I had to make two trips to the car with a filled trolley each time. That year, the décor in my hall reached its apogee. Was a bit, shall we say, *de trop* even for me? But I couldn't have cared less and my pals, glad to have noticed that my shift of mood seemed to be permanent, wisely kept their mouths shut. Women are great pragmatists, aren't they? Certainly the ones I know nearly always have their eyes on the long ball.

I open the back door to let Flora out into the bucketing rain. She's only three, officially an adult but still a baby really, and as she extends a tentative paw into the wet, she turns to eye me: is it all right? Am I allowed? I'm warning you, I'll get wet and it won't be pretty …

'Go on,' I say encouragingly, and she takes off, romping like a young deer, splashing through the puddles and mud. I got her as a pup from a shelter, and until she came into my life, I had no idea how communicative dogs are. Or maybe it's just collies. I watch her as she settles down for a serious sniff along the length of the garden fence. What's been here? Has *a cat* been here? Then, leaving the door ajar, I turn back into the kitchen. I have work to do. Five mouths to feed.

All five of us are *sans* husbands or partners. I've been best friends with Mary since childhood and schooldays. She has never found The One and Only, as she terms her ideal man. Jean and Lorna are widows – well, Lorna is sort of a half-widow. I'll explain later. Mary and I met the two of them when I dragged her along to a knitting group in the ICA headquarters at An Grianán in the hope that she would come down to earth and settle into real life; she was in her hippie phase at the time, talking about going to live in Mongolia. Lorna is quiet, but I always feel there's something big going on under the surface – you know how that can sometimes strike you?

Jean could be described as comfortable in her own skin, impervious to the ups and downs of emotion, you'd think. It's almost like she packed away her feelings with her husband's clothes after he died. She rarely talks about her sons, just smiling her little granny smile over her knitting. She's a great knitter: tea cosies, mittens, winter socks. Her bed is adorned with a king-sized patchwork quilt that took her a year to complete. She knitted me a cover for my mobile phone as last year's present – I mustn't forget to put it on the damned thing. In response to queries about her family, Jean tells us that everything's grand. Except for the daughters-in-law, of course. She doesn't like either of them. Her sons, she says, have been kidnapped by their wives' families.

Leaving Mary aside for the moment, the true exotic among us is Dina – real name Claudine, would you believe? Her parents were obviously romantic types. Like Mary, she never married, although she does have a vivid and entertaining history with men. I met her when she was living in the house next door, more than twice the size of the infill townhouse Derek and I rented on the southside of the city during our first year of marriage. We met when she was between men, as she is at present, and, I think, because we were of an age in a settled area inhabited mostly by older people, we bonded.

Dina is, and remains, tight-lipped about her personal circumstances. For instance, at the time we met, she had seemed to imply that she was renting like we were – although I had asked myself why a single woman would want so many rooms. It was only when I told her Derek and I were moving away that she revealed the house had been owned by her parents and was now hers. I introduced her to Mary and for a while the three of us were a casual theatre- and cinema-going trio.

It was Mary who told me the real story about Dina. On one occasion, when I was up against a deadline, the two of them went without me to the cinema. Over a drink afterwards, Dina confided that it hadn't been only the house that had been left to her. Her mother, who was a widow, had won the Lotto. Quite a big rollover Lotto by the standards of those days: Mary didn't know exactly how much. The mother kept the win anonymous and played it by the book as the Lotto people advised, putting the money into a simple deposit account for three months while she made up her mind what to do with it. And get this! She was on a bus (a bus!) on her way to meet her bank manager, who was going to advise her on how to invest her winnings to best advantage when she had a heart attack in her seat and died later in hospital without regaining consciousness.

Dina had had an older brother but he had died from meningitis at three years of age; she has no memory of him. Anyhow, she inherited the whole kit and caboodle. But, Mary told me, she is ambivalent about her wealth: 'She says it hasn't brought her all that much luck. She's suspicious that the men she goes out with are doing so only because of the money.'

'God almighty, how do they know?'

'Guess what? She tells them.' Mary chuckled. 'It's kind of a test she has. No one has passed it so far. She said I could tell you because she's sick of hiding things. I found her attitudes fascinating. I asked her what were the best and worst aspects of acquiring a heap of money all of a sudden, and she told me that best and worst carry the same weight. Best, she said, is freedom from worry, worst is worrying it'll diminish. "When you have a hundred pounds," she told me, "you worry if it's enough. When you have a million or more, you worry it'll go down by ten pence." Isn't that quite insightful? She presents this giddy front, but I like her, Maggie. More than I did before. She's dippy, there's no getting away from that, but she's honest. I also believe that, as with her men friends, she hasn't come clean to our group because she reckoned we'd all think of her differently if we knew the full story. She said she was taking a risk by telling me.'

'What does she imagine we'd do?' I was astonished.

'I dunno.' Mary shrugged. 'Resent her or something.'

If anyone resents Dina, it's Lorna. She doesn't say anything but I'm certain she's not all that enamoured and it may or may not be about the money. This country is a small village with a very active bush telegraph. Sooner or later everyone knows everyone else's business so she and Jean would probably have known, or at least guessed, about the Lotto money. Lorna has very good manners, however, and almost never lets herself down when she's with us as a group – easy enough, I suppose, since all five of us meet only three or four times a year. Although Christmas, of course, has become sacrosanct, it can be hard to pin us all down to a date.

Lotto or no Lotto, though, I didn't think that, left to themselves, Lorna and Dina would choose to be close friends.

Some years ago, the two of them, along with Lorna's pal Jean, were centrally involved in our Club's split – inevitable, of course, this being Ireland. No point in going into it in detail here, but I don't think it had anything to do with Dina's wealth. Here's a quick summary as to how it started.

It was mid-year and we were all having lunch in Jean's bailiwick, a restaurant in Drogheda. Because we had come up on the train – very enjoyable, I have to say – we had had a few drinks and wine with the food. When the bill came, Dina took it and started to calculate: 'Five ways as usual?'

'Hold on, Dina!' Lorna pointed out that while Dina ('I'm going to treat myself') had had lobster, three of us had had posh burgers and Jean a shrimp salad, all at about a third of the price.

'Yeah.' Jean jumped in to support her friend. 'We're not all millionaires.'

I leave the escalation to your imagination. From such a domestic dispute – as, I think, Patrick Kavanagh once pointed out – epic wars are launched. Ours, with Lorna and Jean on one side, Dina on the other, Mary and I in no man's land, had simmered for nearly a month, via phone mostly.

'I'm not going to put up with—'

'Who does she think she is?'

'It's not my fault my mother won the Lotto. I don't flash it.'

'Why should I apologise? She started it!'

Et cetera. Playground stuff.

I was about wearily to relinquish my mediation role when hostilities ceased of their own accord because Dina fell in her garden, breaking both ankles. She rang me from her hospital bed, the wires hummed and, as women do, we all, including Lorna and Jean, rushed to be helpful: she would be disabled for a good few weeks. We don't refer to the split now because we all know it's wiser not to. Things Were Said.

At least it had brought Dina's financial standing completely into the open.

To tell you the truth, I'm surprised she's kept up her membership of our Club. She did miss one year, away with some swain on a cruise in the Far East, but with that exception, she turns up with bells on, sometimes literally: there was one year when her Christmas outfit jingled with every movement. I wondered if she was making some comment about my own excesses, but decided I was being over-sensitive. (As for the cruise: 'Never again, girls. Full of old ladies with wattles, and diamonds as big as snowballs hanging out of their turkey necks. No men. No real ones anyway.')

On the surface, as I'm sure you're thinking, the five of us have very little in common, except, *sans* Dina, the paucity of male companions and a liking for each other's company. Objectively, it's a bit odd, isn't it? Take Lorna and Jean, two widows with sons and even grandchildren – you'd think they'd want to be with their families, wouldn't you?

Lorna is the group member to whom I'd say I'm the least close. Her son, who is married with kids, is her only offspring; she lives in a large house in Sutton with a sea view. I would kill for it – if I wanted to live that far away from Dublin, that is, and if I could afford to run it. She's a bit touchy about how she manages to do so and up to quite recently was tight-lipped about why she won't go to her in-laws for Christmas dinner, although she claims she has frequently been invited.

Every year I go through the same ritual with her: 'I really don't mind if you want to, or have to, go to Olive's family this year, Lorna –.' Olive is the son's wife.

Every year her response is the same: 'You're really good, Maggie, but if it's all right with you, I'd really prefer to be with you girls – that's if I'm welcome. Anyway, I've already told Martin that I'll be going to your house, if that's all right? There'll be plenty of people at Olive's, you need your friends around you.'

I was slightly insulted. Was I an object of pity? And then one year, during one of these round-the-houses phone calls, she admitted she couldn't stand her daughter-in-law. She has that in common with Jean, who, we all knew from the beginning, can't stand either of hers.

And so we have the two widows, one separatee, or 'Irish divorcée' if you like, that's me, plus Mary and Dina, our two spinsters – although Dina was horrified to hear herself thus described when the word was bandied about by alcohol-fuelled tongues at one of my Christmas tables a couple of years ago. Mary, the other spinster, didn't mind in the least being named as such. She really admires the Coco Chanels and Oprahs of this world; Diane Keaton is her favourite actress, Jane Austen her favourite author and Susan B. Anthony is one of her heroines because of her struggles on behalf of women and votes. 'None of them objected. It's a fine old word – in the past it was because the unmarried women always did the spinning. Bet you didn't know that, ladies! And as for Mother Teresa … '

'But she was a nun.' This from Lorna. 'So she was married! To Christ!'

'Listen, Lorna, being a spinster doesn't mean you're a celibate like she was. Some of us actually like sex. And anyway,' Dina rowed in, 'I hear that woman was really a tough bitch in real life.'

'She lived a real life, Dina. Get real yourself!' For once, Lorna bit back.

'Leave it, the two of you! All of you!' I feared a new split that was, again, about nothing of consequence: 'Eat that trifle. It took me a long time to assemble!' They all got the joke. They knew that while, these days, I turned out a good Christmas dinner, I was what's euphemistically termed 'a good plain cook'. I still am.

I've concluded that they all like coming here because in my house we're free of the familial obligations that afflict most of these sacramental events. That includes me, with Chloë safe in her sanctuary. They're all due this afternoon and Flora and I are delighted to have them. We'll have sherry or gin while we open our presents and the plan is to sit down together for our dinner at around four, timed for when the sun is setting and turning everything in my little dining alcove to gold. Hopefully. If there is a sun. If this bloody rain ever stops. I do like a bit of solar drama, me.

I turn on the oven and go to the back door, calling Flora. 'You little scamp.' I bend down to pat her as she comes in straight away. She's very good like that. 'You're all wet!'

Not any more! She grins at me, tongue lolling, then gives herself a thorough shake, all over me and the kitchen presses. She laps a few mouthfuls of water from her bowl before trotting back upstairs to her room. I'll clean up later: she's a small collie and the spatter didn't reach the counters or anything significant in the food line. Until Flora came into my life I never knew how much you could love an animal but these days I'm a sucker for them. I now donate to every animal refuge and support group that asks me and some that don't. I take the turkey out of the fridge. So naked-looking. I hope it had a good life – I paid enough for it. It's supposed to be organic and free range and all the rest of it, but do you ever really know? And does eating it make me a hypocrite since I'm so animal-friendly in other ways? None so zealous as a convert, they say, and they're right. Even a part-convert.

Too early in the morning for all this soul-searching, I'm committed now. I tear open my packet of sage stuffing. No more mashing and all that palaver Derek used to carry on with and that I killed myself trying to replicate the first time. It's been packets ever since and I don't think anyone has ever noticed. Loads of butter. That's the key. I'll get it into the poor bird so I can have it in the oven before I sit down for my corn flakes.

Corn flakes?

On Christmas morning, Maggie?

I admit it. I'm a sad person.

SIX

Big surprise. We're to be six, not five, at my Christmas table this year. The last time that happened – just after Derek's departure – Chloë had been one of the six and I would never want to repeat that disaster. If I was superstitious – I try hard to convince myself I'm not – I'd be worried. Once every ten years?

When the telephone rang this morning, I was peeling the sprouts. It was Lorna on the other end, sounding stressed. Could she bring someone else to dinner? My automatic reaction was 'of course' – well, you would, wouldn't you, at Christmas? 'Who is it?' Then, hurriedly: 'It doesn't matter who it is, Lorna. All welcome. Any friend of yours and all that … ' The extra guest, I thought, was probably her son. We'd known for ages that things hadn't been great in that marriage of his, not that Lorna had said anything specific: it was the signals we got from her shuttered eyes and her clipped tone any time we asked about him. I'm sometimes glad I had no children. For mothers, apparently, the worry never stops. I suppose I do understand to some extent, since parallels could be drawn between the cares of motherhood and mine concerning my mentally ill sister. But a sibling relationship doesn't quite equate to that of mother and child, with the definition of 'child' seeing no upper age limit. Motherhood, I've gathered, is a life sentence. 'Is it your Martin?'

'No. It's not Martin.' There was a little pause, through which my imagination ran amok. She hadn't specified man or woman, of course, but was there a new man in Lorna's life? That's one for the books. Lorna of all people. I managed to hold my tongue.

'It's a person I met recently,' she said, 'a young man, a boy, really.' Another pause and then: 'He's twenty-two.'

Complete with exclamation marks, the words 'Toy-boy'! and 'Cougar'! leaped into my mouth but I forced myself to eat them. 'I'm happy for you, Lorna,' I said, sincerely, I hoped. This'd be a bit of fun for sure. Of all of our little group, Lorna would be the last person I'd put into the adventurous category, but there's no predicting what humans will do or try: after all, *Fifty Shades of Grey* hit the million-euro sales mark in Ireland during this past year. 'You're a dark horse, Missus. Recent, eh? How long have you been together?'

'I beg your pardon?'

'You and him. How long?'

'It's not like that.' She sounded weary. 'Oh, I'll explain when I see you if I get an opportunity, but I'm not going to make a circus act out of myself with all the others. Ask Jean. She knows – well, she knows some of it. Please make sure nobody will embarrass him, or me, OK?'

'Don't worry. I will.'

'We'll see. Three o'clock, isn't it?' And she hung up.

Not a toy-boy, then? I stared at the phone. I make allowances for Lorna. She's not the easiest person in the world to get on with but there are reasons for that, and her life has not been great since her husband died. Had she another son none of us knew about? The soaps are full of long-lost sons or unknown daughters showing up to create havoc. I'd have preferred the first option but, I thought, we were definitely going to remember this dinner.

One by one, I rang the other three. I got Jean's answering machine – she wasn't crucial anyhow because Lorna had said she knew about the situation – but I explained to Mary and Dina, warning them to be on their best behaviour. 'Nothing in front of this fella, OK? She sounds stressed about it, so no hilarity or teasing or rude questions. We'll all take it gently, as though this happens every day.' They both agreed.

'Never a dull moment, eh?' This was Dina. 'Pity you're retired, Maggie. It'd make a great story for you.'

The others believe that before I was made redundant I'd led a fascinating life. It had been interesting for sure – it certainly beat working in a supermarket or on an assembly line – but it was my interview subjects who led fascinating lives, not me. Fascinating life for me would have been working with turtles on one of the Galápagos Islands or on a Greenpeace vessel, forging through mountainous seas to prevent the slaughter of whales. As a by-product of such work, I would become fascinating to myself then, instead of boring old Margaret Quinn whose passing from this world will leave no trace, except in dusty, crumbling newspaper archives destined, eventually, for the shredder. A by-product of life, that's me.

I won't bore you with how I came to be a journalist, but at

the peak of my twenty years with my newspaper I had enjoyed a certain tepid renown for the way I wrote up my features. That was until the growing fashion for thrusting, opinion-led, star-writer journalism left me behind. I was on the staff, so management couldn't blatantly get rid of me without trouble on their doorsteps. Bit by bit, however, I had found myself assigned to 'quirky' stories, such as fundraising dips-in-the-nip, *Guinness Book of Records* attempts, interviews with radio presenters in their lovely homes, or with new or fading micro 'celebrities', many of whom, God love them, presented themselves in full makeup and kit. Some even turned up with managers and PR people in tow but, reserving my own opinions, I always strove to give them the same editorial attention I accorded to aid workers, archbishops or aspiring authors. I felt they deserved respect, not least for putting their heads above the parapet, and always searched diligently through my recorded tapes for sensible or interesting nuggets behind the trivialities they spouted. And, anyhow, who was to say which of the younger aspirants to fame wouldn't eventually develop into a Bob Geldof, a Jane Fonda or a Michael O'Leary?

By the end of my tenure, with some exceptions, cynicism and scepticism had overcome empathetic human interest in newspapers and even I could see that people like me, who squandered too much editorial time by honing and rehoning pieces, were no longer useful to an independent newspaper competing for readers against huge, highly resourced conglomerates.

So, when the axe finally fell, I wasn't surprised. The weapon wasn't called redundancy but early retirement. Very early retirement since I was only forty-six at the time. But right then I was too weary and too fraught to interrogate my employer on the difference, although I suspected it was to the advantage of the newspaper rather than myself. Although my union would have backed me if I had pushed, my ejection coincided with one of my sister's relapses – the most serious to date – and that alone accounted for most of my emotional and physical energy without taking on the official machinery involved in constructive-dismissal cases. I took the money and ran. In many ways it was a relief: it was becoming difficult to argue for standards, even with myself. Derek was beginning to gain recognition and, with it, a better salary, so money was no longer a major issue in our lives. I could take my time finding some other job. Which, of course, I never did. Not on anyone's staff anyhow!

You may ask why Chloë is not here today. She has her own room in this house, hasn't she? Well, it's because she can't deal with social occasions. I know that's difficult to understand, particularly when the event in question is such a joyful one and when, over the years, she would have encountered all of these friends individually. That doesn't make any difference to her. Meeting them all together is not on. Even one at a time is only marginally OK for her, depending on her mood or medication. I guess you'd need to be closely involved with a mentally ill person to accept that, for him or her, when that's the way it is, that's just the way it is.

On the dot of half past two, the doorbell rings. It's Mary. I have a private arrangement with her that she'll arrive half an hour before the others. It gives us a chance for a chat – and also, if anything still needs doing, she'll help me. Nothing does this year and, although I say it myself, the house blazes with welcome as, accompanied by Flora, I hurry to open the door. 'Come in, Mary! Happy Christmas!'

'Same to you! Happy Christmas, Flora.' She gives the dog

a pat and, stepping into the hall, glances around. 'The usual understatement, I see! Chloë OK?'

'Give over. You say that every year. You know what they say about sarcasm and the lowest form of wit. I might surprise you next year.'

'You and Santa Claus.' We hug warmly.

'And Chloë's grand. Thanks for asking. I'm seeing her tomorrow as usual. How's your mother?' Mary's mother has been suffering from Alzheimer's disease for many years now. She no longer recognises her daughter.

'No change. But she does still sing a bit. We do our best.'

'Poor woman. God forbid it will happen to us, Mary. Give us your coat. As you reminded me last week, ten years! Our eleventh Christmas together – can you believe it?'

'I can. I have to see myself in the mirror every morning – but you look great! Haven't seen that before.' She makes an up-and-down gesture indicating the multicoloured tunic I'm wearing over an old pair of black silk slacks she's seen many times.

'Penneys.' I pluck at the top.

'I don't believe it.'

'Believe it. Fifteen euro.'

'Well, you look terrific.'

'So do you. Red lipstick for a red lady – suits you. Quite daring – and I still like that outfit on you! Very Jackie O. At Jack's funeral, of course!'

'Always the bitther word!'

'Shut up, Mary, you know me and clothes. I don't care what anyone wears. If you wore the same thing every day, if Methuselah's mother wore it, that's fine with me.' On anyone else, her black dress and jacket, black tights and black patent flats may have seemed suitable only for a funeral, but the ensemble accentuates her hair and skin, undeniably mature but still creamy.

'All right. Pax!' She smiles. 'You've said before that you like me in this. We're quite the mutual admiration society, aren't we?'

'Who else would tell us how gorgeous we are? Go on in, the fire's lit. G and T? The champagne is in the fridge. I'll wait with that until we're all here.'

'Just water for the moment. It's going to be a long day.'

Wrong, as it happened, but I didn't know that then.

'Coming up.' There isn't a square inch of undecorated surface in my little hallway so I run upstairs to leave her coat on my bed, then fill two glasses with Tipperary water. I'll join her in moderation: it's early days and there's still a lot of stove time to put in.

An hour later, with Flora snoozing on the rug in front of the fire, Dina, Mary and I, ensconced in my sitting room with our drinks, are indulging in speculation about Lorna. The two of them have gone for the toy-boy option. 'But you didn't hear the stress in her voice on the phone,' I tell them. 'I don't think it's that at all – I wonder will she be last again this year?' Lorna is usually the last to arrive on these occasions because she does Christmas morning rounds of neighbours. Both she and Jean are originally from Drogheda where they went to school together. Jean still lives in the town's hinterland, renting a sweet little cottage in Termonfeckin.

'Good stress or bad stress?' This is Dina, who's wearing one of her own creations: a waterfall of ecru lace over purple tights and pink shoes, topped off with a white feather boa. (She has wardrobes full of this stuff and makes a lot of it herself, probably another manifestation of her ambivalence concerning her money. She takes teasing from the rest of us in good spirits, though. 'Youse can say what youse like,' exaggerating for our benefit, 'youse can look like a gang of oul' aunties at a wake. I'm not old enough yet.')

'Not good stress anyway,' I tell her. 'We can get some of the gen from Jean. Lorna said we could.'

'Not changing the subject or anything, ladies,' I feel we've done enough gossiping about Lorna, 'it's been ten years. And leaving that first Christmas out of it, which was the most memorable one for each of you?'

Mary turns to Dina: 'Remember that one where it had snowed – well, sort of. Frost and sleet on the ground. Real cold, kind of misty too. After the dinner, the five of us took Flora for a walk and just up by that old factory site, we found a rusty gate, hanging off the hinges—'

'Yeah,' Dina lights up. 'You insisted on going in and it was an avenue, kind of forest-y, leading up to this big derelict house—'

'It wasn't derelict at all. We saw lights—'

'I remember,' I smiled at them. 'Halfway up that avenue, Flora wouldn't go a step further – faced the other way. Tried to pull us back.'

'Dogs know things we don't. Wouldn't you wonder how?' This is Dina.

'Did you ever find out who lived there?' Maggie tolerates dogs, but is not that interested in giving them much airtime.

'Plain old squatters. Probably having double-decker marijuana sandwiches that day, because it was Christmas—'

The sound of the doorbell ringing cuts across further discussions.

'Relax. This is probably Jean,' I get up from my chair, 'but if it's Lorna and her friend, you two be good, d'you hear?'

When I open the door, to say I'm stunned is an understatement. 'Good afternoon! Happy Christmas.' I manage not to betray myself – I think.

'This is James McAlinden,' Lorna says tersely.

'You're very welcome, James. I'm Maggie. Happy Christmas – you too, Lorna. Come on in – God! What a day, eh? Come in, come in.' I'm fully aware that my voice sounds higher than normal. Somehow I had been expecting Lorna's friend to be a waif, even if he did prove to be a toy-boy. Well, the jury is out as to the toy-boy option, but this is certainly no waif. His handshake is cool and firm. Then he stoops to pat Flora, who, bouncing over and back between our two latest guests, is wagging her tail off. 'What's her name, Maggie? Is she a collie?'

'Flora. And, yes, she is a collie. Come in out of the wet, you're getting drenched.' As he follows Lorna into the house, James McAlinden trails a faint scent of lemons. Neither is wearing a coat so, having closed the door, I usher them straight towards the sitting room. 'The others are in here. Jean hasn't arrived yet. Go on in.'

Unlike me (I hope) neither Dina nor Mary can hide her reaction on first seeing James McAlinden. Dina's mouth opens in astonishment. In his dove-grey hoodie and pressed jeans, this young man is beautiful. Think 'Darren', the actor Robert Sheehan, the guy with the eyes in RTÉ's crime thing, *Love/Hate*. Shot, and lying possibly dead, dammit, at the end of Series Three. (Although you'd never know with serial drama: I'm old enough to remember Bobby Ewing!)

Well, our new friend is not a replica but near enough. He's a little broader across the shoulders, and his dark, luxuriant hair is collar-length, the shiny, crow's-wing mane of your Native American brave in movies. Or a rock singer who's managed to find a shower. His eyes are large, slightly almond-shaped, and while the exact colour of the actor's is difficult to discern on a television screen as small as mine, this kid's are a pale, startling grey, fringed all round with dark, thick lashes. They're also higher than my own and that, while not unprecedented, is not what I'm used to in men. I tell everyone I'm five feet eleven, but in fact I'm just half an inch above six feet and Chloë is six feet two. Although our parents were not overly tall, Granddad Quinn, a blacksmith from Kilkenny, was huge in all dimensions. I always had to wear flats when out with Derek and even then I was the taller.

Now, you'd think this kid would be a bit uncomfortable in this scenario, wouldn't you? Not a bit of it, it seems, as he smiles at the women in the sitting room, one looking like an ageing Shirley Temple, the other looking as though dressed for mourning, both with a dusting of Hunky Dorys crisp crumbs on their chests. Although neither is overweight, each, I'd noticed with wry understanding, had instantly pulled in her stomach when he had walked in. I'd expect this of Dina, but Mary? Gives you an idea of the effect this James has on women.

Dina gets to him first: 'Hello there!' Having brushed the crumbs off the front of her dress, she holds out her hand. 'I'm Claudine.' We all know that, like a gift, she bestows the name only on those in whom she seeks a reaction, so we don't blink.

Neither does he. 'And I'm James,' he greets her, shaking her extended hand.

'Always James?' she coos. 'Or do we call you Jim? Jimmy, even.'

'If you wish.' He shrugs. 'Or Mac, anything you like.'

'It's James for me. How do you do? I'm Mary,' my best pal says earnestly, using her counsellor voice. They shake.

'I'm fine, thank you, Mary.' He smiles at them. 'Nice to meet you both.'

Lorna, I realise, is still standing a little behind me, watching these performances. For me, right now, this whole thing feels like some kind of weird four-hand reel and I feel I have to intervene. 'I hope you're hungry, James.' I attempt a light laugh but in my own ears it sounds dangerously close to a titter. I don't blame Dina or Mary for their reaction to this cuckoo in the nest: it's impossible not to be affected by his physical aura – but I have to regain control of this. It's my party, after all. 'Don't let a group of oul' wans intimidate you, James.' I include myself in a sweep of my arm around the room. 'We're dying to find out all about you, as I'm sure you can tell, but you should feel free to tell us to eff off if we ask too many questions. Although I have to admit it's great to have – er – someone new in our Christmas group.' Jesus. I'd nearly said 'fresh blood'.

'Sit down, all of you,' I wave them into the seating. 'That's a fabulous coat-dress, Lorna. New? It's great on you.' Then, not giving her a chance to respond: 'Love the fur ruff around the neck. I hope it's fake. Wouldn't want anyone to throw paint over it, ha ha.' As she sits on my little couch, bringing a cushion around to her stomach, I add, 'What would you like to drink, both of you? I think I could find you a beer or something, James.' I was trying to remember if I had any in the fridge.

'What else do you have, Maggie?'

I reel off the options: 'Gin and tonic? Wine, white or red? Sherry? Port? Brandy? We don't have much of a selection, I'm afraid – I know what this lot want, of course!'

'G and T for me, please, Mags,' Lorna says tightly.

'And I'll have one too,' says James, settling himself near her beside the fire on the kitchen stool. (I always have to add to my seating if I'm entertaining more than five people.) Although I'm super-sensitised to accents in general, I can't place James's. A bit of Dublin, certainly, I think, as I go into the kitchen again to fetch the two drinks. There's more than a hint of country, though – maybe the midlands? Could he be a Traveller, by any chance? And since when did young men drink gin and tonic in preference to beer?

I'm leaning now towards the son option because, so far, I haven't detected a sexual haze around him and Lorna. On the other hand, if there had been that kind of connection, it would have been difficult to detect amid the general whiff in the room. I'd better desist with the 'oul' wans' routine, I think: there'd be a bit of sensitivity around that. I know we're all still spring chickens in our fifties – although Jean and Lorna are getting close to the next bus stop. Dina may be sixty already, it's hard to tell. She refuses to have any truck with birthdays. She tells us that for her sixtieth, her plan is to be away on the Côte d'Azur on the day in question, '… hopefully with a toy-boy on my arm, but of course that's far, far into the future.' We all managed to keep our faces straight for that one.

Jean arrives as I'm carrying the G and Ts in for the others. Opening the door, I jerk my head in the direction of the sitting room to signal to her what's in store, but she's ahead of me. 'I know. I saw Lorna's car outside. Happy Christmas, Maggie. This is for you, hope you like it, let me take those – I've left my coat in the car. How's Chloë?'

There's something different about Jean today, I think. The same clothes, granted, the same speech pattern, but she looks, well, healthier or something. 'Chloë's grand, thanks. You do something with your hair, Jean?'

'Nah. Just got a blow-dry yesterday. I had it cut ages ago.'

'Well, it suits you.' It did too. The perm was still evident but it was softer somehow, airier. We swap her present for my drinks tray and she proceeds directly into the sitting room. I drop the gift – soft, something else knitted, no change there – under the tree and follow her.

So here we all are. Five plus the cuckoo, who, I'm surprised to see, has been joined at the foot of his stool by Flora, nuzzled into his pristine white trainers. After first greetings, she is usually quite aloof with strangers.

I had decreed that we wouldn't open presents in front of James since we had nothing for him. So that period of enjoyable time-eating is not an option, but somehow we get through the next half-hour. Usually, when the five of us are together, there's a lot of giggling and banter as we catch up on events since we last met as a group. Today's conversation, episodic for me as I move in and out of the kitchen to check on how the food is doing, is general: too much gloom and doom on the news, the dire, changeable weather, all too evident today as it continues to rain, the austerity budget. James seems to be taking very little part in it but, whether he knows it or not, is presiding.

'You protested, didn't you, Mags?' Jean asks, during one of my visits to the sitting room.

'Yep!' I'm refreshing their drinks. Although I'm not in receipt of a carer's allowance, I had protested in solidarity with the Carers Association outside Leinster House because I have some understanding about what cuts mean to them.

'Well, I did too.' Jean had gone along to the general protest against austerity as a member of a small satellite organisation involving widows.

Dina, predictably, then launches into a rant against all politicians: 'They're all the same. We know that.'

I'm on my way back to the kitchen and, for the sake of it, dissent: 'They're not great, I'll grant you, but they're not all bad and some of them really do care!' That guarantees a few more minutes of outrage from Dina while I take out the turkey and cover it with a tent of tinfoil so it can 'rest'. I do wish chefs would come up with something more empathetic than depicting a dead, roasted creature as merely 'resting' – although I keep such talk to myself for fear of ridicule.

Throughout, the object of all the attention, blatant or covert, sits quietly on his stool, taking no part in the conversation except to answer neutral questions such as this patently silly one from Dina: 'Is gin your default drink, James?'

'No. If it's spirits I'm drinking I like rum, Dina.'

I've noticed that he uses our names a lot – whatever that indicates. It's unusual, though, especially in youngsters who are not inclined to be so formal. What is also unusual is that he has not gulped his drink but has nursed it, refusing all offers of a refresher. I had deliberately given it to him in a tall glass, heavy on the tonic, light on the gin, lacing it with lots of ice and an extra large slice of lemon. Well, you never know, do you? There are a lot of alcoholics in Ireland who scrub up well. I've met them, even interviewed them during my past life as a hack. I don't want things to go wrong today.

Except for her short 'Happy Christmas, Maggie,' routine when she came in, Lorna, ostensibly James's sponsor at this event, has not uttered a syllable. Her tension adds to the curious and novel feel of this year's Christmas 'do'. Although everyone is polite and on the surface behaving sociably, the effect of this new presence in our midst has drifted like fog to the four corners of the house and made a hames of the jolly atmosphere that normally transpires. The air throbs with trying-too-hard, so it's a relief when, just after a quarter past four, I can call them all in to eat.

Miraculously, it seems, just as we're sorting out the seating arrangements, the rain clears away, leaving a legacy of rainbows in a pale, watery sky. 'A double!' Dina cries, clapping her hands. 'That's so lucky!'

I've placed Mary and Dina with their backs to the window and when the sun, now setting, emerges fleetingly through scudding clouds, its pink and orange rays shaft through the glass, giving Mary a Titian corona and dappling Dina's highlighted blonde bob with vivid colour. James is staring at both of them and I'm oddly annoyed. I'd gone to a lot of trouble to provide a nice, celebratory dinner for my friends, but because of him, the whole thing has fallen out of its normal orbit. Lorna's expression is unreadable. Dina, wearing her beatific I-know-a-secret-pathway-to-Nirvana expression, is openly ogling. Jean is looking at James as though he needs to be wrapped in a woolly blanket, while Mary, as far as I can see, is fighting to regain the central position she normally holds, that of Wise Woman to whom we all defer on worldly matters. Without doing anything blameworthy, he has hijacked the occasion.

It's time to lance this. 'So tell us about yourself, James.'

He reacts to the edge in my tone by glancing at me with those amazing eyes of his and, I know this is going to sound totally OTT, dammit, I wither, as if he can see right into my sad soul. I backtrack. 'Sorry. That was rude. Don't mind me, James, all in due course, eh?' Challenging the rest of them, I look around the table. 'Anyone feel like saying grace?'

Shit! Why had I said that? We never say grace.

'No.' Their chorus has a twittery vibe.

'Well, dig in, then.' I start pouring the wine. To them, I hope, I'm back in charge.

SEVEN

At my dinner table, I am ultra-conscious of this year's brighter eyes and more than usually overheated conversations. As an example, even a subject as innocuous as the smoked salmon starter has provoked a spat, initiated by little Jean, of all people, who is just being complimentary: 'Ah, it was worth going all the way to Howth for this, Mags.' But then she goes too far. Forever extolling the virtues of Louth, the orphan county of Ireland, neglected and scorned by its richer neighbours in Meath and Dublin, as she sees it, she mounts her hobby horse: 'We've a great fish shop in Drogheda, ladies – and gentleman, of course.' She nods towards the newest (hon.) member of our Club.

'So you're always telling us – the cheque's in the post, I assume, Jean?' Mary doesn't mean to sound waspish – I know it's just her manner – but Jean, because she has had a couple of glasses of wine, takes offence: 'I'm only saying—'

'Of course you are. We all know that Drogheda is the centre of the universe.'

'Shut up, Mary!' Dina turns towards Jean.

'Leave her alone, Dina Coyne!' Already irritated, Jean, the remains of her perm dancing on her head, always rides shotgun alongside her friend. 'Nobody can be chirpy all the time – and as for that centre-of-the-universe crack, I'll have you know that Drogheda is great. It's just pointy-headed snobby intellectuals like you, Mary Guerin, and – and … ' failing to come up with an acceptable insult, she contents herself with glaring at Dina '… you, Dina Coyne, who look down on the rest of us in the sticks. For your information it was only yesterday I got these shoes in Drogheda. Look at them!' She snatches her napkin off her lap, throws it onto the table and seems about to stand up to show us, when Dina supersedes her.

Jammed in as she is, she nevertheless manages to get one of her own pink delights held up, balancing the heel on the edge of the table so we can all see it. 'Beat this, Jean! Dunnes. Henry Street. Twenty euro.'

'Slumming it on the northside again, Dina?' Mary hates being called a snob. She can be, I admit, intellectually patronising but with good cause: she has the smarts after all.

I steal a glance at James. His smile is still in place. I shoot Dina what I hope is a forbidding glance. 'Put that shoe away, you'll frighten the horses.' To end the bickering, I stand up and start piling plates. 'Everyone finished? Give us all those plates. The soup will be half the size it was this morning.

'Thanks.' I smile at Lorna as I take her cutlery. By contrast to

Jean, who is more animated today than I've ever seen her, Lorna is still sunk into herself. I wish she would confide in us. We'd understand – or would we? 'Don't kill each other, will ye, while I'm away?' I address them in general. 'Won't be long!'

'That was lovely, thank you. Do you need a hand, Maggie?' To my surprise, James stretches out as though to take the dishes from me.

'No worries, kid.' I turn away. 'Stay where you are, but thanks anyway. As you can see, this kitchen is so bijou the two of us would be tripping over ourselves.'

Having turned the heat off under the pot of soup, I take the lid off and, to give the contents a chance to cool a little, get a head start on stacking the dishwasher. I'm hoping fervently that both Mary and Dina, in particular, will pipe down. Mary loves an argument, of course, and both she and Dina pride themselves on being bluntly honest. As a result of such candour, both can unintentionally insult or hurt others, hiding unrepentantly behind the mantra: 'Well, you know me! I call a spade a spade!'

Dina: 'But Chloë looks so normal! She could easily get herself a little job!'

Mary: 'Why do you put up with bad behaviour? Why don't you just kick her back to Merrow when she treats you like that?'

As I've said, Merrow House is Chloë's residential 'facility'.

We all put up with each other's quirks, but we're friends. Friends do that and don't take these altercations seriously, however sparky they are at the time. Clattering away in the maw of the dishwasher, I realise that the sound is very loud; since I left the table, there has been silence. But just as I'm again about to intervene I hear Mary's voice, quite dreamy: 'Leeds, Bradford, Halifax, Huddersfield, Dewsbury, Wakefield and Barnsley ... '

'What's that?' I straighten up to look out at her. The others are all gaping.

'The cotton towns of Yorkshire – remember, Mags?' she calls back. Then, 'Before your time, James,' and for his benefit, starts in on the story of our friendship, and how long it has lasted. Leave it to her, I think, shoving starter plates willy-nilly into the back of the machine. One of Mary Guerin's best traits is her intuition: she's diverting attention from both Lorna and James. The other women know this story but not in such detail – and right now she seems to be starting right back at day one. Order restored!

Of course I remember the cotton towns of Yorkshire, just as I remember the rote-learned poetry – and how to knit. These, along with long tots and English grammar, were probably the only lifetime-useful skills I learned throughout my entire time in school. And I include secondary school in that assessment. Except for Latin. I loved Latin. Such a beautiful, logical language.

I move to the cooker to turn on the sprouts and check to see if the turkey is still warm under its tent of foil. Everything seems well under control and I decide to stay out of the arena for a few more minutes. I need to. Things are pretty weird around that table, but Mary's recital of our early schooldays will keep her companions quiet until I can get back with the next course. In the meantime: 'Everyone OK for wine?' I call. 'Will you look after that, Dina?'

She picks up the bottle.

Mary's considerable gifts owe a lot to her unshakeable confidence, something I noticed from first acquaintance. She is a terrific communicator, but sometimes adopts taciturnity and even tartness for reasons even I can't fathom; as far as I can see, she doesn't notice when people react badly to her more outlandish

83

theories – like her most recent passion, research into the existence of fairies.

Mary Guerin and I met on our first day in second class when, with name badges prominently displayed on our uniform jumpers, we were seated together in the front row of the classroom, 'so I can keep an eye on ye'. Our new teacher, a large, stout woman with iron-grey hair, peered at my badge: 'Margaret Quinn! Your reputation has travelled before ya!' I didn't understand what she meant, so I smiled nervously. She leaned low and poked me in the chest. 'Think that's funny, eh?' Her breath smelt of tobacco, like my granddad's.

'No,' I whispered.

'No, what?' (She pronounced it 'fwhaaht': she was a native Irish speaker and had told us, with an implied 'or else!' that we were all going to love the Irish language.) I didn't know what I was supposed to say.

She sighed noisily. '"No, *a mhúinteoir*!"'

'No, *a mhúinteoir*!' I got it out somehow.

'That's right. I'm the *múinteoir* here. I'm the teacher. I'm in charge. And ye'll all address me correctly. But, Margaret Quinn, for this first week, you're in charge of this wan here.' She shot a wintry smile at Mary Guerin. 'She's new. She's come from a little school where they're all wrapped in cotton wool – that right, Mary Guerin?' And when Mary didn't respond, the woman turned back to me. 'Show her the ropes, Margaret Quinn. Make her understand that she might be living in a big house' – she'd spat the word 'big' – 'but we have no airs and graces here and my classroom runs on respect. "Guerin", eh?' She turned her gaze back on Mary. 'I hear you're a Protestant. English stock, I suppose?'

'No, *a mhúinteoir*.' Mary had emphasised '*Mhúinteoir*'

slightly. 'I'm a Quaker. And the name is Huguenot. French. *A mhúinteoir.*'

The teacher stared at her, but Mary's tone had been perfectly pleasant and respectful. I couldn't get over her guts. This was no ordinary girl.

With pursed lips, our teacher slowly surveyed the class. 'As for the rest of ye, remember, ye're not babies any longer and I won't tolerate any boldness. Ye're big girls now and it's serious business in my class, d'y'hear me? We're going to learn and we're going to start as we mean to go on.' For emphasis, she thumped the desk between Mary and me so the inkpots rattled and our sweet-smelling, arrow-sharp pencils popped out of their grooves.

The atmosphere in Babies School, from Babies right through first class, had not been lax, but it had been humane, mostly friendly, and our teacher, whom we had had for the full three years, had had a soft, musical voice. This one boomed like a man. She terrified me, and even the classroom, with its high ceiling and hard echoes, seemed to warn us that we could expect no comfort. For me and most of my classmates, the transition from Babies to this one had meant merely crossing the yard outside our new classroom window; I felt now as if I'd been turfed out of a warm, soft bed onto a cold floor.

Our teacher turned her back to us and picked up a piece of chalk. 'Now get out yeer copybooks so we can write down a few dos and don'ts.' Heavily, chalk squeaking, she began to write in big, thick capitals: C-I-Ú …

As I scrabbled for the copybook in the schoolbag at my feet, I stole a look at my desk companion. Even at that stage her hair was extraordinary: it sprang out from the hairband under which an attempt had been made to confine it. It was a bright day and in the sunlight her head might have been in flames, like that of the martyrs in the stained-glass window in our church. Staring straight ahead, Mary Guerin already had her copybook in front of her. Both hands on it were open and relaxed as the woman completed her handiwork on the blackboard: '*CIÚNAS*. NO TALKING.' A redundant admonition because, apart from a muffled chant from the room next door, the only sound was a sniffle from someone in the back row.

But then Mary Guerin turned to me and, in a loud whisper, asked, 'What time is lunch?'

The teacher turned round. 'Who said that?'

My heart stopped.

Silence. Then, from Mary Guerin: 'I did.' Again, far from seeming afraid, she looked merely surprised as she raised her hand.

The chant from next door seemed to grow in volume as the teacher and Mary Guerin surveyed each other. 'I'll give you the benefit of the Probation Act on this one,' the woman said. 'Stand up!'

Mary did.

'Repeat after me: "There's no talking."'

'There's no talking. *A Mhúinteoir*,' she added, in a clear, firm voice.

The teacher reached into her desk, took out a bamboo cane and held it up so we could all see it. 'This is my little helper, Cáit. Cáit is always ready to help me keep ye in line.' As she brandished it, I could feel fear, like a hot wind, blow throughout the room. 'Can you see Cáit, Mary Guerin?'

'Yes, I can.'

'Yes, I can, fwhaaht?'

'Yes, I can, *a mhúinteoir*!'

'Sit down.'

Mary sat.

'I have my eye on you!' The woman turned away, placing the cane not in, but on her desk where, like a malevolent snake, it remained horribly in our line of sight. 'Now open yeer copybooks ...'

The morning crawled by, with recitations of addition and multiplication tables, then with transcribing what our teacher had written on the blackboard, a summary of which was: no talking, no whispering, keeping our hands in front of us at all times, no running in the yard, no forgetting our knitting, no excuses for homework undone.

When we had all that down in our copies, she erased the writing on the blackboard, sending clouds of chalk dust flying through the slanting sunlight. She then wrote out our homework, a verse of an Irish poem. And when we had all copied that down, she made us recite it, going over it three times to give us the pronunciation and rhythm, beating it out with Cáit on the wood of her desk:

A dhroimeann donn dílis, *BANG!*
A shíoda na mbó, *BANG!*
Cá ngabhann tú san oiche, *BANG!*
Cá mbíonn tú sa ló, *BANG!*
Bímse ar na choillte, *BANG!*
Is mo bhuachaill im chomhair, *BANG!*
Ach d'fhág sé siud mise, *BANG!*
Ag sileadh na ndeoir. *BANG!*

She translated it, line after line, giving it context. 'That little faithful brown cow, the *droimeann donn dílis*, is our country, Ireland,' she told us. 'Ireland was occupied by the enemy Sassenach. The cow is *síoda na mbó* – *síoda* is silk. So she's the silk of the kine. Who knows what "kine" means?'

Nobody moved. Then Mary Guerin raised her hand.

'You know?' The teacher was genuinely surprised.

'Yes, *a mhúinteoir.*'

'Stand up.'

She stood.

'So?'

'It's cows. It's in a poem, *a mhúinteoir.*'

'And what poem might that be?'

'I don't know the name of it. I know a verse, though,' she added helpfully. 'My daddy and I learned it together. He reads poetry to me in bed at night.'

'Does he now?' The teacher came around to the front of her desk and perched her substantial bottom on its edge. 'Is that so? How lovely. Daddy and you. So, let us in.' Her massive bosoms jiggling as she crossed her arms, she stared at Mary. 'Entertain us ordinary folk with your poem, Mary Guerin.'

Without missing a beat, Mary cleared her throat and then, in a sing-song voice: 'A poem by Robert E. Howard.' She paused, took a deep breath and then:

Now I am but a simple churl
Who loves the kine and grass,
To watch the burning dawns unfurl,
And the fleecy clouds that pass.

'There's more. But that's all I know by heart, *a mhúinteoir.*' Remaining on her feet, she seemed unaware of the sensation her recitation had caused in our class of seven-year-olds. Even our teacher seemed speechless for a few seconds – before reclaiming her dictatorship. 'Sit down, Mary,' she said gruffly, into the hush. Mary did. I glanced admiringly at her. I was in love. And Mary Guerin was mine. I had her, not Brainypants.

Up to this moment, Brainypants had been in charge of everything from Babies through High Babies and into first class. She ran errands, she gave out the copies, she was always top of the class. Not any more she wasn't, and my hope was that some of Mary Guerin's glory would reflect on me. I made a mental note to ask her about her da. Her daddy, as she called him. That would be crucial.

In the my-da's-better-than-your-da stakes, Brainypants was forever boasting to us, whose fathers were milk roundsmen, bus drivers, street sweepers, or porters at Kingsbridge and Amiens Street railway stations, that hers was an accountant. (At the early stages, everyone in my class had had a da, but by the time we left to go to primary school from the superiority of first class, three of the Babies, we whispered, half scandalised, half pitying, had no da at all. Missing even one parent in those days classified you as an orphan.)

To those of us not grand enough to have an accountant in the family, a da was either a good da, an all-right da or a really strict da, who'd take his belt to you. What fathers did when out of the house all day was not really of interest in our little worlds. My own da drove an electric laundry-delivery van, always smelt of bleached cotton and linen, and was a hero to me because, on Saturdays when he delivered, he allowed me to sit in the front seat of his vehicle from where, to the soundtrack of the motor's quiet whine, I had a grand view of the city and suburban streets. The smell released when ironing sheets always reminds me of him.

And before you ask, his laundry had nothing to do with institutions or nuns. It was privately run for the service of the better off.

In his own quiet way, Da was a film buff, and on Saturday afternoons, when he had a half-day, from the time I was five years old, he regularly brought me to matinée performances. Before the age of ten, I was a veteran cinema-goer.

The standouts I remember now are the epics: *Doctor Zhivago* and *Lawrence of Arabia*, for instance and he even sneaked me into various Carry On pictures, where, of course, the innuendo went right over my head but the slapstick was delicious.

But getting back to the classroom that first day in second class and Mary Guerin's budding relationship with authority: 'So now,' our *múinteoir*, said, 'thanks to Miss Genius here in the front row, we all know that "kine" means "cattle". What does "kine" mean, *a pháistí*?'

'"Cattle", *a mhúinteoir*,' we sang.

'Good. And *síoda* is the best of all fabrics. That little brown cow is another word for Ireland. She's the silk of the kine. Because Ireland is the queen of all the countries in the world. But because of the Sasanaigh, the Englishmen, she has to hide in the woods. She's *ag sileadh na ndeoir*. What does this mean, children?'

This was getting beyond me, but Brainypants raised her hand: 'She's crying, *a mhuinteoir*.' Obviously, I thought cattily, trying to regain her crown. No chance.

Our teacher seemed to be impressed, though: '*Maith a chailín*,' she praised, smoothing that girl's path through the rest of her career in that classroom to become her pet. 'Last time now, *a chailíní*. Pay attention. I'll be examining ye tomorrow and ye have to be word perfect. *Arís*. From the beginning ...'

At last the bell rang for lunchtime and we were released into the yard with all the other classes. I took my in-charge duties seriously with regard to Mary Guerin and was prepared to repel all boarders if anyone else attempted to muscle in. I had to get us into one of the prime bits of the yard, and if we didn't run, the corners and all the best lengths of railing would already be bagsed. 'Come with me, Mary. Hurry!' We ran out together.

In the yard, all the good sites were already occupied by Big Girls, but we eventually found a vacant, if lesser, spot and opened our lunch bags. Mine contained two tomato sandwiches and milk in a Baby Powers bottle. Her drink was in a small silver thing, battered and stained and shaped a bit like a larger version of the kidneys we had sometimes for our dinner – I learned at some stage afterwards it was an antique hip flask of real silver. But when she poured the contents into the tiny cup she had unscrewed off the top, I saw she had just plain water. That was bad enough but her sandwich was truly shocking: a slice of turnover loaf creased double over its butter, which was a bit yellow – so it could even have been Stork margarine. Nothing else. Not even jam. Our teacher had implied that Mary was posh. Posh to me meant pocket money, comics every week instead of as a treat, whole bars of chocolate instead of just a square, and a family car. Posh meant Protestant.

'What does your da work at? Is a Quaker a kind of Protestant?' I asked, through a mouthful of bread and tomato.

'My daddy's a cripple,' she said matter-of-factly. 'He used to be a doctor but now he can't work. He was up a ladder and he fell off.'

'Oh, that's terrible,' I said. My heart really melted for her. I couldn't imagine anybody's da not working. In my experience, everyone's da did something.

Mary seemed unaware of my empathy as she bit into her own sandwich. 'And I don't really know the difference between us and Protestants because we only meet other Quakers at meetings. We call ourselves "Friends".'

'Oh? We go to Mass.' Somehow, that felt more serious than simply going to 'meetings'.

'I know,' she said. 'We don't.'

'Do you have to? Is it a sin if you don't? For us it's a real black mortal sin and we'd go to Hell if we missed Mass.'

'It's our own choice. And it's certainly not a sin.' Chewing hard on her thick crust, she shook her head. So she was a Protestant, I thought, even if only a kind of one. Protestants, I knew, could make up their own minds whether to go to Mass or not. They called it 'church', and it wasn't a sin for them either, if they didn't go on Sundays. A Quaker was a new one on me but I knew all about Protestants because there were two Protestant families on my road and, at that time, the two daughters from those houses were my best friends. They had pudding instead of sweet after their dinners, ate supper instead of tea, were always having adventures with the Girl Guides and went 'touring' in their car for the summer holidays. I had therefore gained the impression that money was no object for Protestants so, having seen the state of her lunch, I was wondering about Mary. Maybe Quakers were the poor side of the Protestants. 'Do you have a car in your house?'

'No.'

That sealed the deal. Mary was the first poor person outside of Catholics I had ever met. 'Here,' I said generously, 'I'll give you a bit of my sandwich.' I broke off half of one and offered it to her. She turned red, and, with a furious expression, said, 'Thank you but no thank you. I have my own here.'

'Well, if it's not good enough for you ...' I was insulted. Any other girl, especially a new girl, would have accepted my gift. She just continued chewing but at least she wasn't red any more. I couldn't lose face, though, by getting up and walking away: that would mean she'd won. What she would have won was unclear – I hadn't worked that out. But what was more important, I couldn't risk losing my status of being in charge of her: someone else would have been in like a light. I cast around for neutral conversation. 'So you won't be making your First Communion, Mary?'

'No. Quakers don't have First Communions. To us, every time we eat together is communion with the Lord.' She recited this in a sing-song manner, like her poem.

'So you won't be getting a dress or a veil or white shoes this year?'

'No.'

There was something about the way she said it that, young though I was, I knew it was time to shut up. But I looked at her with further and genuine sympathy. It started to rain, however, putting paid to any more conversation about Quakers or anything else as, all over the yard, girls scrambled to get back inside. As I got my own things together I thought I'd have hated to be a Quaker. The First Communion dress was going to be the main topic of conversation all that year. That and the shoes and the veil, and the handbag to hold the tons of money we'd get from our mothers' relatives and our neighbours. I hoped to get enough to buy a real watch, not one of those stupid Mickey Mouse ones from Woolworths.

Waiting for my sprouts to boil half a century later, I'm only half listening to Mary's version of all this. She, she is telling the group, had always felt sorry for me with my mortal and venial sins, being tempted by Lucifer and all the rest of the stuff I had to carry around. Just as the vegetables come to the boil, Jean, unusually pink-cheeked, passes through the kitchen on her way to the cloakroom. I turn down the hotplate and follow her, catching her just before she opens the door: 'You're in great form today, Jean.'

'It's Christmas, Maggie! Why wouldn't I be?'

There's no answer to that so I turn to the topic of her friend: 'What's wrong with Lorna? She's not herself.'

'You haven't heard yet, I know that, and I'll give you the headlines, but I have to leave the full story to her. She'll tell us if she wants us all to know.' She takes a quick glance over my shoulder to make sure none of the others can see us.

'No worries,' I reassure her. 'Mary has everything under control there.' And indeed she has, as we both hear a burst of laughter, including bass notes from a male.

'OK,' Jean says, in a low voice. 'Martin – you know Martin, Lorna's son?'

'Of course. He's the electrician.'

'Was. He was made redundant by his company five weeks ago and that bitch of a wife kicked him out last week – Christmas week, just before Christmas. Did you ever hear the like?' I had, of course, not like-for-like, but Derek had not taken the season into account when he'd fled to the Arms of Popsy, had he? I didn't say that to Jean, of course. Actually, I was a little taken aback. Jean is usually ladylike and very quietly spoken. It's almost unprecedented to hear her use bad language. Must be alcohol again, I decide, as she darts another glance over her shoulder towards the dinner table. 'He's a bit of a drinker,' she adds, *sotto voce*. 'Did you know that?'

'No.' I shake my head. 'She never said.'

'Well, anyway, he and his wife had some kind of a row, about the redundancy and him being no good and so on, and he reacted by going on a bender for a few days and when he came home the day before yesterday she'd changed the locks. Now nobody can find him.'

'Jesus!'

'Yes.' She nodded solemnly. 'He's missing. Not officially yet, but the guards are involved. They usually take a while to list an adult as missing, so it shows how seriously they're taking this. It's really awful. Don't say a word. It would be better if she could tell you herself. She probably will if she gets a chance. I suspect she won't say much in front of the young fella.'

'What's that all about, by the way? When did she and him happen? How long has it been going on?'

'A couple of months – maybe only a few weeks, I'm not sure. And I'm not sure either that "going on" is the right way to put it. I don't think it is. But I just don't know, Maggie. The whole thing is like a soap opera, if you ask me. I don't want to be unkind, and you know I'm mad about her, but even though I don't know the whole story, I suspect that with this James she's got herself into something that she wishes she hadn't. I'll get her to ring you tomorrow, if he doesn't leave before the rest of us. He hasn't a car so he's probably depending on her for a lift.'

My turn to look over my shoulder. 'He's gorgeous, though, isn't he, Jean?'

'Wouldn't kick him out of bed meself!'

'Jean!' I pretend to be more shocked than I really am, although I am a bit, not because of the words but because they came from little Jean who, you'd think by looking at her, would be the last person to say something so overtly crass.

But why not Jean? We all pretend we're way, way past thinking about sex but give us a few drinks and each other and we're like a bunch of skittish teenagers.

Before I can ask her anything further, I hear the scrape of a chair as though someone else is getting up to leave the table and I let her go.

'Nobody move! Soup coming!' I call, as I get back to my cooker and start ladling.

EIGHT

The stranger at the feast. Clanging, clichéd, but apt. That was how James McAlinden first came into the ambit of poor Chloë's Very Excellent Winter Gathering. And what an entrance!

We're at the coffee stage. Lorna has loosened up over the course of the meal, even occasionally laughing along with the rest of us as we read out the silly jokes in the crackers. The alcohol's helped, although she's been abstemious enough. We all have: none of us has so far breached any significant boundaries either by drinking excessively or trespassing on the James situation. Credit to all, including myself, I think, as I look fondly around the table at these friends, faces soft in the glow from the circle of tea lights around my centrepiece of holly, baby's breath and tiny little chocolate Santas, one of which is listing, probably melting. Outside, the weather remains truly foul.

'Storm's getting worse.' Mary has read my thoughts. 'No taxis tonight, I'm sure. I'm going to need a lift from someone.'

'I'll take you,' Jean pipes up. Her voice, like herself, is light.

These women are all so physically different from each other. Jean, tiny, bird-like, with spectacles and a (relaxing!) permanent wave, is the only one of us who, in my opinion, looks like your traditional Irishwoman heading into grannyhood. Appearances are deceptive, however, because she is stout of heart. I mentioned that she knits – her output is prodigious: she knits for the Chernobyl children, sweaters and ear muffs mostly. (This Christmas, she is involved in the Big Knit, producing teensy woolly hats to put on cartons of Innocent smoothies; in return, the makers will donate to Age Action.) More than that, though, she goes every year to Belarus with Adi Roche's crowd. Talks little about it, except when she's fundraising for medical supplies, to support a medical team or to fix up one of Adi's ambulances. She also touches us to sponsor her participation in mini-marathons or five-kilometre runs. Her endeavour there is for the hospice in Harold's Cross where her husband died. She is probably by far the fittest of our group.

Lorna, Jean's closest friend in our set, is the least blabby and most guarded. This evening she is very quiet, even for her, although she does carry with her the quiet authority that goes with her past as a nurse. Dark-haired, she packs a bit more weight than she should, according to her doctor, but her skin, untouched, it seems, by time or surgical intervention, is the envy of us all.

By contrast Dina, voluptuous Dina with the hour-glass figure and strangely shining forehead, takes advantage of everything science offers women by dint of her hefty legacy. She considers herself a man-magnet, and maybe she is, but whether for reasons already mentioned – fears they're after her money – or not, she tires of her conquests very easily after a few dates: 'Still looking for The One!' She's in her element this evening, cracking jokes, not caring to conceal the attention she's lavishing on the new addition to our Christmas circle.

And as for Mary of the magnificent hair, my truest and best friend, what can I say? Five foot six and a half inches of mystery and unpredictability, brilliant of mind, loyal in friendship, careless with her beauty and in dress. On first acquaintance, you might not guess what an original she is. Asked to guess, despite that gypsy hair, you'd place her as a lifetime clerk or civil servant. Her commitment to her part-time counselling job is firm, but for the rest of her time, Mary is as likely to be checking out the latest James Bond blockbuster as she is a film noir in the Irish Film Institute. She could be immersed in some medieval tome in Marsh's Library, where she's well got, or getting just as excited about the latest exhibition at the Science Gallery in Trinity College, as enthusiastic about her regular ballroom-dancing classes as she is about the individual clarinet tuition she bought last year as a birthday present to herself. And she mounts campaigns: her latest involves writing stiff letters to the Sports Council, demanding a grant so that some urchin she has come across, probably in the shelter, can become an élite cross-country runner.

Mary gobbles facts and research like Billy Bunter gobbled chocs before, like him, getting bored or hungry and seeking more. Her newest academic interest in fairies is too far out for me. It was prompted by a chance re-reading of J. M. Barrie's *Peter Pan*, from which she started ruminating over the passage, 'Every time a child says, "I don't believe in fairies," there is a fairy somewhere that falls down dead.' When she comes up with a conversation stopper like that, what can you do but go with the flow? She is a mind-opener. I can see she's watching James now: lepidopterist fascinated by a new and exotic specimen of moth.

'We still don't know anything about you, James. What do you do for a living?' I'd been so intent on loving my friends that I'd taken my eye off the ball and hadn't seen where the danger lay. Dina is leaning across the table, perhaps to give our star guest the benefit of her considerable décolleté, but if that's her intention, it doesn't work.

'Nothing much right now, Claudine,' he says, picking up his glass and taking a small sip. 'I'm between real jobs and Lorna is helping me find my next one.'

'I think we should leave the poor chap alone. Anyone for more wine?' I pick up the bottle as the wind and rain batter the alcove window so hard that my famous window treatment, now ten years old, flutters a little. 'Is there a draught on your backs there, Mary, Dina? Would you like shawls or something?'

But it's Mary now, heedless, her tongue, like that of everyone here, loosened by wine, who interrupts me: 'Where did you two meet, James?'

He glances at Lorna, who visibly bridles. 'Not that it's any of your business, Mary,' she answers, on his behalf, 'but if you must know, we met in my solicitor's office. And, yes, he is staying with me. He's my lodger! Satisfied?'

'No need to snap at me! Sorry I asked!' Mary sits back in her chair.

'Easy, folks.' I pick up a bowl of After Eights and shove it under her nose. 'Anyone like one of these?'

'Thank you.' Mary helps herself, and as I hand around the chocolates I'm thinking, There is a relationship between Lorna and this kid. Otherwise why would she be so touchy? To break the awkwardness, I stand up. 'I'm going to put on some music. If it's OK with everyone, we'll go back into the sitting room to open presents. Bring your drinks with you – more coffee, anyone?' And when they all shake their heads, I turn to James: 'I'm really sorry there's nothing for you, but none of us knew you were coming until this morning.' I look around the table, challenging them all. 'Next year, maybe?' and to a chorus of 'Of course' and 'Sure thing, James,' I hurry out to the hall to re-energise the CD player. I'm hoping that, as usual, this can be the nicest part of our day, that shiny gift-wrap and ribbons can paper over any residue of communal discomfort. I could kill both Mary and Dina, though.

The present-opening period goes well enough, but to me it's a bit anti-climactic this year. It could be my imagination, I know, but because of James's presence, my impression is that there is less of the customary chortling and exclaiming and hugging all round; even Mary, for whom I had pushed the boat out to give her a Kindle e-reader, seems subdued.

My own haul is much appreciated. A coffret of Jo Malone from Dina, who can afford such things, a huge candle from Mary, along with a handwritten note promising me a free ki massage (she does that too!); Jean, inevitably, gives me a woollen cushion cover in a delicate baby blue. Lorna gives me two presents: the first is an apron made of Irish linen, picturing a jolly Mrs Santa in comfy slippers; the second, a circular diamanté brooch, is from her own collection of costume jewellery – I've seen it on her. 'I love it, it's gorgeous,' I tell her, meaning it. Whatever about the big house and the sea view, I sense that Lorna is not comfortably off although, unlike the rest of us, she never talks about money or how hard it is, these days, to make ends meet. It's possible she had been depending on some help from her son – and now, of course, that would appear to be no longer available and she's worse off than ever. When thanking her, I give her an extra long hug.

By the time she and James leave, first as predicted, none of us is any nearer to understanding the situation. The kid's demeanour throughout had been polite and engaged, not for a moment betraying any boredom, even when we women were discussing the relative merits of different BB creams for our sagging skin. He had seemed to be participating in conversations because of the way he appeared to listen closely to everything being said, swivelling to smile directly at whomever was making a point.

And that aura, or charisma, or whatever it was, never diminished one iota, even when Mary and Dina had put their four big feet in it. Although he never initiated a discussion or offered an independent opinion on any subject, in his own way James McAlinden had dominated all discussion. I even caught little Jean watching him with strangely light-filled eyes. He had certainly got under our communal skin, that's for sure.

Normally, by the time we were eating trifle, the tone would have been rambunctious, even lewd, as it can be when women who have known each other for a long time get together and have a few drinks. Far from it this evening: my little party this year had been the most atmospherically bizarre I've ever hosted. And I include that first one where the food I had produced was appalling and my own distress overwhelming. And you know what happened in the bathroom.

This year, although softened by alcohol, none of us is even the teeniest bit tipsy: the penalty-points system sees to that now, but the leashes are tight. There is and has been an air of restrained energy about the whole event. All afternoon, James McAlinden's presence has been so dominant you could almost have spread it on your bread. Lorna, the only one who knows him, had seemed to be the only one not affected.

While James is shaking hands with the other three in the sitting room, she and I are exchanging thank-yous and laudatory comments in the hall. I open the front door, having difficulty holding it steady against the wind and rain howling directly against it. 'I'm coming up to see you tomorrow, Lorna.' I have to raise my voice against the noise. 'What time would be convenient?'

She blanches.

'I know about Martin,' I continue, before she can put me off. 'Jean told me a little bit about it and my heart goes out to you. She says the police are involved. You shouldn't have felt you had to come today. Everyone would have understood. You should have told us.'

'What would I do, rattling around in that big house with only James and myself in it? I'm really sorry if I've ruined everything for you all and for you in particular, Maggie. It was lovely, really,' she added. 'Every year you go to so much trouble for us.'

'For myself, you mean!'

'Whatever.' She smiles wanly, plucking nervously at one of her eyebrows, something she does when severely under pressure.

'Oh, Lorna.' I want to hug her hard enough to obliterate the world but she's quite a buttoned-up person. Even when I was embracing her in gratitude for her presents, I could feel her stiffen.

'They're trying to contact Olive,' she blurts. 'She's in Tenerife with her sister and all their kids. I knew she was going and I've been trying her mobile this morning to wish the grandkids a happy Christmas and all that but … ' her voice wobbles '… I keep getting a recording telling me that the number is not in service. She must have changed it.'

It's on the tip of my tongue to add: 'Like she changed the locks?' But I manage to bite it away.

We're getting wet and I close the door again. 'Look, there's no way we can talk properly now, Lorna, but I'm your pal and I want to see how I can help. You know I'll do anything I can. You need your friends around you, darling.' To my horror, she bursts into tears just as James comes out of the sitting room to join us. Lorna, the most controlled of us all, is sobbing silently, her entire body shaking, and for the first time since I'd met him, I see a flicker of uncertainty in the boy's expression as he closes the door behind him. Tentatively, he comes towards us, raising an arm as though to put it around her shoulders, but I beat him to it. I'm in danger of blubbing along with her: I'm the type who tears up when seeing people embracing at airports, whether in Departures or Arrivals. 'There are some tissues in the cloakroom, James.' I indicate the tiny room under the stairs.

When he comes back with a fistful of white paper, Lorna has regained control and has batted me away. 'Thank you.' She takes the whole bundle from him. 'Sorry about this. I don't mean to be a cry-baby.' She blows her nose.

I don't want to prolong her distress, especially in front of him. 'Are you sure you're OK to drive, Lorna? It's such a filthy night.' Through the net of fairy lights on the glass beside the door, I peer out at the rain driving horizontally through the halo created by my outdoor lantern. 'Can you drive, James?'

'I'm OK.' She waves both of us away. 'I'm fine. Thanks, Maggie. See you tomorrow. Any time in the afternoon.'

'That suits me. I'll be seeing Chloë in the morning.' Not wanting to set her off again, I give her another, brief, hug. 'See you around four o'clock, all right?' She nods quietly and they leave just as I hear an explosion of laughter from behind the closed sitting-room door. Instead of going straight back into them, to settle myself down, I go to the kitchen and make a fresh pot of coffee. Poor old Lorna, I think sadly. I know there are two sides to every story but that Olive is a piece of work. She's not in the picture anyway: there's no information about Martin she could offer from some beach in the Canaries. Changing her number, though – that was a bit rich. If she didn't want to hear from her husband, she could at least have contacted Lorna before doing that: the woman has a right to wish her grandchildren a happy Christmas.

I mentioned before that Lorna is sort of a half-widow. What happened to her was that she and her husband were legally separated, had the papers ready for divorce, which was due to be made legal in Ireland in February 1997, when he died unexpectedly in December 1996 with just two months to go. At the time of the separation he was unemployed so was unable to pay much maintenance to her, and after he died, she discovered that the only will he'd made had been written many years earlier, when he was twenty-one. His father, a widower, had left the family farm in equal divisions to each of his four sons. On legal advice, each of the four then made a will leaving his quarter in equal portions to the three others. The idea was to keep the farm intact but this situation, typically Irish, was a right mess for poor Lorna. She had to fight for her share, legal costs mounted, and while she ended up with some money, it was a pitiful amount.

More laughing from the sitting room. What's happening in there? Maybe, having been so restrained during the meal, they're letting off steam. Not wanting to rain on their parade, I plaster a wide smile on my face before rejoining them. This works, you know. If you're feeling low or even in a bad mood, forcing your face muscles to lift your lips, cheeks and eyes into a smile really does cheer you up.

The three of them look up giddily, when, coffee pot in hand, I walk in. 'What's going on in here?'

'Oh, give over with the schoolteacher impersonation, Mags!' Mary rises and comes to take the pot from me. 'Sit down there beside Dina and have a drink. We've had a great time and we're still having a great time, so chillax!' It's her favourite new word, picked up, no doubt, from her urchin *protégé*. The one she's determined to send to the Olympics. 'He's made for running, Maggie. His father is Ethiopian, and although the man doesn't run himself, both his brothers ran successfully. It's time this country woke up to see what potential is right under its nose and living on nineteen euro a week in Mosney.' Another of Mary's causes is the plight of asylum seekers and refugees. Mosney is one of the major reception centres for these unfortunate people; they're fed and housed but given only nineteen euro to spend.

'What was all that laughing about?' I do as I'm told and sit.

'We were fantasising about the Incredible Hunk.' Dina giggles.

'Oh, really? Act your age, ladies!' I wasn't surprised. The three of them look at each other as Mary does the rounds of the cups they're holding out to her.

'We thought we'd have a raffle for him – didn't we, girls?' Dina again.

'Did you indeed?' I go along with it, but insidiously, an impish little muscle jumps, just once, in my stomach.

'We did.' Mary is still pouring coffee.

'So who won?'

'You did, mine hostess!' Deliberately, Dina jounces her breasts over her crossed arms. 'We put your name into the hat along with our own. So, come on, Maggie, what'll you do with him?'

'Yeah.' Jean's eyes glisten behind her glasses. 'Your secret's safe with us.'

I have to put a stop to this so I tell them what had transpired in the hall. 'And that's all I know.'

'Oh, God. Poor Lorna.' Dina is contrite. 'But where does James come into the story?'

'I don't know.'

'The police – surely they should have been able to track Olive down.' Mary puts the coffee pot on the hearth and sits down.

'Olive doesn't want to know. Clearly. Someone who changes locks and mobile telephone numbers … '

'But she has his kids!' Mary is getting worked up.

'I promise you, all I know right now is what Jean told me. As for James, all I know is what she told all of us together. She couldn't talk about him, obviously. He was there in the hall when we were saying goodbye.'

'Curiouser and curiouser.' This is Dina again. 'Are the two things connected? Martin's disappearance and James coming on the scene? Is that why the solicitor is involved? Come to think of it, he has the look of Lennie, doesn't he? Mind you, I've seen only photos there. Could be brothers, eh?'

She and Mary turn to Jean, who would have known Lorna's husband.

Jean straightens her spine. 'I don't know any more than you do. But, yes, the police are involved.'

There's silence now as we all absorb this. 'Oh, God!' Mary puts her head in her hands. 'She must have thought we were so unfeeling.'

'Maybe she did, maybe she didn't. She chose not to talk about it, and that's her business, isn't it?' As a particularly heavy barrage of rain hits the glass behind me, a phrase I remember from school – pathetic fallacy, where the weather seems to concur with human feelings – floats into my mind. Appropriate enough. The emotional atmosphere in this room has plunged. 'If she'd wanted us to know more, she'd have found the opportunity,' I tell them briskly. 'She could have warned me on the phone. There wasn't really a chance here with him sitting beside her all the time.

'Look, ladies,' I adopt what I hope is an encouraging tone, 'all will be revealed soon, I'm sure. It's only eight o'clock, still Christmas. And, all right, poor Lorna's gone but the rest of us are together like we always are. None of us can do anything about this tonight. She wouldn't want us to be miserable, would she? And we'll all rally round her. In the meantime, tonight's the night, and has anyone any suggestions as to how we can liven things up a bit?'

'Thanks for the pep talk.' Mary tries to sound sarcastic but she's half-hearted, as affected as we all are.

'Let's get the diaries out for our next jolly, eh, girls?' I'm still doing my best. 'Easter is early next year, the thirty-first of March – that's only three months away. So, when shall we meet?'

None of them have diaries with them so that fizzles out. And while there are a few desultory proposals – Charades, Trivial Pursuit (Truth or Dare from Dina, typically) – no one any longer has an appetite for jollity. The party limps on for another half-hour or so while we drink coffee and eat more chocolates and then they get up to leave, with renewed thanks and promises to keep in touch. In turn I pledge to keep Dina and Mary informed if there are any developments. Jean promises likewise and we all say goodnight.

As I close the door behind them, I survey the remnants of my Christmas. Weeks and days to prepare, all over in an afternoon. I'm used to that, of course, and usually feel it's been worth it, but this year I don't know whether or not this one has justified all the preparations: my highly calibrated Christmas-ometer isn't working. It will certainly be a talking point for next year. If there is a next year, I think, as an image of Lorna's white, stressed face rises to haunt me along with Martin's. At best, I feel, he is lying somewhere in an alcoholic stupor, sprawled on a rural byway in danger of being run over, or in a ditch, facing imminent hypothermia – but alive. Not much of an 'at best', is it?

Standing there, I do something I haven't done in a long time. I say a prayer. For him. For her. For all the poor, stressed, addicted, homeless and mentally ill people in Dublin, Ireland and the world. For all the tortured, starving, abused and abandoned animals. I'm close to tears, dammit, as I envisage a planet seething with pain and misery on this Christmas night, 2012. The alcohol effect.

For heaven's sake! This is self-indulgent, overheated nonsense. Fat lot of good a prayer from me will accomplish anyway.

It takes a good five minutes to turn off all the switches on the extension cords and pull out the plugs. One by one, the strings and swatches of coloured lights go dark. The candles are still flickering in the sitting room. I go in and blow them out. Only the lights in the kitchen are on now.

All over.

NINE

Leaving aside that first disastrous Christmas Day, the one that had started so well with the snow and with Chloë naming our Club, this is the first in the ten years since then on which everyone has left before nine o'clock.

I'm back in the sitting room. I was halfway to the kitchen when I realised I'd forgotten to turn off a table lamp and the gas fire. When all is done, I put the fireguard back. I'm a sucker for marketing, me! I had allowed myself to be persuaded by a young fella in Woodies that this fireguard would transform the experience of sitting by my gas fire because 'Everybody will think it's a real one, Missus. Me ma swears by it, honest to God she does.'

Yeah. Young fellas in the bloom of their strength and virility: I hope you won't find this fanciful but I think their very unknowingness is part of their attraction. They offer not only the possibility of sexual excitement but, for the older woman, the bonus of gratitude on both sides, on his for the teaching, on hers for the confirmation that she still has what it takes. Our world is teeming with potential Mrs Robinsons – you have only to think of what happened here this evening, the simmering lewdness, the laughter about the Incredible Hunk, that so-called raffle and so on.

On the other hand, this was quite sad too. Leaving Lorna, God love her, out of it, James McAlinden's presence reminded the rest of us that we're out of the game. That boy's youth, beauty and, most particularly, the impeccable manners he accorded equally to all, told us in huge neon lights that he wouldn't be remotely interested in any of us. It's hard to come slap-bang up against that. Very sobering. Especially for Dina, I suspect.

Give over. The *über*-seeing little woman who inhabits a section of my brain inside the back of my skull cracks up. *Dina? Who are you kidding? Dina, Schmina. You can fool yourself, Maggie Quinn, but you can't fool me!*

'You're right,' I tell her. 'I do admit there was an indefinable, very male energy in the house and I was as affected as anyone else.'

Indefinable male energy, my foot!

'But it wasn't just us women. Flora liked him. She's usually standoffish with people she doesn't know.'

The dog now? Give us a break. It's called Sex, with a capital S.

'All right, I admit it, I was far from immune to the charms of James McAlinden.' I kick the annoying little woman out of my head, close the sitting-room door and again head for the kitchen, where I pull on a pair of rubber gloves. As though, telepathically, she had heard her name, Flora trots into the kitchen and jumps up to put her two front paws on my hip. What about my dinner, then?

'You've been a very good girl,' I tell her, fondling her ears, 'as good as gold. And I'm sorry you had to wait so long. How about a bit of turkey and ham tonight? You've been so patient, no nagging or anything, and it's still Christmas.'

Together we traverse my trashed kitchen. I feed her and, while she eats, start the clean-up, to the extent that I fill the dishwasher and switch it on. I look around. There's still a lot to be dealt with: the gravy saucepan, the roasting tin, the cut-glass trifle bowl, serving dishes and larger implements, such as serving spoons, all needing to be hand-washed. I can't face that tonight: I'm too tired. It's just after half past eight but I've run out of energy.

So much for sexual fantasies. I'd fall asleep!

I let Flora out for the last time, and when she comes in, I lock the back door and turn out the lights. Another Christmas gone. I'm not sure how I feel. At this time of a Christmas night, we're usually still shooting the breeze, teasing and reminiscing, becoming a little rowdy, and I can't help but feel sad and a little lonely that they've all gone. Flora is great company, but our conversations are somewhat limited. (And, yes, I admit to being anthropomorphic – but where's the harm?)

On impulse, I go out to the hall and ring Chloë but her phone goes straight to voicemail. She's probably having a whale of a time with her pals and the staff, as much as Chloë can experience enjoyment. They do try in that place: they pull out all the stops for big occasions, birthdays included.

Finally in bed, bushed though I am, I can't sleep. You know those nights when you're wrecked, but right at the moment your head hits the pillow, your brain sits bolt upright to conduct a discordant orchestra of thoughts and images? I fear I'm in for one of those. First up on this not-so-merry-go-round, those scenarios I've created around Lorna's son. I don't, or didn't, have all that many dealings with him, but women talk about their children and I feel I know him a little; he was good enough to her until, to her alarm, alcohol began to sing its siren song in his blood. Can I blame Olive? I should probably hold the blame game until I hear her side of the story. Maybe he was pestering her with text messages or something like that. Drunk people see no boundaries.

I try to convince myself that he is alive and well somewhere like Australia, having skipped the country – but I know that's pretty unlikely. Where would he get the cash? He mightn't be the most resourceful of individuals but he isn't a bank robber. And there is the small matter of visas.

Equally unlikely is the notion that he had shacked up somewhere with someone. Martin? Nah. He has no history of straying and he's no catch. Even Lorna would admit that. 'Martin has a beautiful heart,' she would say, 'and that's all that matters in the end.'

The two of them, Martin as a substitute for Jean, who at the time was on the road somewhere between Poland and Belarus in a truck with Adi Roche's charity convoy, had come to my leaving party at the paper's offices to support me. Dina was at a rejuvenation spa in Goa, and Mary, on whom I was really depending, was nowhere to be seen. (It turned out later that she had got the date wrong.) Oh, no! That old memory – go away! But it doesn't. The mortifications do hang around to strike in the quiet times, don't they?

My abiding memory of that evening is of embarrassment, hanging frond-like in the stale air in that newsroom while I listened, toes squinching, to the farewell speech from the paper's deputy editor. Standing in front of my soon-to-be-ex-colleagues, we were both jammed into a narrow space between untidy stacks of back-issues of the newspaper, where the fusty smell of old ink and newsprint was all too evident. Dust tickled my nose so urgently I was afraid I'd sneeze. Lorna, Martin and two more of my less than extensive circle of friends had been politely given places in the front row of those come to support me. From my perspective, I wished they hadn't, being too close to my humiliation. I was glad that Derek had had to work that evening.

Lorna smiled encouragingly at me as, first bestowing on me a toothy smile, the deputy editor unfolded a crumpled page of copy paper. As he did, I caught a glimpse of his key words: 'stalwart', 'bishops', 'dogs', 'Hallé'... Oh, God! Not those hoary old chestnuts.

Fears justified. Chestnuts to the fore.

'First of all,' he began, and we all nodded sagely on hearing that Sir Editor was really, really devastated he couldn't be present. 'Maggie, Maggie, Maggie,' deputy ed. went on, dripping with false affection, 'we all know that you have been a stalwart of this paper since before Noah was a lad ... ' followed by a lot more in that vein.

Oh, how we nodded in affectionate recognition at my successes and laughed at my mishaps throughout my tenure, at the retelling of the time when the deputy himself had humoured me after I had begged to cover the plight of deliberately strayed dogs in rural areas. 'A story,' he reminisced, 'conveyed so passionately by our Maggie' that it had been picked up by broadcasting organisations and had become a public campaign spearheaded by the newspaper in hopes of attracting readership. (It had, albeit temporarily. And in the high hundreds rather than the many thousands.) It had also led to an award for me from the Irish Society for the Prevention of Cruelty to Animals.

But there had also been the time, hadn't there, when our Maggie had interviewed the wrong Archbishop of Dublin, Catholic rather than Protestant, as intended? To the huge puzzlement of the former, this had brought a 'Letter to the Editor' in which His Grace had wondered why I was asking him about his belief that Joseph and Mary had been married and had had additional siblings for Jesus. Wot laughs at that one!

And who would ever forget the occasion when I had been marked to interview a famous English soccer star with Irish roots, had pursued him, or, rather, his agent, for more than a week in London but, failing to nail my target, had come home instead clutching an interview with the leader of the Hallé orchestra. As luck would have it, the musician had sat beside me on the flight home to Dublin, had offered me a drink and, on learning my profession, had offered himself, since he hoped some day to play, or maybe retire, in Dublin, his wife being from Dalkey.

Sir Editor rated cultural matters just slightly above quilting, or instructions for stuffing mushrooms, as subjects for his newspaper – 'An effing orchestra? An *English* orchestra?' – but had run the piece nonetheless as he had space to fill. Sir's deputy raised a lot of laughs with that one.

When, mercifully, it was over, I had accepted my bouquet, my communally signed card and my gift bought from the collection, made, I was sure, by the front-desk receptionist who had been with the paper as long as I had. Somehow (probably by shaming the management into upping its contribution) she had managed to collect enough for a laptop. I didn't have to fake my gratitude when I thanked everyone for that; like everyone in journalism, I was determined some day to write a book, some day being the operative expression. No day as it has turned out!

For the next half-hour, I drank warm cava while fielding

handshakes and too-jolly wishes for my great future. I bridged conversational gaps by introducing Lorna and Martin to colleagues and to two other good friends, one a photographer I used to work with, the other the librarian at the public library in my area.

I've known the latter, a woman of my own age, for yonks. We don't live in each other's pockets but we keep in touch fairly regularly, meeting to go to the cinema and theatre together, that kind of thing. I love talking to her: she's gentle, erudite and intelligent but without a trace of the cynicism that, in my opinion, is ruining discourse in this country. She has had a short story published in the New Irish Writing series in the *Sunday Independent*, and has long planned to write a novel, which she seems to have based around a sort of magic-realism plot involving a librarian and a ghost. Early in our acquaintance, I confessed my own literary ambitions and she continues to be gracious enough to treat me as an equal in the writing field and reassures me that many brilliant authors take decades to write their books: 'But it's always worth it in the end, Maggie.' She, the published author, continues to compare notes with me, the writer *manqué*.

She confesses, however, to be intimidated by the number of excellent authors in her daily charge. 'I could never be as good as the worst of them.'

To that I can but fervently agree.

As for my photographer friend, our history is a tad more complex.

I had always quite fancied Tom (his name is Tom Jennings) but in the abstract, along with most women in the office. There were many times when his ears should have burned as the wistful compliments flew ... He's tall, taller than me, with a long narrow face that lights up when he smiles. We hit it off from the time of our first assignment together but of course our relationship was strictly professional. We were both married. Then, about six months after that first job, his wife was killed in a road accident and that harrowing funeral is one I will never forget. I don't think I have ever seen a man cry so much.

It was about three years later, I think, when we found ourselves on an overnight gig together in a midlands town. We had done most of the work that day, with just a couple of catch-ups to do in the morning so we were relaxed over the dinner – and lots of wine – we had later in our hotel. It was still only a quarter past ten when we'd finished, too early to go to bed, so we repaired to the residents' lounge where we sat at opposite ends of a large, sagging settee to have a few after-dinner drinks. It was midweek, very quiet, and we had the room – tally-ho hunting prints on faded pink and gold wallpaper, worn red carpet, the armrest behind my head pocked with cigarette burns – to ourselves as we chatted amiably about markings, work colleagues and so on.

It was after midnight – and a lot of alcohol – when I wrecked the mood. Opened my big mouth without thinking. As usual.

'Would you ever think about marrying again?' I had meant it casually, I swear to God. Looking back, I suppose we were so easy together I was treating Tom like one of my women friends. But the effect on him, hard to describe to anyone who didn't witness it, was instantaneous. His face reddened – that's easy to envisage; what's not so easy to depict is the reaction of the rest of his body. It recoiled, as though he had been doused with freezing, or indeed scalding, water. He did attempt to shrug, though: 'I suppose I haven't met ...' The mutter faded as he bent his head to look at the floor.

Flabbergasted, metaphorically giving myself a good kicking, I cast around for something to say. I would have always pegged Tom as personally shy but professionally confident, but this was way outside the kind of behaviour I knew. I looked into the dregs of my drink: 'Will we have another?'

'Are you having one?' He was still looking at the floor. He's rangy and loose-limbed, but there was a rigidity about his posture I had never seen before. 'Or maybe not?' Hastily, I put my glass on the raddled coffee table in front of us. 'What do you think? Maybe it's time to call it a night?'

'Maybe.' He didn't look up.

'Are you all right, Tom?'

'Yeah, of course.' But, if anything, he became even more tense.

'You're not. What's wrong?'

He turned to me and in his expression I saw a kind of struggle I couldn't name. Without thinking, I moved up the couch to sit beside him, the creaking of the springs loud in the silence. 'Tell me. Tell me what's wrong.'

'You don't want to know. Truly.'

'Try me?' As I would with any friend, I put a comforting hand on his knee. He grabbed it and held it so tightly that my wedding ring cut agonisingly into the fingers on either side of it. Again, I scrabbled for words: 'You can tell me. Whatever it is. I don't judge.'

It poured out of him. Contrary to outward appearances, my friend's marriage had not been a happy one and just before his wife's death, had become increasingly troubled: 'From day one, we both knew it had been a mistake—'

On the night his wife was killed, the two of them had had a blazing row, one of those marital spats that starts from nothing and ends up being cataclysmic. 'She stormed out and took the car. I ran after her – I needed it for an early-morning shoot and she knew that – but she sped up, screeched away. If I hadn't chased her … maybe …'

'Don't blame yourself.' I used my free hand to stroke his forearm. The muscles were tight as drumskins.

'I do. I do blame myself. No-one could find me to deliver the bad news. Because I was in a mate's flat, getting drunk and making plans with him to leave her and go to Australia. I was there all night. Stumbled home at seven in the morning. Now,' savagely, 'do you understand?'

I did. Those tears at the funeral. Grief, yes, but also guilt and self-loathing. No way to put things right. For the rest of his life.

We stared at one another and under the pressure of his hand, mine, imprisoned, hurt even more. I could feel his blood pumping, but maybe it was my own? There was something else he wanted to say and it wasn't about his dead wife. This could go two ways, I thought, stunned. He's either going to shatter into tiny pieces in front of my eyes, or he's going to kiss me. I needed to think. I had no time to think. 'How did it start?' I blurted.

'What?' His grip on me slackened.

'The row, I mean – how did the row start?'

'About an ironing board.'

'An ironing board?' I felt one of those incongruous, inappropriate, treacherous, alcohol-fuelled giggles tickling the floor of my stomach but managed to stifle it by coughing loudly. 'Sorry,' I said, 'frog. What was the matter with the ironing board?'

'She wanted me to put it away—'

'But you didn't want to?'

'No. I didn't. I didn't want to put the ironing board away.'

In the edgy silence that followed he let go of my hand and I could see that he too was trying to suppress a nervous laugh.

119

Simultaneously, we both gave in and the tension, whatever its cause, imploded and we laughed like drains. Then we went our separate ways to our rooms.

An hour later, still awake but sober in my lumpy bed, I had to give myself a severe talking to. To remind myself that I was a married person. Because, in reviewing the scene, I had found myself half-wishing (and maybe more than half) that he had actually kissed me. It would not have gone further. I knew that. But just a kiss? What harm?

I think we were both embarrassed at breakfast the next morning. 'Sorry about all that last night,' he murmured between sips of his watery orange juice.

'For God's sake, Tom.' I sipped mine. 'Sorry for what? As you know, what happens on the bogs, stays on the bogs. Here. Have a look at the front page of the Indo.' I passed him the *Independent* and he grabbed it as though it were a lifebelt.

Since then, although they continue to hover nearby whenever we meet, such intimacies have been a no-go area and we have kept things casual – the odd lunch, small presents for birthdays.

Along the usual lines ('Don't forget if there's anything I can do?') he was sympathetic about my separation but never went into it in detail, nor did I. These days, we are cordiality personified, verbally always on topical ground. Luckily, we are never at a loss for conversation. Working in journalism gives an endless supply of great work stories, especially from him. As colleagues we were far from equal and he is considerably the more accomplished, having successfully taken assignments through many hotspots and natural disasters in various places throughout the world. But he continues to treat me as though I am still fully in the business and I really appreciate it.

Anyhow, he's always in the background as a really great pal and all of this is by way of saying that it was great to see his smiling, encouraging face in the crowd during that awful night of my departure from the newspaper.

My toes curl in my bed now as I remember how I felt in that room with everyone looking at me. We all did our best to be convivial after the speeches but I was glad to escape early, which was, I imagine, a great relief for most of my ex-colleagues, who could then settle in to having a good time together without having to think of upbeat words to utter whenever they met my gaze. I had refused all offers of going to a pub, from my photographer pal, even from Lorna and Martin. It was difficult to maintain a cheerful expression against my humiliation – and deep fear about whether I would ever again find a job. At my age, I didn't want housework or gossiping to become my main preoccupations for the remainder of my life.

Luckily our house, this house, was paid for; being in Cabra, an unfashionable part of the city at the time, we had bought it as an end-of-terrace doer-upper and it hadn't cost that much in the first place. We'd moved in just a year after we got married, long before house prices in Dublin got silly, and with both of us working, we were able to sort out its defects and, every so often, to throw lump sums at the mortgage. We had the space to add a little two-room extension at the back, one to enlarge the sitting room, the other to form the dining alcove off the kitchen. The only addition I had made since was three years ago when I got Flora. In case she turned out to be a wanderer (she didn't) I had a gate installed across the side entrance so she could be let out safely into the garden.

In fairness to Derek, while the money I get from him is modest, he made no objections to my solicitor's demand that I keep the house; his guilt worked in my favour because he also continues to pay my life-insurance policy, with Chloë as beneficiary, and the health insurance subscription for both of us. I don't feel bad about this. He has no financial worries: the popsy has a high-flying job in public relations, and he himself is now up there in his profession too. In any case he's good with money and has always salted away a fair bit of what he earns towards his retirement.

I don't like to talk about another unpleasant aspect of being spat out of my newspaper, but here goes: I'm ashamed to admit that having work to go to, even work of diminishing impact, had been my respite from looking after Chloë as she became more and more difficult to deal with. Unemployed, without a legitimate reason to be absent from the house for long periods, I wasn't looking forward to becoming her full-time face-to-face carer.

We were children of relatively elderly parents and both had died when I was in my mid-thirties and Chloë was just thirty-two. Both went from heart disease and, believe it or not, within weeks of one another – a tragedy that, as you can imagine, didn't help my poor sister's mental health. As a result, I inherited full physical responsibility for her until, after that seminal meltdown during Christmas 2002, psychiatry stepped in and a five-days-a-week residential place was found for her. Luckily, I had already ring-fenced most of the money we'd got from the sale of Mammy and Daddy's house; it was all intact. Chloë cares not a whit about money and never asks about her share, dwindling now, of course, but there's still enough of hers left to pay what we have to for another few years. When that runs out, we'll use my share – which I have never considered to be mine in any case: money should go where it's needed, is my philosophy.

I can't imagine what will happen after all the money is gone. Should anything befall me, I've stipulated that any balance, plus the proceeds of selling this house and the payout on my life-insurance policy, should go into a special account to pay for my sister's care. I've calculated that if I were to be run over by a bus tomorrow, there should be enough to support her for about twelve years. I don't know who'll take care of her after that. Nothing I can do about it. I certainly can't help from beyond the grave, but if she's still alive when my time comes, my deathbed thoughts will not be pleasant. I don't want to die before Chloë, simple as that; even thinking about it causes despair, and I'm not alone. I know that. Money is a continuing worry for all carers.

These days, I still use my retirement laptop, creaking a bit now but adequate for the bits and bobs of journalism that still come my way. There are still a few features editors of the old school who haven't forgotten me and who commission book reviews, pieces on craft fairs and workers, colour pieces on local events, interviews with visiting celebrities and other 'soft' material. The money, modest though it is, adds to the day-to-day coffers, and is very welcome. As for the putative book, though, while there are several glistering first chapters, none of those novels got beyond the first few hundred words of the second. I might as well have put my novels on Pinocchio's nose as on the long finger because I'm ashamed to say I continue to talk about it with my librarian friend as though it's still a work-in-progress. I suppose we all tell such white lies in the hope that telling them often enough makes them true!

It's easy to blame others for your own inaction. For instance, Chloë couldn't stay away from me when I was writing, wandering into the kitchen hourly, ostensibly to get herself a drink, but always coming into the alcove to peer over my shoulder. 'Is this about me, Margaret?'

'No, sweetie. It's about me, I think. I'm only on the first chapter. It'll all be changed by the end. It could be about anyone. That's how novels work.'

'Well, are you going to put me in it before the end?'

'I have no idea.'

'Why? Why don't you have an idea? Writers have ideas, don't they? Isn't that what they're supposed to do, Margaret?'

After one or two of these interruptions I'd fly off the handle, she'd get insulted, I'd pacify her, and then I'd snap the lid of the laptop shut. Writing over for that day. Again.

My self-righteousness was a sham. If I was really intent on writing a novel, I could have found a way. Or I could have written in bed at night when Chloë was asleep. Women write on kitchen tables when their children take naps. They arrange babysitters so they can attend creative-writing courses. They're so driven by the need to write, they get up at four in the morning to do so while their household snores: I know all of this because I've interviewed the ones who persisted and got published.

What excuse do I have now? Chloë has been with me in the house only part-time for many years now, so what's the problem?

No problem, is the answer, none except my own inadequacy. It took a long time but I've had to face facts: I'm a dilettante. While I have a facility for writing good English, it became more and more obvious I would never make a novelist. I lacked the drive and gave up too easily. As a journalist, I had listened attentively to authors' expositions of plots, ideas and methods of working and many times found myself thinking, I could do that! When it came to my own turn, however, I found that, yes, I could tap into memory reservoirs of advice and tips about how to polish or research but only if I had the raw material!

My main difficulty was that I had nothing of substance to say for myself. The subject matter I wanted most to explore would have distressed Chloë, and since I couldn't do that to her, it turned out that I was neither creative nor ruthless enough to be a professional novelist. Anyhow, led by the librarian, the more novels I read by a worldwide cohort of superb fiction writers, the more depressed I became: I wasn't good enough to get within a mile of the standard of the work I admired, and if I couldn't, what was the point?

For a time, though, abandonment of literary ambition was hard to accept, even harder to talk about. For a while, people in whom I had unwisely confided continued to ask how it was going. 'Trundling along,' I always answered cheerfully, lying through my teeth while simultaneously kicking myself in the arse for my failure – if that combination is physically possible. As the years passed, people stopped asking and I stopped dreaming about becoming Ireland's next Maeve Binchy, or Ireland's first Maggie Quinn. Instead, I settled into my mundane routine of keeping house and looking after Chloë, then, latterly, Flora.

Mind you, even a forced departure from the working world has its advantages, not least of which is that you gain time. To use it productively, despite temptation, I would not switch on the TV until the Angelus was bonging prior to the six o'clock news, forcing myself instead to read. This became a pleasurable habit as, steadily, I started working through the stacks of books I had always promised myself I would take up 'when I have time'. I also had occasional off-peak two-night breaks in modest B&Bs in the country or at the seaside, always fitting them around Chloë's stays with me. I even travelled to Amsterdam and London, taking advantage of cheap city breaks with Aer Lingus or Ryanair.

It doesn't have to be a bad life, you know, being a forcibly retired singleton and potentially the best unpublished novelist in Ireland!

The bed creaks as I throw myself on to my right side. In such a small house, when all-day central heating is added to the build-up from the oven, the heavily worked burners on the cooker and a gas fire in the sitting room, even the bedroom feels like a sauna. But I can't open the window because of the deluge. Irritably, I throw off the duvet and, with just a sheet covering me now, heave back on to my left side, my default sleep side, if you will, but that febrile brain of mine continues to spin.

It's lucky Chloë wasn't here today, I think now. There had never been any question of it, but suppose … My sister's mind is off-kilter but that doesn't mean she lacks physical and sexual reflexes. They watch for that in the facility. Men and women have their rooms in separate houses but there is a lot of communal living and families are warned to look out for what are termed 'special' relationships. If the Merrow authorities detect anything they think is seriously inappropriate, those involved are moved to different houses.

'What about their human and civil rights?' I hear you ask.

I've struggled with that one, but only briefly before squashing it stone dead. Today, if she had been here, would have been a good illustration of why the Merrow House people watch their charges so closely. I want Chloë to stay at Merrow. She's happy there. As happy as she can be. Her reaction to James would have been a nightmare – I can even picture it.

'Stop this! That young man is off limits. And it's not just in the case of Chloë!' I realise I spoke aloud, had shouted, in fact. Flora heard it. I can hear her padding into my room from her own, then pausing in the doorway to survey the lie of the land.

Lorna. Think of poor Lorna. Should I bring her flowers?

Probably not. Too condolence-like. And, anyway, on St Stephen's Day, all I could get would be an old, curling bunch from the buckets in front of a garage shop.

Flora pads right up to the side of my bed and, very gently, lays her chin on the side of my bare arm, her breath warm. Can't sleep, Maggie? I'll stay with you for a while. She settles down, curling up at the side of the bed, her back against the box frame of the divan.

I lean down and pat her smooth head. 'Happy Christmas, sweetheart!' In response, she sighs and stretches luxuriously, all four paws extended, head up, before curling up again. 'Night-night!'

I'll take three deep breaths. That's supposed to help with relaxation.

In through the nose … hold it … out through the mouth.

In through the nose … hold it … out through the mouth.

In through the—

It's no use. I stab my finger on to the switch of the bedside light and get out of bed so fast that I stand on the dog. She yelps in surprise and pain. 'I'm sorry, I'm sorry.' Filled with remorse, I squat to hug her as she forgives me with a small lick. 'It's still Christmas, Flora,' I say, into her warm neck fur. 'Will we go downstairs and have a proper treat? Ice cream for you, but don't tell the vet. And an absolutely huge, gargantuan gin for this stupid, idiotic, fifty-seven-year-old fool.'

I'm telling myself, truthfully, that today was a learning curve, definitive milestone, whatever stupid marker you want to call the realisation that, yes, young men stacking shelves in supermarkets don't turn to look at me when I pass (except to think what a climb that would have been!).

But Flora reckons I've suggested something lovely and bounces in happy agreement. I let her go and the ID tag on this year's Christmas collar jingles all the way down the stairs as she leads the way.

'Was it a good party, d'you think?' Back in the kitchen, with my gin and tonic in a pint glass, I watch her slurp ice cream from her battered green bowl. She's too busy to answer so I answer for her in the refined tone I've given her in my head: It was all right, Maggie – not one of our better ones, I think.

'Of course, you weren't even born ten years ago.' I take a deep mouthful of the cold, aromatic drink. 'Nothing like a G and T, eh, Flora? Here's to a good 2013!'

If someone had told me that evening what the following year would bring, I would have choked on the pips of my lemon.

TEN

Merrow House, Chloë's 'facility', is situated beside a shingled cove in north County Dublin and accommodates twenty 'service users' across four bungalows sited in an arc behind the main house, each consisting of five large, bedsit-like rooms. The place is privately run but part-subsidised by the HSE. Recent cuts to this funding have led to increasingly desperate round-robins from the centre's manager to families, begging for donations, 'however small, so we can continue to offer the same level of superb care to our service users'.

I hate that my sister is known in that way: 'service user' is dehumanising and implies she is nothing but a drain on a resource, the equally dehumanised and depersonalised 'service provider'. Nothing I can do about that, except, perhaps, to start

129

a controversy by writing a letter to the editor of *The Irish Times*, the *Examiner* or the *Independent* but, although I'd dearly like to, I can't go public about anything to do with Chloë because, if she got to hear of it, God knows how she'd react or what she would do. So I keep my mouth shut and my nib sheathed.

'Merrow' is derived from the Irish word for 'mermaid' and each residential block is named after a different sea creature – Anemone, Seahorse, Dolphin and Orca. Because the wind blowing from the Irish Sea frequently cuts rough, all are connected to the back entrance of the central house by four brightly lit, glass-roofed passageways through a conservatory. From a window in one of the aircraft constantly passing overhead, the complex must look like a four-armed squid or octopus. Chloë's room is in Seahorse, with a pleasant view of rolling countryside and of the white post-and-rail fenced driveway curving from the entrance.

On Stephen's Day, as I drive towards the visitors' car park through the pelting rain (yes, still raining!), I wonder if she's sitting behind her window, watching for me. That can be either good or bad, depending on her mood. I'm not optimistic this will go well because I hadn't been able to find her main gift, the iPad Mini she'd asked for. She'd been very particular: it had to be identical to the one a pal of hers had received as a birthday present earlier in December, and although I had Googled, telephoned every retailer, logged on to the online Apple Store, Amazon and all the UK sites, they were sold out everywhere. Although I was prepared to pay any money for a quiet life, even eBay couldn't help me. My mistake had been not to warn her. Don't know why I didn't think of it – I was just caught up in other trivialities, I guess. I knew there was no point in bringing along a substitute.

Once inside, I tap on her door with the car key. Doors in Merrow are never locked but, in deference to her dignity, I always knock. 'Hi, Chloë!' No response. I tap again. 'Can I come in? It's Margaret.' To her I'm never Maggie or Mag or Mags, as I am to almost everyone else. When there's still no answer I push the door open – to hear splashing sounds coming from behind her bathroom door. 'It's only me,' I call. 'Take your time.'

The walls in each of the rooms are painted in different colours, occupants being given a choice. Chloë's are quite a delicate shade of grey, complementing the upholstery of her armchair, an elegant, oversized check in pale apple green and cream. These choices surprised me at the time because she tends to favour clothes in black or dark purple. She has a built-in wardrobe, a bookcase/shelving unit, a large, lockable cupboard for her possessions and a desk-cum-dining table with two pull-out stools, in the unlikely event she should wish to entertain. On her nightstand, she has a lamp and a radio, both battery-operated, but if she wants to watch TV, she has to go to the common room in the big house and fight it out with others as to which channel they'll watch. This is not a bad idea as it forces her to engage socially; otherwise she could easily stay in her room, coming out only for meals, which, I know from the staff here, she wolfs, without much conversation. The nutritionist, who calls once a month, must be fed up lecturing her about eating healthily and slowly, and right now, her room is strewn not only with clothes and used tissues, but with sweet wrappers, empty popcorn and crisp bags and, in the middle of her bed, a half-eaten Mars bar. She's been to the shop. She's overweight, as are many of her fellow 'service users'. I'm convinced that this is due partly to the side-effects of the medications they all take.

I make a mental note to make sure that before she comes to me on Friday for the weekend, I'll have hidden or disposed of the Cadbury's Roses and After Eights.

Ah, the hell with it, I think then. Let her eat what she likes. It's Christmas.

There's no sign of the card I sent her, so carefully selected. I'd spent ages reading the verses inside scores of cards before buying one 'left blank for your own message'. She's touchy and could take offence at something most people would see merely as Hallmarkism. I wonder if she'd got it. Did she tear it up?

But look at that little cardboard tree sporting glued-on baubles made from crêpe paper. And those handmade cards, a dozen or more, strung on a length of tinsel over the head of her unmade bed. My throat constricts. Obviously the products of a Christmas crafts workshop, the type organised by teachers for children on the last day of term before the holidays. Chloë Quinn is in her early fifties. Tears prickling, I put her presents on the table. Judging by the sounds coming from behind the door of her en suite, she is still engaged in ablutions.

'Hi there,' I call again, in case she hadn't heard me the first time. 'Don't get a fright – I'm in here. It's Margaret.' I go to the window from which I can see my car in the car park and some of the rest of the buildings. The rain is now so heavy, it has obscured the sea, and a mini-forest of little silver spears rebounds upwards as individual drops hit the glass roof of the passageway connecting Anemone to the main building. Although Chloë's room is heated, I find myself shivering.

Still the sound of splashing from behind the bathroom door. Doesn't look like she'll be out any time soon.

I turn on Chloë's radio. A presenter is introducing a piece

of music: 'Amhrán an Phúca' – 'The Song of the Pooka' – but after the first few bars, its mournful, sighing melody gets to me and I turn it off. It's hardly Christmassy, is it? Silence now in the bathroom. She should be out soon.

I go back to the window. Staff quarters are on the first floor of the dower house, a relic of past grandeur, refurbished to serve as a hub. Residents of the bungalows enjoy first-class amenities on its extensive ground floor. As well as their dining room, common room and TV room, there is a multi-denominational Room of Reflection. A cubbyhole shop behind a roller blind opens for two hours every day. There are two rooms for hairdressing and quasi-medical appointments, such as podiatry, a large open area with a table-tennis table, fitness equipment and board games, and a small library that includes two desktop computers. When these were set up for Wi-Fi, competition for time on them became so fierce that a system had to be developed whereby, with a time-limited smart card, each resident could log on for just two half-hour sessions every day. Chloë wears hers on a ribbon around her neck along with her library card.

So, you can see why I'm happy that she's here and not in some wretched hospital ward; why I worry that something will happen to take it away from her. One of the criteria for acceptance in Merrow is that the illness is somewhere on the scale between 'mild' and 'moderate'. They don't take 'severe' or 'acute' and, terrified she'll tip over, I am constantly on edge about her behaviour, waiting for a phone call asking me to come in and have a chat. So far, so good, though.

I'm also trying to figure out how best to respond to those begging letters. Chloë is physically healthy and, barring accidents, will live out a normal lifespan. Even with her disability payment, of which Merrow takes most, I pay about half of what I get from Derek towards her keep. And while I can't afford to donate anything significant from my own resources, I'm trying to decide if I should take a big lump out of my savings to ingratiate us. In the subtlest of ways, the management lets it be known that there is a considerable waiting list for rooms here, and I do wonder if there is any possibility that those with deeper pockets than we have could buy into the service at Chloë's expense. Could the management look for an excuse to throw her out in order to take in someone whose family can be relied upon to react to requests for contributions?

The bathroom door bursts open. She's still in her pyjamas. 'Did you not go down for breakfast, Chloë?' It had come out before I could stop it.

'Fuck you. None of your business.' She goes straight towards her wardrobe, kicks a pair of boots out of her way and pulls the door open so violently she loses her balance, totters backwards and lands on her bed.

I don't respond. I don't even look at her. It took a long time but I've learned the hard way that outraged reactions, appeals, even threats have no effect on Chloë when she behaves like this.

I'm convinced that this overt truculence has something to do with the side-effects of one, maybe even more than one, of her medications, which are under constant review. As a result, these outbursts are now rare, thank God, and getting rarer. She's miffed about something, probably nothing to do with me. She'll calm down in her own time. She'll apologise. I'll accept her apology. We'll move on. 'Sorry, Chloë,' I say to her now. 'I've left Flora in the car and I'm worried I've left the driver's window open and she could get out. Anyhow, the seat would be drenched. Take your time getting dressed, I'll be back in a sec.'

She ignores me and I leave the room. Quietly. I'll go back in about ten minutes and everything should be fine. Neither of us will refer to it.

When she was living with us, this used to happen more than it does now. I used to react and we'd have a ding-dong that left both of us worn out. Bit by bit, though, I came to accept that, other than her psychiatrist, I am probably the only person on whom she feels she can safely vent her frustrations so I don't take it personally. A big ask, one that proved impossible for Derek to deal with. He, of course, didn't leave until he was sure there was a young and compliant party to take him in.

Sorry. Chloë is not the only one whose bitchiness breaks out now and then. I didn't really mean that, not now. It's just habit.

Once outside and walking back to the car, I look back at her window. Sometimes, after such an eruption, she'll repent immediately and I'll see her waving – but not today.

You might think there is an element of manipulation here – that my sister is cunning enough to control her reactions with those whom it's necessary to keep onside. Even if that is the case, so what? All it means is that she's learned how to survive in her own world. The way I look at it is the old way: sticks and stones may break my bones but words – et cetera. Except for that one Christmas Day ten years ago when she didn't stop at words, and that's a long, long time ago.

The aspect of her behaviour I have most worried about is her impulsivity. She can be going along as 'normal' and then – wham! She says or does something completely unexpected, occasionally even dangerous: like the time she ran out into the road to stand in front of an oncoming motorhome. She came to no harm: the driver, a German woman, managed to brake in time. But when asked afterwards to explain why she had done it, Chloë could give no satisfactory reply. 'I just wanted to.' She'd shrugged. 'I thought the caravan was cool.' The medication seems to have ironed that sort of stuff out, but the poor Frau was pretty shaken. ('But fy vould she do dat?' she asked me over and over again.) I've thought about the woman often, strangely. I guess she had some stories about the Irish to tell at her Hamburg dinner parties!

Although Mary still asks after Chloë's welfare, even she no longer brings her up when all five of us are together. I don't put that down to what they witnessed that Christmas Day in my house, although there may be an element of that. I think they don't bring up the subject of her illness because of simple bafflement and I understand that from the bottom of my heart. She's not Down's Syndrome or suffering from something like autism, about which there have been heartrending and explanatory documentaries. She's educated to Leaving Cert standard, she can read and write – so why wouldn't she get a desk job somewhere as a file clerk? She's able-bodied, so why can't she get out of the house and stack shelves in Tesco?

So there's an element of frustration – and not just with Chloë but with me for not doing enough in Chloë's interest, for not forcing her to face her own reality. I think, however, the basic reason my friends in the Club no longer ask about her is simply because of tedium. There are only so many times I can reply, 'The same!' to 'And how's Chloë?' or the more impersonal 'And how's your sister?' I accept it's hard for folk who haven't experienced it to know or understand the difference between mental disability and mental illness. Derek, for instance, never did.

Let's get this over with.

Chloë had come to live with Derek and me at Christmas 1992, nearly three years after our parents had died in early 1990. She had lived alone in our parental home in the intervening period, in an increasingly isolated manner, although I didn't fully recognise that at the beginning. Or that their deaths was the beginning of her decline into illness. With the contracts on the house signed and completion pending, I felt we had no other choice but to take her in. Derek had agreed, reluctantly. We'd had argument after argument about it. Our house was too small; she needed more care than we could give her; we were only four years married at the time and still trying for a baby – the walls were paper thin, we'd have no privacy. All valid points from him, but for me it came down to my responsibility for her, that, crucially, she had nowhere else to go, and the professionals I had consulted had told me she should not live alone.

All very well for them, I'd thought bitterly at the time, but when I asked where she was supposed to live, the alternatives offered were horrendous. There were long waiting lists, up to nine years, for accommodation in some of the better places.

After her Leaving Cert, she had worked, happily I'd thought, in a chemist's shop but, out of the blue, had quit some time during 1991. I found this out only when, having fired our original estate agent for lack of action in the sale of our parents' house, I was bringing in a new one to view it and found her in bed at three o'clock in the afternoon. Her room was chaotically untidy and filthy. That was the first time she'd told me to fuck off. In front of the agent, who, to his credit, remained impassive. I was genuinely shocked. More power to him, he tried to reassure me that he saw this all the time with teenagers.

But Chloë wasn't a teenager. At that time she was thirty-three years old.

I don't want to bore you with the ever-changing theories and diagnoses after we'd all accepted Chloë was ill: the waiting rooms, the ups and downs of different medications, the frequent and very worrying catatonia. Then, before we found Merrow House, there was a string of what were, to me, acutely degrading hospital admissions and 'consultations' during which Chloë and I had to sit in front of a group and talk about 'where we're at right now'. During these sessions, notes were solemnly taken of the responses I made to the questions posed by His Current Holiness, the psychiatrist.

I can't tell you how that felt, trying not to humiliate Chloë while simultaneously attempting to be honest about what I really thought, and dreading the inevitable fallout when we were alone again in the car going back to our parents' house where she lived in increasing squalor. (Our mother, to whom cleaning was a sacrament, would have collapsed with horror had she seen the state of it.)

Throughout, in my own home, Derek was generous in intention, but intrinsically furious at the way his life was turning out. He was kind to Chloë each time we had her up to our house, but fought with me after each visit. For month after month, he refused point blank to discuss the possibility that she could come to live with us.

The defining row came just before Christmas 1992 because, with contracts signed for the sale of our parents' house and completion due by the end of January, the issue of Chloë's living arrangements was now critical.

On the day I signed for the sale, I came home from the solicitor's office in a terrible state. It was now or never.

After I'd closed the front door behind me, I sat on the bottom stair and tried to plan how I'd handle this. Only one thing was certain. I was not going to consign my poor, sick sister to an institution, even if a bed could be found for her. Waiting lists there too. (Merrow House is not, technically, an institution, before you get clever on me.)

I took up the phone from the little stool that serves as my telephone table. I knew this was the lull between lunch and dinner for Derek so, picturing him in his whites, perhaps having coffee in the cubbyhole that served as an office – and still not knowing precisely how I was going to handle this – I slowly dialled his work number. He picked up immediately. 'Contract's done,' I said quickly, before he'd even finished the upward inflection on 'Hello?'

'That's marvellous! Congratulations, sweetie! We're in the money! Caribbean in the New Year, maybe.'

He was so upbeat and happy there was no way I could cut across him. 'Yeah, maybe.' I tried to sound cheerful. 'But let's not count our chickens. The buyers can still pull out, you know.'

'They won't.'

'And, Derek, it's not all my money, you know – and if it wasn't for both of my parents dying like that … '

He wouldn't let me go down that road because he knew where it led. 'I know! Of course I know that! But there'll be enough from our half, surely, for one big blow-out and still plenty left. Love the idea of a sun holiday at this time of year. You know you do too. This is great news, Dumpy. No frowning now.' He chuckled and I felt like a right heel. 'Leave it to you,' he went on gaily, 'to turn a fantastic piece of news into a drama. But I love ya. See you at home.'

Slowly I replaced the phone on its cradle.

For years our fantasy had been to sip cocktails on a beach on some Caribbean island while everyone back home was suffering through nights and mornings as dark as pitch, replete with floods, tree falls and black-ice warnings from radio newsreaders and AA Roadwatch. I put my head in my hands. Maybe I should offer to use a chunk of the money to take that trip. He'd see it as a bribe, of course, and he'd be right.

One thing was clear. His reaction showed me that, for him, Chloë didn't feature in my – our – half of the gain. He was too thrilled. This was part of a mind game: while the house was on the market, I had several times suggested that after the sale she would probably have to live with us. Every time I mentioned the prospect, however, it ostensibly fell on deaf ears and into glazed eyes. He simply refused to deal with it, and by treating the latest news as he had, he was making it as difficult as possible for me to tread on his dreams. Sounds as though I'm being cynical, doesn't it?

I didn't blame him, honestly. Chloë was a big ask, but what was I supposed to do? Before we'd got married, with Chloë safely in my parents' care, I had told him that in the future, if and when anything happened to them, I would have to be responsible for her. 'That's years and years away,' he'd always said. 'We'll face that when it happens.'

All right, I decided that afternoon. I would give him the Caribbean, even though it might cost, I calculated, up to fifteen per cent of my half of the house money, after agency and legal fees and all the rest of it. It wasn't a mansion we were selling, but an ordinary semi on the northside of Dublin. If two weeks in the sun would pay for his compliance, so be it.

By the time he came through the door from work, herby aromas were billowing into every corner of the house. I had the table set, with wine glasses, a bottle of red already open and breathing, candles lit and a lamb casserole bubbling in the oven alongside red cabbage from Marks & Spencer and potatoes au gratin. As already made clear, I'm not famous for my cooking, not all that enamoured of the art of it either, but I can do a bog-standard casserole and do it well. 'Sit down, Derek,' I called, as he hung up his coat. 'Everything will be ready in about five minutes.'

'Jeez!' He came into the kitchen and looked around appreciatively. 'Who did you murder, Mags?'

'Nobody. Go on, sit. We'll talk while we're eating. Will you pour the wine?'

'Here's to heat and sunshine.' He raised his glass when we were seated opposite one another in the alcove. 'We're really going?'

We clinked glasses.

'Yes. I'll go to the travel agency tomorrow and get the brochures. Now eat! I went to a lot of trouble.'

'What's going on, Mags?' Suddenly on the alert, or pretending it was sudden, he put down his glass.

'Nothing! Eat, for God's sake.'

But if I knew him, he knew me too, and soon enough we were right into it. 'Buy her an apartment,' he yelled. 'You'll have enough money between the two of ye!'

'You haven't seen the state of that house, Derek. She can't manage on her own.'

'Well, that's not my fault.'

'I never said it was. Who's blaming you? Can you see me pointing the finger at you? You personalise everything, but this is a life event. It's something that can happen to people. Would you be like this if she had terminal cancer?'

He muttered something I didn't catch. His colour had risen.

141

'What? Spit it out.'

'Nothing. I said nothing.' He threw down his cutlery. 'I can't eat this.'

'Tell me what you said.'

'All right.' He lowered his head to look at his plate. 'Remember, you insisted. What I said, was "At least there's an end to terminal cancer."' He looked up again. 'This situation has no outcome, Maggie. She'll bury the two of us. Me first.'

'She probably will. She's younger than us. But that's nobody's fault either.'

'I didn't sign up for this.'

'Yes, you did. For richer, for poorer, for better, for worse. Well, this is "for worse".' I was screaming now, something I very rarely do.

'It sure is, Maggie. It sure is.'

Round and round we went until the food had congealed and we were both wrecked.

In bed that night, he turned to me and gave in. 'All right. We'll try it, and I promise I'll do my best. I'm not going to find it easy.'

'I'll take the lion's share. And we'll go on the holiday. That's something you'd like, isn't it?'

'Yeah.' We held hands, and I'd like to tell you that everything felt better, but it didn't. Not really. What I feared was that I would eventually have to choose and there was no choice.

ELEVEN

We did go to the Caribbean. Had a wonderful time island-hopping, but every morning when I woke to the heat and the sound of surf in the various apartments and cottages we had taken, Derek had already left the room. On going out to check, I could see his sturdy, sports-shorted figure pounding through the shallows as though he was being pursued. He claimed it was for exercise. 'I want to get fit at last, Dumpy. There's a promotion coming up and I'm going for it. I deserve it, but I'll be working harder than I ever did.' The sub-text was in high relief: I'm going to be out of that house as much as possible when she moves in.

Fair dues, though: after Chloë came to live with us, he never took his displeasure out on her, although she gave him plenty of provocation. And in many ways he did step up to the plate. He never complained about what I spent on her. He included her in the meals he cooked and made no complaints if she wouldn't eat them.

I've been so upset about his desertion that it's only now, years later, that I can face up to the genuine turmoil he was going through underneath all that generosity. These days, I can understand his point of view with regard to Chloë. The old Joe South hit 'Walk A Mile In My Shoes' applies. If the situation had been the other way round, if he had brought a difficult brother into the marriage, I'm not sure how tolerant I would have been. And, as I say, he did his very best and no one can do more, can they?

For a while, the three of us muddled along, and while there was tension in the house, everything was calm on the surface, certainly to outsiders. But then another issue emerged, which, at the time, was a bigger one for Derek than having Chloë in the house. It was one that initially, at least, I failed to grasp.

We had been trying for a child – and I had had two very early miscarriages – but when nothing positive was happening, we had had all the usual tests. My gynaecologist had imparted the shattering news that I was the infertile one. He had been gentle, but professional. 'I think you should consider IVF, or adoption.'

That was it for my husband.

He refused to contemplate IVF or adoption, quite unreasonably, I thought, but 'reason' is not objective in such a personal dilemma. And again, as the years flowed on, I have realised something I hadn't understood, not fully, because at the time, to me, it seemed so primeval.

Derek is an only child, and from the day we became serious about each other, I had known he wanted a family of his own, like I did. What I didn't fully appreciate was that his desire was underpinned to a great extent by the fact that he was the last of his bloodline and desperately wanted to continue it. That little item of information had burst through his distress almost instantly as I was giving him the terrible news.

We were in the kitchen where he'd been stirring a Bolognese sauce when I had come in and, still wearing my coat, had told him what had happened.

The explosion that ensued had seemed to me to be out of all proportion.

It had started reasonably enough, just a brief hesitation in his stirring. 'That's terrible news, Maggie. Is he sure?' Stirring resumed.

'Absolutely.' I was still too stunned for tears. 'But he said there are things we can do.' I rooted in my bag. 'He gave me a whole dose of information, leaflets and so on … '

'What kind of information?' Stirring.

'Adoption societies, even foreign adoptions, IVF, this surrogacy thing, donor eggs … ' I put the papers on a countertop. Funny the things you remember: on top of the pile there was a picture of a smiling couple, she holding a delighted-looking baby, he with his arms around them both. The background colour of the leaflet was predominantly blue. The man was wearing a beige sweater. She was wearing a yellow dress. The baby was in white.

Derek, stirring, didn't glance at them.

'Leave that, honey. Let's sit down and discuss this.'

'I can't leave it now. It's about to come to the boil. I don't want it to stick.'

'Turn off the cooker, then.'

'No.'

'Derek? Talk to me, please.'

'I just have to get this going.'

'Derek—'

'Leave it, Maggie.' His ferocity shocked me.

And, of course, wouldn't you know? Chloë chose that exact moment to come into the kitchen. 'Ooh! I love spaghetti Bolognese. It smells great. What time are we eating?' She walked right up to the cooker and, the disparity in their height evident (as I said, it's funny what you remember), stood beside Derek and stuck a finger into the sauce. Derek, maddened, flung his spoon across the kitchen, barrelled out and went upstairs, where I heard him pounding to and fro on the floor of our bedroom. 'What's wrong with him?' Chloë, finger still poised, looked at me in amazement.

'It's private, Chlo, don't worry about it, nothing at all to worry about.' I crossed the kitchen, picked up the wooden spoon and ran it under the tap, but as I did, the blood seemed to drain from the top of my head and I was suddenly dizzy.

'But why is he mad?' Chloë persisted.

I had to sit down. I threw the wretched spoon into the sink, turned off the tap and went into the alcove where I flopped into one of the chairs.

She followed me. 'Margaret?' She was standing uncertainly in the alcove's opening.

'It's just a row, Chloë. We're both very tired and Derek is working too hard right now. It'll blow over.' But even then I felt the glimmerings of conviction that this one wouldn't.

'Would you mind turning off the cooker, Chloë, please?' I could hear the bloody sauce begin to pop and spit.

'Sure thing, Margaret.' She hurried to the cooker and the noise ceased. 'Will I go back into the sitting room?'

I nodded and she left.

My dizzy spell had subsided. Upstairs, the pounding noise had eased into what sounded like pacing and I debated, briefly, whether to go up to him. Without my making a decision, it seemed, my feet carried me there.

'Derek?' I stood in the bedroom door. He was holding his head as he walked up and down in the space between the bed and the wardrobe. 'Don't start, Maggie, I'm warning you. This is serious.'

'It's serious for me too, Derek – it's serious for both of us.'

'I can't talk about it now,' he interrupted. 'Can't you see that? Just leave it.'

Of course I couldn't. I did my usual thing, trying to reason, to pacify, which, of course, infuriated him still further. He went to the door and slammed it shut. 'Right. You want to talk about it? Let's talk about it.' It was then he mentioned bloodlines.

'Your bloodline, Derek?' Incredulous, I slumped on to the side of the bed. 'I don't get it, honestly. It's terrible news, I know, but—'

'But nothing, Maggie. I don't expect you to understand.'

'I don't. Bloodlines. That's a little bit medieval, isn't it?'

'Thank you. Thank you very much for that, Maggie.' He tore off his apron and threw it across the room, narrowly missing a little vase that had belonged in my parents' house and was very precious to me. I knew he hadn't aimed at it and tried not to react. 'I know you're upset. I am too. It's my fault, Derek, not yours.'

'That's really comforting.'

'Look, let's sit down and talk. There are things we can do.' Probably because I'm a woman, I was thinking privately that I could talk him down and he'd get over it.

'I'm not going to sit down anywhere, not now. I'd just say things.' He crossed the room to retrieve his apron and began folding it into a square, then a smaller one, and then a smaller one again until it was the size of a large envelope. 'Maggie, I'm sorry about blowing up,' he said quietly. 'You're my wife and I love you, and I'm doing my best and the whole nine yards, you know that, but … ' He didn't finish. Carefully, too carefully, he put the parcelled apron on the end of the bed and left the room. 'I'm going out for a bit,' he called from the stairs. 'I'll be back in an hour or so.'

It was just as well we didn't talk about it immediately, I thought then, listening to him go and believing that I could, as I said, talk him down when he was behaving more reasonably. And he did come back, again apologising: 'I was out of order, Dumpy. Forgive me?'

'Of course. It's a big blow.'

I bunged up my own grief about being barren for the next few months, talking about it only to Mary, who was understanding. I was grateful, especially because she herself faced no possibility of motherhood – but, then, I thought sadly, the waters under her canoe were at least calm, unlike the emotional rapids under mine.

I met my gynaecologist and, without telling Derek, discussed ways out of the situation. None was easy, all were expensive and I didn't broach any of them for a few months after that initial row. To me they were always on the cards and the next logical step. We could afford it, and it would give him what he wanted, surely.

I was aghast to discover that I was wrong. Artificial intervention, by whatever means, was not an option for him and would never be. Neither was adoption – that bloodlines thing again.

I continued to push; he continued to balk. To use a hackneyed phrase, a child, or lack of one, became a third person in our marriage. The fourth, I suppose, if you count Chloë.

One evening, about a year after I'd been given the news, we were eating what in jest we called our Annual Review Dinner. Each October, just after Derek filed our income tax return, we'd go to a high-class restaurant to talk about our finances and plans for the following year. You might think that going to restaurants had to be something of a busman's holiday for Derek but it was more of a treat for him than for me. He loved comparing the work of starry, colleague chefs with his own.

Chapter One was the Review venue that year. Of all the top-class places through which we annually rotated, it was the one Derek most favoured because, he said, the food was sublime and the service was as service should be, attentive and knowledgeable without being intrusive. I'm no gourmet: I eat when I'm hungry and as long as the food tastes good and is well cooked, that's all I need. So I find it very hard to make these comparisons. I had loved the airy spaces in Guilbaud's; I'd enjoyed L'Écrivain when we'd gone there the previous year. But I also loved the steaks, the onion soup, the jam-packed clutter and personal attention in the Trocadero where we went for birthdays and anniversaries. All had their charms, and I could go along with what he said about this place, packed today as always, yet with waiting staff seeming supremely relaxed as they moved quietly among the tables and murmuring clientele.

We'd finished talking about money and, tongue relaxed by wine, I had again mounted my carousel, trying to persuade him, even openly demanding, that we go down the scientific route to have a family: 'You know we both dearly want this, Derek. Lots of people do it. It's very successful – I can let you see the percentages. I've downloaded a lot of material. We might even have twins, get it all over in one go. Wouldn't that be great?'

'Will you stop going on about this?' Fiercely, too fiercely, he cut into his pheasant. 'Don't ruin a good meal. I've said I'm not doing that. Why can't you accept it, Mags? We've enough on our plate anyway, with your sister.'

'I'm not going on about it. I haven't mentioned it for weeks, months, even. And you know why I haven't accepted it. I want kids, Derek. Just like you. This is the way to get what we want.'

'How many times have I to tell you that, for me, it's not natural?'

'And how many times do I have to explain to you that of course it's natural! The basic material, your sperm, my egg, comes from us, from both of us. What's the problem with that? We'd just be getting a small bit of help, that's all, like ...' I cast around for some apt simile. 'It's like getting an expert landscaper to come in and sort out your garden or a top chef to sort out your difficulties with a soufflé.' I looked hopefully at him. Far from being helpful, I'd completely wrecked things.

Over his fork, stalled on the way to his mouth, his eyes were wide with horrified disbelief. 'Sperm, eggs, gardens? Soufflés? Is that how you see this? Throw in a few ingredients, stir them all up and whoop-di-do, we have a child?'

'I know, I know,' I said quickly. 'That was a dreadful way to put it, an awful image. I'm sorry to be so clunky but I was trying to explain. It's just an intervention, an aid to a natural process.'

'No. And that's final.' He resumed eating. 'Nothing natural about it. It's against Church teachings!'

I gaped, too stunned to argue. I had never pegged him as orthodox. The subject of religion was rarely, if ever, mentioned in our house. Or if it was, it occurred to me now, it was usually brought up by me in the context of child abuse by clerics, or some edict I thought fatuous. We didn't go to Mass. Or did we? Did he go without telling me? How was that possible? Maybe I didn't know my husband as well as I thought I did. 'Church teachings, Derek?'

'Yes. Church teachings. You have a problem with that?'

'Of course not. Each to his own is my attitude, as you so very well know. I'm respectful of all religions unless they—' I stopped, thinking it wiser not to go into what I found hypocritical about 'Church teachings'. 'But since when are you so orthodox?' I tried to sound reasonable.

'Since when have you noticed anything about me? You're so taken up with Chloë—'

'Oh, here we go! This has nothing to do with her.'

'No? Everything in our lives is to do with her, Maggie. I can't turn around in my own house without bumping into her. She's everywhere – you don't even see me any more. I don't count.'

'That's not fair.'

'Isn't it?' We had been hissing at each other in low voices, and although the tables in the restaurant were well spaced, he looked over his shoulder. The white-haired couple nearest us were eating studiously. 'For Christ's sake, you're making a show of us, Dumpy.'

For a while we continued our meal in silence. Our glasses were refilled; Declan, the general manager, came to chat and, of course, superficially we brightened. When he left, taking advantage of the cheeriness he always trailed, I regrouped: 'Derek, please tell me, what does religion have to do with this? I'm genuinely asking. For instance, we got married in a registry office, which seemed fine to you.'

'You don't want to go there, Dumpy.'

'Why not? Are you telling me that you wanted a church wedding all along?'

He looked at his plate. 'At the time I wasn't sure about marrying you, Maggie. Registry office didn't mean anything to me. Piece of state paper. Church would have.'

'Jesus!' I was stunned. 'Are you saying – are you still not sure, Derek?'

'What do you think? I've stayed with you all these years, haven't I?' He placed his knife and fork carefully beside each other in the exact centre of his plate. 'I did warn you not to go there.'

'But you haven't answered my question. Are you still not sure?'

'I'm sure. I would have walked out long ago if I wasn't.' He raised his eyes from the plate and I believed him. Probably because I wanted to. In any event, I made a huge effort and parked this new revelation. I took a deep breath. 'Let's go back to what we were talking about. Please, Derek. Just hear me out. Let's forget all the hi-tech stuff. Adoption isn't against any teachings, is it? There are Catholic adoption societies – and whatever about bloodlines, the child would have your name. Will you at least think about it?'

His expression was unreadable. 'Enough. Any more of this and I'm walking out of here. I mean it, Maggie.' A little muscle pulsed in his jaw just below the ear and I knew him well enough to see what that meant. He was so furious, he might indeed leave. I had to accept defeat.

Although I continued sporadically to bring up the subject, it was half-hearted, he recognised that, and no longer flared about it. As a result we never again had a discussion of such intensity about the matter, but I realised that something basic was missing whenever we made love. It wasn't that he was just going through the motions, that would be inaccurate. Derek is a loving man and a generous sexual partner, but although I never mentioned it – feared the consequences, if the truth be known – I could tell that, for him, sex between us had lost a degree of relevance. It's clear now that, alongside my husband's all-too-understandable difficulties concerning Chloë, it was the news of my infertility that shot the lethal torpedo into our marriage.

On the surface, this might seem unreasonable on his part since no one could be held to account for it, but my view is that both partners in a marriage have the right to expectations. Like Chloë's condition, mine is what it is.

From the perspective of hindsight, our union, like most, had flowed like a river, encountering rapids and rocks, flooding over plains, exploring new channels, its eventual destiny being the quiet sanctuary of the sea. Long before that, however, it had plunged fatally over a waterfall. It's ironic, I think now, that despite all the fighting and undertows, it wasn't Chloë, sailing on, oblivious, who finished Derek and me.

Ironic, too, that his three children are girls, but maybe he and Fiona continue to try for a son. If so, I hope for his sake they have one. And, by the way, they all go to Mass together. Mary ran into them in Marlborough Street. She was on her way to the Municipal Gallery for a lunchtime chamber-music recital and they were coming out of the Pro-Cathedral. So he hadn't been kidding about the religion thing. Funny that you can live with a person for so long and remain blind to what really matters to him or her.

I don't mean to whinge about Derek and, truthfully, I don't blame him. His intentions were good; he's a good man. He was caught up, as I was, in events outside the control of either of us. He handled the Chloë situation with as much grace as he could for as long as he could, but the dam in my womb, as I now think of it, proved too high for him to surmount. It's sad but, hey, that's life.

Again I look towards Chloë's window in the gable wall of Seahorse. It's a neat coincidence that today is Wednesday, the day I normally visit her. I think I can see her outline, but I doubt if she can see me in the back seat of the car with Flora's head on my lap.

Our routine works by and large: the Wednesday visit, the Friday pickup to come to stay with me, the return on Sundays in time for what they term high tea, a meal Chloë really enjoys because it includes poached eggs, toast and hot chocolate. 'You know, Flora,' I scratch behind one of her ears, 'some people stay in bed on St Stephen's Day. Other people's worst problems are having to eat cold turkey, or that their telly goes on the blink, or they can hear their ancient lush of an uncle snoring in the spare bed.

'But we're not some people, are we? We have Chloë, we've no kids around the place, and we still have to go to Lorna's. You like her. You'll be there for her like I will. Maybe we'll get James to give you a drink of water. You remember James? You liked him.' I test the reverberations. Hardly anything. Just that residual bit of regret. The fantasies would have been nice – but what was I on about? Those stirrings of lust were genuine. I'm not ashamed of them, don't disown them. At least they proved there's life in the old girl yet.

I shift Flora off my lap. 'I won't be long. Honest!' She knows that phrase and makes no attempt to follow me as I open the door. But, bestowing on me a reproachful glance, she gets to her feet, circles and flops down again on the car seat with her back to me.

As I walk out of the car park, I look again towards Seahorse and see that my sister's hands are splayed against the glass of her window. Two little starfish.

TWELVE

The second stint with Chloë on this St Stephen's Day is almost as short as the first.

The plan had been to see her briefly, give her the Christmas presents, go to Lorna's, then back again to Merrow House to take her home for the night. But as I approach her room for the second time this morning, I'm not optimistic. She has probably opened her presents by now and knows the bad news. I had teared up on seeing those starfish hands against the window. I fear now that they could have been glued to the glass with anger. Outside her door, I take a deep breath, then plaster on that smile, the one that seeds others.

She's sitting on the bed, adding to the general untidiness in the room, surrounded by shredded wrapping paper, ribbons and tattered bows.

'Before you say anything, Chloë,' I get my spake in first, 'I tried everywhere, literally everywhere, to find you an iPad Mini. You'll have to believe me. We're on all the waiting lists and they'll be back in the shops early in the New Year. You'll get it as soon as it's in. I'll pull out all the stops. I promise.'

'It's not fair. Delphy got hers months ago.' Delphine – 'Delphy' – is the pal.

'Not for Christmas, she didn't. She got it for her birthday earlier this month. It wasn't launched in America until October and there was the usual lag in it coming to this country. Listen, Chlo, how would I know all that unless I did try? And, anyway, doesn't Delphy's dad work for Apple? Of course he was able to get one for her. I even tried Apple in Cork for you. I'd have driven all the way down there, but even they had none left. Look – see this?' As a precaution I had brought along a newspaper cutting dated 18 December, advising those seeking the gadget not to waste their time. 'It was even in the newspapers before Christmas. It was on the radio. I heard it myself. They were sold out everywhere in a couple of days – read it.' I thrust the cutting into her hands. 'Be reasonable, Chloë, you asked for it only after you saw Delphy's, and that was already too late.'

She gazes at me. She's overweight, as I told you, but she's so tall she can carry it off. Her best feature has always been her large, luminously blue eyes, and she turns them on me now. 'All I wanted was an iPad Mini.' Her tone is not belligerent: it's wistful.

'Do you like your other presents?' I remain cautious.

In response she raises one foot, making little circles with it in the air. 'See? I liked them.'

I'd bought her an innocuous selection of unremarkable things: scented soap, gloves, a man-sized cashmere sweater from Tesco, a tiny shower radio and a new pair of sheepskin slippers from TK Maxx, one of the few places I could find them in her size and within my budget. They're men's, but who cares? 'Are you sure you like them? I can change them – I've kept the receipt. And you'll have the iPad Mini as soon as I can lay my hands on one.'

'I know, Margaret. Don't go on about it.' She takes both slippers off and that was it, believe it or not. My fears about tantrums have been a waste of good energy. I just never know what's coming, do I?

She helps me clear up the torn gift-wrapping and we put it all into the gift bag in which the presents had been packed. Then, holding a second paper bag filled with the sweet wrappers and other debris, we walk together to the recycling area at the end of her corridor. Two Irish giantesses, heading for a bin: not for the first time I wonder what strangers would make of us.

Not to push my luck, when we get back to her door, I stop at it without going in: 'I'll be back in a couple of hours to pick you up. Don't forget to pack extra, Chlo – remember, you're staying a bit longer this time. Right over the New Year, so you'll need the bigger bag.'

'Thanks for the little radio. You're the best sister in the world.' To my astonishment, she throws her arms around my neck.

'It's for the shower – did you notice that?'

'I'm not stupid, Margaret! I'm not a baby. My brain does function, you know, and when I see S-H-O-W-E-R written on a tiny little radio, and a loop out of the top of it, I know what it means! Pshaw!' She puffs a disparaging little moue in my direction. 'Delphy has one.' Her face changes when she smiles, and with her fair hair, shining after her recent shower, her almost flawless plump skin and those wonderful eyes, she looks beautiful and far younger than her chronological age. As I return the hug, I remember why, despite everything, I love her. Why I'd crawl over broken glass to rescue her from harm.

Back in the car, instead of heading straight to Lorna's house, I drive past the turn-off to her road and instead aim for Burrow Beach. It's still only two o'clock, and although Lorna had said anytime in the afternoon, I'd meant 'mid'. I park illegally – surely there's leeway on St Stephen's Day? – and release a thrilled Flora, who's had her main walk already today, from the car. When we get on to the strand, however, we find half the population of Sutton and Howth traipsing along the wet sand, half of them with dogs. Although I have brought a tennis ball with me, I'm afraid to throw it. A lot of the local dogs are Labradors and our experience with that excitable breed is that, as far as they're concerned, it's finders, keepers with other dogs' toys. Flora is disgusted with me, trotting backwards a few feet in front of me, dashing forward from time to time to nose at the hand holding the ball. She gives up to make her own entertainment only when I force the bloody thing into the pocket of my slacks.

Although there's no wind, the rain continues to fall relentlessly, obliterating the horizon, melding sea and sky into a quilt of undifferentiated grey. My showerproof coat lacks a hood, and although my hair is already wet from walking between Seahorse and the car park at Merrow, I turn up my collar. Quite soon, though, cold, shivery wet fingers are creeping under it, down the back of my neck, and after just ten minutes or so, I've had enough. I'm also pissed off. What do I look like with these streels and thick mats hanging around my face? My hair is a dark ash blonde, according to my tactful hairdresser, 'mousy', according to the realists (Mary!) among my friends. It goes black when wet. My size is horsy enough without adding to the drama with a black, unkempt mane.

I'm annoyed with myself all over again for thinking about my looks in the midst of poor Lorna's distress. What age are you? I scold myself. 'Back to the car!' I yell irritably at Flora, who is now in the sea up to her shoulders, gambolling up a storm alongside a spaniel and pretending to be deaf. 'Flora!' This time she responds, charging out of the water and shaking herself vigorously before cantering up to me, an innocent expression on her face: You called?

Fifteen minutes later, I'm pulling up outside Lorna's. It's a solid, double-fronted fifties house in red brick, set back a little in its own grounds, with an inlet just across the road behind a low sea wall. Usually I would just drive in, as the gates are permanently open, but today there's a garda car parked just inside them.

I forget about my stupid hair as I crack open one of the rear windows; it's cold and there's no danger of suffocation for Flora, but in weather like this, she fogs everything up, especially when her coat is wet. 'Back soon,' I call to her. She's staring hopefully at me from behind the dog grille. Life for Flora is one long game of follow-the-bouncing-ball. Where will it land next? Walk? Play? Food? Nap? Hugs? 'Be good,' I say distractedly as, with one eye on her and the other on the squad car, I close the driver's door and zap the locks.

My heart is thumping hard as I walk in. The seats in the squad car are empty: the cops have gone inside. Good or bad news? Don't jump to conclusions, but my pulse accelerates. It might be OK. With next-of-kin Olive off the radar, they could be here to tell Lorna they've found Martin in a hospital. Or he's been arrested for vagrancy, or on a public-order charge. They could just as easily have him in custody for his own sake, literally to dry him out; most people's experience with individual gardaí is that they turn out to be quite human. Isn't that the case?

Or they could be here just to tell Martin's mother that they've managed to find Martin's wife. At least that would take some of the heat off. Surely, being married to the poor guy, Olive has some legal, if not moral, responsibilities. My imagination is running away with me now: any news, however relatively 'soft', would be preferable to the news I fear.

The front door is ajar but I ring the bell anyway. Best not to gatecrash.

It's a garda who answers, her dark, bulky gilet leavened by the jaunty blonde ponytail bouncing at the back of her head as she takes a quick up-and-down look at me. Up mostly. The top of her head doesn't even reach my shoulder and, to me, she looks about fifteen years old. Her huge grey eyes are sharp enough, though. 'Hello?'

'My name is Margaret Quinn. I'm a friend of Lorna's. She's expecting me. Is everything all right?'

'I'll let her tell you herself.' She widens the door opening. I do a quick mental calculation: she doesn't seem all that upset. But this is my first such experience with gardaí. Do they reflect the emotions they deal with? Or are they trained to remain impassively professional at all costs?

I can hear the sound of a man's voice coming from the drawing room on the left of the hall and, when I get inside, find it's coming from her colleague, large and uncomfortably perched on one of Lorna's spindly antique chairs. Like all her other antiques, it's shabby, its patina neglected. He stops talking when we come in.

Seated in front of him on the couch are Lorna and, to my

astonishment, Mary Guerin. None of the three looks too badly upset, although Lorna has a ball of tissues in one of her hands. 'What's the story?' I ask, addressing none of them in particular.

'I'll get us all a cup of tea, will I, Lorna?' Mary stands up and leaves the room. She is my best friend and I love her dearly but woman-to-woman relationships are complex, and as I look after her, some residual, ridiculous shards of jealousy, hangovers from schoolyard arguments, surface. What's she doing here? I'm the Designated Rescuer today. Not her.

Before I have time to analyse this, however, Lorna's voice cuts through that shaming conceit: 'They haven't found him, Maggie,' she says, in a quavery voice, 'but they think he might be somewhere in the UK.'

'Well, that's hopeful, isn't it? At least he's not—'

'A man of his description took the ferry from Larne last Friday.' The girl garda cuts swiftly across me. 'And just before you came, Miss Quinn, I've been telling Mrs McQuaid here that we have a good line going through the PSNI to the police in Scotland. I think we'll trace him all right.'

'He was drunk, Maggie,' Lorna says tearfully. 'They nearly didn't let him on the boat. That's why people remember him.'

I move over to the couch to sit beside her. 'Some news is better than no news, isn't it, Guard?' I address the man. I know its sexist, and even youth-ist, but with that ponytail bobbing around, this girl is so young-looking and pretty I'm finding it hard to take her seriously, even though she was the one who saved me from putting my foot in it by uttering the word we all fear: 'dead'. She was also the one who addressed me as 'Miss': no flies on her, she'd copped I wasn't wearing a wedding ring. She takes an armchair and we all listen for a few moments to the sounds coming from the kitchen at the end of the hall as Mary clanks around with crockery and spoons. Otherwise the only sound is of the old house ticking away to itself and the hiss of the gas fire fitted incongruously into a grate built for logs. These cops seem to have all the time in the world for us, and I find this consoling. I'm sure Lorna finds it doubly so.

The silence lengthens. Then: 'I think we've taken as much information as we need for the present,' the male garda says gently to Lorna. He lumbers to his feet. 'You have our cards, OK? All the contact details are there. And our colleagues in Howth or Raheny stations are available all day up to nine o'clock.' He and his colleague exchange glances. 'Cutbacks there, too, I'm afraid. We used to offer a lot more hours – but we always give priority to cases like this. And we've both put our mobile numbers on the back of the cards.'

'Will you not wait for your tea?' Lorna's voice remains shaky. 'I'm sure it must be ready.'

'No, thank you,' the male garda says. 'I'm sure you'll appreciate that the sooner we get on this case, the sooner you'll have your son back with you and we can all relax.'

'So ring either of us at any time, day or night, Mrs McQuaid,' the girl adds. 'If we don't answer it's because we're out of range. You can leave a message and we'll get back to you. Feel free. Honestly. And of course if you hear from Martin, be sure to let us know as soon as you do. OK?'

'We've a good record in catching up with people,' the man takes up the running again, 'despite what you might read in the newspapers. As I told you, the fact that Martin used his Visa card to get cash on Christmas Eve in Glasgow is a very good lead and we're on to it. All right?' He glances at me, then back at Lorna. 'Take care of yourself, Mrs McQuaid. Nice to meet you, Miss

Quinn – no, don't get up,' as Lorna makes efforts to stand, 'we'll let ourselves out.'

The two of them go towards the door but then have to stand back to let Mary in with a tea tray set for five. 'At the risk of sounding like Mrs Doyle,' she says, 'you won't have a cup?'

'"Go on, go on!"' He smiles. 'Not right now but thanks all the same. You have good friends, obviously, Mrs McQuaid.' They leave, closing the front door quietly, almost tenderly, behind them. A class act, I think, as I remove my coat, then help Mary with the tea things while Lorna sits, mute and miserable, in a corner of the couch. Given present circumstances, its loose covers, with a riot of peony roses in an exuberant pink, don't strike the right note. They are a new acquisition, the only upgrade she has made to her décor in yonks, and this is the first time I've seen it. 'Not to change the subject, Lorna, but I have to say that I love the way those new covers lift the whole room. Milk?' I pour some into her cup and do the same for Mary's. Then, casually, 'James still with you?'

Mary's head jerks round. Holding the teapot in one hand, she had been placing a tea towel on a side table to protect it before lowering the pot. 'Of course he is, Maggie!' She stands staring at me now, with it and the cloth in hand. 'You know that. You saw him only yesterday. Where did you think he went on Christmas night?'

'Just asking.' Carefully, I add milk to my own tea, sit, and then, to Lorna: 'You see, I have to pick up Chloë and take her home with me for the night, Lorna. Otherwise I'd stay the night with you. That's why I asked. It's her usual Wednesday, you see. Just a coincidence that it's the day that's in it. So, although I'd love to, I just can't I'm afraid.'

I'm over-explaining, earning myself another hard glance from

Mary, who says, 'He's gone for a walk. He said he wouldn't be long.'

Her manoeuvres with the teapot completed, Mary sits too. 'Sorry the first cup is a bit weak, Lorna. I'll let that draw for a while and hotten you up. Would you like me to stay tonight?'

'I'll be fine. Honestly.' But Lorna glances uncertainly from Mary back to me. 'Don't either of you worry about me. I'll take one of Mother's Little Helpers and go to bed early. And, yes, James will be here to get rid of burglars.' She attempts to laugh and fails. 'Sorry. Don't mind me. I don't know whether I'm coming or going.' Her face crumples and I can see she's very close to tears.

'Well, we're all here for you, you know that.' I sip my tea. She sips her tea. Mary sips her tea. Then we all go on the qui vive as we hear the front door opening. It's as if he had heard us discuss him. He and the gardaí must have crossed paths in the driveway.

Lorna drops her pretence and puts her hands over her face. 'I just can't deal with him now. He's grand, no trouble really, but I just can't.'

'I'll head him off.' Decisive as always, Mary gets up and goes into the hall, closing the drawing-room door behind her.

I can hear muffled voices but the walls in this house are thick and I can't make out what's being said. Lorna has removed her hands from her face and is concentrating on her tea. And although I, too, am looking into my cup, as Mary comes back into the room, I can feel her gaze on me as we all hear him go upstairs.

THIRTEEN

Mary Guerin and I became best friends quite quickly after those first few shaky days in school but it wasn't a calm-seas sort of friendship: it was the kind where we vied with one another about trivialities, such as whose mother was the best-looking. And, I seem to recall, there was a long-running dispute about which of us had the daintiest ankles. No contest in the hair stakes, of course: I wasn't even on the track. Throughout our schooldays, Mary's extraordinary hair remained relatively short and cut as though by hedge shears, but for me it had a fascinating personality of its own. I was seriously jealous of it because my own, fine and limp, could never by any stretch be admired. Wet, Mary's hair rested close to her head each morning when she arrived in school. But then, like a shoal of tiny, exotic fish, as it dried throughout the day it emerged slowly to quiver and dance with each movement of her head so that by the time the final bell rang for us to go home, she was again in full haloed glory.

The edifice of our friendship, built in primary school, survived the earthquakes of secondary, which was a sort of miracle because while I went locally, Mary was sent down the country to board. Perhaps, without knowing it, we had ironed out our differences early. There were countless heated 'You said', 'No, you said' spats; I couldn't enumerate the times one of us said, 'I'm not speaking to you!' or, in the school yard, 'I'm not best friends with you any more. I'm going to play with [girl X],' followed by stompings off to join someone else's gang. Reconciliations, though, were swift. Although neither of us was good at apologising, we got around this. For example, after one such tiff, I, with what I had thought was sophisticated subtlety, plonked my last two squares of chocolate in front of her at Little Lunch: 'Here, I'm not hungry. You might as well eat this for me. It's Fruit and Nut.'

'Thanks,' she'd said, and, knowing quite well why I was giving it to her, broke off one of the squares and gave it back to me.

By fourth class, we had been separated within the classroom and I, unfortunately, continued to be placed in the front row, sharing a desk with a girl we all pitied but shunned. Having contracted polio as an infant, she limped badly and, with casual cruelty, we called her Hopalong, or the Gimp. Her rocking gait and clunking calipers would have been bad enough, but she held her head high and sideways, rotated on her thin neck as though her cheek had just been forcefully struck. This unnatural, strained position led the ligaments (or tendons, or whatever they are at the front of your neck) to bulge like thick strings. The poor thing's overall appearance was of martyrdom, an image not helped by a lazy eye, quite a common phenomenon in those days, behind round, wire-framed spectacles. Remember them? The type always referred to by my mother as 'dispensary glasses', held on by wire hooks instead of earpieces and distributed to the poor.

I've forgotten almost all my classmates' physiognomies from those far-off days, but not hers. I don't mean to dramatise this but from time to time her poor, tortured body and face still rises to haunt me in the middle of the night, that four-in-the-morning wakefulness when, with toes curling, you stare at the ceiling reading your non-eradicable list of embarrassments and regrets.

When I look back at how I sniggered about the Gimp with others behind her back or patronised her to her face, I'm deeply ashamed. I hate thinking about how, sheep-like, I went along with the mob, not deliberately ostracising her – that would have been too obvious – but never, for instance, sitting beside her to have lunch unless the only space left was on her bench. All through those early days, that poor girl was never willingly included in any yard games, never picked for a team event, unless forced on us by a teacher. After yet another of her frequent absences with illness, I was the one who had to show her what she'd missed and made only token efforts to hide my resentment.

I really don't know why I behaved like this. If it doesn't sound too psycho-babbly, I suspect her quiet, non-combative acceptance of her treatment at our hands served only to spur us on towards some sort of mob mentality, 'group think' I believe it's called now, but that's no excuse. While there was no physical manifestation, it was bullying at its worst and I deeply regret it. It has even occurred to me, in those later sleepless hours, that my having to look after Chloë now might be some sort of karmic revenge.

The Gimp had the last laugh, I discovered, and I'll tell you about that in a minute. Right now, though, I'm dying to illustrate how simply, at the other end of the scale, a childhood friendship can be sealed for ever.

In fourth class, aged ten, while my growth in height had inexplicably stalled, Mary had put on a spurt and was taller than me; in fact, I was temporarily of average height with my classmates as we became eligible for slapping by the archbishop on Confirmation Day. I dreaded it. While other girls dreamed of their first grown-up visit to the hairdresser and debated whether they should have shoes of white leather or black patent, knee or ankle socks under their costumes, hat or no hat (most said yes to the hat), I lay awake, terrified at the prospect of that slap. Would the holy man draw back and deliver a haymaker? Would he even knock me down? How much would it hurt?

There was more. My unshakeable image, no matter how hard anyone tried to convince me otherwise, had been garnered from the holy pictures we circulated among ourselves. In these manifestations, the Holy Ghost was a little red and yellow flame balancing on a child's head prior to entering the child's soul where He would burn for all eternity. Mine was the first hand up when our new *múinteoir* asked our class who had further questions about the forthcoming ceremony. 'Will I feel the flame of the Holy Spirit coming in through the top of my head?' She assured me, or tried to, that He wasn't a literal fire, but to me she sounded a little shady and I wasn't convinced. So how, I continued to worry, could I be the same person if I had a bit of fire burning all the time in the middle of my chest where my soul was?

'No, sweetheart,' the *múinteoir* persisted patiently. 'The Holy Ghost is a spirit. The flame is just a way of explaining how He will enter your soul and inspire you for the rest of your life. It's not a real fire. But He is real. It's a matter of faith.'

'It's a mystery, isn't it, *a mhúinteoir*?' Brainypants called smugly, hand raised and flapping. With Mary Guerin's sanctioned non-participation in religion class, Brainypants was undisputed top dog. Or bitch.

It sounds bizarre now but my Confirmation stress was absolutely real, and nobody, not my parents, not our latest *múinteoir* – only recently out of training college and, thank God, a Bambi when compared to the gorilla we'd had before – could reassure me. I was still very far from being a Strong and Perfect Christian, obviously, and the archbishop would see that in my eyes; he would probably test me to see how hard a slap I could endure. What was more, no matter how hard I studied and recited, I just knew that on the day I would make mistakes in answering the catechism question he would ask me.

On the day before the Confirmation ceremony, Mary, in whom I'd endlessly confided how worried I was about what was facing me, walked me to the door of the Pro-Cathedral in Marlborough Street where the ceremony was to be held. We were going in for last instructions and naturally, as a Quaker, she was excluded from the entire event. I was ambivalent about that: while I would have liked her to be with me, at the same time (another source of later shame) I had something over her. She and Brainypants were always vying with one another for top slots in the class, leaving my results in third place. Now, in this one thing, two if you count First Holy Communion, I had leapfrogged her, a victory that wasn't all that impressive, however: she got two days off school, I got slapped by an archbishop.

Mind you, she thought a slap was a small price to pay for new clothes, a bagful of money and being treated to lunch in the Gresham Hotel. But on the day before the event when she linked me to the Pro to have a run-through, I would gladly have swapped with her. We stood together in the windy portico of the church and Mary wished me luck as sincerely as though I was setting off on an Arctic expedition. 'Here!' She produced a small white box from her schoolbag and handed it to me. 'I got this for you with my pocket money.'

'For me?' I was bowled over. 'Can I open it, Mary?'

'Yeah. I hope it's the right kind. The man in the shop said it was.'

Inside was a Confirmation medal. My mother had already bought me one but I didn't tell Mary that. 'It's perfect, Mary. I'll wear it and think of you all day tomorrow.'

'Don't forget your catechism, though!'

'I won't.' I had been designated to sit on the outside of a row, so chances were I would be asked a question by the archbishop. Before he slapped me.

'I'm glad you like it. You can keep it in the box afterwards.'

'I won't keep it in any box, Mary. I'll wear it for ever,' I said fervently, meaning it.

'Ah, you don't have to go that far.' But then something struck her: 'I hope you won't be different after you get confirmed.' She looked worried.

'Well, that's the whole idea, sort of.' I hesitated. 'But I wasn't different after First Communion, was I?'

'This isn't like that,' she said. 'The whole point of Confirmation is that you're supposed to change, sort of, inside. I was looking it up in the encyclopaedia.'

Mary's family owned, she'd told me, a full Britannica at home. She was the only person I knew who had access to such a resource and I was looking forward to seeing the volumes when I went to tea in her house at the end of the week. 'Don't worry about it, Mary. I promise I won't change,' I said to her. Then: 'See you the day after tomorrow. I'm dying to go to your house and see the Encyclopaedia Britannica.'

I really was. During the first two years of our friendship, I had repeatedly asked her to tea in our house, but she had always declined, giving various excuses: her mother needed help with something; she had to go with her brother to the doctor for a check-up; one or sometimes both of her sisters were sick; her father had set aside an evening to help with her arithmetic homework, and so on.

Eventually, it got through to me that she simply did not want to come and I stopped asking. I was miffed for a couple of days but then forgot about it. Anyhow, in some respects, I was relieved: my sister's behaviour, especially at the table, was atrocious and I had been banking on the novelty of Mary's presence having such an effect on Chloë she would stay calm, at least for the duration of the meal.

'Good luck, Maggie,' she said, and before we went our separate ways, we hugged shyly while the wind whistled. Somehow I knew right then that our friendship would survive anything life threw at us. Do you think that's likely at the age of ten? I'm telling you, cross my heart, that for me it was more than likely: it was certain. I just knew, deep down.

Inside the Pro, I scanned its vast interior, softly lit from multiple banks of candles in front of all the statues and shrines in the side chapels. I was to sit beside the Gimp and saw her immediately, leaning sideways as usual in one of the pews towards the front. Painfully aware of the sound of my footsteps ringing through the holy hush, I went up and slipped in next to her. It was just after three o'clock on that sleety February afternoon and, apart from the girls in our class drifting into the pews in dribs and drabs, there were perhaps three or four dozen grown-ups dotted around. Some dangled rosary beads, others knelt with heads bowed into their hands, a few, the dossers, were probably just resting in the relative warmth. A woman dressed in black shambled around the stations, her voice echoing as she gabbled Glory Bes at each stop, their rhythm almost like that of a pop song:

GLORYbetotheFather
andtotheSON
andtotheHOLYGhost
asitWASinthebeginning
isnowandeverSHALLbe
WORLDwithoutend
a-MEN.

As though accompanying her, in the creaking choir loft, an organist was testing the keys, running little trills and chords, time lagging and clashing against each other, waves of curling notes advancing and receding against the hard surfaces of stone, marble, plaster and mahogany.

'Where do you think we'll be really sitting?' The Gimp's whisper was deferentially low.

In the gloom, with her head twisted away from me so I couldn't quite see her gammy eye, she had quite a nice face, I thought generously. 'We'll know in a minute,' I whispered back. 'Iníon Ni Ghrógáin is up there with her list, see?' I pointed to our young *múinteoir*, who was standing in front of the altar studying a list. 'I think she said we'd be about halfway up on the right-hand side. I know I'm going to mess up on the question he'll ask me tomorrow,' I confided. 'I just know. I'm really afraid.'

'But you're one of the brainboxes!' The Gimp, whose real name was Pauline, looked at me in astonishment. At least, I think she was looking at me. It was always hard to tell.

'Shut up!' I snapped. 'Doesn't mean I know everything! Anyway, we're not supposed to be talking.' And I turned a cold shoulder on her. Stressed as I was that week, I took offence easily and I didn't like being thought of as clever. That was pressure. Standards to be kept up and all of that.

Secretly, though, I had always cherished my reputation as 'third brainiest in the class'. It was comfortably prestigious but the pressure was low – I could leave the jousting for top slot to Mary and Brainypants while at the same time behave in a lordly way with the underlings who scrabbled around beneath the three of us for the rest of the marks.

I shouldn't have been mean to the Gimp – she had been paying me a compliment after all – but there was just something about the way she crooked her suffering face that seemed to invite you to have a go. I turned back to her. 'Sorry!'

'That's all right,' she said, with her wonky smile. Sometimes, I thought, I wish she'd hit me.

The Confirmation next day passed off without incident, although I ruined my new patent shoes in a puddle. I answered my question perfectly. The slap was just a stroke on the cheek. My mother didn't notice I was not wearing her medal but Mary's, my father gave me a pound note, and the neighbours on either side of our house gave me a half-crown each. The lunch in the Gresham was great too, largely because it was just the three of us, Mammy, Daddy and me. Chloë wasn't there: her private school was running normal hours that day, so I could bask in the individual attention.

At that time I didn't know whether to be angry or relieved that Chloë attended a different school from mine. My parents, having decided that she needed to be in a class with a high teacher-to-pupil ratio, rather than struggling to find her feet within the battalions where I was, had sold their car to enrol her in a private school. 'You wouldn't do something like that for me,' I sulked, when I was told. The good bit about it, though, was that she was out of my hair and I had no responsibility for her during the day.

Privately, I thought she was a spoiled brat. Various medics my parents had consulted about her had told them she would grow out of the temper tantrums and bad behaviour; 'Chloë's doctor says' became the refrain in our house whenever I protested that she was allowed to get away with murder, which wasn't fair. So that day in the Gresham, I took full advantage of my parents' good humour. I knew my father was a nice da, but that day I found my mother, away from her worrying, was, underneath, quite a nice person as well. Surprising, too. Because I hadn't known until that day that she had worked before she became Mammy. I hadn't asked – to me she was just always there, in the kitchen or the sitting room, wearing an apron and worrying all the time about Chloë, talking about Chloë, thinking about Chloë, answering me distractedly whenever I asked a question. So to find she had worked as a secretary in the Dublin office of a film distribution company before she was married, and right up to the time Chloë was born, was just mind-boggling.

She had even met a real film star, Barry Fitzgerald. 'I think it was about 1959. You were three, Maggie,' she said to me, as we waited for our third course, 'and we were expecting Chloë. I even remember the name of the movie: it was *Broth of a Boy* and they were all in it, all those great Abbey actors, Harry Brogan, Philip O'Flynn, Marie Keane, the Golden Brothers and people like that. D'you remember when we used to go to the Abbey, Eddie?'

'Of course I do, you daft brush! The Abbey company was playing in the Queen's then, in Pearse Street,' he explained to me, 'because their own theatre had burned down. It was a lovely place, a bit bockety, but with red velvet seats and a great orchestra pit. That's where I met your mammy, actually.'

'We found ourselves sitting beside each other and he bought me a packet of Rolos.' She took up the story.

'1952,' he added. 'Mackintosh's Rolos.' He sounded wistful. 'I've kept the wrapper all these years.'

I detected something passing between them, although it was gone in a flash. This whole thing was revelatory and quite wonderful. For the first time in my life I could see them as real people, with a real history.

'Of course I thought Barry Fitzgerald was ancient,' she said then, 'and he *was* ancient. I think he must have been around the seventy mark at that stage but to me he looked around ninety. Yeah,' she said slowly, eyes misty with remembrance, 'it was lovely. The reception, I mean. We were all invited to the premiere, even old Mrs Madigan who cleaned the office. It was the first time in my life I had ever tasted smoked salmon. And the first time I had a glass of champagne. Do you remember, Eddie?'

'Of course I don't. I wasn't there, love! I was minding today's film star!' He smiled at me, but the arrival of our apple crumble and ice cream dissipated the bubble of nostalgia as they steered the subject towards what a great meal we were having. Anyhow, by late afternoon on that Confirmation Day, life had sagged back to normal. When we got back into the house, Chloë was already at home with a babysitter.

For me, though, Mammy's stock had risen immeasurably as a result of that lunch. There was no question but that I was the second-class child in our house, but I don't blame them – not any more, because now I understand. I do miss them, both of them. And I can't look at a packet of Rolos these days without experiencing a little pang.

Let's get back to the Gimp because I promised you a story about her.

Long after Mary and I and the rest of our classmates had grown up and wouldn't have recognised each other in the street, I heard that, believe it or not, the Gimp had become an award-winning particle physicist. Mary had gone to a lecture on astronomy in Trinity College. She hadn't recognised the name of the lecturer but there she was, the Gimp, up on stage, wearing a floor-length skirt to hide her deformity while talking with great authority about the beauty and order of our own galaxy and the entire universe. 'I didn't know it was going to be her,' Mary reported. 'I didn't make the connection until I saw her and even then it took me a while. It's a complete transformation. She looked absolutely fabulous, Maggie. We had a chat afterwards and she was asking for you.'

'She remembers me?'

'She says you were kind to her. Helped her every time with her catch-up when she came back to school after one of her numerous operations.'

This was hard for me to take in. 'Does she still limp? Is she still wearing glasses?'

'The limp, yes, still quite bad, but the way she used to look sideways at you? That's fixed. And no glasses. She had surgery there too, so no more crossed eyes. Contact lenses. I'm telling you, Mags, she's completely open about it all and she'd put us to shame. She was even laughing about that dreadful sadist of a teacher we had in second class. Remember her? Ugh!'

'Do I what! And I don't laugh, actually.'

Mary let that pass. 'And as for the lecture,' she went on, 'very impressive. She's a bloody phenomenon.'

'Oh, God – we were horrible to her, Mary. I've been feeling guilty about that for years.'

'Maybe *you* were horrible to her! I wasn't – anyway, don't sweat it. It obviously didn't affect her. She said something about maybe getting together next time she's in Dublin. She's here a good bit because her mother isn't well. She's based in Harvard.'

'Good God!' I stared at her. 'Who'd have thought?'

'Not me anyway. And my conscience is clear about that horrid time you allege we gave her. She made no mention of it at all. She gave me her card, one for you too.'

It was March 2004, and we had come into town to watch the St Patrick's Day parade and were having a cup of tea in Bewley's, crammed and steaming with wet parade-refugees, their green flags and sodden leprechaun hats strewn at their feet. From the floor beside her chair, Mary pulled her voluminous handbag on to her lap and, while rooting in it, expanded on the Gimp's astounding emergence from grub to butterfly. 'She qualified originally as a doctor, something in psych, I think, but then decided there wasn't much she could do for the human race in that field. So she switched over, took further degrees in physics and ended up as this award-winning research bod. You'd want to see the string of letters after her name. I found it hard not to look at her without my tongue hanging out.'

I would have argued with her about her clear conscience and, indeed, the collective conscience of our whole class, but didn't have the energy. 'Ah, here they are!' She pulled out the cards. 'Recognise her?' She handed me one. It bore a tiny photograph of Dr Pauline Dwyer, the name followed by the string of qualifications Mary had mentioned. I studied her, a blonde woman with a wide, confident smile full of American teeth. 'I wouldn't know her, Mary.' I went to hand the card back to her.

'Keep it,' she said briskly. 'She gave it to me for you. We might meet her some day, the two of us, next time she's in Dublin. She's terribly interesting and I think you'd like her.'

'I'd probably be intimidated.'

'No, you wouldn't. She's really nice. Honestly. I'm going to meet her anyway. I found her fascinating. Think about it?'

'Maybe.' But I knew I could never face the woman.

I was left with no choice as it happened.

Two days after the national feast day, I was pooching around with a piece I was writing, or trying to write, about traditional Easter rituals. This wasn't a commission, but if I could come up with something original, I could probably place it in a Sunday newspaper: editors are always looking for themed colour pieces. I had decided to do an 'Easter Celebrations Around the World' article but wasn't having much success. Easter bunnies and eggs, chocolate, processions, carnivals (Rio), church celebrations, and variants of same, were all I could find. 'Just start!' I said, in such a firm voice that Flora got a fright and scrambled to her feet. 'Sorry!' I said, ruffling her ears. 'Nothing to do with you.' I poised my fingers over the keyboard:

Did you know that in France, fish and the ringing of bells are the main symbols of Easter? Or that in Bulgaria, you play

*conkers with eggs, taking turns tapping your eggs against
the eggs of others and that the person with the last whole
egg will have a year of good luck? In Brazil, it's the Macela
flower.*

The phone rang. Thank God, I thought, I was boring even myself.

It was Mary, sounding pleased. 'Get your coat on. We're
meeting Pauline in town. She's going back to Boston tomorrow so
this is our last chance.'

'Pauline? Who's Pauline?'

'For God's sake, Mags. Pauline Dwyer. The Gimp.'

'But I'm working.' My stomach clenched. The woman would
have a go at me – with good cause.

'You can work when you get back. Come on. You can purge
your stupid guilt or whatever – but she has nothing against you.
Honestly. So don't go apologising, d'ya hear me?' (My mother
had always added 'd'ya hear me?' to the end of her sentences
when giving out. I heard it as 'd'ya Hermy', and until I was about
eight years old, I thought 'Hermy' was a word in the lexicon of
scolding.)

Anyhow, this was how, half an hour later, I found myself
sitting with coffee in front of me in the library nook off the lobby
of the Fitzwilliam Hotel opposite St Stephen's Green, along with
Mary and the far from Gimp-like Pauline Dwyer. Fair dues to
Mary for recognising her, I thought. I certainly wouldn't have.
She had been waiting for us when we arrived so I hadn't had the
opportunity to judge her gait for myself. Otherwise she was a
good-looking woman. She was also charming – and funny, with
a gift for mimicry. We had been talking about the difference
individual teachers can make to the psychological well-being of

their classroom charges and she had given us a wickedly accurate manifestation of that first terrifying teacher. 'Poor woman,' she said at last, when we had laughed ourselves silly, adding sympathetically, 'I figure she had to be menopausal or, at the very least, had been jilted at the altar. What do you think?' She looked from one to the other of us. Then, to me: 'Mary told me about your poor sister, Zoë, is it?'

'Chloë,' I muttered, glaring at Mary. I didn't like my private woes being aired in public. Then I remembered: hadn't Mary mentioned that before she became the paragon she was now, the Gimp had been 'something in psych'? This was a set-up. But I couldn't object, not really. So I gave Pauline Dwyer a truncated history of Chloë's troubles and a summary of what had happened at Christmas. 'And she's still in a psychiatric unit?' she asked, gazing at me, both eyes in synch. Whichever surgeon had done them, they'd made a really good job of it, I thought. 'Yes. They tell me they're putting a release plan in place.'

'And she's coming back to live with you, Maggie?'

'That's the idea.'

'How do you feel about that?'

'Fine,' I muttered, again glaring at Mary who, innocent as an Easter lamb, was admiring the toes of her shoes. 'Look,' I said, 'you're very good to take an interest but you're a physicist now and—'

'I keep my hand in with psych matters. Sort of a side-hobby. I've kept up my registrations too. You'd never know what the future holds – have you heard of a place called Merrow House?'

'No.' I was taken aback by the swift change of subject.

It turned out that Pauline had at first gone to Trinity, graduating in medicine with the woman who had subsequently opened Merrow and still managed it. 'She's a close friend and it's a good place. The best in the country, from what I know. If you ever need to talk to her, in the future, of course – or if you'd like me to put in a word ...' Delicately she let that hang, then: 'Mary gave you my card?'

'Yes.' I was astounded at this development. At that time, I was indeed worrying about how I would deal with Chloë when she came home to me from hospital. It was a huge responsibility, particularly as I knew she wasn't all that keen on taking her medication.

'Thank you, Pauline!' I was fervently grateful, yet guilty too. This was my little sister we were talking about putting in a home. (I've described Merrow to you and it's far from the workhouse we tend to picture when the word 'home' is mentioned in Ireland, but I didn't know that then.)

Pauline Dwyer proved to be as good as her word. Later that year, when I just couldn't cope any longer, I rang her in Boston and she set up the interview with the owner of the facility.

Deep down, I despise nepotism or pulling strings of any sort and here I was now, not only a member of a Club, but of an old girls' network.

I tried to reassure myself that everyone did this in Ireland – men had been at it for years. In my case, this was for my sister, on whose behalf I would have begged the Pope of Rome for help if I'd thought he could do anything; as a mendicant I would have climbed Croagh Patrick barefoot. But after Chloë made her (difficult) transition from my house to her new home, I have to confess that, although tempered with deep sadness and even stronger guilt, the unease I felt about how it had been achieved had yielded to relief.

What complex emotional lives we live these days.

Meanwhile, I knew that never again would I even think of characterising Pauline Dwyer as Hopalong or the Gimp.

FOURTEEN

On a late afternoon in November 2012, Mary and I were sitting in front of the living-room fire in her flat on the Navan Road. It was late afternoon, and the Irish winter held full, horrible sway: it was another chronically wet day. This, it seems, is what global warming – or climate change, as the boffins now seem to prefer – is increasingly going to be like in this country. When that all started, I remember having conversations about how great it was going to be: Marbella-sur-Dollymount all year round. Far from it, it now appears. Great for trees, this weather: maybe we should all move to Leitrim and plant forests.

She had rung me at lunchtime to ask me to go to a matinée of Bernard Farrell's *Bookworms* at the Abbey. I had initially demurred: 'Have you seen today's weather, Mary?'

'Don't be such a wuss. A few showers won't hurt you – make

your hair curly! Anyway, we both need cheering up and Bernard is always good for a laugh, plus he tells us a thing or two about ourselves. Two for the price of one! Come on, you've nothing else in your crammed social diary, have you?' I hadn't and she knew it. Unusually, Chloë was not with me. She was one of a crew working on a Christmas pageant and had elected to stay at Merrow to help with painting the cyclorama. So, really, I had no excuse.

We had both enjoyed the play but, on the downside, had got drenched on the way home. Mary's room now reeked of wet wool – while she had been able to change into her dressing gown, my coat steamed on the radiator under one of her windows.

I suppose the flat could be classified as a large bedsitter. Newly insulated by the landlady, who had also upgraded the bathroom and installed a storage heater to augment the weak central heating, it had been modernised to a degree. Although that bathroom is a proper one, the flat has no separate bedroom and its kitchenette sits behind a flimsy stud wall. It runs over the entire first floor of a two-storey house, so the main room is huge, by flat, or any other, standards, and Mary sleeps very comfortably, she says, in what used to be called a Murphy bed, built into the wall between two of the three large windows in her main living room and pulled down each night. Don't know what a Murphy bed would be called these days. Something dreamed up by a marketing department. Super Sleeper Space Saver?

Outside, the traffic whooshed by through the puddles and gutters, emphasising our companionable quiet. We had long ago achieved that stage in our friendship where silence is rarely awkward and even less frequently a threat. Then Mary, out of the blue, asked, 'Do you get lonely, Maggie?'

'Do you?' I was astonished at the question.

She hates it when I answer a question with a question. 'I asked you first.'

'What age are we? This isn't a competition.' Then: 'I haven't thought about it much. That's the truth. I suppose it can get lonely. At night especially, after you close your front door and that's it. You've vanished from others' lives. From the world, I suppose.'

'At least you have your own front door and at least you have a sister to worry about. What do I have?'

'Mary!' This was so unlike her. 'Would you care to swap? Sure you don't have a spare minute with all your causes and interests. And, anyway, you do have a family.' All three of her siblings had departed long ago to work in better weather; all are married and have children, probably grown up by now, so Mary also has a squad of nephews and nieces. She never talks about any of these relatives, though, which I have always found odd.

'I don't have a family. Not really.' She shrugged. 'Since my parents died, when last did any of them bother to come home to see just me?'

'Be reasonable, it's a two-way street. When last did you go to see them? They have kids. You're freer than they are.'

'Would you get a grip, Maggie! To Sydney? To Durban? To La Jolla?'

The brother, who lives in California, Jeffrey, is an IT bigwig in Silicon Valley and, as far as I know, the two sisters, Naomi and Jennifer, don't work outside the home. With Mary here in Ireland, it seems that this family chose to emigrate as far away as possible from each other. It's certainly past time for reunion. 'Why not go to them, Mary? You have the time.'

'But not the money. Anyway,' she added quietly, getting up

185

again, this time to switch on a table lamp beside the fireplace, 'they don't want to know.'

'Why would you think that?'

She sat back in her armchair and appeared to consider this for a moment or two. 'You're not to tell this to a single person, Maggie. I mean it. Not to any of the others in the Club. Nobody.'

'I promise.'

'I mean it. It's too humiliating. I'm trusting you with this.'

'Cross my heart. What is it, Mary? You're driving me mad.'

'I wrote and asked them if they had any plans to come here,' she said slowly. 'Three letters, three addresses. I used this Gathering thing for 2013 – I even enclosed that government leaflet we all got about it – but it was just an excuse, really.'

'Outside the Gathering, were you clear in telling them you yourself would like to see them?'

'Of course I was!' But something about the way she had blurted it led me to think she had not been all that emphatic about it. I could picture what she wrote: 'There's this Gathering thing next year. We're all supposed to be asking our long-lost relatives to come home to Ireland for a visit in 2013. Relieve you of a few dollars in the cause of our country, ha ha!' She was staring into the fire. 'Not one reply. Can you imagine how that feels?'

I can envisage the humiliation, I thought. How about being barren and having an ex-husband who walked out on you, then rubbed your nose in it by having three children in quick succession with a new, fecund partner who named them Crystal, Marjorie and Sunniva? (In my head, when I'm thinking about them, they're called Poverty, Chastity and Obedience, but I wouldn't reveal that to anyone, not even to Mary). And although I genuinely didn't and don't resent those little girls, the fertility bit, the comparison between the divine Fiona and myself, continues to sting. But this was Mary's conversation, not mine. She had made an admission of vulnerability, a condition she very, very rarely entertains, or at least confesses to. So I contented myself by telling her that I could feel for her. 'How long ago did you write?' I offered. 'Maybe it's taken a long time for them to get the letters. Maybe they've moved.'

'Six months. I put return addresses on all the letters. They didn't come back to me. As for moving, they haven't budged, any of them, according to the directories I've consulted. You can find anyone these days. Not just on Facebook, there are online directories. Just put in the names, approximate places, and there you go! For a fee, of course. That's for the accurate ones.'

'They've cut all ties with this country?'

'So it appears. The house is still there, as you know, but the rent we get for it goes directly to the nursing home. My mother's pension tops up the fees and she still has a couple of euro pocket money. Not that she needs it. What's to spend it on? How much soap can one old lady use?'

'But,' I persist, 'if that's the case, the home should be in contact with your brother and sisters.'

'The agency that deals with getting tenants, contracts and so on handles the whole thing. They have authorisation to replace and repair. I'm just their local contact if there's an emergency. So far,' she knuckles the wood of her coffee table, 'so good.'

'Did you try Facebook?' I try another tack.

'Yup. The two girls are there, large as life. Happy in their nappies. Of my brother, the IT expert,' she sounded bitter, 'there is no sign, would you believe? And before you suggest it,' she held up a hand, 'yes, I did try LinkedIn. He's there, of course, but as one of the stars of his company. No home address and only the company phone number.'

It did occur to me that she could ring him. All three of them. But to mention it would be further to expose her feelings, obviously raw, about this.

When we were children I, who had only Chloë, fractious as she was, had privately envied Mary, who had three siblings. But there had been an undercurrent of awkwardness between us about our families.

'You have no idea how much it cost me to swallow my pride and ask them to come over here,' she said quietly now.

I did. I know my friend whose fierce independence is equalled only by that pride of hers.

It's only in novels, you know, that you can really 'share sorrow', that you can put out an arm, or two hugging arms, and everything improves. At that moment, I was tongue-tied, bereft of anything useful or comforting to say, other than an inadequate 'Oh, Mary! I'm so sorry. I didn't know.'

'Why would you? I didn't tell you.' She got up yet again and went to each of her windows, drawing the curtains to shut out the filthy afternoon. She came back and, without looking at me, said, 'I'm the one who's sorry. I shouldn't have opened my mouth. I'm just being sentimental. It's no big deal.' Having confided in me, she had now pulled up her drawbridge.

'It *is* a big deal, Mary. I think it is anyway. I can't come up with a single reason why a person wouldn't bother to reply to a letter like yours, let alone three people. Do they have anything against you?' I'm cautious. 'Could you have said something, inadvertently, of course, to offend them? Anything to do with your parents?

Your dad's will, for instance. You know what they say about wills – "Where there's a will there's a row."'

She stared witheringly at me and I braced myself for a put-down. Then her expression cleared and, deadpan: 'They all think I'm bats.'

This struck my funny bone and I had to give way to one of those attacks of giggling that catches you off guard. 'Sorry,' I spluttered. 'I can't help it. You *are* bats!' I was just beginning to get myself under control when she too started to giggle. 'I am, amn't I?'

When we had quietened I looked around. 'Not changing the subject, but I've always loved coming into this flat. It's so cosy.' It was, too, with the fire chuckling in the grate, reflecting on the twin bronze urns she had lugged home from Crete, and on books from all around the world on shelves built into both sides of the fireplace. Her fairy books, children's included, winked at us from a large brass tray-table beside her reading chair.

She sighed. 'Yeah. Cosy. I suppose.'

'I see you're working on your fairy thesis.' Nodding towards the books, I was careful to sound neutral.

'Yup.'

'How's it going these days?'

'Not bad. Fits and starts, I suppose you could say. Mostly folklore so far – fairy reels, forts, trees, raths, banshees, changelings, all the rest of it, but I'm looking forward to getting out and talking to a few old codgers in the sticks. They're the ones with the real stories. That'll be the enjoyable bit.' She got up yet again, this time to put a briquette on the fire, then had to step back a little as a shower of sparks exploded on to the hearth. We lapsed again into silence.

Bats, yes, I thought, but endearingly so. The kind of bats and quirkiness friends treasure about each other; the kind that, when you're thinking about your friend, puts an affectionate smile on your face even as you shake your head in bemusement.

The first conversation Mary and I had had about her little friends had not been all that convincing. Earlier this year, she and I had been walking home, this time having been to an afternoon showing of *The Best Exotic Marigold Hotel*. (I'd loved it, she hadn't. She had liked the performances but thought the thrust of the thing was patronising.) We were waiting for the green man at the Doyle's Corner traffic lights when she'd turned to me. 'I'm thinking of doing a paper on the place of fairies in medieval Irish society. What do you think, Mag?' Impatiently, she pressed the crossing button for the second time, then had to jump back as a lorry ploughed through a puddle in the gutter. 'Wanker!' she yelled after him. 'So what about it?' she asked, in a more normal tone. 'Should I have a go?'

'I'm the wrong person to ask. You know that. I don't believe—' I stopped. She always became immersed, almost obsessively, in any new interest and I didn't want to wreck her head.

'I know what you were about to say. But how do you know, Maggie? Just because you haven't seen a fairy doesn't mean it doesn't exist. Your religion believes in angels. Have you ever seen an angel? Ever seen a photograph of one, even?'

'You don't see them, Mary.' Jeez, I thought, she's forced me into implying I believe in angels. I did when I was a child, but now? 'Angels come in various forms, you know,' I added feebly.

'And fairies don't? So what's the difference? Is it because religion tells you to believe in angels but not in fairies? Are you so thick that you'd go along with that?'

'What about miracles, though?'

'What about them?'

'Do you deny that miracles happen, Mary?'

'Do you deny the power of suggestion? Of the human spirit? Of the body's power to heal itself? And if you accept that miracles are caused by angels or saintly intervention, who's to say that they can't happen because of intervention by fairies? Where's the proof to cut them out? You can't see or hear or feel them either, can you?'

'You're just being ridiculous now!'

Luckily for me the lights changed and we started to cross, but then had to dash aside as a little Peugeot with go-faster stripes crashed the red and almost mowed us down. Mary was livid: 'Did you see him and his effing little baseball cap? He was about fourteen!'

'All right,' she began again, when we had safely navigated the junction. 'It's clear I'm on my own with my fairies. But step outside the box for a moment. Do you think that to write a thesis on them is theoretically a good idea? They believed strongly in fairies in medieval times—'

'And burned witches!'

'Point taken. But they wouldn't have burned witches if they hadn't believed in witchcraft. Eh?'

'Willya give me a break, Mary? My brain's hurting!'

'Thanks for the support. Much appreciated!' But we continued on, past St Peter's Church, in relatively companionable silence. We're both used to these exchanges. Fairies represent only the latest spate in Mary's rivers of enthusiasm. We could equally have been sparring about the fate of orang-utans in Borneo, mining inside the fragile Alaskan environment or, appallingly, why it's acceptable to eat dog in certain cultures. You can imagine how I feel about that one!

Another bus splashed past outside. I looked at my watch. 'Time I was thinking of making a move.' I was so relaxed and comfortable, though, that I was reluctant to face again into the horrible evening. 'It's been lovely, Mary. Thanks. As usual.' Then, teasing: 'Speaking of bats, Mary, do Quakers believe in fairies?'

'I don't actually know.' Instead of rearing up, as I had expected, she sounded intrigued.

'When last were you at a meeting?'

'None of your business.' That had got to her. 'When last were you in Lourdes?'

'*Touché!*' This wasn't the first time she had hit me with that. In the immediate aftermath of Chloë's suicide attempt, I had unwisely confided my long-ago promise. 'It's still there, Mary, that ambition. I just haven't had the time.'

'Too many articles about peplums being "the new essential for the coming festive season", eh?'

'That's not fair.' I was startled.

I was, I admit, a tad shame-faced about that particular last-minute filler piece. 'But that was – what? This time last year? I can't believe you saw it.'

'I was tidying Toddy's waiting room and saw your by-line on the cover of one of the magazines. And you're right, it isn't fair. We all have to make a few bob.' Mary supplemented her part-time counsellor's income with shifts as a receptionist in a large dental practice to cover holidays or when one of the full-time girls was sick. 'Sorry.'

'Apology accepted. And I will go. To Lourdes. Maybe next Easter? "Easter 2013" has a nice ring to it, don't you think?'

Again she surprised me as, after a moment, she said tentatively, 'I might even go with you. It's a place that has always intrigued me. Not necessarily from any religious perspective,' she added hastily, 'it's just that, from what I know, it seems to inspire so much human goodness.'

I decided not to be flip. After all, it could be another thesis-in-gestation. 'That would be terrific,' I said warmly, meaning it. 'I'd love to have company.'

'Easter is four months away. We'll talk about it, OK?' We lapsed again into silence.

'Will I turn on the news?' After a few minutes, I again looked at my watch: it was coming up to six o'clock and the remote control was on the lamp table between us. I stretched out to pick it up, but she stopped me.

'Nah. I've had enough friggin' news to last me for the rest of my life.'

'No problem.' But this struck me as decidedly odd. She's such a livewire and so curious about every aspect of human life that not to want to be up with the play, both nationally and internationally, was uncharacteristic. What the hell was going on with her today? She'd tell me in her own time, I supposed. 'Yeah. You're right. Why disturb ourselves with all that shite?' I settled myself deep into her cushions and looked around appreciatively.

Mary's taste in décor is eclectic. Her walls are a deep, unusual shade of pink, close to coral. She had found her Oriental carpet, its geometrical pattern on a faded, mustard-coloured base, in a charity shop; her curtains, bought at a house-clearance auction, are of heavy red velvet and she had covered her armchairs and couch with afghans and ethnic throws in eastern colours, reds, indigos, emerald greens and ochres. I have never been to the Middle East, but to judge by the bazaars you see on TV and in movies (usually in scenes where the protagonist is fleeing from some baddie or other), the effect here, I'd guess, is souk-like. 'I love this,' I repeated, 'so …' I searched, but again '… cosy,' was the best I could come up with.

'Yeah.' She sighed and, sounding sad, said, 'We're all getting older, Mags. I can't stand the thought of getting ancient and sick, with all that that entails for people on their own. There's no way I'm going to find myself in some awful nursing home. I'm joining Exit. Tea?' She got up and went through into her kitchenette.

It was only then that the peculiarity of this entire conversation struck me. 'Exit?' I was horrified. 'Is there something you're not telling me, Mary? Are you sick?' Although she was less than ten feet away, I had to compete with the running tap. Her water pressure, unlike mine, is fantastic.

'Don't be an idiot,' she yelled back. 'If there was anything to tell, you'd be the first to know.' She filled the kettle and turned it on.

'You've worried me now.' She really had. She was sick. I'd bet on it. This was why she'd tried to connect with her brother and sisters. 'Mary! Please tell me there's nothing—'

'There's nothing, honestly. Don't be such an old Cassandra. We were talking about loneliness, not death.'

'I didn't say you mentioned death. You mentioned Exit. That's Exit International? The assisted-suicide thing? Death is what you're thinking about, isn't it? It's on your mind, Mary.'

The kettle popped and crunched noisily beside her and she gave it a vicious smack. 'Effing useless piece of tin!' She was irritable now. 'I'll have to change it. Again. Don't know what's in the water but they all go like this.' This was good. This was Mary, not that strange, sad person I had seen before the laughs – the malign spirit in Mary's clothing who'd talked about age and death and nursing homes.

I knew better than to badger her right away. But when I had put on my coat, still damp but warm at least, and we were standing in the open door of her flat peering down on the staircase leading to the ground floor, I brought it up again, deliberately not looking at her: 'You're sure, now, Mary, there's nothing I need to be worried about? You would tell me, wouldn't you?'

'Of course I would, you eejit!'

'So what's all this about Exit, then? Just another new interest, eh?'

'Insurance, that's all. Like loads of people. You should think about it yourself, kiddo! None of us is getting any younger.'

That wasn't the response I had been hoping for: it was more of the same. 'Mary!' I rounded on her. 'You have me really worried now!'

'You're the type who would worry about ducks going barefoot. Will you get outta here, Maggie Quinn!' She thumped me affectionately. 'You'll miss your bus.'

'I'm walking. Such great weather! Who wouldn't?' After a beat, I was able to match her tone.

'Who wouldn't, indeed!'

'How is that fairy thing coming?' I had hoped to catch her off guard and I did.

'Slow,' she replied. 'Why do you keep on about that?'

'Just interested, that's all. But it is happening?'

'Stop fishing.' She recovered. 'Goodbye, Maggie.' Giving me a little shove, she closed the door.

I was slightly, only slightly, encouraged. My Mary is such a positive, thrusting person; that other Mary back there, the one talking about Exit and loneliness, wasn't even a distant cousin. As I descended the stairs, I made a mental note to keep enquiring about her thesis, or paper, or whatever it was. I'd be happier if she was still involved because then she couldn't be dying, could she? Those fairy books open on her table were a good sign, I insisted to myself. A thesis takes a long time and you wouldn't start it without a prospect of finishing, would you?

Or would you? Mary might …

After that, I watched her closely when we met, but every time I broached the matter she answered in the same vein I did when responding to her enquiries about Chloë: 'It's going grand.' Or: 'A bit slow, but it's coming.' Physically, to me she seemed absolutely fine. I could see no changes. Maybe she was a tad grumpier than usual, flared up more often, but that could be put down to the execrable, horrible, grey and greyer, wet and wetter days and even worse nights we were having to endure. My photographer friend had always referred to this type of weather as Celtic Gloom, and Mary hated it even more than I did.

For me, of course, Christmas was the light on the horizon. Let it flood, let it bucket – there was always a Christmas to come.

And when this one had, there she'd been in my little house wearing her well-used black outfit, feisty and Mary-like as always and as taken with James McAlinden as the rest of us. There's life in that old bird still, as there is in us all. Right?

I don't know what I'd do without her.

FIFTEEN

St Stephen's Day, 2012

There is no encounter in human life so joyful as that between your dog and yourself after even the shortest of separations.

Flora exhibits a further twist to this trait. Even though she has been in the car while I've been driving Chloë home from Merrow, as soon as I open our front door, she rushes in ahead of us then turns to welcome my sister: Hell-oooo! Where've you been? We missed you so much – come on in! This way! She leaps on to the first step of the staircase to guide my sister to her room. Collies, I'm told, if not given work to do, always find work for themselves. In addition to her self-appointed role as my dearest companion, welcome at all times and everywhere in the house, Flora's other gig is as a sort of tour-guide-at-home for visitors, in which classification she now includes Chloë.

'Hi, Flora!' Chloë bends low and affectionately pulls one of the dog's ears. Then she straightens up and delivers two firm thumps to the door jamb. She performs this ritual each time she arrives home with me and when, many moons ago, I asked her why, she shrugged. 'I just do. I suppose I'm saying, "Hello, House!"'

'Do you like this house?' I asked her.

'Of course I do, Margaret! What a question – it's home, isn't it?' and she made that scoffing little 'pshaw' sound.

'See you later, Chlo!' We part ways – she bumping her suitcase upstairs one step at a time, I to the alcove where my laptop, on charge, is blinking to itself. I have to complete the 'My New Year Resolutions' feature I was asked to do for one of the provincial newspapers. The deadline is nine a.m. tomorrow for publication on Monday as a two-page spread. I have already transcribed all the phone interviews I did with a number of the mini-celebs in my contacts book, the ones who will accept my calls without going, 'Who? Who did you say you're working for again?'

I'm not proud. I'll take any gig. This newspaper pays promptly and 100 euro is 100 euro. It's pretty poor recompense for two full days' work and a significant addition to my phone bill, but it will feed this household for a few days.

In the run-up to Christmas, though, I had better things to do than spend multiples of ten minutes each on trying to persuade puffed-up little reality-TV-show runts and other one-trick ponies to talk to me. As for trying to sweet-talk a bunch of B-list social climbers who tell you they talk only to journalists they 'respect', life's too short. So I had gone back to my old reliables. Twink, for instance, has never forgotten I was kind to her when she needed a bit of a gee-up. She's loyal: top of my list when I need good quotes in a hurry.

Before I can sit, Flora is back downstairs, standing four-square in the archway leading into the alcove and giving me the Collie Stare. This is unnerving: she stands very tall, ears pricked, eyes totally focused on mine (I guess it's how, in the field, these dogs intimidate their sheep charges). 'What do you want now?' I say to her, trying to sound authoritative. 'It's all very well for you but I have to work. You've had your outing, it's not dinner time yet, so sit down and relax. OK?' Instantly her stance changes. She turns her back on me and, as though all her bones have jellified, collapses in a heap, swishes her tail and tucks it around her front paws. Whatever it was she wanted, it can't be urgent. She was probably trying to con me into giving her an early dinner.

As I sit down, I can hear Chloë humming loudly as she unpacks upstairs. She's been put on new medication and although it's early days yet, and allowing for the odd blip such as what happened at our first meeting this morning in Merrow, so far it seems to be working pretty well. We've been down these roads before, though, and I'm never complacent. To deal with her without flipping out myself, I've learned to rejoice during the good days and accept the bad. While I can never again allow the kind of behaviour that sent her into psychiatric care ten years ago, I can now ride Chloë's ups and downs without exacerbating either.

Help comes in unexpected guises. For instance, if this isn't going to sound too pat, I have adopted four lines of Kipling's much-quoted poem 'If' as a comforting mantra, shamelessly copying and pasting them onto a page to tuck into my laptop case.

Where my relationship with my sister is concerned it's not just

If you can meet with Triumph and Disaster
And treat those two impostors just the same ...

It's also:

> Or *watch the things you gave your life to, broken,*
> *And stoop and build 'em up with worn-out tools ...*

Patience. Tolerance. Acceptance. These are my personal tools, my Three Wise Monkeys, whose pedestals are worn but not worn-out. If I can keep them in good condition I'll be doing well and, for me, that third pedestal, Acceptance, is key. Even in the case of Derek.

During the immediate aftermath of Derek's desertion – and the 'spectacular' that Chloë pulled on that Christmas Day – I would lie awake at night for hour after desperate hour. During those short days, I went about in a half-daze, visiting Chloë, dealing with insurers (who, incidentally, refused to pay for the water damage because Chloë's was 'a deliberate act') and working with Mary, who helped with the clean-up. The spoilage, mercifully, proved to be minimal; even the Christmas lights survived intact, and the electrician I brought in said that the sockets had escaped too. So, after the carpet was taken up and removed, all we had to do was, despite the snow, open the windows to dissipate the smell of damp wood from the floorboards and banisters, order a new carpet and do a bit of revarnishing and repainting.

Such grunt work helped occupy me during that first terrible week between Christmas and New Year 2002/2003.

Then, early in January, possibly the day after I had had the bath taken out and had gone on my sightseeing trip to north Louth, I came home, after another difficult visit to Chloë, to hear the phone ringing inside. I rushed to answer it. It was Derek.

My heart turned over, sickening me. 'Don't hang up!' he said quickly. 'I don't want a row with you, Dumpy. I'm ringing only to discuss our financial arrangements. I won't see you stuck, I told you that.'

I did hang up. Then took the phone off the hook in case he called back. I rang Mary, who was sympathetic but forthright. 'You have to engage with him about money. You just have to swallow hard, Mags, and deal with it.'

'But you don't understand.'

'Probably not. I never had a husband. I don't have a very sick sister. One situation would be tough enough, two together have to be unbearable. How could I understand? It doesn't mean that I don't want to look out for you, sweetie. Ring him back.'

I hung up again. I was doing that a lot when someone was kind to me. They all were, Dina, Lorna, Jean, Mary, of course, other friends, acquaintances. I even had a phone call from an ex-newspaper colleague, a woman I hadn't been close to when working there, but who had heard, somehow, about my situation and wanted to offer her help – 'Even if you just need to talk to someone who's been through a marriage break-up, Maggie. Time will heal, honestly. And sometimes the perspective of a relative stranger can really help, so don't hesitate. A cup of coffee, maybe … ' I thanked her, but that night I had again gone to bed leaving the phone beeping to itself as it sought its cradle.

She had apparently told Tom, my photographer friend, who was away on assignment in Eritrea and his was among the notes and cards I got at that time. He had enclosed a quotation he had been given by some Irish missionary nun he had met out there. *I hope you don't think this is icky,* he wrote, *but I was thinking about you and your sadness. Throw it out, do what you like with it, but know you have friends. See you soon, I hope. Will bring photos! This is an amazing place. We think we have problems?*

He had copied the quotation onto what seemed to be rice paper.

It is easy to love the people far away. It is not always easy to love those close to us. It is easier to give a cup of rice to relieve hunger than to relieve the loneliness and pain of someone unloved in our home. Bring love into your home for this is where our love for each other must start.

I Googled it some time later and up it popped. Mother Teresa as author. Not a surprise.

The Derek situation did resolve itself, materially at least, quite quickly. He was so abject about what he had done to me and the reasons for it, that I was able to dictate terms. I don't mean that to sound harsh or mean: I firmly believe that women and men alike are free agents and that there is no point in trying to handcuff a person to yourself if he or she does not want to be there. But my own means being meagre, and bearing Chloë's needs in mind, I had to be practical.

I consulted Mary. She is not only astute and all-too-familiar with my particular situation, she is a better researcher than I am, far more forensic and patient. So I asked her to find information about my entitlements to maintenance payments and so on. As a result of her briefing, I told Derek that I did not want either a legal or judicial separation, just a simple agreement drawn up by my solicitor. This would be private between us and would be no business of any outside agency such as a court, and would be of no interest to the Revenue Commissioners. As a result, any regular money he gave me would not be subject to tax (nor would he be entitled to claim it from the taxman) since it was still a simple passing of funds from one spouse to another.

Mary did warn me, however, that only four years of living without 'normal marital relations' (not just 'living apart') need elapse before Derek, or indeed I, would be entitled to file for divorce. That was a bit of a surprise to me: just one drunken night or a 'reconciliation' weekend might, given the circumstances and a good solicitor or barrister, reset the clock! So far, thank the Lord, he hadn't uttered a peep about divorce. And I certainly didn't want him to. I hated the idea of the financial wrangling and heartache of a legal case: all that 'Statements of Means' stuff, accounting for every penny you spent, and in the process reducing a marriage to entries on a ledger.

To this day, I am surprised that there has been no push in that regard: I know that if I was in the popsy's position, with three of his children, I'd certainly want to regularise my situation.

Since those days, Derek and I have spoken on the phone from time to time, usually about some standing order glitch at the bank, or delay in applying the cost-of-living indexing, and over the years, while you couldn't call them cordial, the conversations had become less tense until I no longer dreaded having to telephone him about something. Hence, I suppose, the exchange of Christmas cards. That had been a first, of course, but for now, at least, the apple cart is stable. Long may it last. And while I still bear a residue of grudge about his reaction to my infertility, I have genuinely come to understand his point of view about Chloë.

By the way, in the context of my sister's suicide attempt, when she was calm and on her first weekend home from the hospital, I asked her why she had done it. 'What possessed you? You scared the living daylights out of everyone that night.'

She could come up with no reason other than: 'You all looked so happy.'

'But you looked happy that night. You even christened us "The Winter Gathering", remember? I thought you were doing so well.'

'Yeah. You thought.' She shrugged. 'You were there with your friends, having a great time. I had no friends. And you're all getting on with your lives. What life do I have? Nobody cares.'

'But— Ah, it doesn't matter. Never mind.' I couldn't see the point of continuing along that line. There was no way I could reassure her that her life was going to improve, was there? Hope always glimmers, I suppose, but absent a miracle, my sister's refrain made absolute sense. 'Please, Chloë,' I contented myself with keeping things simple, 'I don't want to go through that again. Ever.'

'Do you think I do? It's not about you, Margaret. Not everything is about you.' I was learning the hard way that poor Chloë's reality was not my reality. In a later conversation, she revealed that the reason she had seemed so upbeat that Christmas Day was that she had deliberately gone off her dumbing and numbing medication. 'Just to feel happy for one day. Like you and your friends, Margaret.'

I'm blue in the face telling her that stopping the meds makes the crash inevitable. She knows that already. But, deep down, how can I blame her?

To get back to the present, ninety minutes after sitting down at the laptop, Flora snoozing beside me and dinnertime fast approaching, I have completed the second-last section of my newspaper commission. This segment is graced with the title: 'The Plans and Resolutions of Bobbie Comerford (aka 'The Belfast Belle', as per headlines in the *Irish Sun*, because she – geddit – 'rang up' a stack of money on British TV's *Deal or No Deal*).

The Belle's main resolve? 'Now that I've that under my belt,

I'm going to get on to the American version in 2013 and win that too.'

Finally, I get to Scintilla. Honestly! Only one name. She and her publicist tell me she's the new star on the tweeny pop horizon.

Her resolutions? To buy an allotment, grow flowers and be a better person. She was lovely, I thought, when I spoke to her: she claims to be nineteen, but in her photo she looks about eleven under all those waist-length extensions, braids and dreadlocks. (How does she wash it all? Does she wash it?) And to judge by the number of times she mentioned his name, she's totally in thrall to her hatchet-faced mentor, whose photo she also sent me. I was supposed to give equal wordage to each of my interviewees but she was so sweet I'm planning to sneak in an extra fifty for her.

I'm just setting out on the first paragraph when the telephone rings in the hall. 'Shift, Flora, shift!' I nudge her with my foot, but she's reluctant to move from her warm spot on the rug beside my chair so I step over her. This has to be Mary or one of my other Club friends. Although we all have mobiles, they're for emergencies only and we seem to be the only people left on the planet who use landlines day to day. I don't really know why. Given that you have to rent your line as well as pay for the calls, the costs are much of a muchness, but, hey, nowt so queer, or in our case as hidebound and fuddy-duddy, as folk.

It's Jean. 'Can you talk, Maggie?'

She sounds strangled. She's been crying. 'Of course I can, Jean. Are you all right? What's happened?'

'Poor Lorna. Her Martin—' She can't continue.

I can hear fumbling noises, as though she's dropped the phone and is trying to retrieve it. 'Jean, please, what about Martin? I was in that house just a couple of hours ago when the police were there.

They said they'd tracked him to the UK. They were quite optimistic.' I realise I'm talking to the empty air. 'Jean! Jean? Are you there?'

I have to hold the receiver away from my ear as she comes back on and blows her nose, hard. 'I'm sorry.' She sniffles. 'It's just that I only heard a minute ago. She rang me herself but she was too upset to speak and Mary's there with her and she took the phone. Thank God she wasn't on her own. Mary asked me to ring the rest of the –' her voice cracks '– the – the Club.' She takes a shuddering breath. 'So that's why I'm ringing.'

'Please, Jean, are you telling me they've found Martin?' I try to speak calmly and quietly as Chloë, again humming loudly, comes down the stairs and into the hall. I nod and smile at her and indicate she should go on into the kitchen.

'Sorry, Maggie, I'm OK now.' Jean is in my ear again. I hear her take another loud, shaky breath. 'Yes, they've found him. They don't know yet whether he fell or jumped or was pushed. But he was on a Tube platform in London. And, reading between the lines, Mary says this anyway, she thinks he must have been drunk. Bothering people. And that's why they don't know how he ended up under the train. Anyway,' her voice gets stronger, 'it really doesn't matter one way or the other, does it? I suppose it does matter to poor Lorna how he – he— He's dead, Maggie. Will you ring Dina? I can't face it.'

'I will, of course. Poor Lorna. Does Olive know, d'you think?' I'm a slow burner. Unless it's about Chloë, for whom I'm permanently on watch, I don't immediately fire all engines on hearing bad news.

'I don't know and I don't care.' Jean's voice rises in pitch. 'I don't give a sugar about that bitch, may she rot in Hell! I blame her for a lot of this. If she had been a bit more supportive – no! I'm not thinking for one minute about her. I'm thinking only of Lorna. Her only son. I couldn't live if it happened to one of mine, but of course you'd have no idea what that's like—' She stops. Then starts crying, making no attempt to hold back. 'Oh, God! What am I saying? I'm gone in the head. I'm sorry, sorry, sorry, Maggie. After that lovely day you gave us yesterday – please forgive me. I didn't mean it. Call Dina, will you?' She hangs up.

Dina's reaction is calm, on the surface at least, so much so I have to remind myself that the shock reaction will come later for her too. 'That is absolutely terrible news, Maggie,' she says quietly, 'the worst. How is she going to survive this? She has nobody now.'

'She has us, Dina. Mary's there. And she has the grandchildren. Plus she has James with her, if that proves to be of any benefit.'

'Are you going over there?'

'Probably later. I was there earlier and she was in a bad way, but the police were being quite optimistic about the whole thing at that stage.' I lower my voice: 'I can't go right now. I've just got in with Chloë. I need to settle her.' White lies aren't a sin if you're telling them for good motives: my sister can't be dragged into this.

'Oh, right, right, of course. Today's Wednesday, isn't it? How's she doing?'

'She's fine.'

'She'll probably have a crowd in at this stage – I mean Lorna, of course, not Chloë. Sorry, Maggie – neighbours and so on. And I believe that the gardaí are great, terrifically supportive in these circumstances. And Mary's there too, of course. You said she's there?'

I can almost hear the gears grinding in Dina's brain. 'Yes.'

'Well, no point in piling on the pressure. I'll go over to her tomorrow. Is there anything you think I should do? Or bring?'

'Just follow your instincts, Dina. I have to go now.' I hang up. What did she want? A map? My irritation is irrational. We all find someone on whom to take out our distress, isn't that right? She hadn't sounded all that grief-stricken, though. As I continue to stare at the phone, Chloë comes back out of the kitchen, carrying a can of Coca-Cola. She is heading for the sitting room and the TV. 'I had a nap,' she calls back over her shoulder.

'What do you fancy for your tea, Chloë?' I hope I'm sounding normal. Underneath, though, reactions are revving up as I try to figure out how to manage the evening. I should go over to Lorna's. But we have a sacrosanct Wednesday routine here, Chloë and I. Wednesday evenings, we allow ourselves to have a TV tea: we eat on trays in front of *Fair City* and we like to watch Rachel Allen afterwards. *Cake Diaries*. Scrumptious. She's always smiling and nice.

This being St Stephen's Day, though, I'm not sure what's on. They muck around with the schedules on RTÉ. They're certainly not concerned with people like Chloë who, when she's here, sets her routines by her favourites.

The news? Nah. News boring. We never watch the news together. We usually try to find an episode we haven't already seen on reruns of *America's Next Top Model* for Chloë while I go out and do the dishes. I don't even have to go back in to her if I don't want to. As long as we've had our hour together, it seems, that's grand and for the rest of the night, save for coming in and out making cups of tea and so on, each can do her own thing. For her, TV is the queen of the attractions in this house: she can watch her own choice of programme and doesn't have to fight with other Merrowners, as she calls her fellow 'service users'.

She probably doesn't even notice half the time whether I'm

here or not. I've watched her watching the screen, and she hardly blinks.

She's in fine form this evening, mellow even, and I'm unwilling to upset her by bringing her into a house filled with mourners. I'm equally unwilling, however, to leave her here alone for so many hours. Her suicide attempt will never let me do that.

That was then and this is now: I have to get back to facing the reality of Jean's phone call and poor Lorna's loss. I can't telephone her to sympathise while crying off going to see her because of – well, because of You Know Who.

Maybe Mary has her mobile phone with her. To hell with the expense, I take out my own machine and punch in her number. She speaks so quietly when she answers, I'm not sure it's her. 'Mary? Is that you?' In the background I can hear some chatter.

'Yes? Who's this?'

'It's Maggie. How's she doing?'

'Hold on.'

A few seconds later, she comes back on, speaking more clearly. 'Sorry, I couldn't talk to you in there. How do you expect she's doing? "Devastated" doesn't even come close, I'd imagine, but you'd never know by looking at or talking to her. Unnaturally calm – too calm I'd say, dispensing cups of tea to callers.'

'I'm in some difficulty for coming over there.'

'I know. It's Wednesday.'

'She's here until after the New Year, Mary. There's very little I can do about it.'

'You'll have to make up your own mind about that. There are plenty of us here anyhow. Jean will be arriving soon, I'm sure. She's completely shattered. There are neighbours and so on. And James, of course. He's very attentive. He claims he's Lennie's son, by the way. Jean was right. He'd been adopted out as a baby and came looking for Lorna – that's where the solicitor came in. Lorna told me the story after the police and the priest had left and we were in the kitchen together to get tea for the first batch of neighbours. I don't know how people get to know these things – the squad cars and so on, I suppose.

'Anyway, James popped his head in to tell us that there were two new arrivals, and when he'd left, she told me about him as though she was telling me who kindly gave her the chocolate Kimberleys she was arranging on a plate. That's what I mean about her unnatural composure. Look, I'd better get back in there,' she adds quickly. 'That doorbell's ringing again. See you when I see you. OK? I'll tell her you rang.' She hangs up.

I know Mary. I know how she communicates disapproval. She has left me in no doubt about what she thinks of my priorities. She's right, even if, for once, she wasn't blatant about it: first things first. This is Lorna we're talking about, the Lorna whose 'real' son is lying in a morgue somewhere on the other side of the Irish Sea, the same woman and sterling friend who, with her skill and quick thinking, saved my sister's life.

In the sitting room I find that Chloë, having discovered a channel showing non-stop *Simpsons* episodes, is entranced. 'Listen, Chloë,' I sit within her line of sight, 'do you remember Lorna? My friend Lorna? The one I went to see this morning?'

'Yes.' She doesn't take her eyes off the screen.

'Well, she's very upset. Her son has just been killed.'

'Oh, yes?'

'Yes … Look at me. Do you understand what I'm saying, Chloë?'

'Yes. Lorna's son has been killed.' She doesn't move her gaze from the TV. 'That's terrible, Margaret.'

The television emits a burst of laughter. 'It is.' I hold my cool although I want to throttle her and Marge Simpson both. 'It is terrible. I have to go and see her. Do you mind? I can give her your sympathies.'

'Yes. Please. That would be great.' More laughter from that damned TV.

I know she's not being deliberately obtuse. In her more communicative moments, she has told me that the medication numbs her. This was corroborated by one of the myriad psychiatrists she has had over the years: 'Good news, bad news, it's all the same. Don't be upset by this. It goes with the territory and, let's be honest, some of it is as a result of the medication. It's trial and error but the aim of prescribing is to create an optimum balance between highs and lows. You could tell her you'd won the Lotto. She'd say, "Great". You could tell her your mother had been massacred by a chainsaw gang and she'd say, "That's terrible." She would mean both but it's within her own ambit. You'll find that, to her, ups and downs flow past in the same river. She's sincere in what she says and it doesn't mean she doesn't care, it's that she can't. She will try to meet expectations about her reactions by using appropriate language. But for now, until we find something better to control her symptoms, this sort of equable middle ground is the best we can hope for.'

'All right, Chloë.' I stand up. 'Thanks. Flora will be company for you while I'm gone. I won't stay long, I'm just going to pay my respects. There's a ton of food out there in the kitchen.'

'Thanks, Margaret. I'll see you later.' She smiles widely in the direction of the TV as Lisa Simpson, her favourite, once again gets exasperated with Bart.

SIXTEEN

11 January 2013

London is as cold as steel this wintry morning, as hard on the skin as those railway tracks were on poor Martin's body. I'm first down to the hotel lobby, one of those in which electronic check-in desks with their harsh blue screens are the most prominent furnishings and where the smell of grease and rashers permeates the air. The wall-hung TV is silently running Sky News, a small huddle of Americans (those 'tan' wash-and-go slacks!) peer at the flight screen beside it, and the ATM is constantly beeping as businessmen and -women, tilting under the weight of laptop cases, withdraw funds for the day. The Merrion Hotel it ain't.

I don't mean to be carping, honestly. My grumpiness is because of fatigue, pure and simple. The drawn-out tragedy of the previous weeks has taken its toll but in addition I had difficulty sleeping during the night – no blame to the bed, which was a double and perfectly clean, or the room itself, heavily insulated from plane noises. The fault lay with my own brain, wheeling through one of those high-alert nights. I was worrying about Lorna, worrying that I had said something that offended Mary because she seemed a bit offhand with me – worrying about Flora pining in the kennels, worrying about my finances: you name it, I worried about it. The only absentee on last night's roster was Chloë: I knew that at least she was being looked after in Merrow House (thank you, Pauline!), and that night and day, along with her iPad Mini, she was probably playing with her new iPhone. She had been due an upgrade so we had gone together to the phone shop. She had rung me four times yesterday to wish me bon voyage to London, sent me a message she would see me 'soon', then confirmed it on voicemail to say she would be ready for pick-up first thing on Saturday.

Rather than get up, however, or read, or do something sensible like switch on CNN, a channel that always sends me off, for some reason, I had lain there rigid, checking the time every half-hour or so. When five o'clock finally dawned, I had tumbled out and into the shower and here I am, at twenty minutes to six, coffeed up but very tired, waiting for the others. We're due back at the airport at six.

Martin's body is being flown home this morning. One of the reasons for the delay is the habit of Ireland Inc., endearing or frustrating depending on your perspective, of shutting down for a fortnight over the Christmas period. As a result, the paperwork has taken a long time. Also, since this is high season in the Canaries, Olive, according to herself, hadn't been able to get a flight back, with her sister and their combined kids, until three days after poor Martin's remains had been taken from the Underground. The details of what had happened to him had dribbled in during the last two weeks. Courtesy of Mary, who, typically, knew someone who knew a pathologist in London with access to the information, we had been able to bypass Olive.

Lorna was avid for information, no matter how horrible it seemed to the rest of us. It was as if, by knowing exactly how he had behaved before he died, what happened immediately afterwards, who removed him from the tracks, where he was taken, what the post-mortem had shown, she could hold on to some of him until he vanished completely from her life.

According to what we had learned, he had been unlucky in his fall (or jump) from that train platform. 'Only the inquest will tell us for sure what really happened,' Mary told me, when she phoned me a few days after that St Stephen's night. 'A lot of Tube stations now have pits dug out beneath the tracks, which means there's quite a good depth between the train tracks and the ground. They've been put in for drainage, but they're actually known as suicide pits or dead man's trenches, and if you fall into one of them, you have a good chance of survival because the trains aren't usually travelling at speed, even if they're not stopping at that particular station.'

'How did you find that out?'

'You can find anything, literally anything, on the Internet. You know that, Maggie. Don't be stupid! But it was my guy in London who told me – I just checked it online. Anyway, I told you I have a contact who knows someone in London. He confirmed it for me.'

I let the insult pass. 'So what happened, then?'

'Not all of the stations have those trenches and this one didn't. There's no doubt he was pretty badly mutilated. Chances are that he was electrocuted by the third rail, the electric one.'

'I hope he was so drunk he didn't suffer.'

'It was probably very quick.'

'Yeah. Probably. I hope so.'

We all hung on to that as a silver lining in the days intervening. Overcome by the enormity of what had happened, we speculated about the hows and whys with each other and, as tactfully as we could, with Lorna. Maybe the inquest would prove he didn't do it to himself but was pushed, inadvertently or otherwise. That was our main hope. For sure we knew two things: he was drunk and it was quick. Ergo, we decided, he couldn't have felt much.

But those crumbs of comfort didn't stop my febrile little brain interspersing the manner of Martin's death with my other worries while I'd lain there last night: Brain had hooked up with Imagination to re-create the horror of the poor man's last few moments on earth. 'Suppose it had been Chloë?' Brain suggested slyly. 'It could have been Chloë, couldn't it?' Imagination supplied the image and we were off again on another round.

For me, the worst aspect of all had been that Martin had been identifiable only from dental records. He had been carrying a passport but it was explained to Mary – and relayed – that a likeness to the photograph could not be determined and there was no proof that the passport had belonged to the cadaver. I leave it to you to form your own picture of the smashed, limp, dripping corpse I saw in my mind, with someone or something probing his poor, misshapen mouth to get at what was left of his teeth. I don't want to discuss it with anyone: I see it clearly enough every time I close my eyes.

On St Stephen's night, after Jean's phone call, I had gone to Lorna's house. We were all there except Dina and, in her absence, had included her in an informal rota, which accommodated our personal situations, such as mine with Chloë. The aim was that at least one of us was always with Lorna overnight during this awful waiting period. I was reluctant to put Flora into kennels during my own stints, although the proprietor assures me she makes no trouble whatsoever and that she's one of their most popular regulars. (I'm sure she says that to everyone!) Anyhow, there was no need to go to the trouble and expense. Flora took quite happily to sleeping on the floor beside me in one of Lorna's spare rooms during my nights 'on'.

The coffin would be closed. This was not just because of the condition of the body, but because repatriation regulations require it to be lined with lead or zinc and sealed. This new information added exponentially to Lorna's grief, already exacerbated by Olive's dictum that there was to be no removal or wake. Thank God I was there to hold her hand as she wept and wept: 'I'll never see his face again. Ever.'

Privately I thought that, given what her son's face probably looked like, not only because of the accident but because of the length of time it was taking to get him home, that was not a bad thing. I tried to comfort her but was clumsy about it: 'Just remember him as he was, Lorna,' I put my free arm around her shoulder, 'your lovely shining boy.' I set myself off with that and it was hard to say, as we held each other, which of us was now the more upset.

By Olive's decree, Martin was to be taken straight from the airport to the crematorium in Glasnevin. 'It's easier that way for everyone,' his wife had insisted, when I phoned her to ask her to change her mind. 'Whatever he did, Olive,' I had pleaded, 'he deserves a good send-off. Everyone does – even criminals get good send-offs from their families. Surely Lorna deserves a little time with him before she loses him for ever. She's heartbroken.'

But she had been implacable. 'That woman wouldn't even spend Christmas in my house. She has no right to ask me to do anything. I'm sorry she's upset, of course I am, we're all upset, but it's a bit late for her to be telling me how to conduct me own husband's funeral.'

We knew that Olive's sister had taken her children back to Ireland with her own kids and I piled on the pressure: 'But that's the point, Olive. Your way means there's no funeral at all. She's Martin's mother. Grandmother to your children! Don't they, at least, deserve a little time to say goodbye too? It's not right to deprive them of their memories of their father in this way. People remember funerals and who was at them for the rest of their lives—'

'Lookit, Maggie,' she interrupted, 'you're a nice woman and all the rest of it but, apart from anything else, I don't want my kids to be exposed to all that church mumbo-jumbo. All that being "in the Arms of Jesus", and being "welcomed home" stuff. That's all crap.' She has a thin, shrill voice at the best of times but now, raised and slightly distorted as she competed with traffic noises at her end, I was holding the handset a few inches from my ear to make out what she was saying. It was hardly a dignified way to conduct a conversation about her recently dead husband.

'He's dead and there's nothing nobody can do about it now,' she continued. 'I've told my kids and, yes, they're terribly upset but they have to come to terms with it. He disgraced them, have you forgotten that? He knew what he was doing when he fell off the wagon. He knew he was on his last chance with me – I'd made that clear. I know this sounds tough and that you and your little gang of happy clappies think I'm a bitch for throwing him out and so on, but youse never think of my side of the story, do youse?' Her voice was rising in tandem with her anger. 'What I put up with, and what the kids had to put up with too. Martin made his bed and he can lie in it wherever it is.'

There was a screech of brakes her end, and I heard her drop the phone. 'I'm sorry, Maggie,' she said, more calmly, when she had retrieved it. 'I got a fright. Some idiot crashed the lights. Martin's mother and the rest of youse blame me, I know yiz do. Did it ever occur to any of yiz that I lost Martin McQuaid a long time ago? And it's not what youse all think, that I got rid of him just because he lost his job. Or even because he fell off the wagon – again …

'I'm not an ogre, Maggie. Martin and me were going nowhere for a long time. And you're probably thinking where's all the tears on my side? Well, I've done me crying and mourning long before this.'

She stopped, and then, more quietly: 'Look, I know you mean well, but I've made the decision, I've booked the undertaker, and I've told him to organise the crematorium. End of!'

I argued further with her, managing at least to secure the name of the undertaker she was using. I also persisted in trying to wring one further concession: 'Having the coffin driven straight from the airport cargo section to the crematorium is too cold-blooded, Olive. Even leaving Lorna out of it altogether, it's what your kids will remember, that their daddy, whatever his faults, was carted away like an imported carpet or disposed of like a box of rotting mangoes.'

'Don't give me that. It's a bit OTT, isn't it?' She's getting angry again. 'They won't know anyhow. They're with my sister and their cousins – they're not coming to the airport. She's organising a minder.'

'They mightn't know now, but they will in the future. They're kids. Kids ask questions. When they're old enough they're sure to ask about their daddy's funeral. They won't thank you for this, Olive. What about the airport chapel? Just a rosary, Olive. Please.'

Despite the continuing traffic noise behind her, wherever she was, I could hear her audibly exasperated sigh. 'All right,' she said. 'I'll do that much. I'll book the airport chapel where Lorna and the rest of youse can do yizzer praying for a few minutes, but that's the end of it. OK?'

I retorted that this had nothing to do with praying but with respect. Then, fearing I'd given her an excuse to backtrack, I said quickly, 'Thank you, Olive. You won't regret it.'

'Don't push it,' she warned. 'Just a rosary, mind – no speeches, all right? I'm going against me own judgement here.'

'Thank you again, Olive.' Then, because I know how to quit when I'm ahead, I said goodbye and broke the connection. It was a small enough breach in her wall of opposition but it was at least something to bring to Lorna. And I had to admit that, although she had been bolshy, Olive had been open enough at least to listen and to give a little. It's easy for us all to judge, but none of us had been in her house, living with an alcoholic, as Martin was. It could not have been easy. I had taken on Lorna's side of the story 100 per cent and will still support her with all my strength, but that conversation with Olive had at least given me a glimpse of a different scenario.

I had phoned Lorna to tell her the (relatively) good smidgen of news about the undertaker and the airport chapel. And that night I had rummaged around in my bedroom and found my mother's old mother-of-pearl beads. I had even remembered to pack them yesterday when getting ready to come here to London.

On the afternoon of the Monday following Martin's death, armed with the knowledge that the funeral would not be quite so peremptory as originally planned, all five of us had met in Lorna's kitchen to help her compose the death notice for the newspapers. It happened to be New Year's Eve but none of us, not even Dina, mentioned it.

I love Lorna's kitchen. In keeping with the rest of her house it's a shabby but impressively huge relic of ould decency, as my mother would have put it. Along with the modern fitted cupboards and so on, it retains its heritage, dominated by a large, old-fashioned dresser, a rusting Aga, and a floor laid, in an intricate pattern, with Victorian tiles. Some are cracked and stained, but have not lost their beauty.

Most intriguing to me, however, is the row of small iron bells hanging alongside the hearth. Fancifully, on each visit, I itch to get my hands on them to summon the housemaid. Can't you just imagine, the morning after a party, ringing one and when it's answered, saying, 'Clean up this mess, please, Molly!' In real life, even in the last century, I'd never have rung such a bell. I'm the type of wimp who would get up early to clean the place so as not to trouble the maid!

That afternoon, we were all, even Lorna, glad to have something to do as we sat on the mismatched chairs around her long oak table. But as Mary, self-elected note-taker, opened her bag and took out a pen and pad, I couldn't help but reflect that this was where, as a child, Martin had had his tea, done his homework, probably argued and fought with his mother about small and big things, about his missing father, perhaps. This was where, I imagined, she had been sitting when he burst excitedly in to give her the good news of his acceptance as an apprentice to the electrical trade.

We turned our attention to the death notice and, after much discussion, agreed that Lorna's son had 'died unexpectedly, following an accident in London'. As mourners, we listed not only Olive and his children, Lorna, Olive's sisters, brothers and parents, but also Martin's employers (this had been at the insistence of loyal Jean: 'Let those feckers see what they've done!') and the names of specific friends among the GAA players in the club where, before his fall from grace, he had coached youngsters. We were leaving nothing to chance in ensuring that when news of his death did come through, anyone with any interest in him, or indeed in Lorna, would know that her son had died.

'Thanks very much, all of you.' Her voice was hoarse from crying. 'As far as I'm concerned, I wouldn't mind if Olive vanished up her own—' Always ladylike, she pulled back and her eyes, probably for the hundredth time that week, filled again. It was terrible to see. This woman, the most reserved of our five, was coming apart. Jean immediately went over to her, nestling against her like a chick under a hen's feathers, and Lorna turned to her, openly sobbing.

'I'll make a fresh pot.' Dina got up and headed for the kettle. God only knows how many cups of tea we had consumed since we'd first got the news. From what I had drunk that day alone, my insides must be curing nicely, I thought, as I watched Dina go. She wears very high-heeled shoes, the kind in which I definitely could not walk (or would not: I'd be even more freakishly tall than I am already) and probably because of them, today's pencil skirt, drawn tight, emphasised her swaying behind.

Poor Dina, I thought that afternoon, all that sexuality and nowhere to park it, despite the parade of men. 'Is James coming? Where is he, by the way?' I had lobbed in the question without thinking, but then, secretly, waited for my tummy to squeak at the sound of his name.

No squeak.

Not even a pip.

Silliness vanquished. Sense and dignity restored.

'He's at work.' Lorna disentangled herself from Jean. 'I haven't seen him. He left early. I asked my solicitor to take him on for a few days because, with everything else, I just couldn't cope with him being here all day and every day. He's been given three weeks to clear up a backlog of filing in the office.'

'No worries.' I was as brisk as a new broom and felt as clean. 'He's working? That's good news, isn't it, girls? Will you want to bring him to London?'

'He has no business being there.' Mary was using her sensible voice. I have to say she was looking a bit peaky that afternoon. She would never admit it, of course, but she was probably more affected by what was happening than she was letting on. 'All right, even allowing for the fact that he's Martin's brother, they didn't know each other. And he's been on the scene six, seven weeks? In my opinion his appearance at the funeral – or this "thing" for Martin, whatever it's to be called – would set off a fluttering in the dovecotes, an upsetting one, and we don't want that. But,' she turned to Lorna, 'the decision is yours. Think about it. We don't have to decide right now.'

'I – I don't think we should.' Again Lorna hesitated. 'Include him, I mean. Mary's right. I haven't told any of my own family about him turning up out of the blue like he did. They're a bit, well, conservative.'

To accompany, or perhaps cover, the clatter she was making, Dina now turned on Lorna's sink-side wireless, which was tuned to Lyric FM. 'Will I leave that on?' she asked, and we all agreed, fervently on my part as I bathed in the slow, peaceful piano piece spreading through the silence in the kitchen. As I did, I became ashamed of the facile mental sketch I had made of Dina a minute earlier. Who was I to caricature this well-off, single woman? She could, for cash, renew her house furnishings, even the house itself, without giving it a thought. Who was I to sneer at her hedonistic lifestyle, her Botox, her numerous holidays, her seemingly inexhaustible supply of sexual partners? Could I be just that teensy bit jealous?

It was not an appropriate time to go there so I didn't.

In any event, since Martin's death, Dina's behaviour had been a revelation because, after that slow start when I had telephoned her to impart the news, she had proved to be as loyally attentive and devoted to Lorna as any of the rest of us. For instance, she had daily hefted large bags of goodies from the Butler's Pantry deli, so Lorna wouldn't have to lift a finger in the kitchen. Additionally, she had insisted on paying for the insertion of the death notices, which, because of their numbers and length, was very expensive. Further, she was adamant that she would pay for all flights to London and overnight accommodation at an airport hotel – this hotel – which was necessary because of the early departure to Dublin.

I look at my watch. Where are the others? It's five minutes to six now and we're due across the way in the airport at six. Right on cue, I see them, all four coming together through the glass door into the lobby; they must have called into each other's rooms.

SEVENTEEN

The airport terminal is hopping.

In contrast to our sombre little group, a plethora of high-spirited, sun-bound holidaymakers, a huge proportion of whom are obviously pensioners, crack jokes fore, aft and across the ropes as they drag or kick full-to-bursting suitcases through the snaking queues. The Americans, dressed for comfort and with their money belts tightly strapped around their waists, are again very obvious. Young backpackers, many in deliberately frayed denim, are either sleeping on unused baggage belts or sitting in rough circles on the tiled floor as they wait for desks to open.

We can be numbered with the more soberly dressed and less burdened as we pull our wheelie-bags behind us but we're just a sub-group since, unlike almost all of our fellow cabin-baggers, none of us is staring at the screen of an iPad or smartphone. The place resembles a sort of mad, anything-goes party, with even the check-in staff at adjacent desks discussing future getaways as they tag the bags destined for the hold. The high good humour and the cacophony – the chatter and laughter, the loud shouting into phones, the almost unceasing announcements on the Tannoy – are ear-splitting and none of it feels right. To me, Martin McQuaid's presence is everywhere and I feel people should pipe down a little to offer proper respect while Olive and one of her brothers are finishing the paperwork for the coffin in the cargo terminal. None of us mentions it, but that piece of knowledge isolates us, hanging about our group like grey vapour.

As for Olive, when she and her brother join us at the Departures gate, I had expected the atmosphere between her and her mother-in-law to be as frosty as ever. To my surprise, it doesn't seem too bad. I can't say they're warm with each other, but I detect a bit of a thaw on Olive's side. The only seat left in the gate area, as it happens, is beside Lorna's and Olive takes it while her brother goes to fetch a coffee. She and her mother-in-law, facial expressions not unduly antagonistic, I see, certainly greet each other, but because I'm in another row and way out of earshot, I can't hear what they're saying. Maybe it's a start. Maybe, having had to deal with the coffin and so on, the reality that it's her husband and Lorna's only son whom she's about to consign to eternity has finally dawned on Martin's widow.

As for the weirdness of being on that flight, knowing what's beneath us in the hold, that's a whole other story.

The only equivalent experience for me was when, in my journalistic days, I was sent to Lourdes to cover the repatriation of the body of Monsignor Horan, the cleric who, almost single-handedly and against serious opposition, even ridicule, succeeded in bringing an international airport to a windy field in Knock, County Mayo. He had died during a pilgrimage to Lourdes, and the reverent atmosphere during his flight home could not have been more different from this. That day, up and down the plane, the passengers had recited the rosary, all fifteen Mysteries, with even the Aer Lingus hostesses carrying their beads to join in and the flight-deck crew dispensing with their normal 'On the left side you can see …' announcements in favour of empathetic condolences to all.

By contrast, on board today, passengers are listening to iPods, summoning drinks, selecting chicken-and-stuffing sandwiches from the trolley, buying perfume and cosmetics. A large group of men at the back of the aircraft is obviously bound for some kind of sporting occasion: they are wearing identical tracksuits and in such high spirits that we can hear their laughter and loud joshing all the way up the aisle to where our group is sitting.

At one point, when we suffer through a short period of turbulence, tossed seriously about, I find myself wondering about Martin. Is he being further disfigured?

Or is there a precautionary procedure for this eventuality, with undertakers packing their clients very tightly into their carapaces? With what? Papier-mâché? Does the body make a mould of itself? That image is one I find utterly repulsive and, looking across the aisle at Lorna's white face and tightly shut eyes, I order myself sternly not to share it. As you know, I'm sometimes, no, frequently, wont to blurt this kind of thing without thinking of consequences. Beside me, Mary, who is also a bit green around the gills, is possibly asleep.

Before leaving Dublin yesterday evening I had checked all the papers, and Martin's death notice had been displayed as written,

Deirdre Purcell

prominently because of its length. So when, after the very short
flight the plane makes its descent into Dublin, it's of some
consolation that anyone with any interest in Lorna's son should
know where they can come this morning to wish him a final God
speed.

The undertaker had organised a funeral car to follow the hearse
and all seven of us, Olive, her brother and the five members of our
Club, squeeze into it. It takes only a few minutes to get across the
campus to the chapel and I will never forget Lorna's reaction as we
drive into the small car park.

The day is bright, breezy and, for once, dry, but it is very
cold and most of the sizeable crowd present have bundled up
with hats and scarves. As we draw up to the front of the chapel,
however, many of the men present remove their headwear. That
mass gesture of respect, so insignificant in normal circumstances,
finally undoes Martin's poor mother: she collapses into my arms,
sobbing bitterly. Even Olive is dabbing at her eyes.

I spot James McAlinden. Wearing a trench coat, he is hanging
back, behind a cluster of other men.

Not just because of what I saw, or thought I saw transpire
between them in Departures, the behaviour of Lorna's daughter-
in-law this morning has continued to afford me cautious hope that
Martin's death may, after all, bring some sort of rapprochement
between herself and Lorna. It would be too much to say she is
a transformed woman but, right now, there is little trace of the
bolshy, snippy Olive I had spoken to on the phone so recently. She
is hard-faced at the best of times and the bright sunshine does
her no favours; that being said, I find it difficult to equate this
woman, teary as she embraces and is embraced by those offering
condolences, with the person who had changed the locks and

thrown Martin out on his ear. Perhaps on reflection, with hearses and closed coffins in three dimensions right in front of her and a reiteration of condolences from such a sizeable crowd, she can at last allow her defences to be breached. For whatever reason, having all morning been prepared for further confrontation, I'm glad to find there is none.

She is definitely affected, even softened. It could be grandstanding, I suppose – kindness from others frequently has that effect – but I don't think so. For her, the emotions today have to be terribly confusing. It's all very well, I would imagine, to bawl out your drunkard husband and then, your patience having been tested for years, to evict him because he has lost paid employment, meaning he has brought poverty to your door. Could her behaviour have been just a temporary fit of justifiable rage? She had said on the phone that their relationship had been deteriorating for years. On the other hand, when, shortly afterwards, your husband dies in horrible circumstances such as these, the emotional complexity must be inconceivable to all but those who have gone through something similar.

I try to picture how it would be for me if Derek died. Unlike Olive and Martin, we've been apart for more than a decade. I've shucked him off but he's still my husband, and not just legally. I know that will sound odd, but he's the one I smiled at across the lilies through the wedding ceremony during which each of us, forsaking all others, promised a step-locked future. I meant those promises. Should he die now, how would I react? At his funeral, where the emphasis, naturally, would be on Fiona and his children, I would legally be chief mourner, but morally would probably sit with also-rans. Half of the congregation, though, the half who knew me from when we were together, would be furtively sympathising with me when they thought his current partner wasn't looking. This is Ireland.

What would the dominant emotion be? Would I feel tragically bereaved? No.

Upset? Yes.

Angry that he has put me in a situation where I'm upset? Yes.

Nostalgic for the early years of our marriage when we were still in love? Maybe. Not sure about that.

Regretful I took his love so much for granted I didn't see the possibility of his infidelity? Probably.

Jealous of Fiona? Yes.

Furious that he did the dirty with someone younger, prettier and, crucially, fertile? Yes, I'd be furious about that, but not, oddly, with him. In that instance, I would have to accept that biology is biology.

So who could I blame? God?

God, if there is such a being, has enough real tragedy to deal with without worrying about one barren woman. He should be glad that, unlike Derek, I've done my bit to keep the population of the planet in check.

Anyhow, see what I mean about complexity and confusion? Olive's situation is not analogous (I nearly referred to her there as 'poor Olive': I wouldn't go that far!). There isn't another wife, quasi or otherwise, and she can demonstrably have children, yet she must be as befuddled as I would be, particularly if Martin had died by suicide. As she sits just a foot away from his polished coffin, it's likely, in my opinion, that she's questioning where it all went wrong in her marriage. Where it went wrong for her man. Is she blaming herself for not having done more about his drinking? This was clearly more of a problem than Lorna had indicated.

For the first time, I empathise with why she didn't want a funeral. In public she has to play the part of the Grieving Wife, while fully aware that most of the people in the chapel must know the true story and that some, watching her reactions, will ask themselves and each other if she isn't a hypocrite. If I'd thought this through before ringing her to gainsay her decision about not having even a small ceremony such as this, maybe I wouldn't have pushed her so hard. But, weasel words, I can't be sorry. Olive is not my responsibility. I did it for Lorna. My vote will always be with my friend.

Stop thinking, Maggie. It's less than two hours after the plane carrying us and Martin took off from London, there's a whole day to go and I'm already wrecked.

I look around the little airport chapel from my seat in the third row, behind Lorna, Olive and their respective families in the first and second. Believe it or not, almost all of the pews are full. I have no experience of counting crowd numbers but there must be more than a hundred people here. And in fairness to Olive – this new Olive – despite what she had said to me over the phone, she has made sure that her own children and her sister's are here. Two of her brothers and their wives have brought theirs as well, so quite a gathering of small people is leavening our ranks. It includes Jean's grandchildren because her two sons and their wives have brought them along.

Also there for Jean are some of her Chernobyl colleagues, last seen by me shaking buckets at a fun run in the Phoenix Park. A few of Mary's refuge people are here, as is Roddy, the dentist for whom she works occasionally. I had seen Dina greet quite a number of people, and I'm astonished to recognise my librarian friend and two of Chloë's carers from Merrow. Including ourselves by name in the death notices had obviously been the right thing to do.

Craning to look behind me, I see that James is in the back row. I'm just about to call him up – he should be with the family or at least with us – but then I remember that Lorna, who must have seen him among the crowd, hasn't made that gesture and it's not up to me. I've done enough interfering in this family.

The ceremony is short and moving, the celebrant referring, neutrally, to Martin as 'a loving son, father and husband, whose troubles are now over and whose spirit is now at rest'. He mentions the parable of the Prodigal Son, and, with delicate allusion to the manner of Martin's death, lapses into Irish with the self-explanatory saying: *Bíonn grásta Dé idir an diallait agus an talamh*. The grace of God is found between the saddle and the ground. It has been the only mention of the Divine. In this instance, I think, Olive must have got to him, because other than the ritual prayers, read quietly, with no histrionics, there has been no reference to angels, 'the arms of Jesus' or, with the exception of that exquisitely tactful Irish *sean fhocail*, even to God. The recitation of the rosary decade is gentle and when, before the exit of the coffin, I see the entire congregation queuing up to shake the hands of Olive and her mother-in-law as chief mourners, I am so moved by the whole affair that my own tears, the first of the day, flow at last.

Lorna's neighbours have done her proud, showing up in numbers, and during the milling around that always follows such ceremonies after the coffin is borne out, she introduces us to them. She also brings us around to at least fifteen, maybe as many as twenty, distant cousins and their kin, some related to Martin, some to herself and him, who had travelled to Dublin from country places all over Ireland. There are three politicians: urban and county councillors from her area.

Martin's death, of course, made the news: 'A thirty-year-old Irishman has died in London, having fallen from the platform of the Underground railway system to be hit by a train, Jenny MacGuffin, or McShane, or McLaren reporting. It had been a two-day wonder for radio, made small inside paragraphs for the broadsheets and was a main story for the *Irish Daily Mail*. This is why a representative from Pieta House, the organisation set up around suicide and suicide prevention in Ireland, is also in attendance. She comes up to introduce herself and to offer assistance to both Lorna and Olive, adding, 'And, of course, anyone who is affected, no matter what the inquest says.'

Ireland is a good place to die, I think, as I watch Lorna's grandchildren throw their arms around her and weep with her and their mother. People in this country understand death and accord it a reverent and prominent place in life. Dissonance is shelved, even if only temporarily, as we all recognise what is real and, for that time at least, think as one.

Mary is talking to Jean a few yards away and I am walking over to her so we can go together to my car in the short-term car park when again I spot James, walking slowly (my imagination uses the word 'dejectedly') out of the church car park towards the main road. 'James!' I call before I can stop myself. Dammit, I think, I wish I could stop doing that. It usually gets me into trouble.

'Hello, Maggie,' he says. 'Nice to see you again.'

'Are you going back to Lorna's? Mary and I could give you a lift if you like.'

'Thanks a million, but I have to get to work. I had just some of the morning off.'

I look carefully at him, uncertain about his tone. After all, this young man's brother is dead. The brother he had never got to know. Who is minding him? 'Where's work?'

'Fairview.'

'Sure that's on our way. Hang on a second, I'll just get Mary and we'll be off.'

'Thank you.' The strong sunshine picks out a couple of zits on his chin and renders him hopelessly young-looking, albeit still spectacular and, although the light is so bright he has to squint, his eyes seem more extraordinary than ever. But, thank God, he arouses only maternal instincts in me now. 'I'm sure you have very weird feelings about today.' Impulsively I touch his arm.

'You said it!' The veneer of sophistication, so evident in my house just two weeks previously, is nowhere in evidence. He's just a boy, really, I think. And if Olive's confused about her reactions, what must it be like for this kid? He gets up the courage to go and find his family and discovers that his father is long dead, his stepmother in bits, his half-brother, the one to be consigned to the flames, was a drunk, lost his job, went missing, then threw himself, or was thrown, under a train in London. Instead of meeting a father and half-brother, he's attending a funeral where he's treated as an outsider by the remainder of his 'real' family. 'Have you spoken to anyone this morning, James? Lorna? Olive?' What I mean, of course, is, 'Has anyone spoken to you?'

'No.' He shakes his head. 'I don't know how, Maggie. I don't know what to say. I'm not staying with Lorna any more. It was too … ' I can see him searching for a word. 'It was too hard. I've gone back to my adoptive family.'

'That's sensible for the moment. Look, James, all of this, like everything in the world, will pass. How do you get on with your parents?'

Again he shakes his head. 'They're grand. But they want me to be grateful all the time, and it's very difficult. I didn't ask them to adopt me.'

'I'm sure they love you.'

'Yeah, sorry, that was childish. They do, and I am grateful. They gave me a good life and a good education and of course I love them, and they love me.' Then, with a flash of the self-possessed James I remember from my sitting room: 'What's not to love?'

'Exactly! Hang in there, everything will work out. You'll see.' I say it confidently although I cannot remotely see how things will work out for the poor chap, for the present anyhow. I doubt strongly if either Lorna or Olive would fully accept him into their problematic lives right now. Being me, though, I plough on: 'Listen, I'll have a word with Lorna but not now. OK? Nothing can happen overnight, she's too lonely and upset, but if you take it handy, you'd never know. This is going to sound terrible, but there's a vacancy in Lorna's heart, although she doesn't know it quite yet. Right now she's in the blackest, deepest hole anyone could imagine – but in time I truly believe she'll accept you as a stepson.'

He stares at me, his expression as nakedly hopeful as that of a child waiting for a turn on a fairground ride. 'You really think so?'

'I do. And don't forget, you do have real-deal blood family – Martin's kids are your half-niece and half-nephew. There were a few others here at this funeral today who were your father's relatives from the country. In time I'm sure you'll be able to get to know them. But you have to understand, James, that Olive

234

has just lost her husband in a rotten way and her life is askew right now. Take your time with this, although it's not going to be easy. Along the way, there'll have to be horrible invasive things, like DNA tests and all that. I'm only guessing here. Maybe not. Maybe, if you wait long enough, they'll just accept you. Right now, James,' I touch his arm again, 'I don't need any tests.' I give him the sunniest smile I can summon. 'I'm absolutely convinced you're Lennie McQuaid's son. How did you find out about Lennie, by the way?'

'My parents, my adoptive parents,' he corrects himself, 'they got me in touch with the right people. He's on my birth cert, just as L. D. McQuaid, no occupation or anything like that but it did give his age, and the social worker who does this tracing thing told me that to have his name, even like that, plus his age, was a great help. My birth mother is dead. She was a druggie. I was taken into care when I was born and when she died – she was only twenty-one – I was put up for adoption. Her name was Charlotte. Charlotte Rowan.' He says it flatly, with no rancour, but I suspect that this aspect of his parentage had not been an easy discovery. 'McAlinden is the name of my adoptive parents.'

I park that. To dive into something so tragically personal is not my business and I don't know James well enough. I had seen photographs of Lennie, a red-faced man with a very short, supremely unflattering haircut, but had never met him. I had gathered, however, from listening to both Lorna and Jean, that he was phlegmatic, a man of few words, and could not settle in the city. The older I get, the less I am surprised by human behaviour, but the vision of him with that wretched slip of a girl – who had such a romantic, euphonious name – makes me shudder. Not with revulsion but with empathy. 'Look,' I say, 'I think that, deep down,

Lorna knows you're on the level. Why else would she have taken you in like she did and got you a job?'

'To keep me out of her house during the day?'

'No. You have to accept that this is hard for her. Listen to me, James. I can't say it enough. You have to be patient. Her own son, her only child, has just died and just before he did, you showed up and she learned that her dead husband, the one she didn't even get the satisfaction of divorcing, was unfaithful to her. Can you imagine how that feels, James?' I hope that didn't sound too harsh but now I can see Mary coming towards us. 'Right. Here's Mary. We'll talk again.' A reporter's habit never far from home, I fish my pocket-sized notebook with pen attached from my handbag, scribble my telephone numbers on a blank page, tear it out and give it to him. 'Any time. All right? What's yours?' He gives it to me. I enter it and put the notebook away.

Mary joins us and in greeting her, before my eyes, that chameleon boy sheds the vulnerability he has shown me and adopts the easy, confident manner he had displayed in my house just three weeks before. He would be a great psychological study. Maybe I could get Mary involved with him as a project, I muse, as the three of us, lost in our own thoughts, walk to the car park, Mary dragging behind a little. 'Tired?' I link her and slow down. The image of my own lovely bed, with its snuggly duvet and bargain-priced but wonderfully soft down pillows, is dancing in front of my eyes.

Traffic is light and we get to Fairview in less than a quarter of an hour. I let James out under the pedestrian bridge. 'Don't forget what I said.' I smile at him as he levers himself out of my less-than-spacious back seat. 'Patience pays!'

'Thanks, Maggie.' In public mode, he blazes that smile of his that, some day, will slay some unwary woman, probably many unwary women, and in the full brightness of day, I indulge in a little Psychology 101 and confirm the obvious to myself. What, three weeks previously, I had taken to be extraordinary self-confidence and sang-froid is a mask, sculpted and perfected over many years as a defence against the world. Like Dina, who is suspicious of motives because of her money, James could perceive his beauty as the enemy. Who wants him for himself? Look at how we five mature, middle-aged women behaved on Christmas Day. Raffling him, no less!

'What was that all about?' Mary, whose eyes have been closed throughout the journey so far, comes out of her reverie as we drive away. 'What's he thanking you for?'

'Ah, nothing. Just a bit of rubbishy female advice I gave him.'

'I saw you pass him a note back at the chapel, presumably your home number. I hope you're not still smitten.'

'For God's sake, Mary,' I snap, a little too vehemently, pissed off that she had even noticed my brief, very brief, diversion into Fantasy Land. Then, more conciliatory: 'Look, I admit I was taken with him just like the rest of us. Maybe not you, though.' I look across at her but she's staring ahead. 'You have to admit he's gorgeous, Mary. We all agree on that. You'd want to be a dead woman not to at least ask yourself what it would be like with him. And, yes, I did discover that I, for one, am not dead yet in that department. I'll admit to a bit of daydreaming. For about two minutes. But I got sense, as I'm sure everyone else did. Even Jean was giddy. She said to me, believe it or not, that she wouldn't kick him out of her bed! It was the drink, Mary. It was Christmas. It was lights, alcohol, action!'

'Count me out of the James McAlinden Appreciation Society – that's a troubled young man. And if you're wise, you won't get involved. I'll say that only once, Maggie. Take it or leave it but, believe me, I know what I'm talking about.'

'Message noted.'

'But the advice contained therein not to be taken.' She closes her eyes again. She has to be as wrecked as I am. And she does have a point: from her work at the shelter she is in a position to make value judgements on people. She was given training.

By three o'clock, we're again in Lorna's kitchen.

There had been no formal, soup-tea-and-sandwiches invitation for the mourners after Martin's consignment at the crematorium: the relatives had departed for the four corners of Ireland, the friends and neighbours had dispersed and Lorna had invited just the four of us back to her house. She had asked Olive and her side of the family too, but had taken it in good part when her daughter-in-law had declined, saying that having been away from them in London, she needed to look after her children. 'Of course,' Lorna said. 'But please, don't be a stranger.'

'I won't.' Olive's arms had twitched as though she was about to embrace her mother-in-law but, at the last minute, she had let them fall back to her sides and there was an awkward little shuffle between the two of them. I was standing beside them when this happened so I can verify that, yes, the beginning of an entente was in progress. Early days, but wouldn't it be great?

Mind you, I may lose a member of the Club: Lorna, no doubt, will choose to be with her grandchildren. If so, so be it. We've had a good run.

We've been in Lorna's kitchen for about an hour or so when she pushes back her chair from the table and stands up. 'Thank you,' she says shakily. 'I don't know how I would have got through this without you all. I don't want to go over the top about it but,' she addresses each of us in turn, 'thank you, Mary. Thank you, Maggie. Thank you Jean. And thank you, Dina. Thank you for your generosity. I'll never forget it. And neither will Martin, wherever he is. I know I'm repeating myself, but I couldn't have gone through it without – thank—' She can't continue and sits down heavily.

'What else could we do? We all feel so helpless, Lorna!'

'I'll-make-a-fresh-pot-of-tea' Dina Coyne gets up and goes towards the kettle and, once again, I feel mean about thinking badly of her that St Stephen's night. The generosity to which Lorna had referred had been financial and Dina's alone. That she could afford such largesse was neither here nor there: it was the gesture that counted and, in my opinion at least, she was making a solid effort to bridge the mysterious gap between herself and Lorna.

Martin McQuaid's second miracle! Two rapprochements in one day! Now all we needed was the third, for James.

We talk and cry together well into the afternoon. Lorna pulls out her old photo albums and we talk with her about the individual snaps: 'That was Martin's first day at school – would you look at the Brylcreemed head on him?

'And that's him, the mucky pup, coming home from football practice. That washing machine was running night, noon and morning ...'

'Oh! I'd forgotten about this one. This was him and the first girl he had a crush on – at least, she was the first one I got to see. She invited him to her Debs. He was only a fifth-year. God, the nerves, the excitement ...'

We pass around the photos, listen and talk until the light begins to fade outside. I'm reluctant to break this up but I have to collect Flora from the kennels before six o'clock and they're strict about their timings. We had agreed together that Jean would be the one to overnight with Lorna on Martin's first night released to the skies from the crematorium chimney. I had Chloë with me the next day and Sunday so wouldn't see Lorna again until Monday. 'Is it all right if I go?' I push back my chair. 'They lock the gates of those kennels at six.' 'Fine,' they chorus.

Then Mary stands up too. 'I'm absolutely bushed. Would you mind, Lorna, if I take a lift home from Maggie? I'm not sure I can face the buses right now.'

'Of course.' Lorna joins us on our side of the table and takes one hand from each of us. 'How can I ever thank you, both of you?'

'You can swallow one of those pills Jean got for you and have a good night's sleep.' Mary kisses her cheek. 'You know we're all here for you. You can certainly ring me any time of the day or night.'

'I know that. I really do. Thank God you two came to An Grianán that time. Someone up there,' she pointed to the ceiling, 'must have been shining a light on me that day.'

'The pleasure's all mine,' Mary and I say simultaneously, as though we've rehearsed it, and then we leave.

All the way down the Black Banks Road, Mary is unusually quiet.

'Didn't sleep well last night, Mary?'

'Not really. And it was a tough day all round.'

'It sure was.' I let her be. We're just approaching Clontarf when again I break the silence. 'Yeah, it was tough, all right, but it went well, considering. A lot of it is thanks to you, Mary. You kept us all going with your flow of information. It really helped.'

She doesn't reply, and at first I think she's asleep, but when I glance across at her, I see that her eyes are trained on me. 'What's the matter? What have I done now? You're making me nervous.'

'Pull into this next car park,' she says quietly.

'Mary! You're frightening me. What's going on?'

'Will you just pull in, you eejit? You'll miss the entrance – it's right here!' She taps on her window.

I brake hard and swerve, coming to a stop within just a foot of the little kerb separating the car park from the promenade. Across the sea inlet, named, incongruously, at one stage by some Pollyanna as the Blue Lagoon, the lights are on in all the windows of the East Link Business Park; behind its bulk, I can see the funnel of a cross-channel ferry. I turn off the engine and the car's headlights. 'So? Here we are.' I look across at her through the sudden darkness. 'What's up?'

She rolls down the window and inhales deeply. 'Ah! Ozone and sewage. A potent mix, non?'

'Mary!'

'All right. I don't want you to freak about this and I don't want you to tell any of the others. Not yet. Do you promise?'

'You know I do. Mary. Will you just get on with it? I'm dying here.'

'Funny you should say that.' Her smile is a little lopsided. 'I have cancer.'

EIGHTEEN

Later that evening
I have cancer. Cancer. Cancer have I: a series of sentences making a sentence palindrome.

The Big C word, spelled backwards, is recnac, did you know that? Appropriate, eh? Say it aloud. Recnac. While 'cancer' is soft, like a flower – just reverse those liquid Cs and the word is hard. Unyielding as concrete.

Spelling backwards in my head is a habit I still fall into from time to time, developed in primary school. I do it particularly with people's names: Mary, for instance, is Yram. I thought that was lovely. Exotic. When I pronounce Yram (I-ram) in my head, I see a doe-eyed carpet weaver in an Arabian Night. And as her eclectic interests expanded in adulthood, to me it had seemed Yram became more and more apt. I don't think I ever told her about this tic of mine, or if I did, I've forgotten. She's certainly never mentioned it.

Spelling backwards. Yeah! Yeah! Yeah! Pauline – the Gimp – was Eniluap, multi-syllabic, not so euphonious as Yram, but when pronounced E-neye-lu-ap it suited her hopalong gait perfectly, as though I'm urging my mount to go faster. Giddyap! Eniluap!

In our class, Brainypants, whose real name was Mairead, was to me Daeriam. We had a Neelie and an Asil – and, as far as I was concerned, their backwards names suited them even better than their real ones. The Neelie rode a bicycle to school; 'Neelie' sounded to me like a bicycle freewheeling down a hill; Daeriam was top swot.

Although not in our top three, the Erdried, a serious, spectacle-wearing girl, was close to it. As for the Asil, her backwards name was the most apt of all. *Asal* is the Irish for donkey, or ass, and our Asil was dipsy and pretty and the class dunce. She made the papers in 1975 by marrying a sixty-year-old Eastern European hotelier with an aristocratic pedigree. Her wedding, in Dromoland Castle, was the Irish social event of the year, attended by Prince Rainier of Monaco and some of his chums, plus a real Arab sheik from somewhere mysterious, the name of which escapes me now. The German hotelier died in 1990 and Asil, lauded for 'unstinting charity work', appears now and then in the Social and Personal columns where she is styled the Rt Hon. Mrs Lisa Something Unpronounceable with a lot of consonants and few vowels. (Whether she is a Rt Hon. or not is open to question according to hacks and hackettes on the more snide side of journalism.) It is true, however, that she resides, not lives, like the rest of us, in her palatial apartment in Monaco.

I know stuff like this because I go to hairdressers and dentists and I have the kind of ragbag mind that delights in hoovering up random facts. A lot of the really trivial stuff can stick, you know, and you'd be surprised at the effect some of it has. Years and years ago, in some magazine in some waiting room, I read an interview with Peter Finch, still one of my favourite actors. He died in 1977 when I was only twenty-one, so it's that long ago. Anyway, in the piece, he said this: 'Good acting should teach people to understand rather than judge.' To this day, it affects how I view cinema and theatre performances; it also, I think (says she, blowing her own trumpet), informs my journalism. Did, anyway, when I was doing those interviews. Maybe not so much when I'm writing about the New Year resolutions of the wannabe class.

Funny what sticks, isn't it? Even funnier what goes through your mind at moments of crisis. It's as if the brain pulls down shutters and won't allow reality to seep in.

For instance, here we are, Yram and me. Sitting side by side in my car, parked on the seafront in Clontarf, while the wind ruffles the surface of the Blue Lagoon.

And she has just told me she has cancer.

And what am I doing? I'm mentally surfing, that's what.

'Are you all right, Maggie? You're very quiet. You did hear what I said?' She looks at me. She sounds concerned.

She's asking me if I'm all right? 'I'm fine, thanks, Mary, never better – how the hell do you think I am?' I'm not consciously parsing my feelings, but as soon as I say it I realise anger is uppermost. 'My best friend has just told me she has cancer and I'm supposed to be all right?'

'I'm the one who has the cancer,' she points out. She knows me inside out, as I do her. She knows that I will probably scream and shout but at some ungodly hour, probably three or four in the morning, will wake up in a blue funk. 'Look,' she adds, 'I'm getting cold sitting here. Let's wait until we get to my flat. You can come in and have tea, or cocoa, or we could even have a real drink. I'll tell you the whole story.'

'We're not going to your flat.' I make a decision, start the engine, turn the heat up full and grind into reverse gear. 'We're going to my house. I'll have to leave early in the morning to pick up Chloë but, no arguments, you're staying with me tonight – unless you want to subject me to sleeping on the floor in your place. You'll probably be sharing with Flora. She won't mind, I'm sure. Flora's very generous like that.' I glance across at her and, to my relief, get an answering smile.

It's only when I mention her name that I remember I'm now going to have my work cut out to get to the kennels on time. 'We have to go via the kennels. Is that OK? Are you hungry?'

'No.' Her tone is wry. 'One of the little-known benefits of cancer, I believe, is that for some people, including me, it seems, it deals with any weight problems.'

'How long have you known?' I indicate to pull out; while outbound traffic is bumper to bumper, townbound is light. 'Are you sure? Did you have the tests?' The questions tumble out as the shutters finally open, allowing my fear and me to stare together at my Mary, too weak to talk, her lips white and cracked, her skeletal hand holding one of mine as I attend her deathbed.

'Which question do you want answered first?'

'Them all, actually. How long have you known, Mary?'

'Suspicions or fact?'

'Both. Don't play with me. This is serious.'

She doesn't answer, and as a bus brakes to let me out in front of it, I realise the enormity of what I had just said, what we face and how I'm making this very, very difficult for her. I'm being selfish in the extreme. 'I'm sorry, so sorry, Mary, please forgive me. I'm acting like a cretin. I didn't meant to talk to you like that. I'm so frightened. Why the hell didn't you cry off the Club? You must have been feeling dreadful all through that giddy bloody dinner. And all that stuff about James McAlinden, that must have—'

'I'm still alive, Maggie. My sense of humour hasn't vanished with this diagnosis. Neither has my sense of friendship or enjoyment. I'm still me! So will you stop this? And before you ask me anything else, it's ovarian. The cancer is ovarian.'

But I can't stop. Not yet. I'm appalled at what my friend must have gone through, nursing her secret while being surrounded by innuendo and Dina's flirting and our stupid, silly giggling. 'You had the perfect excuse not to put yourself through that day. Everyone would have understood. You told me years ago that in your branch of your religion you didn't celebrate Christmas. You said that, for you, every day was holy, that Christmas and Easter and the Resurrection and all the rest were to be celebrated every day.'

'Sssh!' She reaches over and puts a restraining hand on my arm. 'Calm down. I'm an *à la carte* Quaker. I take a drink, don't I? And, like all the *à la carte* Roman Catholics in this country, I try to be a good person and cut out the Church's organisational shit and edicts. I celebrate what my friends celebrate and it's a big part of my life.'

'But—'

'Maggie, if you don't stop, I'm going to get out of this car at the next traffic lights. I mean it. There's a bus about three cars behind you and another a few yards behind that. They're all going into town.' Her quiet, authoritative tone finally shuts me up.

'I'm sorry,' I say meekly.

'If you insist on going on about Christmas,' she said then, 'I

246

know how much it means to you and I didn't want to spoil it. Anyway, a few days wasn't going to make any difference. Stop panicking, will you? I know it's a shock but I've had a few weeks to get used to the reality of it—'

'A few weeks? You mean you've known the full diagnosis for a while?'

'Got the test results the morning of Tuesday, the eighteenth of December.'

'I don't believe it. That was the day—'

'Yes. That day. We were in the Merrion that day.'

'But why didn't you tell me?'

'I couldn't. It was too fresh. I had to absorb it. And I knew that nothing was going to be done in the Christmas period.'

Her narkiness in the Merrion that day, at a level unusual even for her, made sense now. 'And there was I, going on about shagging decorations and Christmas— Oh, Mary! Why didn't you stop me? I could kill you for not telling me.'

'You mightn't have to,' she said drily, then: 'Sorry. Forget that. I'm just being melodramatic – must be catching!

'Look, it was good that day in the Merrion, Mag. It gave me a dose of reality and a foundation to stand on. I'd suspected since long before that, and while it would have been nice to have my suspicions negated, in one way it was good to have them confirmed. Now somebody else is in charge and, in a very weird way, I can relax. Life doesn't stop. Christmas happens. People celebrate a wedding or a christening in one hotel function room while next door people eat sausages after a funeral. Real life doesn't stop just because of a cancer diagnosis. It has to be inserted into the whole package for one third of the population of this country, every person when you add in family and friends. My reality is my so-called work, my music tuition, my friends, shopping, Christmas, Lorna, poor Lorna, Jean with her little bobble hats, even Dina with her fantasies and fur coats. Recession, the news, work, entertainment, that doesn't go into freeze-frame, you know. Cancer doesn't become your whole life. I'm determined that for me, anyhow, it won't. Accepting you have this illness is just something else to be dealt with. Treatments. Time. Regular doses of other aspects of your life. I'm not going to give things up, Maggie. I'm just going to add another.

'And by the way, don't think for a second that I'm alone with this. I haven't been since the beginning. The consultant's diary is packed, back to back. He was run off his feet that morning he saw me. That's real life too, the community of people facing this disease. And I don't think I'm going to die in the next few months so all I ask of you is to be my friend and let me deal with it. You don't have to suffer along with me. Although, knowing you, I'm not so sure you can achieve that!'

The traffic lights at the junction of Amiens Street and Talbot Street are red, and as I wait to turn right, I notice the home-going office workers racing each other up the long escalator towards the railway platforms. How great to be one of them right now.

But then the little voice at the base of my skull swings into action: How can you pick out the ones who are battling depression? Or going home to violence? Or taking the Dart to Dún Laoghaire to catch a ferry crossing to an English clinic in order to sort an unwanted pregnancy? Or who are, like you, facing an existence as an adjunct to a friend's cancer diagnosis? A possible, well-flagged bereavement?

'This is what all that stuff about loneliness and Exit was about, isn't it? And Lourdes?' I keep my eyes on the escalator with its endless, ant-like stream of competitive commuters. 'That afternoon we were together in your flat, you said you'd written to your brother and sisters six months previously. That's seven and a half months ago now.' I'm getting worked up again. 'You knew at that stage? Seven months ago, Mary?'

'I had my suspicions, yes.'

'But seven months … ' The implications of the delay are clear and I turn now to glare at her.

'I won't warn you again. I'll get out right now if you don't shut up. Anyway, the symptoms are vague. They could be as a result of all kinds of things, benign things, like eating the wrong food. I looked them up. They didn't seem all that serious.'

I'm furious with her. That delay could have been crucial. 'It must have dawned on you that it was serious, Mary. Otherwise why would you even think of asking your brother and sisters to come here? What kind of benign symptoms?'

'Bloating around the middle, indigestion, constipation, all that kind of perfectly normal stuff and a lot more besides, like low back pain. Sure that could be just getting older. It could have been a whole load of things, as simple as eating too many white-bread sandwiches.'

'And Lourdes? You mentioned Lourdes to me. Do Quakers even believe in the Virgin Mary?'

'You're incorrigible, Maggie Quinn. As if it matters. Yes, if you really want to know. Quakers do believe in Mary as the Mother of Jesus,' she said quietly. 'Where do you think I got my name? My parents were Quakers. The Waiting Worship, old-fashioned kind, where God works through everyone equally.'

'So it's not against your religion, then, to go to Lourdes?'

'Nothing is against my religion, as you put it, except not loving my neighbour, and that can encompass a whole encyclopaedia of real crimes. Listen, Maggie, are you going to respect me or are you going to behave like my mad aunt for the next six months? Because that's how long I've been told the initial treatment will take, longer if I have to have surgery. Are you going to be my friend, Mag, or behave like a female Attila the Hun? If you are, I'll find another friend! Fatigue is another symptom, now that you ask. And you're making me quite tired, to tell you the truth.'

She doesn't mean that badly and we both know it.

'Is that why the fairy project is so slow? You don't have the same energy?' Mary's enthusiasms usually send her dashing headlong into projects.

'Probably,' she admits.

We pass the rest of the journey to the kennels in relative silence until, when we're less than a kilometre away, she reveals that she has started her chemo treatment. 'Monday mornings. Second one next Monday, the fourteenth.'

'So soon? When was the first?'

'New Year's Eve.'

'Hold on a second. We were in Lorna's doing Martin's death notice that afternoon.'

'I know. I found it a little – eh, weird.' She's choosing her words. 'Listen, Maggie, I'm fine at the moment, truly. But for completeness,' she smiles wanly, 'I'm told that, especially after the later goes, there is a possibility, just a possibility, Maggie – are you listening?'

'Yes.'

'A possibility that I'll be feeling a bit crook. There's no telling, apparently. Everyone reacts differently. And before you ask, there'll be eight altogether, two weeks apart. They'll move it to three weeks apart if I'm having a bad reaction. And then surgery if it doesn't work and then radiotherapy. To tell you the truth, right now I forget which comes first. I'm living in the moment. I've joined the community of the therapised!'

'Don't trivialise it, Mary.' I glare at her again.

'OK. Sorry. Without the surgery, he tells me the whole thing should take twenty-two weeks. Twenty-four if there are any delays. Only twenty or twenty-two to go from Monday – so, one way or the other, I'll be grand for your birthday party in July.' She smiles at me.

'Right.' I swallow. Hard. The thought of her having her first chemotherapy on her own, then coming to Lorna's to write a death notice is too horrific to take in. 'No arguments, Mary, from now on.' I try to sound bossy. 'No more heroics. You're to leave Lorna to the rest of us. You have to think about yourself now. The others will understand, Lorna will understand. There'll be plenty of us around to hold Lorna's hand.'

'We'll see. But I do take your point. It's important that I mind myself, not to get too tired or stressed. I'm supposed to get plenty of sleep and to keep up my nutrition levels and so forth. And not to sunbathe. That bit'll be easy anyhow.' She glances through her window at the darkness, punctuated with the sickly yellow of the sodium street lighting. 'I'll apparently be in danger of infections. So, if you have a cold coming on, Mags, you're to tell me. And, by the way, for the moment not a word to the others, OK?'

'OK. But why not? They're our friends, Mary. They'll want to help. All this secrecy – why?'

'Promise?' She ignores my question. 'I'll cut you out of the deal altogether, Maggie, if you tell the others. I'll tell them myself when I have to, when it becomes obvious, but in the meantime – I couldn't stand to be at the centre of a circle of pity and concern.

I look at the way we're all treating Lorna and I see the same for myself in spades. So I mean it. No telling.'

'Shut up, Mary. Don't keep going on about it. I said I'd keep shtum and I will. How are you actually feeling about all this? The truth!' I glance sideways at her profile.

'Well, congratulations, Maggie.' Her tone is acerbic. 'The first time you've included that in your list of queries – sorry. I shouldn't be sarcastic. Obviously,' she adds slowly, 'I've had time to think about it and have taken it as far as the ultimate.' Then, sensing my horrified reaction, she turns to me full on. 'Before you jump in again, just listen. Listen, please, Maggie!'

I zip it. And when she's sure I'm not going to interrupt, she continues: 'If that's to be the case, if I am going to die soon, I'm more or less reconciled. Not to run the usual clichés, I've had a good innings. I've had a fantastically interesting life. I've done most of the things I would have bucket-listed as things to do before I die. Now that's the hard bit out in the open. Are you still listening?'

I nod. I can't speak. The prospect of my life without Mary is too hard to take in and I'm refusing to do so.

'Good,' she goes on. 'Now the better bit. The bit that's probably far more likely to happen. I'm probably not going to die, not in the near future anyway, OK? Still with me?'

I nod again, but the red lights on the back of the car in front of me have blurred as tears glaze my eyes. I dash them away. I make sure I sound calm as I say, 'Go on.'

'The better bit,' she repeats, 'is that these days there is some good news. I'm fifty-eight this year. I'll probably – no, make that definitely – see sixty, even sixty-one. That's regardless, the consultant says, although he does hedge his bets. Every sentence out of his mouth includes phrases like "we hope" or "we expect" or "there should be" coupled quickly with "there could be". Even if this first round of chemo doesn't do its work, I can have surgery. And I can have another round of the stuff. I don't intend for that to happen. I'm thinking positive right now and I intend to continue down that road.

'I don't want to know the average length of survival for this particular cancer, Mags, so please don't go rushing to find out. Even if you insist on doing it, keep it to yourself, but I don't recommend it. I'll look it up some time, but you can take it from me that I don't need any consultant to tell me I'm lucky to be diagnosed in this era. It's not like the old days. He tells me there are many new and better-targeted treatments coming all the time and he'll be calibrating with colleagues all over the world to individualise mine. They do that nowadays. The Internet and Skype and so on have revolutionised their intercommunications. He won't give me percentages but I gather that, right now, he plans to enable me to have a very long and fruitful life. So will you take that on board and stop worrying? Your worry will not increase my chances one whit. In fact, the opposite is the case. Glass half full, eh?'

'I'll try. And you shouldn't be comforting me, Mary. I'm sorry about the way I've reacted. Really. From this moment on, I'll be your little ray of sunshine. OK?'

'Not too bright, I hope. I couldn't bear it.'

'Just a little glow on your horizon.'

'Perfect. Thank God!'

'Thank God?'

'I was dreading this conversation. Thank God it's over.'

'Am I that difficult?'

'You're that loving, Maggie. You're that much of a friend.'

We pull up outside the gates of the kennels just as the owner is coming out to lock up. As I hurry out to intercept him, it occurs to me that if this were fiction, Mary and I would have hugged tearfully after that kind of an exchange. We hadn't. We don't. It's all very well to mutter, 'Love ya!' during a hello or goodbye embrace, but the real thing is harder to express. And when it's expressed as she just has, physical contact would have opened the floodgates.

NINETEEN

There had been tears, I won't deny it. But I had had a long, emotionally eventful day and, despite my best efforts to stay awake for my friend's sake, my eyelids are now drooping in the warmth of my sitting room as the two of us, with Flora dozing on the rug between us, sit on opposite sides of the gas fire, hissing away to itself in the fireplace.

One image is haunting me. While we were still eating, Mary had dug into her handbag to show me three sets of large hooped earrings she had bought, blue enamel, pearly white and, poignantly, in light of what may happen to her glorious hair, a pair in fire-brigade red. 'I picked them up at the airport on the way back today,' she had said, 'just on a whim,' and, pushing back her hair, held a red one to one of her ears. 'I won't be getting a wig, I don't think I could bear it, so I hope these will distract from my baldy head. What do you think?'

'Very gnick, Mary,' I'd said, again fighting an onrush of tears. The sight of those cheap, bold hoops had brought home to me more than anything else what a tough road she faces and how bravely she's stepping on to it. Although Mary has never openly admitted it, she's proud of her mane. 'You might be lucky.' I hoped I sounded cheery. 'Some chemos don't affect the hair.'

'Not this chemo,' she'd said matter-of-factly. She'd packed away all three sets. 'I asked.'

'Some of the wigs are very good nowadays. You'd hardly know … '

The look she gave me had spoken volumes and I'd faded.

'I'll get us another drink, OK? I need one anyway.' I got up and went into the kitchen to clink and clank around and to have my cry in private.

'You must be knackered, Mary.' I could hardly get the words past my tongue when I returned to her.

'Not really. For some strange reason I seem to have loads of energy right now. Must be psychological. Not looking forward to, you know, Monday. I had the choice of every two weeks or every three weeks. The three weeks gives you more time to recover, but the two weeks means that it's over sooner. The consultant did say that the real test will be the radiotherapy. Everyone feels as flat as a pancake for that. I'm not to do any work during those weeks because I won't be able for it.'

It sounded truly scarifying but her tone of resignation was the most upsetting aspect for me. Mary resigned? I wanted her to be as angry as I was. I wanted her to fight. But now was not the time to attack her. 'Maybe it's a golden opportunity to read up about your fairies. Can I help in any way? Do a bit of research in the

National Library? They have everything there, every kind of book and periodical going back years and years.' I was desperately trying to find the bright side, any smidgen of lightness. I was even prepared to tell her that there were fairies everywhere (even at the bottom of my garden) – I was all over the place.

When we had been driving home from the kennels and the news was still roaring around in my stomach, I had wanted to roll down my window and shout at the top of my voice at other drivers: 'Don't you know, you stupid people? Mary has cancer!'

Needless to say, I hadn't done anything of the sort but had truly resented the way everyone else bowled heedlessly along the thoroughfare as if nothing had happened. I was so mad at them all I nearly called 999 when I saw a ponytailed blonde in a four-by-four (what else? What a cliché!), driving with one hand around a roundabout while jabbering away into the phone she held to her ear. If I can afford Bluetooth for the little tin-can I drive, she certainly can for an expensive behemoth that takes up half the road and has one Baby on Board strapped into the middle row of her seven effing seats.

I remain frightened, emotional, you name it, and, on Mary's behalf, totally freaked out by the notion of the body changes she'll go through. I'm angry with her, too, for the delay in seeking help: I'm terrified she's going to die. In fact, it's absolutely clear that I'm far more upset than she is. Or seems to be.

Women die from ovarian cancer. Unfortunately I didn't need to look that up. I know it all too well because in my journalistic days I interviewed a sufferer in a hospice when she was within days of her death. The only other thing I remember about the poor woman, who was in her fifties, like Mary, like me, was that the cancer had spread into various other organs. They performed surgery on her but it was too late and, in her words, delivered almost jauntily: 'They opened me, had a poke around, and just sewed me up again.'

Does Mary's doctor know what he's doing here?

And do sufferers from illnesses such as this have any idea how it affects friends? Everyone empathises with family. Family members are consulted gravely by medics. Family members are advised and counselled. While they are offered tea and sympathy, along with 'if there's anything I can do', close friends are permitted merely to cheerlead from the sidelines. In my opinion, however, those cheerleaders can be affected just as much or even more than family, when illness strikes so heavily. And, yes, I know about the ARC drop-in centres, great resources as they are for anyone connected to a sufferer or even worried. But I'm talking about the generality. If I'm your daughter and you have cancer, even my employer will ask about you and be tolerant. If I'm 'merely' your friend, life goes on as normal.

Mary has no next of kin in this country. I haven't brought it up yet, but could she nominate me? I want to be involved. I'm her closest friend; when I was with Derek I spoke more intimately with Mary than I did with my husband. I couldn't have imagined trusting anyone else with some of the confidences I've divulged to her. Certainly not my mother – nice enough as she was underneath all the buttoned-up closeness she displayed in her own domain – and Chloë was never an option. I have to be involved with this.

What kind of stuff have Mary and I talked about during our long friendship? Child's stuff. Teenage stuff. Ersatz teenage stuff, young-woman-in-love stuff – instance my phone call to her following the first time I had clapped eyes on Derek after which I could barely breathe, let alone speak. 'Guess what?'

'What?'

'You'll never believe it!'

'Maybe not. Do keep me in suspense, though.'

'I think I'm in Heaven.' I'd let her stew for a few seconds. I'd wanted her to guess. I'd wanted to prolong the moment.

'Let me guess.' She doesn't let me down. 'You've met someone.'

'Yeah!' I yell. Then, more quietly: 'But I don't know if he's met me, if you get my meaning?'

'Stop talking in riddles, Maggie. You met someone but he hasn't met you? How is that possible?'

'I saw him. I saw him in a restaurant. He was only inches away. He gave me a coffee. Oh, Mary, he has the most fantastic eyes. And great hair.'

'And he bought you a coffee? The last of the big spenders.'

'No, stupid. He made me a coffee. He was behind the counter. It was just the way he looked at me. Oh, Mary … '

'Jesus wept. The way he looked at you? You're Sally O'Brien now?'

That TV ad of many moons ago, probably the late seventies, early eighties, was for Harp Lager, if I recall. It starred a laughing colleen, so vivacious, so curly, so dancy – and so far from yours truly that this, from Mary, bored right into the insecurity bone. 'Shut up, Mary. That's not fair.' I could hear myself sounding like a ten-year-old. *Pro-tem*, in my heart, I was a ten-year-old.

She sighed. 'All right, Maggie. So how did he look at you, then?'

'I dunno. Kind of sideways. He has these great eyebrows – he's absolutely gorgeous.'

'Great eyebrows? How's his hair? Oh, sorry. Great. You said.'

Of course she was being ironic but at the time this was lost on me. 'Kind of – let's see. Gosh! Kind of crispy.'

Her silence at the other end of the phone spoke louder than

words. At that phase in her life, Mary was working in the Department of Health as a 'junior ex' – junior executive officer, the first rung of the civil service executive promotional ladder, or it used to be. Great things were expected of her in the new, thrusting civil service where women had been discovered actually to have independent thinking organs named brains, but she was bored out of her tree by the work she called 'mindless', which largely involved, she said, the reviewing of files and attending endless meetings. She was constantly threatening to leave – and did, the day she graduated with a social services qualification, having taken night classes at university. In the meantime, she was inclined to take out her frustration on her friends. On that occasion, I was too euphoric to react to her sarcasm, whether expressed, implied or silent, and chattered on. Derek had said perhaps ten words to me in the coffee shop that day but, if memory serves me now, my conversation with Mary had lasted for the guts of two hours.

And then there was the time of our first marital row, when I thought the world had opened to spit fire and consume me. No one had ever, ever been so hurt, so offended, so insulted and abused as I. Mary had talked to me or, more accurately, listened to me for two hours on that occasion too.

In fact, now that I'm looking back like this, it hasn't been an equal relationship. I had turned to her not just during the crises but during every tittle-tattle affecting my life, whereas she …

I look across at her, nursing her drink. When had I fulfilled the equivalent role in her life? I couldn't think of a single instance. Her life had always seemed so interesting, not without hassle, no one can escape hassle, but without any drama I would consider critical enough to need my intervention.

Well, it sure is my turn now. I decide to bring up the next-of-kin thing. 'Mary, say no to this if you like, but with your sisters and brother away and your mother – eh – incapable, if that's not too harsh—'

'Ga-ga.'

'All right, ga-ga. I'm wondering if you could nominate me as next of kin. Does it have to be a relative?'

'I doubt it. Never thought about that. I don't see why not. I haven't been asked anything like that so far. I suppose that could be sorted out on Monday when I go in again for the chemo …'

She trails off and I could kick myself for my timing. 'Forget it for now. We can talk about it anytime.'

'No. You're right. Who else is there? A couple of cousins, but I don't even know them. I've met them maybe twice or three times and not for many years. I'd be very grateful if you would, Mags. Thanks. You can be my sister. I'll tell them the truth, that you're only an honorary sister, but I'll treat you like a real blood one and I'll make sure everyone else does too. Would you come with me on Monday? Last time a few of the patients had companions with them. They seem to allow that.'

'Of course I will. But there's one more thing, Mary.'

'What?'

'There is no way – and I'm not entertaining any objections here – you're going to bus it to chemo or radiotherapy. Starting on Monday, I'm driving you and I'm picking you up and, yes, I'll stay with you if you don't kick me out, and that's that. From the little I know about it, you're going to be in that hospital for hours. There may be a couple of days, if you or I have other appointments, like on Wednesdays or Fridays when I have to drive Chloë, but we'll work around them.'

To my astonishment, she agrees to this too, without a quibble. 'Thank you, Maggie. I appreciate it.'

We're quiet then, both locked in thought. That had been an unusual exchange – Mary always rebuffs offers of help: it's almost automatic with her. I'm going to have to be careful. The ground has shifted. Nothing like cancer to bring real life right up against your nose.

Despite everything, Mary's news, Lorna's bereavement, the evening together had been pretty mellow, considering the circumstances. Resonating with 'do you remember', we had talked of childhood experiences, of hops, showbands and, latterly, dinner dances we had attended together. The conversation has wound down naturally and we're now quiet together. 'I wish that was a real fire like you have in your flat,' I say now, as Flora, whimpering and with paws twitching, chases something in her sleep.

'Yeah. It's great company, like you with the dog, I suppose.' Although Mary would not be in the front rank of animal lovers, she leans forward to pat Flora's head. 'You have to treat a fire like a child, don't you? Feed it, mind it, clean it, dress it up for the next day. And the sound is great when there's nothing decent on the telly.'

We lapse again into silence. To anyone coming upon us we would appear peaceful, but I'm still churning inside. I can barely imagine how it is for her.

During our earlier conversations, she had revealed that while there are many factors involved, the risks of developing her particular cancer can be mitigated a little by giving birth. I've often wondered if Mary would have made a good mother. I've never, of course, initiated such a discussion, even though she had given me a few openings, letting it slip from time to time over the years that it had been a source of sadness to her not to have married and borne a family. Although I had made the right noises (I hope), I had remained unconvinced. She's such a free spirit, so engaged in life and the goings-on all over our planet and beyond, would she have been able to settle down to domesticity?

My only encounter with Mary's own family had been instructive but I had been very young and had taken in the implications only in retrospect. Even at the time, though, I had found them pretty odd, which was peculiar in itself because she had insisted that, religion apart, there were few differences between her family and my own.

Before going to Mary's house for tea, I had consulted my mother and Daddy about what I could expect. I found their views about Quakers to be pretty vague and I believe now they were confusing the Friends with the Amish. However, as a result of their ignorance, when finally I had accompanied Mary to her house on the Friday of the week I had been confirmed, I was expecting to see her mother in a modest grey dress with a kindly wrinkled face and a plait around her head or maybe wearing a frilly bonnet. Her dad, the crippled doctor, might be wearing a funny stovepipe hat and be driven around in a horse-drawn buggy.

We had been friends for at least three years before she had issued her invitation: 'My mummy says to ask you if you'd like to come home next Friday after school for tea. Naomi and Jennifer will be there but we don't have to eat with them.' Mary's two sisters were weekly boarders and came home for weekends on Friday afternoons.

'Will Jeffrey be there?' I was ten years old. I was beginning to notice that boys were exotic and made you feel all funny.

'Don't think so. He has cricket practice.'

By then, I was used to her reticence about her home life; she always clammed up whenever I asked her a direct question about her sisters. Probably because I was such a blabbermouth about my own sister, it was something I had vaguely resented at first – why couldn't we trade complaints? The leniency and special treatment accorded to my sister in our house drove me bonkers. In my view, our Chloë was completely spoiled and was let get away with murder, whereas I was killed for the merest hint of cheek or giving back-answers. 'It's just not fair,' was my mantra, repeated almost daily to Mary.

I had figured that Mary's secretive attitude about her home life must have something to do with status. She was posh, according to that teacher in second class, who had very quickly taken a scunner against her and was bent on bringing her down a peg, employing a combination of sarcasm and the services of Cáit on the least excuse. But I had seen Mary's lunches every day and I understood what her problem was, or so I thought, because I suffered from a rough equivalent. By reputation, she was (a little bit) posh; by reputation I was (a little bit) brainy. Neither was true but we had to keep up appearances. In my case fear – of punishment, of letting people down, of humiliation – was the spur to staying near the top of the class. Her fear, I had reckoned, was that someone, even I, her bestest friend in the whole world, would find out, or even guess, the real story in her house. Her secret? She wasn't posh at all. That was my theory anyway, and I was avid to see if it was borne out in the flesh, as it were.

So. Confirmation over, money spent – on a little bracelet, with the rest in the post office 'for the future' – I had something to look forward to. Whatever they were like, Mary's house and family were bound to be different from my own. A real excursion into exotica. And only two days away.

TWENTY

On the Friday afternoon of the visit to Mary's house for tea all those years ago, I thought she was a little nervous as we travelled together on the bus to Glasnevin. We alighted at a stop beside Iona Road, a street of substantial, bay-fronted red-brick houses with large, well-kept gardens and parking for quite a lot of cars. It was a road I knew, having passed it often enough on my way home to Ballymun, about a mile further north.

Her house, when we came to it, was on a side road, perpendicular to Iona Road and, even larger than the houses there, lived up to my expectations. It was detached, with a good-sized porch and ornamental railings fronting an immaculate garden.

'This is it.' She sounded peculiar.

'What's wrong, Mary?'

'Nothing. Come on.'

She pushed open the gate and I followed her towards the door, painted a shiny black and sporting a brass knocker, letterbox and knob, glittering in the weak spring sunshine. Instead of using a key, as I expected, she veered left through a side gate, leading me around the house in the direction of what was obviously the back door. 'My mother doesn't like us to use the front door. It lets in draughts. And germs,' she added quickly. 'They're a bit pernickety about germs.'

'Of course.'

She opened the door to reveal the kitchen and a girl sitting at a white Formica table pushed up against one wall. She was small, slim, blonde and very pretty. Her school uniform was pale grey, her right arm was in a sling. She looked the two of us up and down: 'This her? The famous Maggie?'

'Don't be rude, Naomi.' Mary reddened. 'You promised.'

'I did, didn't I? Come in, Maggie, do, please, come in.' The girl got up from the table, turned on her heel and left the room.

'Sorry about that.' Mary turned back to me.

'Don't worry about it. Look, if this is awkward … '

'It's not. Naomi's a pig, that's all. Come on in. Please, Maggie.'

'She doesn't look a bit like you.'

'Neither of them do,' she said shortly. 'Jennifer's not too bad. Of course she's the younger.'

'Will she be here?'

'Yeah. She's at Pony Club this afternoon. Naomi sprained her wrist last week and couldn't go today.'

Pony Club was definitely posh.

I followed her into the kitchen. Leading from it was a huge conservatory spanning, I saw later, the full width of the house and contained a farmhouse table with eight chairs; that room was as big as the entire ground floor of our house in Ballymun. 'This is gorgeous, Mary. You're so lucky. Do you go to Pony Club too?'

'Put your schoolbag on the bench there and give me your coat – do you want to do your eccer now?' She ignored my question. 'We could do it either here or in there.' She indicated both the Formica table and the larger one in the conservatory. 'Or would you like a snack first?'

'A glass of milk would be nice.' I shrugged off my coat and gave it to her. Homework was the last thing on my mind.

'I'll put this in my room.' She took it. 'Back in a sec. Sit down.' She left the room, clattering up the flight of uncarpeted stairs I could see through the door she had left open.

I took stock. They had a fridge: although they were becoming commonplace in the sixties, our family had not yet risen to one. We still used a meat safe hung on the wall outside the back door, and kept our milk in the scullery, which was cooler than the kitchen. I listened hard to detect if Mary was coming back and, as all was quiet, tiptoed across to open the fridge's impressive white door. This would give away their status once and for all. If it was stuffed with food and goodies, there was some very dark mystery about Mary getting only bread and water for her lunch every day.

Initial inspection proved inconclusive. There was food, all right, but nothing extravagant: eggs, butter, milk, lettuce – and, interestingly, they kept their bread in the fridge too. Two Johnston Mooney and O'Brien sliced pans sat side by side on the top shelf. My tummy rumbled. I'd absolutely love a bread-and-butter sandwich, I thought, when I heard a sound behind me. I spun around to find a petite blonde woman, as perfectly elegant as a china doll and wearing a tweed costume of duck-egg blue. She was coming towards me with hand extended. 'You found the fridge. Good. You must be Maggie?' Her eyes were startling, as blue as her suit.

Shame-faced, I closed the fridge and took her hand. 'Yes, that's right, Mrs Guerin. Mary said it was all right to get myself a glass of milk.'

She fingered the string of pearls around her neck. 'Of course it is, Maggie. Let me get it for you. Sit down there at the table.' She crossed the room towards a row of cupboards. 'Did you have a good Confirmation?'

'I did. And I love my medal.' I touched it, hanging beneath my collarbone. True to my word, I hadn't taken it off since donning it on the morning in question.

'It was Mary's idea, truly.' This woman – no wrinkles, no bonnets, no plaits – took a glass from one of the cupboards, went to the fridge, filled it with milk and brought it to me.

I thanked her but, even at this remove, it's very hard to describe the feeling I got from her. Her words, written as they are here, seem friendly, hospitable and welcoming, but there was something about the tone in which they had been delivered that belied them. 'Well,' she said now, 'I'll leave the two of you at it. Do help yourself to anything you need. Tea will be at half past five.' She smiled at me as she left, but I definitely felt anything but welcome. Even after her departure, the air in the kitchen seemed to maintain a chilly impression of her. I think, looking back, I was a bit afraid.

In fact, although there was nothing I could put my finger on, in its order and sterile perfection, the house made me feel uncomfortable. There was nothing on any of the kitchen's surfaces. The fridge gleamed, the floor tiles gleamed, the Aga gleamed, the taps over the sink gleamed, and as for the sink itself, the porcelain was blindingly white under the rays of the low sun shafting through the window above it. There was a door beside the Aga and behind it I could see one of those newfangled twin-tub washing machines. I was always a fanciful child and to me, being there felt like being on the set of a horror movie where, in the next frame, the creepy music would start. I wished Mary would come back.

I contrasted this modernity and hygiene with our tiny, messy kitchen, colanders balanced on saucepans in my mother's makeshift press under the sink, just two shelves behind a sprigged cotton curtain she had sewn herself. I pictured the chipped jugs and the old enamel bread bin on the shelf above the blackened rings of the gas cooker, the mangle outside the back door, the jam-jar vase on the table filled with dusty artificial daisies. Mary's mother, I thought, would have a heart attack if she came to our house where, obviously, germs held ceilidhs in every corner.

Curiosity was, even then, my middle name and I was speculating like mad about what was going on here.

Here's another thing, I thought. Naomi was obviously taking after her mother, with her blonde hair, blue eyes and tiny fragile wrists and ankles. As I've told you many, many times now, Mary was a Red – and how!

When my pal came back, she was businesslike: 'You OK? Good. You got milk?'

'Yeah. I met your mam. She gave it to me. She's very pretty, isn't she?'

'She is.' She looked hard at me as though she were trying to detect whether or not I was being ironic. Then: 'So where'll we do our eccer? In here or out there?' She indicated the conservatory. Without hesitation, I opted for the light, for the relative normality.

The winter sun even illuminated a patch of dust the sweeping brush had missed under the big wooden table.

We emptied the contents of our schoolbags on to the table and got busy. Because it was a Friday, we had a lot of homework. Our (nice) Iníon Ní Ghrógáin always gave us extra, 'to keep the brain in tune, *a chailíní*, but – deliberately, I always thought – the assignments she gave us were on the more pleasant spectrum of school work, for me anyhow: drawing maps, translating simple tracts of Irish, doing long tots – or, my favourite, writing an English essay. It was nice to be there, in the warmth and light, the only sounds the scratching of nibs (we had graduated to fountain pens) or the shuffle of paper. We didn't need to talk. Being together was enough. Within half an hour or so I had forgotten my earlier ... fear? Too strong a word. My earlier discomfort.

And I couldn't fault the tea, when it came. Precisely at half past five, Mary's mother came into the conservatory. She was carrying a tray on which stood a two-tiered cake stand, two plates, two knives, butter and jam dishes and two glasses of milk. She placed the lot almost soundlessly on the table between us. 'I hear you like tomato sandwiches, Maggie.' She smiled, indicating the display of them, dainty, triangular and crustless, on the lower plate of the cake stand. The top plate bore two scones and two slices of Battenberg cake.

I was delighted. Battenberg cake, pink and yellow chequerboard inside a marzipan coat, was one of my favourites. To me, it spelled treats, luxury and rewards for achievement. The taste of marzipan still brings me back to the day my mother made a Battenberg to celebrate the one and only time I came first in the class for an English essay, beating Mary into second and the Gimp into third. (In truth, my success was phoney: Brainypants, who, it was felt, was destined for a Nobel Literature Prize at the very least, was having her appendix out that week, but I basked in the glory and at home kept the appendix a secret.)

Interrupting this messy interlocking set of reminiscences, I glance at Mary now as she sits, eyes closed, hands loosely clasped in her lap, feet crossed on the footstool in front of the fire. She is breathing quietly, as though she is asleep. I know from experience that her chair is very comfortable but just as I'm wondering whether I should get a blanket and leave her there or wake her, Flora, as if catching the thought, stands up, stretches, ambles out of the room and Mary's eyes open. 'Where's she gone?'

'To bed. She's had enough.' We listen to the sound of paws trotting upstairs. 'Time for us to go up too, Mary. I was just remembering that delicious Battenberg cake your mam gave us when I went to tea in your house that time.'

'Yeah, way back when, eh?' She gives me a strange look. 'Listen, Mags, I'm sorry for not telling you the full story about her, about us all in that house.'

'What are you on about?' Although I'm puzzled, again I'm remembering my initial reaction to the atmosphere. 'What about her?' I ask cautiously.

'Ah – nothing.' She looks away.

'It's not nothing. I can tell it's not. What's on your mind?'

'Nothing. I told you. It's late, we should go to bed.' Then, wearily: 'Oh, what the hell, who cares now?' And she lets me in on a secret she has kept from me for nigh on half a century. She tells it in clipped sentences, every one of which hits me like a mallet because I'd had no idea. Not. A. Clue.

In summary: Mary was adopted, or half adopted. She was the progeny of her real father, the paraplegic doctor, and some woman with whom he had had a fling, long before his accident. Her adoptive mother, the china doll, forgave the fling, until, after three further children, Jennifer, Naomi and Jeffrey, her father strayed again. Mary was five years old, going on six.

This time, the doll threw her husband out. One night, however, less than a month later, he attempted to come back, via a ladder he took from the shed in their garden and placed against the bathroom window, which was ajar at the back of the house.

The doll, roused from sleep by the sound of scraping against the concrete wall, rushed to investigate and burst into the bathroom, startling Mary's father. The ladder slipped, and the good doctor fell twenty feet onto a concrete pathway.

In hospital for more than a year. Paralysed from the waist down.

'Oh, Mary, I had no idea.'

'Why would you? I haven't said this to anyone outside the family. But d'you know what? What I've just told you is the official story. I think she pushed him. I really do.'

'Mary!'

'I know, I know. But it's possible and no one will ever know. He's dead, she's ga-ga.'

'Did you ever ask her?'

'Are you mad? She barely tolerated me. We rattled around in that house during the week – Naomi and Jennifer were there only at weekends, as you know, and Jeff was rarely at home. If it wasn't rugby, it was cricket or orienteering. He was the sporty type. Anyway, that pair were not the brightest lights in the light shop and they weren't all that enamoured of my so-called academic successes.' She pulls a face. 'But there was one time, during the summer holidays, when we'd been swimming and we were getting on OK, I thought. I was eight or nine, and I did bring it up. You know me, things just burst out of my mouth. They immediately told her what I'd said. You can imagine what she thought of that!'

I could. 'How about Jeffrey? Or your dad?'

'Never mentioned it to either of them, although I'm sure the girls did. So, as you can gather, m'dear, from my perspective, things were not exactly hunky-dory in my house and, for certain, I was not the house favourite.'

'But I always thought—'

'Yes, I know what you thought. Quakers. Gentle Friends. Why amn't I being asked to tea? The Mystery at Mary's Manor. So now you know. At least there was no violence, no abuse, no beatings. Nothing like that. That, at least, was a blessing, I suppose. No fire, just ice.'

It all makes sense now, the atmosphere in that chilly house with the perfect kitchen and the perfect doll presiding. No wonder poor Mary hadn't wanted to invite me. My instinct is to get up out of my chair and go across to hug her to death. But I don't. Lost in her story, she has spread her hands and is gazing down at them as though checking for cracks in the skin.

'Anyway,' she continues, 'she took him back when he was discharged – she had to, really. For her, it was all about appearances. Within her circle of bridge players, she was the magnificently forgiving wife, rearing her husband's illegitimate spawn. Agreeing to adopt me: *quel héroïsme*. And there she was now, saddled with Wheelchair Man, the man who had betrayed her not once but twice. This additional burden to bear. Talk about heroic – this was epic! *Magnifique!*

'As far as the outside world was concerned, that woman was a saint. She dressed me up for Friends meetings and outings so I looked just as well cared-for as Jennifer and Naomi. What a lovely little parade, so brave! And the poor doctor in his wheelchair – such a brilliant career cut short! The three little princesses in their simple but beautiful dresses, and Jeffrey the little prince with his shoes all shined. All for show. At home, the woman blanked me.'

She looks up from her hands and, although I'm normally good at deciphering expressions, this one beats me. 'Too much information, Mags?' she asks softly.

'But why did you never tell me?'

'What could you have done? What would you have done?'

'I don't know.' I didn't.

'Remember that day you mentioned Pony Club?' she continues. 'Did I go to Pony Club too, you asked. Well, no Pony Club for me, no ballet, no tennis. Nothing the other two girls did. Why do you think I became so bookish? Why was I nearly always top of our class at school? I know that first sadist of a teacher made my life miserable, but she taught me to be resilient and not to give in. As well as that, there was some sort of connection in my life, even if it was negative. I had got under that woman's skin in some way. It was better than being ignored and I survived it. What doesn't kill you, and all the rest of it. Without knowing it, she was teaching me life skills. As for my mother, she, also without knowing it probably, was doing me the same kind of favour. She taught me how to have a life of my own without involving any of them.'

'But did your father not intervene? Surely he could see what was going on, the unfairness of it.'

'My father?' She laughed and it was not a pleasant sound. 'My father, for all his brilliant intelligence, didn't notice what was going on in his house, or maybe he did and decided to bury it. By the time he came home from the rehab place, he was already writing scholarly papers on medicine, getting published in the journals.

Nothing else mattered to him. I suppose it's understandable, really, if you think about it. He was being well cared-for, physically at least – I'll give her that much – but he stayed in his room most of every day and, except for Sunday dinner, always a big deal in our house, he didn't even eat with us.'

I'm reeling and yet, despite my shock and sympathy, both of which are genuine, my half-moribund journalistic instincts have kicked into life. What a story! You wouldn't use it as a plot for a novel because critics would deride it as incredible, but it would make a cracker of a yarn for a Sunday newspaper. I can almost see the two-page spread, the front-page pics – Alfred Hitchcock calling—

Stop it! I snap back to reality. 'I just can't believe this, Mary. I'm knocked for six. Not very Christian, is it? Not very Quaker? She could forgive him but take it out on you?'

'Funny enough,' she's looking into the fire now, and goes on slowly, as though working it out, 'when I became old enough to think for myself, I understood why she treated me differently from my half-sisters. It's obvious. I was the living embodiment of her failure to keep her husband onside, yet when you say it wasn't very Christian, it was, in practical terms. She did her Christian duty. She provided the basics for my father and me: shelter, food, clothing for both of us, education for me. The only thing she left out of her litany was "Comfort the afflicted." I knew I was going to escape some time. My father knew he couldn't.'

'And yet you're the one left looking after her? What kind of karma is that?'

'Number one, I'm not looking after her, the nursing staff are. Number two, my father's punishment for his transgressions was lifelong. She was in full control of him.'

'How did he die?'

'On the operating table. A simple thing. He was taken in to have his gall bladder out, but didn't survive the operation. It happens. Something to do with the anaesthetic.'

'But at the funeral … ' I vividly remembered her dad's funeral: the simplicity, the long silences, broken every so often when a member of the congregation stood up to share his or her thoughts on God. On life or death. On the man himself. For a Roman Catholic accustomed to defined and communal rituals, it was serene but disorienting.

'All that time, though, Mary! All those years through primary school when we talked about ourselves incessantly, all those phone calls when we were teenagers. I still can't believe you didn't tell me.'

'If you think about it,' she's wry, 'you were doing most of the talking. About the injustices you suffered because, in your house, Chloë was the pet.'

'You're right. I'm sorry.'

'Forgiven. Forgotten.' She waved airily. 'We were little kids. All kids are me-me-me.'

'I'll make it up to you, Mary.'

'For God's sake, Mags. You and your dramatics. It's water under the bridge. No need to make it up to me, as you put it. Aren't you now my honorary sister? That's something you're going to have to live up to, pal. Anyway, as I said, keeping all that to myself meant I had to become self-sufficient and I did. If you can believe this, it turned into a sort of benefit-in-kind because it became a matter of pride not to have to depend on anyone.'

'But, Mary,' I'm still trying to absorb some of the details of this amazing narrative, 'why do you go to visit that – that woman in the nursing home?' I'd been about to use the word 'monster' but managed to zip it in time. 'You can't love her.'

'Somebody has to visit. I'd be afraid she'd get no care at all, or much more casual care, if someone wasn't keeping an eye on how things were going. And, anyway, it wasn't all bad. She did adopt me. I could have been in an institution. And, believe me, with all the news about what went on in those places at the time, I appreciate that. And although it was only to Leaving Cert, the education they organised for me has stood me in good stead for a lifetime and gave me the desire to go on further. So she deserves a bit of credit. It took me a long time to see it, though.'

'I really can't get over the fact that she took him back.' I'm still mulling over the details. 'Was it because of his condition? Did she feel sorry for him or something?'

'Who's to know? Guilt? Hiding the fact that she pushed him?'

'Wouldn't he have said?'

'You didn't know him. He was probably feeling guilty about his own behaviour. And, anyway, he needed her to care for him. Which she did, again to give her some credit. I'd say the situation was extremely complex. Even if she didn't push him, her motivation to care for him might have been partly material. I think he got some insurance money – so they were in it together – and before you ask,' she had seen me take a breath and open my mouth, 'I don't know what story they concocted about why he was up a ladder at the dead of night. I did hear something in the early days about him forgetting his keys. Anyhow, Mummy would probably have calculated that she couldn't bring up four children by herself in what were straitened times in Ireland. In law, remember, I was now hers too.

'If I was being generous, some of her motivation could even

have been religious: condemn the sin, love the sinner, sort of thing. Or she might have, believe it or not, genuinely loved him underneath it all.

'A goodly portion of it, though, was definitely the martyr-stroke-heroine status she enjoyed in her circle of friends. I'll never know the whole truth. Nobody will now.' Her sigh turns into a yawn. 'And, anyhow, who can know the truth about someone else's inner thoughts and reactions? Look at you. You've forgiven Derek, haven't you? I haven't heard you going on about him for quite a while now.'

'Change of subject noted!'

'Well,' she ignores that, 'have you?'

'I had no choice, Mary. It was let it eat me up or get over it. He never offered to come back anyway, did he? He's perfectly happy with Fiona and his three little girls. I accept that or not. It's my only option now.'

'It's "Fiona" now, is it? That's progress – but would you take him back? If the circumstances were right, I mean?' Then, seeing the expression on my face, she desists. 'Sorry. Forget I asked. I'm tired.'

'It's a question that doesn't arise, Mary.' Too prim, I think.

'I know, I know. I'm just being tactless, as usual.' She yawns again. 'I'll sleep for a week. Will we go to bed? It's been quite a day. Too many questions, no answers, eh? And poor Lorna. I hope Jean is minding her.'

'I'm sure she is. Jean is stronger than she looks. And, Mary, don't be afraid. I'll mind you.'

'Come on.' Again she ignores me. 'Let's go upstairs.'

Half an hour later, when finally I get into bed, I'm glad to welcome Flora who, having decided to cede temporary ownership of her room to Mary, comes in and gives me just one wag of her tail (hi there!) before whumping against the base of the divan. Like Mary, I'm utterly beat, but I doubt I'll sleep much tonight, and the dog's steady, sturdy presence will be balm.

Tired as I am, my brain has perked into action. How badly had I let my friend down by not guessing what was going on in her house when we were children? By not probing a bit more? By being so self-centred and whiny about Chloë? But, as she said, so many questions, no answers, and absolutely no amends to be made at this remove. But I will mind her now, as I promised. I'll make up for my whingeing little self when she was young.

It does speak volumes about the depth of her fears, currently expressed or not, that her self-sufficiency had stretched to accepting my help. And even more poignant, now that I know the whole story about her childhood and her current crisis, was her earlier confession that she had asked her three siblings to come to see her. What must that have cost her?

I do wish she hadn't brought up Derek, though. Now I have to figure out if I've forgiven him.

As I lie there, thinking, with the dog snoring gently on the floor, I make a new discovery: at a certain stage, it is actually less exhausting to give up a grudge than to maintain it.

TWENTY-ONE

14 February 2013

Martin has been dead for six weeks now and it has been two weeks since his Month's Mind. Yes, before you ask, Olive had agreed to this and, to be fair, it had been a relatively positive experience. We did have the tea and sandwiches this time, in Lorna's house because Olive's is too small. The buzz was cordial, aided by the natural ebullience and interaction of all the children present. James did not attend either the Mass or the afters.

It's now a mid-February Thursday and Mary and I are at present on our way to Drogheda to meet Jean. Why is still a mystery. She wouldn't tell me when she rang last night: 'Can't talk now, but can the two of you make it?' I had nothing else on and I knew Mary was getting cabin fever so, on behalf of both of us, I agreed. 'Will Lorna be there? Dina?'

'I can't raise Dina, just her answering machine. Lorna's babysitting for Olive.'

The mystery deepened. What was so urgent that it couldn't wait until all of us were available? 'Give us a hint, Jean.'

'No hints. You'll just have to restrain yourself until tomorrow, Maggie. Isn't it great about Lorna and Olive?'

'It sure is.' The slow but steady repair of that relationship was a genuine marvel to the rest of us. 'I haven't seen her for over a week. She doing OK? And by the way, with everything that's been happening, we have no date for our next quarterly meeting. Do you think Lorna will be up for it?'

'She's so-so right now,' Jean tells me. 'She has her good days and her bad, mostly bad at the moment, unfortunately. But the grandchildren,' she adds, 'are a tonic. They keep her going. As for the date of our next meeting, I'll have a chat with her.' Although she had lowered her voice to speak about her friend, underneath she sounded bubbly, not an adjective I would normally have applied to her. 'Jean, are you sure you don't want to tell me why we're meeting tomorrow?'

'You'll see.' I had to be content with that, but as I hung up, I made a mental note to telephone Lorna. I had been so taken up with Mary I had neglected the others somewhat. But if the experience of my own bereavements – my mother and father being the closest to home – was anything to go by, Lorna was probably at the stage right now, funeral and Month's Mind complete, when the rest of the world flopped back into its own business and she most needed people around her. Although we don't, as I've explained, live in each other's pockets, we do make efforts to keep in regular touch.

Secretly, I envy her the grandchildren: they are the unspoken absences in the life of a childless woman. As a reward for the more trying times of parenting, natural parents enjoy the love and relatively stress-free delights of their children's children and this is something I will never know. Of course, I have no idea what I would have been like as a mother, but that loss is more than doubled by having no prospect of dandling grandchildren on my knee. And I think I would have been a good granny. Granny Maggie. Has a great ring to it. I don't even have a niece.

Oh, stop with the whingeing, Maggie Quinn. You have a lot to be thankful for: health, a house, a great dog, food in the pantry and, most of all, a squad of lovely friends. Cool the jets, as Dina would say.

A lot has happened since Christmas Day. It has been a very long six weeks, it seems, since Mary began her cancer treatment, four since I learned the truth and became her taxi person to take her to and from the Mater Hospital. Like Lorna's, her spirits are up and down, but that's understandable and so far she's managing the ordeal well, which is just what I would have expected. In a way, it's a help that there is a roadmap, a calendar of appointments and tests and consultations to follow. Luckily for me, chemo treatments are always on a Monday morning so our schedule can fit around my obligations to Chloë. The routine has become almost like a part-time job for both of us.

She had taken that point: 'Yeah, you're right, but it's kind of in reverse for me. I'm not actively doing anything, dammit. Everything is being done to me and for me. It feels very strange, but what is so surprising is how quickly you can fall into a routine of dependency. I'm so bloody passive, Maggie, I've become a leech.'

This had been, as you have probably guessed, on one of her down days, and before all this happened, I would have argued with her, insisting that such a negative view of herself was preposterous.

But I had learned that the better way to deal with her during this period was to act like a counsellor. So instead of taking her on, as I would have during more normal times, I had responded quietly: 'I know. It must be hard for you, of all people, Mary, to feel so dependent on others and to accept others' decisions about your body.' Trite, trite, trite – I knew it, she knew it, glancing at me with eyes narrowed as though spoiling for a fight – but because you can't fight Pollyanna without making yourself look bad, she had withdrawn the claws.

In theory she could have continued to work, although there would have been a kerfuffle about sick pay and so forth, to which, in law, I thought she should have been entitled. But she had decided simply to take a sabbatical from the shelter.

She is still mulling over the issue of dependency: 'I do hate this position, as I said, but if I'm honest, in some ways I probably needed a reality check. It's the first time I've ever realised that a person can become too independent, you know, Mags. I suppose it has given me time to assess everything. I've realised the hard way that, in one second, my life and the way I live it can turn 180 degrees on a five-cent copper coin. And another thing: I'm very committed to the shelter, as you know, but now I think I've probably been working there for too long. The misery is getting to me. It was anyway, long before this.' She thumped her chest as though it was the seat of her illness. 'Maybe it's time to rethink. I don't want to let down the people who do such fantastic work, but they'll be managing without me anyway for a few months. We'll see what happens. Maybe it's time to let those waters close over me.'

She still takes shifts on the low-stress reception desk in her dentist's surgery. Although that's cash-in-hand (don't tell the

Revenue!), what she gets paid there does not come close to covering her rent. Mary has always lived frugally, however, and she does have some savings, so I'm not all that worried about her on that score. Not yet. She had a quiet word with her landlady, who lives on the ground floor of the house, and the woman, knowing what a solid meal ticket she'd enjoyed for the guts of fifteen years, has told her not to worry about it for the present and, believe it or not, even halved the rent, '"Until you're well again, Mary"! Wasn't that really good of her?' Surprised by the woman's generosity, Mary had been touched. 'People do step up to the plate, eh?'

They do, I assured her, sometimes. But I also reminded her that she had deserved such consideration: she had been a great tenant. The woman was wise not to want to lose her.

It's late morning and we're northbound on the M1, about, I'd say, thirty kilometres or so from Dublin, on our way to meet Jean. We're in the middle of another argument about Mary's hair. I don't want her to shave it off, not yet, but she's determined: 'Every morning it's like waking up on a bear's chest. There's chunks of it all over my pillow! I'm not listening to you any more, Maggie. I'm going to the hairdresser tomorrow and that's that. I can't look any worse than the half-baldy freak I am now.' She puts a hand up to her head, pulls, and a long, thick strand comes away in her fingers, leaving an open patch of pale scalp. 'See?' She brandishes it under my nose. 'Like a dog with mange!'

'OK – enough, enough!' I give in. 'It's your hair. I'll be sorry to see it go but sure it'll grow again. Oh, here's the exit.' Just in time, I turn off where Jean had indicated. When going to Drogheda I like to drive across the Boyne Bridge, further on, especially at night. I'd love to know whose idea it was to light it up like a Christmas tree. I defy anyone to cross that bridge and not experience a mood lift.

'You feeling all right, Mary?' I ask her now. 'Not sick or anything like that?' I'm sneakily enjoying my triple role as companion, nurse and chauffeur, and Mary's uncharacteristic compliance with my advice and bossy oversight of her daily life. She hasn't become meek, that would have been too much of an aberration, but these days she goes along with virtually everything I suggest. Was this, I had wondered more than once, how it felt to be a mother?

'I'm fine. Never better.' Her tone is dry.

'I wonder what she wants to see us about.' We're buzzing through Julianstown now. 'She tried to get Dina. Lorna probably knows already, whatever it is. I hope it's not bad news. She didn't sound depressed, though, on the contrary.'

'Probably wants a donation for a one-legged camel shelter in Egypt.' Her illness has not extinguished Mary's mordant sense of humour.

Jean had given me directions to where we were to meet on the south side of Drogheda town. On the way we passed one of the sights of Ireland at this time of year: acres of commercially grown daffodils, just about coming into flower. There are some for sale at the farm gate and, impulsively, I stop and buy an enormous armful: twenty euro buys me twenty-four bunches of the little buggers; I'll give Mary and Jean a third each, keep a third for myself. I absolutely adore daffodils, harbingers of hope and sunshine to come. 'Some of these are for you, Mary.' I toss the lot onto the back seat.

'Christ, you've made me cry again now.' She bursts into tears as she roots violently for a tissue in her handbag. That has been happening a lot lately; her emotions are very close to the surface, probably, we're told, as a consequence not only of her plight but of the stuff being pumped into her system. I'm used to these emotional outbursts and don't get upset except when she blurts something that makes me wonder if she really is on the way out.

Less than a quarter of an hour after leaving the motorway, Jean's daffodils at the ready, my charge and I are seated in a little coffee shop, attached to a bakery to judge by the array of unusual scones (Parmesan and caramelised red onion, anyone?) and sinfully beckoning cakes. It seems to specialise in the colour red. Among the butter icing and cakes in full wedding livery, there are heart-shaped cakes, buns and biscuits, even a pile of heart-shaped loaves. Probably Danish. They go in for that kind of thing. A very romantic place, anyway, not very Jean-like.

Once seated, I pretended I needed something from the car. The 'something' was the hank of hair Mary had pulled out and left on the floor, now safely wrapped in a tissue and in my handbag.

The shop has two seating areas to the right and left of the entrance doors, and with Mary behind me, I had headed for the area on the right so hadn't spotted Jean in situ at the lefthand side. When I got back in, she was standing in front of Mary. 'Thanks for coming up. We've a table on the other side – will you join us?'

'I thought the others weren't coming? These are for you, by the way.' I give her the flowers.

'Oh!' She seems taken aback. 'You're too good, Maggie.'

'Just a few from the roadside. No big deal.'

'You robbed them from the motorway?' She's alarmed now, then, hastily: 'That came out wrong. It's just that I didn't see they were out yet.'

'Jean! As if!' The picture of myself, hazard lights flashing on the hard shoulder as I brave the whizzing traffic to pluck daffodils from the meridian, is almost comical. 'Of course I didn't.'

Then, talk about surprise! At the table to which she's obviously

286

headed – it's a small place – is a man who stands up on seeing us approach. He's not one of her sons. 'This is Jerry,' she says, and I'd swear she's blushing. 'He's one of the truck drivers for the convoys.' Her voice flutes as she gazes up at him. 'We've known each other for a year.'

Jean? Little Jean? Of the knitting and the perms and the pearls without which I have never seen her even when waving her off on one of Adi Roche's convoys. 'A year an' a half,' the man corrects her affectionately. He's big, at least three or four inches taller than I am – and burly, with a fisherman's or farmer's ruddy complexion. His tie might be strangling him because even as he's shaking hands with Mary and me, he's inserting a finger of the other hand behind his collar, pulling it away from his neck. 'Nice daffydils.' He nods towards the flowers and in his mouth, the mispronunciation sounds tender.

We all sit down. They're clearly an item but, of course, the first thing I see is an image of the two of them in bed. The missionary position? She'd be toast! In case she's thinking the same thing, I don't dare meet Mary's eyes.

For me, however, the penny has dropped: Jean's unusually loquacious form on Christmas Day? The bad language – she had called Olive a bitch, I seem to remember. Her spirited confrontations with others on behalf of Lorna – she'd referred to Mary as 'pointy-headed' – and hadn't she said something about not kicking James McAlinden out of bed? Talk about coming out of her knitter's nest! I think I remarked on it at the time but had put it down to the drink and had forgotten it until now.

'I've been wanting to tell you for ages,' she dives in when we've settled, 'but with James there on Christmas Day, then poor Lorna and Martin – and I didn't want to land Jerry on your doorstep without an invitation, and it's not the kind of thing you tell someone on the phone, now, is it? Anyway, I did want you to meet him in person – you can take that tie off now, Jerry,' she interrupts herself, laying her tiny hand on his huge one, and while he hacks gratefully at the knot, she resumes: 'I wanted to give you plenty of notice. You see, Jerry has a motor home—'

'It's only a camper van, really.' He's still pulling at the tie. 'I built her on the chassis of one of the lorries' – he pronounces it 'lurries' – 'but she goes like a train and she's comfortable enough. Jean likes her anyway, doncha, love?'

'This is the thing. This is what I couldn't tell you on the phone. Oh, you tell them, Jerry.' Eyes shining, Jean settles back into her seat to enjoy our reaction to what's coming next.

'OK,' he goes. 'Well, ya see, me and Jeanie here are havin' a year off. We're takin' the ferry to France and, with the help o' God, you won't see us again for a year!' He pronounces it 'yee-arr'. 'So what d'ya think of that, girls?'

He beams at us and again I have to refrain from looking at Mary. Whatever about being ironic among ourselves, it's been a very long time since I was called a girl by someone else, and I'm sure the same applies to Mary. 'That's amazing.' I really mean it. 'I had no idea.'

'Dah's right ['ri-att']. We're goin' travellin'.' He's still gazing at her with an expression not far short of adoration. 'Like little Willie Nelson. Except it's nuttin' to do wit' de Cihy of Noo Orle-ans, we're off in the van. It's France,' he begins counting off on his fingers, 'it's Spain, it's It'ly, it's Greece and Albania and Montenegro an' de Baltic. We'll be in Pehersburg midsummer for dem whih nihs.'

'Do you know that during the white nights they never have to turn on the streetlights? Can you just imagine that?' Jean, transfigured, butts in, then, to him: 'Sorry, love. Go ahead.'

'Den it's a bih of a trek t'rough Russia and back t'rough Lapland and Finland and Sweden.' In little curves, he's running one finger through the air as though following a map he sees in his mind. 'We're goin' to stay nort' for the Nordern Ligh's in Norway and den Scandinavia and Germany and Holland buh we're goin' ta skip Belgium.' Like a child, he makes zigzag gestures with both fists on an imaginary steering wheel. 'Scooh right t'rough it. We're noh interested ['inther-eshted'] in Belgium. Thah righ', Jeanie?' She nods in enthusiastic agreement. He drops his steering wheel again to renew the battle with his tie. 'An' sometimes it'll be ferries and sometimes we'll have to leave de Lady Jean ashore to take a smaller boah.'

'That'll be in the Scottish Highlands.' Excitedly, she takes up the running again. 'I've always wanted to see the Highlands, the Mull of Kintyre, Skye and Iona and – and, oh, everything! And that's what he's called the van, the Lady Jean. He's painted it on the bonnet! Isn't that lovely? We've it all planned. He has the maps all ready and marked and he's programmed the satnav.'

Little and Large, Mutt and Jeff, they're as excited as a pair of junior infants bound for Disneyland. I don't want to sound in any way patronising but it's lovely to see.

'Jaysus!' he explodes, wrenching at the tie. 'Dis bloody t'ing! Sorry, girls, for de curse words.'

'Here, let me.' Jean stands up and, nimble fingers to the rescue, undoes the offending article and sits down again.

'T'anks, love.' He smiles down at her. Even sitting, he is impressively large. His chair is spindly. I hope it can hold him. 'She's a greah girl, isn't she?' He turns his smile on Mary and me. It's impossible to resist and I find myself grinning back as widely as a delighted baby.

I'm astonished, but genuinely happy for both of them. 'Does Lorna know you're going away, Jean?'

'She knows we're going but she doesn't know when. We've been taking her into consideration, of course we have. She knows about Jerry, but I swore her to secrecy because I didn't want all the gossips cackling on about it until I was sure he wasn't after my money, like some people we all know! Sorry, Jerry.' She turns to him and gives him a little puck, like a child pucking a dray horse. 'That's an inside joke. No offence!'

'None taken.' He continues to grin.

I hadn't even thought irony to be one of Jean's talents. The woman continues to surprise. No more than the rest of us, she hasn't a bean.

'Anyway,' she turns back to us and, earnestly now, 'we've talked about it and we're not going right away. We were originally planning to go on the first of this month, St Brigid's Day. Spring, all the rest of it. I love spring, don't you? Then, when Martin died, we changed it to May because I hoped that by then Lorna and Olive will be proper pals, but she's so down in herself that we've now decided to go on the twenty-seventh of July. We tried for earlier that month but the ferries were all full. What recession, eh? So I'll be still here and able to wish you a happy birthday, Maggie!'

'I hope you're not staying just because of that!' My birthday is on 22 July.

'No, it's for Lorna. To give her a real chance. I know the rest of you in the Club will look out for her but she and I are best pals and we want to give her a decent chance to get used to the idea that I won't be popping in all the time. Isn't that right, Jerry?'

He nods. 'The ferry people were understandin'. They didn't mind the change. I've been a good customer for years.'

'But you're not going to vanish from our lives for a full year, Jean, are you?'

'Of course not. Well … ' she considers '… all going well,' she makes a fervent sign of the cross, 'we won't be back in Ireland, please God, for a full year, but don't worry, we'll have our mobile phones. Jerry's used to travelling off pissed—'

'Off piste, love.' Then he winks at us, his big face creasing merrily. '"Off pissed". She's greah crack, isn't she?'

This would be sickening if it wasn't so adorable. (Can't believe I said that. I take it back.)

'Yeah, whatever.' Jean waves airily. 'Jerry'll be looking after all of the official stuff. He knows how to Skype and everything. He has a little camera on his laptop and if you get one on yours, Maggie, we'll be able to talk to the whole Club in your house on Christmas Day.'

Mary and I look at each other. It had probably occurred to her, as it just had to me, that with Jean off the roster as well as Lorna, probably, that left just Dina, herself and me. Not much of a gathering.

I couldn't bear to ruin Jean's obvious excitement, though. 'Of course. We could change it for 2014. Jerry, you could come too, and maybe we could all go to Lorna's. She could have Olive and her grandchildren there too. Like a real big Christmas. You can't control what's going to happen and it's still only February. Who knows what's going to happen between now and next December? But,' I include him, 'I'm really thrilled for you both. It's terrific, isn't it, Mary? This calls for extra special coffees all round.' I start to get up but Jean's boyfriend (manfriend?) reaches across the little table and puts his Great Dane paw on my shoulder. 'Siddown there for yerself, Maggie, girl. I'll go up. You stay here, girls, and have a bih of a nahher. I'm sure ye have a lot to talk abou'. Coffee for everyone? And a few of dem nice-lookin' fairy cakes, mebbe?'

'That would be lovely, Jerry,' Mary says demurely, the first time she has uttered a word since coming in. Before getting out of the car, she had wound a scarf, turban-style, around her diminished hair, but it suits her. In fact she looks like an extension of her flat: rug-sized, the scarf is one of several jewel-coloured head coverings she had bought in an ethnic shop in Moore Street and is probably of African origin. It is a dusky pink with a swirling emerald green pattern and lights up her face. She has not taken off her coat. Perhaps because of her treatments, she feels cold even when she's sitting at her own fireside.

Jean waits until her beau is out of earshot before leaning across the table. 'I was dying to tell you all at Christmas, but then Lorna brought James and she was so upset and it didn't seem right, somehow. Please won't you mind her?'

'We will, won't we, Mary?'

'Yeah.'

'Oh, Mary.' Jean's eyes widened with remorse. 'You must think we're so awful. Here we are going on and on about our big adventure and we never asked you how you were. How are you? I haven't seen you since I found out about your troubles. How's the treatment going?' Mary had lifted her gagging order, relenting the day after she'd imposed it (goes to show how unusually distracted she is) so the other three in our Club had been filled in on what's happening in her life.

'It's going. That's all I can say. And thank you for asking. It means a lot ... ' Mary hesitates. 'But, Jean, this guy, what's his background? He's nice and all, I'll grant you, but how well do you know him? It's one thing the two of you travelling across Europe

292

to bring help to the afflicted, but there are plenty of other people in a convoy. It'll be just you and him for a year in a confined space. You might start irritating each other after a bit. Everyone needs personal space. Everyone gets on everyone's nerves, no matter how much in love they are. It's his van after all. Do you trust him enough not to dump you somewhere in Siberia after a row, leaving you to walk home? Do you believe he'll protect you in some of those very dangerous places you'll be going through? He mentioned Albania, for instance. Have you any idea what's going on there these days?'

'Jerry? You're talking about Jerry?' Jean, genuinely amused, laughs her little silvery laugh. 'Mary, I know the world. I'm fifty-nine years old.'

'Exactly. He could see you as desperate. Last gasp and all the rest of it?'

'Give over, Mary. The chap seems lovely.' I think her innate cynicism is getting to her. To me, that huge guy is on the level.

'Thanks, Maggie.' But Jean is gazing compassionately at our friend. 'Like me, Jerry has a grown-up family, Mary. He's a widower. He knows I've nothing except my pension and the few pound I have left in my savings. He knows I don't own the place where I live. I've met his kids – they're all married and settled and they like me. They don't want us to do this. Their idea is for us to go on a cruise. They think their dad works too hard. One of his sons is a consultant gynaecologist and he says he'll pay for any cruise we want. The Caribbean, the South Seas, anywhere. No way, José. I'd be bored out of my tree.'

'What about your own family, Jean? How do they feel about this?' Mary persists.

'They're delighted. My sons are anyway – I don't give a hoot about the wives, as you know, although in fairness, they seem to have fallen in with the general excitement. Maybe this will sort us all out. As for the kids, they can't believe their luck at Jerry's being a truck driver. He's promised them a little overnight trip in the camper with us before we go away for real.' She pauses for breath. Then, chin jutting: 'It must be awful for you, Mary, what's happened to you. I know you must be suffering and I'm really sorry for you, but do you have to see the worst in everyone?'

'No. Only in people who might harm my friends.' Mary locks eyes with her and I can see that Jean is searching for a suitable riposte but I am the only one who has noticed that Jerry, having ordered our coffee, is just a foot away and must have heard what Mary last said.

He doesn't sit down and the grin is gone. 'I'm a professional trucker,' he says softly, addressing her, 'and it's true dat people like me get lonely on de road and a few of us don' have all dat greah a reputation. But I love dis woman, Mary. She's de first woman I can say dat abou' since my own wife died. And as far as doin' Jeanie harm ['harr-um'] you can sleep aisy in your bed. I'm goin' to marry her.'

Jean nearly falls off the chair.

He catches her and, when he's sure she's stable, picks up one of her hands. Right in front of Mary and me, the two astonished servers behind the counter and the three elderly and now open-mouthed women at the next table, he lowers his considerable bulk to one knee. But because he's so big and the space so limited, he bumps against the table, rocking and threatening to overturn it.

Still on his knee, he drops Jean's hand, steadies the table, takes her hand again. 'I was goin' to do dis in Paris but now's as good a time as any wih your friends here as wihnesses. Jean McKenna, on dis Valentine's Day tew t'ousand and t'irtee-an, will you do me de greah honour of agreein' to becomin' my wife?'

Valentine's Day? Of course. How had I missed that? Because I'm a sad person, that's how, so sad I had even been blind to the plethora of hearts and rosy redness in here.

Nobody else here had been so myopic. When Jean leaps to her feet and throws herself against him, almost knocking him over, despite her slightness, the applause at first ripples politely and then becomes raucous all over the shop, which is, except for the man on one knee, populated this morning entirely by women. Mary bursts into tears again. Jean is already in tears. Jerry is in tears. I am having difficulty keeping myself in check. But the three elderly ladies beside us totter to their feet and cheer. Throughout that café, the smiles could have powered a small town.

TWENTY-TWO

25 February 2013

A dull day, with a fine net of drizzle.

It's bang on eight o'clock in the morning when I drop Mary off outside the Mater where she's due to undergo her fifth round of chemotherapy. As she gets out of my car, she is carrying her 'chemo bag'; its contents include woolly socks and slippers because her feet get cold, tissues, moisturiser and sucky sweets to take away the metallic tang on her tongue arising from the toxins. This morning's headscarf, cherry red with blobs of violet and purple, is vibrant, even a little gaudy, a brave little banner of battle against the effects of the chemo, which is beginning to bite. She had a short but unpleasant reaction after her last dose and they can't promise it won't happen again or at what intensity. Her hair has all gone now: she got the last of it shaved last Friday and is as bald as a stone. She professes not to care but I don't believe her. If she doesn't care, why is she so assiduously covering her scalp with such colour?

I think I am more upset about her hair than she is, although I haven't said it to her and certainly wouldn't now. To me that hair had defined her, reflecting the steady, valiant fire burning in her soul. Without it, and despite the bright scarves, to the eponymous man- or woman-in-the-street I would imagine that she is just another average, middle-aged woman: invisible. As for me, I'm not invisible, just overlookable. I still see men giving me the once-over, but fleetingly: That'd be some challenge. Then, on looking closer: Ah, here! Too many miles on the clock.

As I watch my friend go up the steps without a backward glance, like a mother seeing her infant off to school, I have to swallow hard. What is it with me these days? I think, pulling away to find a place to park. I've gone soft.

The new Mater car park is full this morning. Since it opened, the area around the hospital is a little easier to negotiate and I have developed a pattern.

Engine running and flashers on, I double-park at the top of Eccles Street, wait for someone to ease out of a space somewhere further up, then drive like hell to get to it first. That usually works, my little tin-can being such a pitiable little vehicle that (a) it can get into a half-space and (b) to others, it's clearly being driven by one of those batty old ladies who arouse either chivalry or wariness. ('Let's give her the space, Harry, you'd never know what she'd do.')

When I get into the Day Oncology Unit, Mary has already been hooked up. Even on dull days such as this, the room is bright. It is referred to as twelve-bedded, but to my eyes, the 'bed' in which Mary sits is a sort of recliner.

The first time I came here with her, I was expecting a funereal, almost mortuary-like ambience and was petrified – until we got into the room where first impressions were that, leaving the drips and medical devices aside, this could be a hobby shop or activity centre.

I know that sounds trite but it's what I saw. With specialised nurses moving among them, quietly checking monitors and drips, patients were reading, knitting, poring over books of crosswords, Sudoku or other puzzles. Two, eyes closed, listened to iPods; the thumbs of a youth, aged about eighteen, I'd guess, flew over the screen of some kind of games gadget while he studiously ignored his mother beside him, quietly embroidering a cushion cover. There was one patient there that first day from a species I now characterise as Laptop Man: those who, along with being tied to their cannulas and poison-dripping tubes, wish to stay tethered to their careers.

Mary's overall attitude remains positive: 'If I didn't think this was going to work I wouldn't do it, Mags.' Being her, she has researched all the alternatives, or as many as she could find in a plethora of medical studies and reports, and it has all come down to this. It is awe-inspiring to me that someone as analytical and independent as Mary has been able to put her trust so completely in the expertise of strangers. I'm not sure I could – but, mind you, I don't have cancer.

We have as usual been among the first to arrive and so far there are only five other patients here this morning, including a Laptop Man. 'Right,' I say to her now, pulling up a chair beside her apparatus. 'Got a parking space first thing. Must be my lucky day.'

'Mine too. Another Monday. After this only three more Mondays, six more weeks, and we're done with it.'

She's one of the readers in here so her entertainment, the Kindle I gave her for Christmas, is already to hand. Little did I know to what use it would be put; she did, of course, and I still find it hard to forgive her for not confiding in me.

I flash a smile around the room. Relationships within this room are a little surreal, with numbers and constituents constantly in flux and, like an avenging angel with wings folded – for now – the Big C hovering over us all. There is chat, some laughter, even ribaldry occasionally, and it is possible, I suppose, that the person sitting in the chair-bed next to you could become a lifelong friend because of shared experiences, but somehow I doubt it. I haven't bonded, for instance, with the mother of the teenaged boy with the games gadget, although she is probably of the same age or thereabouts and quite friendly. I don't want to. I want this just to be over. Similarly, if I were one of these patients, I think I would want to get back to my 'real' life and the people in it as quickly as possible.

I lean into Mary. 'I'm going to nip into town for an hour or so as soon as the shops open. You'll be OK here?'

She nods. 'Anything exciting in mind?'

I glance around the room to make sure no one is eavesdropping but they're all engrossed in their own business. 'Well, yes, not exciting but specific.' I lower my voice: 'This morning, when I was getting dressed, I stood in front of the bedroom mirror wearing only my underwear. I don't do that often, too gruesome. Anyway, I did this morning, and maybe it's because of you and your hair and the poison going into your body and all the rest of it, but anyhow, for the first time in months, maybe years, I saw myself properly. You know how that can happen? Like when you're passing a shop window and you catch the reflection of yourself without having had time to put on your mirror face or, indeed, mirror body.'

'Let me guess. You're going for a makeover? Left it a bit late, haven't you?'

'Yeah, right.' I take a deep breath. 'Lookit, I'm going for a bra fitting. The first one I've ever had. I was really shocked when I saw myself in that mirror. The ugly bras I buy for comfort? So secure. So old-lady! And the sensible white cotton knickers I buy five-to-a-pack in Tesco? I looked like an Eastern European shot-putter, no offence to any of them. It's time I did something about it. By the way, did you know what the word for "bra" is in German?'

'No. But I'm sure you're going to tell me.'

'*Büstenhalter*. Doesn't that say it all? Certainly describes my collection of orthopaedic aids.'

She raises an eyebrow. 'Jean and Jerry and their love-in on Valentine's Day got to you, then?'

'No. Of course not.' But I had been oddly unsettled lately. It had occurred to me that Mary's cancer had wreaked havoc with all the suppositions and acceptances of my own life. But she hadn't been the only one, had she, who had kept her private life private during the Christmas just past? Jean too. She had said her relationship with her beau had been going on for a good while. And Lorna had kept her secrets. Am I the only one in our Club who blurts it all out? What's going on with Dina, for instance? Must give her a call and unleash a bit of the third degree.

Now, however, is not the time to whine at Mary. 'Let's face it, isn't the thing with Jean and Jerry just marvellous in it's own, er, unusual way?' Then I can't resist it: 'Do you think they've already done it?'

'Of course they have. Don't be ridiculous.'

'God! That picture of them in bed together – can you just imagine it?'

'Talk about *Raiders of the Lost Ark*. Will he find it, will he not?'

'Mary!' I'm shocked, but I'm having to suppress a giggle. We've been talking in subdued tones but I shoot another glance around the room. All calm. Nobody's paying us any attention.

'Personally, I'd prefer not to think about it, thank you very much.' Mary slides the switch on the end of her Kindle, but as the device obediently flickers into life, she grins.

'You're awful!'

'So are you. That picture of you, all six foot of you in your orthopaedic bra and sensible knickers, is not something that's going to leave me in a hurry. But, please, don't go the whole hog with thongs or red satin frillies. Ugh!' She pulls a face. 'Couldn't stand thinking of you poncing about in ridiculous underwear just so you can look good in your bedroom mirror. Moment of truth, old friend. You'd look like an ageing totem pole. And, anyway, who's interested?'

'Thanks for the vote of confidence.'

'That's what friends are for – no one else would tell you and, anyway, no one can fight with me. I'm a poor cancer victim! Now, if you don't mind … ' She depresses the page turner on the side of her machine and, within a millisecond, is absorbed.

I open my own novel, but as I settle into it, from across the room there's a tinny blast of orchestral music; the ear buds of Laptop Man opposite have slipped out and fallen to the floor, taking his iPod with them. 'Sorry, ladies.' He smiles at the two of us while reaching for it but, because of the restraining cables and drip deliveries, can't get to it. 'Here, let me.' I stand up, retrieve the thing and hand it back to him. 'There you go, no worries.' He thanks me and I go back to Mary's side. That had been a good illustration of how this place is fuelled – alert politeness among all parties.

Over the next hour or so, Mary and I read our books, and when it's time for me to slip away, the pace of activity has increased and the room is nearly full. 'Won't be long.' I touch her forearm. 'You all right?'

'Fine.' At first she doesn't look up from her little screen, then, with a wry expression, 'Never better!'

I won't go into too much humiliating detail of what it felt like to have my naked, sagging, differently sized breasts – left bigger than right – measured and assessed with narrow eyes by a stout woman using her tape like a weapon. 'Don't worry, Margaret,' she murmured, first names being apparently de rigueur in lingerie fitting rooms. 'Most real women are lopsided.'

I hadn't been worried. Until then.

Maybe it's routine to most women, but I found it deeply embarrassing to be left, literally, to hang out while the woman, tape now around her neck, bustled in and out of the fitting room with bunches of brassieres drooping like wilting lilies from her hands. She didn't let her tut-tuts out for air but, like a flock of disapproving crows, they flapped over her head, cawing at my arrant stupidity in choosing to wear garments so unbelievably wrongly sized. Let's just say that now I know what size I should have been buying for the past forty years, I won't be going through this ordeal again. I accept two of the cheapest specimens she has suggested, pay the cashier, and flee from the shop.

At least the drizzle has stopped, if only temporarily: the sky remains low and threatening. I pull the collar of my anorak up around my mouth and, head low, hurry back towards the relative safety of the Day Oncology Unit.

I'm going up the steps towards the glass doors of the hospital when, hand outstretched to pull one towards me, I can see a man coming across the lobby towards them. He's wearing a well-cut dark suit and an open-necked white shirt. He's ten feet away and closing fast. Shocked, I withdraw my hand, but it's too late. He has seen me. It's Derek.

I haven't clapped eyes on, let alone met him, for many years. I don't want to meet him now but there's no way to avoid it.

'Maggie!'

'Derek!' I'm conscious of my worn jeans and jacket – and of the pink shopping bag I'm carrying with its coy, girly logo under the pink satin ribbon. I've waited for him to emerge and we're just outside the door but the hospital is busy this morning and, to keep access clear, we now have to perform an awkward sideways shuffle on to the concrete wheelchair ramp beside the doors.

The shirt is of heavy linen, I can see. I have also seen his eyes dart to the underwear bag.

'How are you, Derek?' I am civil but curt. My instinct is still to get away from here as quickly as possible.

'Getting there. Look, it's starting to rain again.' He glances up at the sky. 'Have you time for a coffee? I'll buy.'

Patronising prat, I think. I can afford to pay for my own coffee. But rather than appear childish, I peer ostentatiously at my watch. 'I suppose I have a few minutes for a quick one. Thank you.'

We go inside and into the hospital coffee shop just inside the doors. 'This is a present for the person I'm visiting.' I indicate the pink bag before dumping the bloody thing beside the leg of the table and sit down.

'So?' He's still standing.

'I just thought I saw you looking at it.'

'None of my business, surely, who you buy underwear for, Maggie.'

'No, of course not. I just thought …' I'm flustered. 'Look, this is a bad idea.' I pick up the shiny bag again and get to my feet. 'I have to go.'

'You have five minutes, Maggie. Everyone has five minutes. Or are you afraid?'

'Of course not.'

'Good. Is it coffee or tea?'

'Coffee.'

'Right. Sit down again. Take it easy, Dumpy, it's just a cup of coffee.' I flinch at his use of the diminutive. He searches my expression and then, without further comment, goes up to the counter.

What the hell am I doing, sitting here? Then I remember the *détente* I myself engendered with my Christmas card. As he had said, it's only coffee. I watch as he waits for the cups to be filled. He seems to have lost a bit of weight, or else the suit is handmade for him and is very good at disguising his chef's belly. Confirmation he's doing fine.

When he comes back with the two cups and sits down, I occupy myself with pouring milk into mine and then, carefully, very slowly, dissolving two packets of sugar into it. I don't take sugar.

He's the one who breaks the awkwardness: 'Who are you visiting?'

'Mary Guerin. You remember her?'

'Ah, yes, the Virgin Queen! Sorry, but that's how I think of her. I have no idea about the virginity part of course.'

'Don't be disgusting, Derek!'

304

'The queen bit certainly fits, though. She didn't like me one bit and, boy, did she let me know it!'

'She's a brilliant friend, Derek. She's been a wonderful support for me all through these years since you—'

'I was wondering when we'd get around to what a fucking bastard I am – speaking of which, how's Chloë these days?'

'Remember where you are.' I look over my shoulder to see who's heard. No one has, it appears. 'Keep your language for your kitchen.'

'Were you always so pompous?'

'Were you always so crass and vulgar?'

We glare at each other but somehow, having vented, the tension has dissipated. 'Sorry. I'm sorry, Maggie.' He visibly relaxes. 'Your friends are your friends and I know, to my cost, how loyal Mary is.'

'I'm sorry too. It's just such a shock seeing you. You were coming out. Were you seeing a consultant?'

'What makes you ask that?'

'The good suit. The linen shirt.'

'Mm. Still sharp, I see. Yes.' He stirs his coffee. 'I was seeing a consultant. He wants me to have tests.'

'They all want you to have tests these days. They're afraid they'll miss something and you'll sue them. I read something somewhere about the huge numbers of unnecessary tests being performed. What tests are you having? Don't tell me if you don't want to, I'm just curious.'

How many times had I used the words 'tests' there? Maybe Mary was right and Jean had affected me, so much so I was channelling her speech patterns. 'I'm just curious,' I repeat.

'Stomach trouble. And, yes, I have been eating my own food.' He grins.

He's always had an infectious smile and I relax. A little. 'Chloë's doing fine. Everything is working well. Thank God for Merrow House.'

'Are the finances OK there? I could maybe up the money I give you?'

'No, thanks. We're fine.' I gaze at him. 'Money was never the problem, was it? But let's not go there.'

'You're right. Let's not.' He lowers his head so I can't read his expression.

'Look, Derek, I hope, and this is sincere, the tests go well for you. I'm sure they will. You look in the pink anyhow. How are the girls? And Fiona?' To slow myself down, I take a mouthful of the coffee, so sickly sweet I almost gag – and I've put so much milk in it that it's barely lukewarm. And had I said 'in the pink'? Talk about drawing attention to the bag at my feet.

Why does what Derek thinks, or observes, or comments upon matter one whit, for goodness' sake?

It matters because it's underwear, I answer my own question. He had seen me so many times in my underwear. He liked to take it off, slowly, with his sensitive chef's fingers. He had liked to uncover my breasts, one at a time, then turn me over to uncover my bottom, turning me back—

'They're grand. The girls are growing up real fast.' He raises his head again and drinks, then grimaces and puts down the cup with more force than necessary. 'There's no reason why hospitals should serve slop like this. With the machines on the market these days, it's possible, you know, to offer a decent cup of coffee. It's not rocket science. And, by the way, thank you for the card.'

'Thanks for yours. It was nice. The robin, I mean.' I'm glad to be discussing cards and robins. What the hell is up with me today? Sitting down with him was a mistake. A very bad mistake.

'Robin – I know what you meant, Maggie. What's wrong with Mary?'

'Cancer.'

'That's rough. Is she having chemo?'

'That's what's happening right now. It takes hours. This is her fifth dose and she's relaxed enough, happy to read and so on, so sometimes, rather than sit there, boring her with my tittle-tattle, I take advantage of being in town to do a bit of shopping. For her, of course. The present is for her.'

I'm gabbling again.

'Of course. You told me that already, Maggie. Although, unless she's changed, she wouldn't have struck me as the type for frivolous underwear.'

'How do you know it's frivolous?' Rather than being defensive, I'm becoming annoyed now. 'And define "frivolous".'

'Still the wordsmith, I see.' And then: 'I know it's underwear,' he says, with a smile I can't interpret: nostalgic? Sad? Even a little bitter? 'I know exactly what type of underwear that shop sells because Fiona used to buy hers there. Sometimes I used to buy it for her, for Valentine's, Mother's Day, that kind of thing.'

This is absolutely none of my business. It could even be considered a little sick for me to be discussing his mistress's underwear with the man who is still, after all, officially my husband, but there has been an undertone to this that I don't understand. 'She doesn't like the place any more? Was there a falling-out or something? Or did she just go off the kind of stuff they stock?'

'The falling-out is between me and her. We're in the middle of separating.'

'But the Christmas card?' I'm shocked. 'That was just two months ago. It was from all five of you.'

'It was from me. I just happened to call into the house to collect my post on the day it arrived and I recognised your handwriting among the cards on the mat. She wasn't in, so I took it. I didn't want you to know, Maggie. I couldn't bear the thought of you gloating about it – although you'd be entitled to – but now that you do know, you might as well know the whole story. I moved out last September.'

TWENTY-THREE

27 February 2013

I haven't told Mary about meeting Derek. Not yet. I'm not ready for her take, sensible and grounded as it would be, on what happened in that hospital coffee shop two days ago. Most of all, I don't want her advice about how I should be reacting.

That's what I don't want.

It's harder to know what I do.

This morning, while driving Chloë and her iPad Mini between Merrow and the house – she had spent the whole journey tapping on the thing – I was debating whether or not to ring her and come clean, just to break the ice before we met again in the afternoon. After all, I had excoriated her for keeping momentous secrets, and here was I, all wound up inside because of one conversation I had had with my not-officially-ex-husband.

Sorry to be going on like this, but we're going to see Mary's mother later today and I doubt I'll be able to spend that time with her without Mary noticing how distracted I am. Although, in my favour, she herself is fearful about this visit. She has not been to the nursing home since she started the chemo and is very guilty about that. 'It's not her I worry about, Mags, it's the staff. She recognises me only once in a blue moon anyway, and I don't think she'd notice if I never came, but my fear is that the staff will capitalise on my neglect, and will bump her lower down the priority list.'

'I'm sure they wouldn't do that.'

'Well, you read all that stuff in the newspapers, tying patients to their bed and even hitting them.'

It's unusual to find Mary so fretful but, as I've said, she has shown peaks of anxiety recently and I've learned to let them pass without trying all the time to take her emotional temperature. 'That's all in the past,' I soothed, operating in a vacuum, of course, because I do not have a clue about any of this. My only personal experience of institutions or 'facilities' is Merrow, a place that does not house geriatric patients and is too new to have any permanent residents who are even remotely close to reaching that status. I suppose time will tell what happens to them, but Chloë is far from being near that front line and I'm assuming, like Dickens's Mr Micawber, that Something Will Turn Up. Welcome, Poverty! Welcome, Misery! Welcome, Homelessness, Hunger, Rags, Tempest and Beggary! Mutual confidence will sustain us to the end!

That's me.

By the time we had reached the house, I was still no nearer deciding whether or not to spill the beans.

As usual, I had taken Flora with me to pick up Chloë and when the three of us get into the house, they both perform their little rituals: Chloë thumping the door jamb, Flora acting as tour guide. 'Let's have a cup of tea,' my sister suggests. I agree, a little reluctantly. Before going out again to fetch Mary, I had been hoping to finish a piece for the *Irish Daily Mail*, a paper that, unlike some other newspapers, pays promptly and quite well; its deadlines, therefore, are not to be missed.

When we were settled in front of our tea and the tin of Afternoon Tea biscuits, a carryover from Christmas, Chloë launched into a long complaint about a row between herself and her ex-friend, Delphine. Delphine had said something, Chloë had said something back, emails had been exchanged via their iPad Minis and now they're not talking to each other. 'I'll never speak to her again, Margaret. I hate her.' Chloë took two biscuits from the tin, then added another, for luck, and began to munch.

'That's a pity, Chlo. Friends are essential, you know. Do you miss her?'

'Yes. But it's all her fault. I did nothing.'

'Well, if we could find a way to make it right, would you be interested?'

'I suppose so. But she'd have to say sorry first.'

'If she said sorry, would you say sorry too?'

'Maybe.'

For the next few minutes, as I debated with her which way we should go to repair the damage, I was on autopilot, not really thinking of the spat. Instead, standing back a little from the conversation, I was mourning how, in some ways, prolonged use of medication had narrowed my sister's life and outlook. She was certainly calm and biddable most of the time now, with the exception of sometimes inexplicable outbursts of fury, usually directed at me.

There are some in Merrow, I know, within whom intelligence and acuity still shines and their situation is far more tragic than Chloë's. At some level, they recognise their plight and are still fighting for their lives. On the surface, to outsiders at least, this cohort should have been able to live independently, with careers and so forth, but, despite many experiments, they simply couldn't manage. They are highly frustrated, frequently oppositional and always first in the queue for time on the computers.

Chloë, on the other hand, professes occasionally to 'hate' her life in Seahorse, but the hatred is transient, usually arising from something akin to the falling-out with her friend. She rarely questions her status as an inmate, not for the past several years anyhow. I am no medic and I'm certainly not criticising those who care for her, but I've been dealing with my sister for a long time. I now think it's a pity that the cocktail of medications she takes, some of it sedative, has not only reduced her ability to feel either deep pain or transcendent joy, as I think I've already mentioned, but has seemed to muffle what had been, in childhood, a high and alert intelligence. She had always been difficult, very difficult at times, but very bright. Now she is less difficult, easier to handle, but also much less tuned in to subtleties. In general, it seems to me that her world is reduced to like or loathe, love or hate, expressed in simplistic language and experienced emotionally as if in one dimension.

For instance, if pushed to it by me, she will watch nature programmes, but truly enjoys only *The Simpsons* – without appreciating the context or the politics – or *America's Next Top Model*, without being in the least bothered about the glaring differences between her own physical appearance and the contestants'. When she was younger, Chloë had the stature, the cheekbones and the stick-thin physique to be a catwalk model and, before she became ill, was truly good-looking. At present, despite the belly fat and pouches on her cheeks, she could still be rated 'handsome'.

I am not in a position to pontificate about her intelligence, which is probably still intact, although she has become as intellectually lazy as she is physically sedentary, but her personality has been muted and she has definitely regressed to adolescence.

I don't know for sure but I reckon all of this is probably harder for me to observe than for her to go through.

By now she has run out of complaints, so I take the biscuit tin and put it away. 'Do you want another cup of tea, Chlo?'

'No, thanks. I think I'll watch telly.'

'You do that. Now, remember I've put sandwiches in the fridge for you? You won't forget?'

'I won't.'

'Because you know I won't be here this afternoon. Remember I told you I'm taking Mary to see her poor mother in hospital?'

'Yes.' She's sliding off her chair and I can see her attention is already on what she is going to watch.

So, why haven't I told Mary about Derek? I can't really say. I think it has something to do with aftershock, or needing to absorb the situation before I share it. Because after those initial skirmishes, he and I had talked for the guts of an hour in what is usually termed a full and frank manner. I believe now that I didn't want to expose some elements of that conversation to Mary's forensic analysis until I knew what I felt.

When I got back to the ward, she was ready to be taken home. I had gone into the room full of apologies but with no plan as to how I would gloss over my lateness. She had held up a hand to stop me before I could even start. 'You don't have to apologise to me, Maggie. You're the one doing me all these favours and I'm very grateful. Anyway, I'd think that what you went through this morning with a bra fitting would be for me the deepest circle of Hell. That's enough torture for one day.'

'Not for the young ones, though.' Relieved, I took her arm and, as we left the room, then the hospital and walked together towards my car, gave her a blow-by-blow, dramatically enhanced account of the horrors of the bra-fitting room – and a totally fictitious story about my lengthy vacillation over which bras to pick. 'But, Mary, there was another fitting room. The girls in it hadn't bothered to close their door and through it I could see them, bare-chested, advising each other and jiggling themselves about as they tried on these bits of lace and satin.'

'Frillies. Are you going to show me what you bought, Maggie?'

'Later. Not here. I think our generation is the last ever to have been taught that modesty about our bodies is not only polite, it's a virtue.'

'Such an old-lady thing to say.'

'Yeah.' I had laughed ruefully. 'Let's change the subject. You feeling all right after this morning? Think you'll be up for going out to the nursing home on Wednesday? Chloë's fine with that, by the way. I told her I'd be home by teatime.' We were in the car now and heading for Phibsboro.

'Yeah. I'll be fine. Sorry you're going to have to drive me again so soon. I could take the bus.'

'I told you at the beginning of this that there's to be no buses.'

'Well, maybe I'll just leave the nursing home for another day.'

'Not a good idea. No point in putting it off if you're feeling strong enough physically. The longer you put it off the more difficult it will be. You'll just end up feeling guiltier and guiltier. You know I'm right. I'll be there, I'll go in with you, it'll be fine. You'll feel better having done it.'

'I suppose I will.'

And I suppose, I think now, as I open my laptop and start to type, I'll feel better having shared my dilemma.

It arose at the end of my conversation with Derek. He had asked me to have dinner with him in Chapter One: 'For old times' sake, Dumpy. No stress.'

'That's ridiculous. We have a history. How could there be no stress?'

'I mean it.' He gave a lopsided grin. 'I'm just a guy looking for a good meal with a friend.'

'That's so cheesy.'

'You liked it when we saw Julia Roberts saying it to Hugh Grant.'

'That was toe-squinching and you know it. Anyway, that film was before … '

'I know. You saw that with Derek BO.' His grin widened.

I got it, or thought I did, and it had nothing to do with body odour. In the years before things went sour between us because of Chloë, he had teased me about looking like a 'mightier' version of the film star Bo Derek, who, incidentally, is eight or nine inches shorter than I am. 'I'm fifty-seven years old, Derek,' I retorted. 'I've moved on from that woman and that kind of – of … ' I was temporarily lost for an adjective to describe what I figured he was doing: trying to drag me back to the good old days, so-called. 'And before you go any further,' I added bluntly, 'let me put a stop to this and be very clear. There will be no dinner.'

'BO stands for "Before Outrage". Derek Before Outrage. Keep your hair on, Dumpling!'

'I hate that name now. Please do not use it!'

'All right. I won't. Sorry.'

Behind the counter, someone dropped a cup or a plate: something breakable anyway. There was a flurry of activity and we both turned to watch. 'There's a few bob gone out of some poor sod's wages,' he said matter-of-factly.

'"Poor sod" is right. Is that what happens in your place?'

'So, if I promise not to,' he ignores my question, 'will you come to dinner with me?'

'Not to what?'

'Call you "Dumpling" ever, ever again.'

I stare at him. He's doing his little-boy trick, sideways head, wide eyes. It used to work.

'If you don't want to go to Chapter One,' he says then, 'we could go to Eddie Rocket's. I don't mind. It's not the food, it's the company. Isn't that what you used to say all the time, Maggie?' He was bestowing on me another blast of the old Derek charm, the kind I'd fallen for so many years ago in the coffee shop where I'd first seen him.

The awful truth was that it was working again – well, a little bit. Because of his perfidy I had forgotten how sexy Derek can be. He's always had a skill that not many people enjoy: he can make you feel, for that moment at least, that you're the only person in the world who matters to him. He had had it that very first day when I was a kid on one side of the counter and he was just a coffee server. Being a head chef has obviously consolidated that trait, however you would define it.

316

Time to knock it on the head, I think. 'How are the three girls reacting to you being gone?'

'Nice move, Maggie. Smooth change of subject.'

'Well, how are they?'

'They're fine. We're in the process of organising access, all the rest of it. I miss them.' For an instant, his expression clouded. 'Would you like to see a photograph?' He made as though to reach into his inside pocket.

'No. It's all right. You're grand.' The last thing I wanted to see was a snapshot of the three children that should have been mine.

'Sorry,' he said quietly. 'That wasn't very tactful of me, was it?' And there it was: the elephant, tap-dancing across the room.

'No. It wasn't, Derek.'

'Forgive me? Or have I wrecked my chances of feeding you? So, what about it, Magser? Dinner? A public restaurant? People around? No danger – you still eat, don't you? What's the harm?'

'I have to go.' Too much feeling washing around now. Too difficult to deal with. 'Mary will be waiting. I've to give her a lift. Thanks for the coffee.' I got to my feet and was rushing towards the door when I heard him call after me. I turned round. He was dangling that wretched pink bag in the air.

All of this is buzzing in my head this afternoon when, article completed and emailed, thank goodness, I collect Mary, who is very subdued. 'You're quiet this afternoon, Mary.'

'So are you!' she retorts, with a flash of her old spirit.

'Why don't we turn on the radio?'

'Fine by me.' For a time, we listen to the parade of other people's problems on Joe Duffy's talkathon, *Liveline*. 'That poor woman.' I depress the volume when Joe takes an ad break. 'It probably puts other stuff in perspective, eh?' We had just listened to the life story of a caller to the programme. She suffered from epilepsy, two of her children were autistic, her husband had committed suicide, she hadn't been able to pay her mortgage for more than two years and was living in fear of repossession.

'Yeah.'

Mary's head, unusually, is resting on the passenger window of the car. I doubt she's paid attention to anything she had heard. 'Are you dreading this, Mary?'

'What do you think? I don't even like the woman.'

'Look, when it's over, we'll harden our arteries with cream buns. Deal?'

She merely nods. Now, I thought, is definitely not the time to raise my own trivia.

When we get to the nursing home, purpose-built for sufferers of Alzheimer's and other forms of dementia, I am impressed. It is a long, low building, surrounded by pleasant and well-tended gardens, dominated by old trees and, at the moment, the underplantings of daffodils are well in evidence, although, unlike those I bought in Julianstown on the way to meet Jean, not yet blooming. 'This will be lovely in a few weeks' time,' I say cheerily, as I drive into one of the parking spaces but, again, she doesn't reply.

Inside, we're told that Mary's mother is with some of the others in what is called the Big Room, used for recreation and communal activities.

When we get there, we stand just inside the door and immediately I try to identify the person I still think of as the doll among a crowd of, perhaps, thirty or so, about half of whom are wearing 'real' clothes; the rest being in dressing gowns or tracksuits. Possibly as many as a third are asleep with heads fallen sideways or on to their chests. Two are mumbling incomprehensibly to themselves, and an attendant is lovingly wiping drool from the face of a woman so shrunken and wrinkled that her sex can be discerned only by the bright pink cardigan she is wearing. They all occupy either wheelchairs or those high, wing-backed chairs common to all such institutions for the elderly, and have been arranged in a semi-circle to watch, or at least aim at, a long-haired young man in the centre of the room. He is trying hard to engage with them, smiling around the gathering while playing an Irish jig on his guitar.

I can't figure out which is Mary's mother, but I haven't seen her for decades. After that one visit to the Guerin family home, I had never been invited again, and Mary had moved out of it at the earliest opportunity.

One gap in my friend's life is, to me, inexplicable – although her personality is so singular that maybe it's not all that odd after all. She has never been interested in seeking out her birth mother, or even in determining who the woman is or was. The best I could ever get out of her was a curt 'I don't need to know, Maggie. Now can we talk about something else?' I did ask on one occasion if she had ever broached the subject with her dad. 'No,' is what I got, in such a tone that I didn't pursue it.

The young man finishes the jig and now holds the guitar in the air. '"Daisy"!' he cries. 'What about "Daisy"? Who knows "Daisy"?'

A man half raises a trembling, claw-like hand.

'That's great, Roger. Will we have a go? All join in now! Don't let me down! You'll know it when you hear it.' He begins to sing, very slowly and softly, watching them all, gently strumming, smiling encouragingly at individuals around the room.

Dai-see, Dai-see,
Give me your answer, do –

One tiny old lady, almost lost in the mound of coverings over her in her wheelchair, is first to join in, her voice high and quavering. 'Good girl, Betty!' He breaks off, then resumes:

I'm half cra-zee
All for the love of yoooou –

The old man who had first reacted begins to caw tunelessly along – the few wisps of white hair on his liver-spotted scalp trembling slightly as he moves his head to a rhythm different from the guitarist's.

It won't be a stylish marriage –

A few of the others now add their voices. Two of the women attempt to wave their arms in the air.

I can't afford a carriage –

It's now a feeble chorus, barely audible above the young man's sweet tenor. It's out of tune, it's weak, it's pathetic and noble at the same time, and deeply affecting. I turn to Mary and find that there are tears running down her face. 'I didn't know she knew that song,' she whispers. 'And I don't suppose she notices now, but she absolutely hates being called Betty.'

But you'll look sweet –

'Is that her, the first little one who sang?' I whisper back.

Upon the seat –

'That's her.'

Of a bicycle made for two!

The young man finishes with a flourish on his guitar and then: 'Will we go again?'

'Who's that?' shouts one of the men, thumping his walking stick on the parquet floor.

'Eamon. I'm Eamon,' the young man responds cheerfully. *'Tús maith leath na hoibre.* A good beginning, half the work, ladies and gentlemen! Now that we've made such a good start, we'll have another go. OK? Everyone ready? Right. Here we go. "Daisee Daisee …"'

'I can't stand this—' Mary bolts from the room.

I follow her and, for the first time in all the years of our lives together, I hold her and try to comfort her. The scarf slips off her head and she grabs it, but there is a moment when, with her baldness and her contorted, weeping face, she, like me, like any of us, could belong inside that room. Youth and health, I think, are mere cloaks worn over the constantly ageing selves waiting to emerge. I'm shaken at the thought and, out of the blue, a memory blast from my childhood culture bursts through. Dear God, I supplicate over Mary's head, dear God and Your Holy Mother, let me not end up like that. Let Mary not end up like that either. Sacred Heart, St Joseph and St Jude, please take us before that happens.

She calms down after a bit, goes to a nearby bathroom to clean herself up, and then we wait outside the room until the music session is over and the young man comes out. 'Hi,' he says cheerily. 'They're in good form today. Who are you looking for?'

'My mother, Elizabeth.' Mary sounds like her old, resolute self. 'She was singing with you.'

'Betty? Oh, Betty's lovely. You can go in. They'll be there for another while.' He goes off.

'You ready, Mary?' I put an arm around her shoulders.

When we walk back into the room the attendant is aiming a remote control at the massive TV set in a corner, now showing a rerun episode of *Location, Location, Location*. She comes towards us. 'Can I help you?'

'I've come to visit Elizabeth Guerin. She's over there.' Mary points.

'Great,' says the girl. 'She'll be delighted to see you. I'll get her for you, give you some privacy.' She goes towards the tiny lady, who doesn't even look up at the approach, or even when the girl crouches low to talk to her. We're still too far away to hear what is being said but Mary's mother does not react at all, not even when the attendant points us out.

'It's all right, thank you.' Abruptly, Mary seizes the initiative. 'I'll take it from here. I know where her room is.'

'Great! Bye-bye, Betty.' The attendant stands up and waves as Mary seizes the wheelchair and comes towards me. 'Have a lovely visit!'

'Her name is Elizabeth!' Mary whirls to confront the girl. 'Get that into your stupid head. "Elizabeth"!'

'Take it easy, Mary.' I shoot an apologetic smile towards the attendant. 'Your mother doesn't know—'

322

'That's not the point!' But Mary stops and, leaving the wheelchair, goes back to apologise to the girl, who takes it in good part.

There is little point in going into too much detail about what happens during this visit in the old lady's room, except to tell you that our get-together was rather brief. Sitting there on the bed, watching Mary's efforts to break through what I can only describe as the gauze that surrounds her mother, I feel like a spare wheel. The woman exists in a dream world. What's more, I can see no similarity whatsoever to the impeccable, icy little person I had encountered in Mary's house. Only the eyes, maybe, vacant now, a little faded, but still that extraordinary blue. 'She likes singing, obviously,' I suggest in desperation. 'Will we try a song?'

'If you like.' Mary's tone tells me she doesn't have much confidence in my brainwave. Desperately, I start up, quite lustily: 'Daisy, Daisy, give me your answer do ... '

For a second or two, nothing. Then the woman, eyes now wide with horror, looks at me, back at Mary, and towards me again. 'Nurse!' she screeches, picking up a little hand bell and whacking it frantically against the side of her locker.

Mary and I retreat, the din diminishing behind us as we hurry down the corridor and into the front lobby of the place. 'I didn't know I was that bad,' I say breathlessly when we're outside, making for the car. Luckily she sees the funny side too and we both subside into schoolgirlish giggles when we collapse into the front seats of the vehicle. 'We shouldn't be laughing.' I wipe my eyes, then insert the key into the ignition. 'But see it from her point of view. This enormous woman shouting her lungs out in her little room ...'

'I certainly shouldn't be laughing. I'm supposed to be the

dutiful daughter. But thanks for coming. Honestly. I'll try again in a week or so. It's for the staff, as I told you. I want them to know that she has someone in her life.'

'You're doing the right thing.' I slot the car into gear. 'Now! Cream buns?'

'Ooh, yes! Will Chloë be all right?'

'Fine. The telly is on and I've left sandwiches for her. She's not expecting me till teatime and that's flexible. Flora's the one to be missing me. She's usually fed by now, but I'll give her a bit extra. She's a very forgiving animal!'

Over the coffee and buns I confess, telling Mary about my encounter with Derek. She listens without comment until I end up with the quandary I face. Or think I face: 'He wants to bring me to dinner. To go, or not to go, Mary? I can't make up my mind. I know that, compared to your illness and your mother and everything, as a problem it doesn't really amount to a hill of beans, does it?'

'So why did he leave? Did he tell you?'

'Karma, Mary, although I did manage to resist pointing that out to him. It seems that the popsy, Fiona, found another suitor, some rich businessman with property here and business interests in Dubai. He also owns a helicopter, that rarity in recessionary Ireland. It's true love.'

'Don't be so cynical.'

'You? Telling me not to be cynical?'

'Anyway, what are you going to do about it? He's a bolter, Maggie. Pure and simple. All you've heard is his side.'

'I know. But – oh, I dunno. He was so – so real. I haven't seen him for so long. I had this image in my head, him laughing at me or something. But …' I trailed off. 'What do you think I should do?'

She's not buying it. 'For God's sake, Mags, would you listen to yourself? It's not my life, it's yours. And it's clear you're not going to do nothing. You want to explore this. You're going to have dinner with him, aren't you?'

'I shouldn't be bothering you with this, Mary. You've enough on your plate.'

'The cancer hasn't affected my brain, you know, not yet anyhow. I'm still a sentient being. So, are you or aren't you taking him up on his invitation?'

'I can't make up my mind.'

'You've already made it up. All this will-I-won't-I is just for respectability's sake, and for the sake of having a back-up to blame if it proves to be awful. Well, I'm not going to be back-up this time. It's your decision and I think you've made it.'

I gaze at her. 'You're right.' I'm shamefaced. 'On all counts, you're right. I am using you as a backstop. And I am going to have dinner with him.' It was the first time I'd actually admitted it to myself. 'What harm can come of it?' I begged, then realised I was parroting what Derek himself had said. 'No strings,' I rushed on. 'Definitely no strings.'

'So this conversation has been a complete waste of time and energy for both of us. You had already agreed?'

'No. I just left him sitting there. I said you'd be waiting for your lift.'

'What are we going to do with you, Maggie Quinn?' She sighed. 'Leopards don't change their spots. And this one is obviously needy. Don't fall into the trap of being his lifesaver. Be careful.'

'I will, honestly.'

'I mean it. Really and truly mean it.'

'I know you do.' To get on safer ground, I ask her if she thinks the Club is about to break up. 'Like, with Jean away, and Lorna, I'd say, choosing to go with the grandchildren next Christmas.'

'I've thought of that. Would you be very upset?'

'A little. But, you know, we've had a good ten years. Everything changes. And the way things have been going, I don't look beyond tomorrow at the moment. Next December is very far away. Anything can happen.'

She looks steadily at me. 'Are you worried I'll be gone too?'

'No,' I lie. 'Of course not. What I meant was that anything can happen to anyone at any time – and frequently does!'

'Hmm.'

We finish eating and are silent on the way to her flat, that last exchange pulsing between the front seats of the car. 'By the way, how are the music lessons coming on?' I ask her, as we pull up in front of the house. To my astonishment – and admiration – she is keeping up her clarinet tuition during her treatment because, in her view, she has to have some outside distraction and her tutor is very understanding if she becomes too tired, or if, in her own words, 'I run out of puff halfway through.'

'Actually quite well,' she tells me. 'We're both surprised, my teacher and me!'

She is some woman, this friend of mine, I think, as I drive off. But I remain worried. Suppose all this treatment doesn't work? It does happen.

A few minutes later, I let myself into my own house, calling, 'Yoo-hoo, Chloë, I'm back!' while automatically waiting for the sound of scrambling paws.

No paws. But the sitting-room door is closed. Flora must be in there with my sister. She never barks, except at cats. She's probably behind the door.

As I go towards the sitting room, I notice that the hall is very cold, although I'd left the heating on. I remind myself to look into that. Must be the radiator. 'Hi there.' I push open the door where my sister, predictably, is still sitting in front of the television, the remains of her sandwiches on the floor beside her chair. No dog. 'Everything OK? Where's Flora?'

'Dunno.' She shrugs. 'Probably upstairs?'

'Flora? Good dog!' I call, climbing the stairs, but when I'm halfway up, I see that the door to 'her' room is open. She would have come out to greet me if she'd been in there. 'She's not there,' I call to Chloë, as I come back down. I'm puzzled. This is entirely uncharacteristic.

But when I go into the kitchen, I realise why the hall is so cold: the back door is wide open. The first twinges of anxiety pull at the pit of my stomach as, calling for Flora, I hurry across the room and go into the garden. If she'd been out here, she would have rushed to meet me on hearing me come in – even on hearing my car.

She's not in the garden. And the gate across the side entrance is swinging in the wind.

I run into the sitting room. 'Chloë, did you let Flora out into the back garden?'

'Yeah.' She doesn't take her eyes off *The Simpsons*. 'She wanted to go out.'

'When. How long ago?' I seize the remote and turn off the television. That gets her attention but she merely shrugs. 'I dunno.'

'Think, Chloë, please think.' I'm getting frantic. 'Was it an hour ago? Two hours?' Then I have an inspiration: 'What was on the telly when you let her out?'

Again she shrugs. I want to shake her. 'Was it *Neighbours*?' I persist.

'I think so.' She frowns. Then: 'I went to get my sandwiches and Flora came out with me. I let her out then.'

'Did you open the side gate when you let her out?'

She looks at me, puzzled. 'What side gate, Margaret? Is there a side gate?'

This is a useless exercise. There is no advantage to be gained in barracking her further. She's not being clever. There is no reason for her to know about the side gate. She never goes out when she's here, even in summertime, and that gate was installed to coincide with Flora's arrival just three years ago, long after Chloë had been ensconced in Merrow House.

That gate is opened only by me, by men delivering furniture, or by the young lad who cuts the grass for me during the spring and summer months. I haven't ordered furniture. It's February and the lawn is dormant. Whether stolen or strayed – and she's such a home bird that the latter is unlikely – my dog is gone.

TWENTY-FOUR

2 March 2013

It's been three days now and no news of Flora. I'm devastated.

I didn't tell Mary about her that first night. I was panicked and, as always in a crisis, my initial instinct had been to make the phone call as soon as I realised Flora had vanished, but I had held back. She had had a rotten day all round and it wouldn't have been fair to land her with yet another of my dramas. In any event, I suspect – actually I know – that she tolerates Flora for my sake – and for my sake would be upset to learn she was missing – but wouldn't understand what all the fuss was about. A dog is a dog. It dies or strays. Buy another or go to the pound and select a handful if that's your bent.

I didn't have to tell her. She found out.

I had not been all that surprised by her emotional outburst in the nursing home. I had been reading up on possible psychological side-effects – on top of the physical – suffered by patients undergoing cancer treatments. I had eliminated many that, given the bedrock of Mary's personality, were extremely unlikely and had been left with a mental checklist of possibilities:

(a) Panic attacks: no. None that I saw anyhow.

(b) Loss of physical energy: a little but not too obvious.

(c) Anxiety: not really. The attempt to contact her siblings might have been a sign of her apprehension when she was keeping her suspicions about her illness to herself, but I had seen no evidence of an increase since she'd started the treatment.

(d) Irritability: possibly, but even at the best of times she's liable to flash.

(e) Loss of motivation: probably, as in the slowing of work on the fairy project.

(f) Changeable emotions (sudden crying or anger; irrational exuberance): definitely. As had happened that afternoon after the visit to her mother. Totally uncharacteristic behaviour in the Mary I know.

Anyway, side effects of chemo or not, she had had a horrible day all round so for that first night, at least, I had not laid my burden on her shoulder.

In my distress, I did think of ringing one of the others in our little circle but who? During my last visit to Lorna a couple of days previously, she had been on a crying jag, absolutely inconsolable. Lay on her my worry about a dog? Inconceivable.

At the other end of the scale there was Jean, the brand-new

cloud-nine fiancée. Couldn't do it to her either. Couldn't bring her down that way. Anyway, she had enough on her hands with poor Lorna. As her best friend, Jean was there more than the rest of us.

That left Dina. Dina and I just didn't have that kind of one-to-one relationship. In the way that Mary was the substance of the coffee, Dina was the froth. She had come out of the period surrounding Martin's death well but, in general, that had been as part of the group. Don't get me wrong: I like her. In many ways I wish I had her attitude to life (and, of course, I wouldn't mind having her money) but as a confidante in my distress, I don't think she would ever be my choice, except as a very last resort.

So I was on my own in a way I hadn't been for a long time. I even thought, briefly (for about a millisecond), of trying Derek's mobile but when I recognised the thought, I laughed out loud, a little shakily, at the absurdity.

Chloë is back with me for the weekend and I have had to call on all my inner resources not to scapegoat her, while in the meantime doing everything in my power to recover Flora.

That first evening, I had immediately gone up and down the terraces on both sides of our road, knocking on doors and asking if anyone had seen her or noticed anything peculiar. All except one of those who answered my knock said they hadn't, and the old, arthritic man four doors away, who thought he had, was rather vague: 'I saw a white van. You know the kind? There were two men in it, but I couldn't say if they went into your house. It parked up on the path out here.' He indicated the area outside his own gate. 'I don't like them white vans, d'ye see, but by the time I got to the window, they were gone. They weren't here for no more than two or three minutes.'

Everyone was very kind: many said they would recognise Flora, having seen her with me on her lead, and that they would keep an eye out. But this is Dublin city and even in such a traditional, cheek-by-jowl terraced area such as ours, I know very few of my neighbours other than to comment on the weather as we pass on the road or encounter each other in local shops. A lot of the little houses had been acquired during the boom years as buy-to-let investment properties and are inhabited by a transient population, many of whom are young people, and I'm not convinced that they, well meaning on their doorsteps, will follow through on any promises.

I can't adequately describe what that first night was like. After I got back from questioning the neighbours, I had, of course, called the gardaí – forgetting that, with cutbacks, station closures and so on, there was not a warm body to be had. And even I knew that to dial 999 would not be appropriate in the case of 'only a dog'.

My second call was to the emergency number of our vet. 'I'm just looking for advice,' I said to the veterinarian on duty, a Spanish girl whom I knew very well and who was profoundly sympathetic.

'Tomorrow, you bring photograph of Flora. We put it on our wall and we tell the local newspaper, eh? She is micro-chipped, your Flora?'

'Yes.'

'That is great help. If she is taken for the pet trade, or for traffic to England, sooner or later the chip will be read.'

Pet trade? Trafficked to England? I was horrified. I had seen items on the TV news about puppies being taken from puppy farms to go to England, but the impression I'd had was that, while they weren't treated very well in transit, this was a legitimate trade. 'Could that have happened to her?'

'You come in tomorrow with photograph. You have nice clear photograph, yes?'

'Yes.'

'So, tomorrow John is on duty. He will have good chat with you. I leave him a note on his desk right now when I hang up this telephone. He will advise you.' John Malone is the lead vet in Flora's practice. He has known my dog since I got her; it was he who microchipped and vaccinated her. Even the sound of his name calmed me a little.

I used my printer to photocopy a snapshot of Flora, printed out thirty copies and added a handwritten description of her and my phone numbers to each page. Then, with Chloë's help, I slotted each of them into one of those transparent plastic page sleeves for use in box files.

I suppose you could categorise my sister's reaction to all of this as dutiful rather than empathetic. I had yelled at her initially, but then had simply ordered her to help me with the notices. She had complied without objection. I think that's the best I could have hoped for in the circumstances.

At one point, however, she had surprised me: 'Sorry, Margaret,' she said, when the last page had been slotted into the last sleeve and I was shuffling them into a pile. She had opened her arms and given me an awkward hug, patting my shoulder. 'There, there, Margaret. Everything will be fine.' Was this organic or was she repeating what she had seen and heard so often on TV? It didn't matter. I choked, turning away so she wouldn't see it. 'It's all right, Chlo,' I muttered, into her shoulder. 'I hope you don't feel guilty. It's probably not your fault.'

Immediately she released me. 'I think I'll go back to watch telly.'

'Go ahead.' I left her to it and went out into the night, leaving my flimsy cries for help in corner shops and taped to lampposts all over my area until the stack ran out. When I got back to the house (no skittering, no paws, no delighted whimpers of joy), my sister was watching another rerun of *Friends*.

That night, instead of joining her, I twisted up and down the radio dial, tuning in to each of the local stations I came upon, writing down its phone-in and texting numbers until I had nearly twenty. I texted and phoned them all – but to little avail. I was told over and over again by the frontline researchers who take the calls, 'We don't do lost dogs.' In vain did I try to persuade them: 'But this isn't a "lost dog". I'm a journalist myself and this is a real news story. Dogs are being snatched from people's gardens. You could run a feature on it.' All those girls and boys were dismissive, qualifying their lack of interest with a sop of politeness: a wish for good luck in my search.

I got a sort of hearing from just one, the penultimate, when a girl with a heavy country accent (Cavan? Deepest Meath? Cavan/ Meath border?),who sounded as though she was about twelve years old, took my phone number and said she would pass it on to her producer. To judge by the sounds behind her, her station, Clash FM, was broadcasting from a barn because at one stage during our conversation I heard a distinct moo.

I was too upset at the time, though, to think this funny or even quaint. And I had little hope of a result. My hunch was that Clash FM was one of those pirates with no licence, too insignificant and too infrequently on air to attract the heavy hand of the licensing authorities. The station's 'researcher', I felt, was merely following her instructions: 'All you have to do is take the name and the phone number and pass it on.' As I hung up after the 'no' from the last station on my list, I realised I had run out not just of options but of ideas.

Later, in the dead of that dark, rainy night, with Chloë's rhythmic snoring cutting through the silence on the landing between our rooms, I imploded with grief and anxiety, too upset even to cry into my pillow. Flora was – is – very far from being 'only a dog' or canine companion to me. That little collie's spirit has imbued this house with love, loyalty, fun and forbearance of human peccadilloes. She had demanded nothing in return except food once a day, a few outings and my presence – and if any of those was not forthcoming, she was willing patiently to wait. She was – is – my only child, my loving consort, the beating heart of my home – and if that sounds anthropomorphic, wildly sentimental or even bonkers, so be it. It's how I felt as the hands of my bedside clock seemed not to move.

And during those long hours of darkness, when I was boiling the kettle for yet another cup of tea or refilling my hot-water bottle, or brushing my teeth for the third time, I would forget for a few seconds and look around to check if she was behind me as usual. Going up or down the stairs, I would see her, just in front of me, heralding my arrival at my chosen destination, checking over her shoulder every couple of seconds to make sure I was following. Entering the kitchen for the umpteenth time in the early hours of the morning, I would see her look up from her food bowl and give me the customary brief, distracted wag: I see you, but I'm busy just for the moment. Talk later?

The nearest I came to outright weeping was when I noticed that her water bowl was still full. I had filled it before going out to collect Mary for the visit to the nursing home.

My imagination, haunted by the old man's report of the two men in the white van, ran riot. I could see Flora's eyes wide with terror, confusion and bewilderment as she was (*if* she was) bundled into the vehicle. Was she now tied up? Trussed? Cowering in a cage? Alone in a filthy shed somewhere?

Or, if the white van was not implicated, had kids taken her to tie her to a lamppost for BB-gun target practice? Could they have thrown her over the wall of the zoo as food for some predator? My house is quite close to the Phoenix Park but it had been a long time since I had been to Dublin Zoo and I was hazy about the new geography, African Plains and so on, but that night, my mind's eye saw no boundaries.

Had she been taken in order to 'blood' larger fighting animals and was she even now cringing in the corner of a dog pit? She is such a gentle soul, she would put up no fight, not even to defend herself. In our three years together I had never seen a single hint of aggression towards human or animal; even her routing of cats was pro-forma. On the many occasions she saw off feline trespassers in our garden, it was with barking and a pretend dash, stopping short when they mounted the garden wall, then coming back inside with a triumphant grin. Piece of cake, Maggie. Safe to go out. All clear now.

It was in vain I tried to cut short these repetitively unreeling horror films until, by seven o'clock in the morning and with the sky lightening, sheer fatigue gave me a break and I dropped off into a deep, dreamless sleep.

I woke again at about a quarter to nine and immediately rang the vet to see if John had arrived yet, to be told he was due at nine.

I showered in record time, pulled on a pair of old jeans and a jumper and was in the car twenty minutes later.

John Malone is a big, sandy-haired man who, after a quarter of a century in Dublin, retains a trace of his original Scottish burr. He was at the reception desk when I came in, and immediately took me into one of the examination rooms. He wears a seen-it-all-before aura but in no way could this be interpreted as cynicism. 'Sit down, dearie,' he said, closing the door behind us. 'Tell me what happened.'

'You remember Flora?'

'Of course I do. That's a lovely little collie.' His sympathetic tone and use of the present tense brought me dangerously close to blubbing, but I managed to bite it back. I explained what had happened, and when I mentioned the white van, I watched closely for his reaction. His expression did change, became sombre. 'Oh – well – I see. There's a lot of that going on, I'm afraid. But listen, Maggie, don't lose hope. Sooner or later some vet or other will see that dog and will identify the microchip. We've got a lot of dogs back that way, but I have to warn you that it usually takes a bit of time.'

'How long?'

'Depends. If she's been taken, I suspect it's for the pet trade rather than as a working dog because she's untrained. I mean for sheep or cattle.'

Thinking of poor Flora and her self-appointed tasks, I could only nod.

'Well, then, if that's the case, it could be local, you know, the North or whatever, but it's more likely it's for England and there's no physical checking between here and there. But new owners will at some stage have her checked out. Is she the type to pine? Not eat and so on?'

That was something I couldn't answer. 'She's been to kennels a couple of times and seemed to give no trouble, according to the people there.'

He gazed at the sleet now sheeting the air outside the window. 'We have to hope. I'm assuming you've done the usual stuff – postering, checking with neighbours and so on?'

'Of course. But …' I hesitated '… how good are our chances?' I had liked the plural.

'I don't want to be pessimistic, Maggie, but I don't want to give you false hope either. Each case is unique. The fact that she's microchipped is a huge plus. If she wasn't, I would say your chances are minimal. Are you sure she's been taken and not just strayed?'

'She has no history of straying – but then she's pretty confined at home.'

'Look,' he said, coming around from behind the examination table where he'd been standing and putting his big, consoling hand on my shoulder, 'I have to go – there's probably a queue forming outside. Keep the faith, dearie. She's a lovely little dog, great temperament, well cared-for and in good health. We'll put up her picture on our rogues' gallery here and on our website, and we'll spread the word as we always do. If she's been taken, the chances are that she'll be put up for sale, be snapped up by some family and will be identified in due course. The authorities all over Europe are on alert for this kind of thing. So don't lose heart, OK? Are you on Facebook?'

'No.' I shook my head. I could have kicked myself. I'm a bloody journalist, or so I call myself. Why hadn't I thought of that? Because I'm an idiot, that's why. I've been resisting social media for no good reason other than that I believed it would be a bothersome intrusion. All that trawling, all those demands on your attention – all those viruses!

'Well, it might be a good idea,' the vet, unaware of my self-flagellation, continued. 'And you should use Twitter too. If you're new to this kind of thing, Josepha will set you up and show you what's what. She's a right little cracker on social media. Give her a ring – I think she's on again tonight. In the meantime, try to take things easy, Maggie. It sounds like you've done all you can, and so far all the right things. It's going to be hard but you'll have to have patience. And don't forget, we're all rooting for you and Flora. And do get online, now, won't you?'

I thanked him but I left that examination room under no illusions as to the parlousness of my little dog's position. I managed to keep it together when leaving her snapshot and description with the receptionist on duty, but on the way out, I had to pass through the waiting area where I was appraised by something small and furry in a cage, a cat, and two dogs, a cocker spaniel and a huge multi-gened black thing with paws the size of small frying pans and a lolling tongue. Tail wagging furiously, he lunged towards me to tell me how glad he was to see me and was restrained only with great difficulty by the woman at the other end of his leash.

The tears came then.

I cried all the way home and then, because Chloë must not see how upset I was, instead of driving straight there, I parked a few houses down and, to calm myself, turned on the car radio.

It was about five minutes to ten and Miriam O'Callaghan was winding up before the news at ten o'clock on RTÉ Radio One, my default station. She had been interviewing some singer, whose name I didn't catch – who was now singing a really mournful thing about loss and heartbreak.

Christ, I thought. Is there absolutely nothing on the blasted radio that doesn't remind me of Flora's plight? I stabbed for

Lyric, this time to find someone singing mournfully about caged green finches and linnets while wondering if the creatures are actually singing or screaming. Larks, the singer tells us, don't sing at all after entrapment. I turned off the radio. The universe, Dina would say, was conspiring against me this morning.

I took three deep breaths, reminding myself to get a grip: some perspective might be in order. Although, right now, I was on the floor, this had to be a mere taste of the agony endured by the mother of a missing child, or by the wife of a missing husband. Having given missing persons only cursory attention via newspapers and TV news, I had never fully appreciated until now the depth of that sorrow.

I put the tin can in gear and moved it slowly to its usual berth in front of my own house, noting, as I drove in, that the side gate was still open. Let it swing now for ever, I thought.

Once inside, I listened for sounds from upstairs. While I could no longer hear snoring, there was dead silence. Chloë was having a lie-in.

I could resist it no longer. With no Flora, the quiet felt as though it was pressing in on all sides. I had to talk to Mary.

Her phone was engaged, and although food was the last thing on my mind, I went into the kitchen to do something about my breakfast.

Of course the first thing I saw was the bloody full water bowl.

It will give you some idea of my state of mind that morning if I tell you I hesitated before picking it up to empty it and put it away. My brain said, Of course you have to do it. My heart told me that to put it away was to accept that Flora was gone for ever: an admission that any further effort to find her was a lost cause. In the event, I went for a halfway house: I emptied it, dried it carefully with a tea towel but then left it in plain sight on one of the counter-tops. Trivial though it was, that little sequence of actions brought all the emotions to the surface again. I was coming apart.

When I dialled Mary this time, she answered on the first ring, her tone surprisingly light, even joyful, I thought. 'Hi, Mags. Glad it's you,' she said, before I could launch into my tale of woe.

'Oh? Glad?' I was confused. 'What's up? How are you this morning?'

'Fine. No problems, nothing new anyhow, but guess what?'

'What?'

'I've just put down the phone from a long call. Very unexpected. One of my nieces rang me from Boston, would you believe?'

'No!'

'Yes. Ramona. She's Jeffrey's kid, in Boston University, and coming to Ireland for a semester at a university in Dublin – there's some kind of a reciprocal arrangement. She was asking me about accommodation but I think she was hinting that she'd like to stay with me. "You're my only relative except my grandma, Auntie Mary," she said, "and of course you know all about her." It's the first time in my life someone's called me "Auntie"! I love it. And, Mags, she told me that Jeffrey was the one who told her to call me. He showed her my letter – I asked her if he might come to visit after all and she didn't say no. She said that if everything worked out he might come with her for a few days to settle her in.'

'That's great, Mary.' I was wondering why on earth she didn't see the irony in him showing his daughter the effing letter when the bastard hadn't lifted the phone or replied to it. I swallowed hard: 'Are you going to put her up?' I was thinking of Mary's one room and the Murphy bed.

'I'll try to sort something out. I'll talk to Mrs M downstairs and see if we can't manage. I couldn't expect her to sleep on the floor, could I? Anyway, it would be too awkward sharing just the one room. I hope we can come to some arrangement.'

'Did you say you would? Put her up?'

'Not quite. Oh – more or less.'

'When is she coming? How old is she?' I was trying to match her lightness of tone.

'She sounded a little vague about dates, but we're going to talk again when she gets her schedule. As for how old – you know, I haven't a clue. Isn't that terrible, Mag? My own niece!'

'But I thought Jeffrey was on the west coast, not in Boston.'

'Oh, you know the way Americans work.' She was determined to brook not a smidgen of negativity here. 'Kids go away to college and live in dorms, all the rest of it – and there was I moaning and groaning about them all. Isn't it brilliant, Mag?'

'I'm delighted for you.' I was genuinely pleased. Or I hoped I was. I should have been. Some spoiled brat inside me, thwarted because she couldn't break into Mary's euphoria with her own tale of woe, was shouting treacherously: What about me? What about me? This isn't fair. I need you. It's my turn now.

'You sound really excited, Mary,' was what came out of my mouth but Spoiled Brat was prompting me to consider whether this was 'irrational exuberance' on her part, yet there was no doubt that she seemed absolutely re-energised by this.

'I *am* excited. What a great thing to have to look forward to, after all this cancer mess is laid to rest.'

'When did you say she was coming?' I was once again calculating in my head. By my last reckoning, without surgery, the treatments were not to be over until July. 'I didn't.' Now Mary was getting irritated with me. 'Try to concentrate for once, will you, Mag? I told you she hadn't firmed up her arrangements yet.'

'Oh, yeah. Sorry.'

'Look, would you have an hour to spare today?' Her tone changed. 'I was going to ring you anyway but you beat me to it.'

'Chloë's here.'

'You could spare an hour, surely. What age is Chloë again?'

'You know perfectly well what age she is. But you also know that this is not the point with Chloë.' That was Spoiled Brat speaking. I was acting like the female equivalent of a bollix and I knew I was. What selfish, horrid little imp had got into me? 'I'm sure I can,' I said quickly. 'Of course I can. She's asleep anyway, probably won't be up for ages. I'll leave her a note. Any particular reason?'

'I'd like you to look at my flat with fresh eyes,' she said eagerly. 'My so-called décor is certainly not suitable for a college student, is it? It's very old-lady.'

'Mary, it's gorgeous. I love it.'

'Exactly. Old-lady. I rest my case.'

I arrive at Mary's flat thirty minutes later, having given myself a severe talking-to on the way over. Do not rain on Mary's parade, was the gist, and when I see the light in her eyes, I'm completely ashamed of my previous self-centred line of thought. Seeing her like this, rejuvenated, pink-cheeked, how could anyone, most of all me, not be glad for her?

'Right.' She pushes back the curtains as far as they'll go from the glass of all three windows in the living room and we both come to stand in the centre of her room. 'Be objective. Be totally frank.

I won't be offended. If you were a young woman, say eighteen or nineteen, maybe twenty, and you were a college student from Boston seeing this for the first time, what would you think?'

Obediently, I shove poor Flora to the back end of my consciousness and try to do as Mary bids, to be objective about the brasses, the redness, the rich, almost medieval tapestry of the furnishings. The earlier sleet had gone the way of all sleet and, with her windows facing south-east, that rarest of rare commodities this winter and spring, bright, unforgiving sunlight, strikes sparks from the brasses and shiny inlays and illuminates bald spots I had never before noticed in the rugs and carpets. It also makes a yellow brick road along the dust drifting quietly through the air. 'You sure you meant it about not taking offence, Mary?'

'Of course.'

'Well, the first thing we have to do – sorry.' I stop. My mobile phone is buzzing in the pocket of my jeans. Because of Flora, I'd made sure to have it with me today. 'Sorry, Mary, I may have to take this.' I can see she isn't best pleased as I fish it out.

'Hello?' I hadn't recognised the number.

'Is dat Flora?'

My heart falls towards my stomach: 'I beg your pardon?'

'Is dat Flora?' The voice, male, cigarette brown, is rich with a country accent.

'No, I'm afraid you have the wrong number. This is Maggie Quinn.'

'Oh.' There's a bit of fumbling, then, 'Maggie. Sorry, Maggie. Of course. Dis is De Big D Programme on Clash FM, de real country station for de real country, and you're on de air with de Big D himself. I have great news for ya, Maggie Quinn, you're today's winner.' There followed a deafening blast of some kind of hooter. I held the phone away from my ear. 'What part of our lovely country do ya live in, Maggie Quinn?'

Bemused, I put the phone back. 'I'm from Dublin. What have I won?'

'Well, whaddya know – Clash FM's first Jackeen winner. De big smoke, wha'? We got listeners everywhere, folks. Are ya partial to a good steak, Maggie?'

'I love steak, yes.'

'She loves steaks, folks!' The hooter goes off again. 'Well, you're in luck, Maggie.' He comes back on as the noise dies away. 'As today's winner, you and a friend – d'ya have a husband or lover, by any chance?'

'Not at the moment.' I glance at Mary, who had sat down and is now tapping her foot.

'D'ya hear dat folks?' shouts the Big D. 'Bachelor alert! Dere's a jackeen on the loose! Well, Maggie, you and a friend,' he emphasises, 'you and your friend will be dinin' in style on a date and at a time of yeer choice. De best steak in Ireland, a bottle of wine, de whole damn t'ing in McGarry's Fine Dinin' Steak and Grills Restaurant on Main Street Drumcattlin.' He lowers his voice to an intimate pitch: 'And t'anks to de great folks at McGarry's Fine Dinin' Steak and Grills Restaurant, for such a great prize. McGarry's of Drumcattlin, fine dinin' at regular prices!

'When d'ya t'ink you'll be able to get up to us in Drumcattlin, Maggie?' ('Broadcasting' tone.)

'Do I have to choose right away?' I glance again at Mary, who seems intrigued now.

'Not at all, not at all. We'll put your name in for ya wit' John dere over in McGarry's and you and your friend just turn up on de day. No need to bewk. We'll put a word in. And youse can be sure youse'll be treated like rilety' (voice lowered), 'and t'anks agin to McGarry's Fine Dinin' Steak and Grills for supportin' De Big D. Couldn't do it widout ya, McGarry's. T'anks.

'And t'anks to you, Maggie Quinn. See ya soon – who's Flora, by de way? It says here on dis piece of paper, "Flora".'

'Flora is my dog. She's missing and, you see, that's why I—'

'Lovely, lovely, well, all de best, Maggie, to you and little Flora and see ya soon in Drumcattlin. Drop in and say hello to de Big D when you come up from de Big Smoke. Aisy to find us. We're right off Main Street over Francie McRory's butcher's shop. No one's a stranger in Drumcattlin. Youse'll be as welcome as daisies, isn't dat right, folks?

'Now back to business. Comin' up later, we have Big Tom and Larry Cunningham, Margo and Sandy Kelly, equal time for de ladies on Clash FM, eh? We have de parish dets at the top of the hour, and dat broadcast is sponsored by McQuillan's undertakers right here in town and t'anks to dem, but right now, here's Declan Nerney, wit' his mega hit 'De Marquee in Drumlish'.' There was a blast of country music and the line went silent.

As I stuffed my phone back into my pocket I was figuring that the parish 'dets' had nothing to do with money: local 'deaths' and attendant obsequies were one of the most popular slots on all local radio stations. 'Have you heard of a place called Drumcattlin, Mary? Any idea where it is?'

She was staring at me. 'Flora's missing?'

TWENTY-FIVE

4 March 2013

Mary and I swap concerns. Her idea: 'Fresh eyes, Mags!' Just the thought gives me a lift.

I had underestimated my friend's perception of my attachment to Flora and, after a predictable barney between us as she excoriates me for not telling her – 'I'm not made of tissue paper. I'm not a baby!' – she had promised to pull out all the stops in an effort to find my dog, and I had promised her similarly that I will strain every nerve to help her refurbish to a standard fit for her niece. Buoyed up, I offer the kicker: that when her place is fully redone and Flora is back home, she will be my chosen friend for the trip to Drumcattlin to eat my winning steaks in McGarry's Fine Dining Steak and Grills Restaurant.

So, for the rest of daytime Saturday and almost all day

Sunday, we live in one another's tasks, she working on Flora's disappearance, I on the makeover of her flat. Although I had loved the womb-like quality of her existing décor, I had agreed with her (the dust, the threadbare rugs), regretfully, that her room could do with an uplift. Although I know the distraction is temporary, helping her gives me something productive to do, while knowing that someone I trust is on Flora's case.

Her first port of call requires my co-operation. It is to one of the women in the shelter where she had worked. She had remembered that this lady had run a dog sanctuary before she herself had sought refuge and might have some insight into how dog-napping was organised and where the selling markets are. I drive Mary to the shelter but unfortunately the woman has left and there is currently no trace of her. She is now, like Flora, off the radar.

I take Mary home.

We split up then, and while she settles in to ring every shelter and pound in the country, both public and private, north and south, I go home briefly to make sure Chloë has enough microwaveable food to tide her over lunch and dinner if that proves necessary. Then, leaving her to her own devices, I go into town to take a benchmark pricing on floor coverings and furnishings in Arnotts and Clerys, then tour the big north- and westside shopping centres to check out the less expensive options.

IKEA, of course, is going to be my Holy Grail, especially since Mary's visitor will be young and, presumably, have a youngster's taste. But I reserve that for the Sunday, and will take Mary with me. Believe it or not, she has never been there.

I'm not too hopeful driving back to the flat. She would have telephoned me, I think, if she had made any breakthrough. And so it proves when I get back and we settle down over tea and sandwiches to compare notes.

There is one aspect of her quest still outstanding, however, and I cling to that. I am, as you know, continually surprised at the breadth of Mary's networking contacts and she has telephoned a detective friend. He couldn't help her straight off but he has, however, promised to dig out any existing arrest records of criminal rings who have turned their attention to dog-napping. He explained that where pedigree breeds are concerned, this is now a lucrative enterprise and has told her he will follow up anything he finds with colleagues and parallel police forces in other jurisdictions.

The ISPCA and the Dublin SPCA were helpful: they had checked their records but no collie bitch of that description had been received to date by their shelters. Like the vet, they had told Mary that the microchip would increase Flora's chances of coming home but, again like him, also warned that we should not expect early results; in addition, they told Mary that Flora's colouring, relatively unusual in a collie, could prove helpful.

Next, she told me that while there was no point in phoning any official government departments or agencies because it's a weekend, she has made lists of relevant numbers and websites on both sides of the border 'so we can be ready for Monday'. The horsemeat scandal, where some beef products had been found to be partially equine, has been in full cry on all media outlets recently, and she has spent some time trying to work out a way to connect into this as a concern. 'They eat dog in some countries, Maggie,' she says, frowning as she flicks through her notes, but when I don't respond, she looks up and, seeing my expression, hurriedly backtracks. 'Don't worry. I haven't heard a thing, not one thing, about anything like that in this country. Sorry, Mags. I didn't mean to upset you.'

But the image she has conveyed – it had not arisen in my worst nightmares up to then – is so hideous I find it difficult to quash and it takes all my willpower to concentrate on my side of the bargain.

'Right,' I say, forcing myself to concentrate on the task in hand. 'My turn.'

I dump my load of papers, leaflets and colour charts on the table. 'Let's start with these.' I add the collection of home and living magazines I had bought by the armful from newsagents. I had also bought an index file and, as we tear out illustrations depicting 'one-room living' and 'living in small spaces' rooms, colour concepts, features on accessorising, we file them. We pore over the colour charts and end up arguing over whether soft dove grey is preferable as a wall colour to blue-grey. I have to admit that the more we look at these idealised illustrations, the shabbier and more old-fashioned Mary's room seems.

Such a pity in many ways, I think, but she doesn't agree: 'I can't believe I haven't done this years ago.'

Irrational exuberance again? But this time I'm not being bitchy. I'm genuinely concerned. 'There's plenty of time, Mary, don't get carried away. And all this is going to cost money, you know.'

'I'll manage.'

If it hadn't been for Flora's constant pull at my consciousness, the day would have been very enjoyable. In fact, I have to admit it was enjoyable, to a degree – until at around teatime, the detective rings Mary to tell her he has very little information to give her. 'Dead end,' she says sadly, as she hangs up.

Suddenly, it's seven o'clock, time for me to go home. Not having slept the previous night and once again larded with stress, I'm suddenly overcome with a wave of tiredness. 'Here.' Mary gets up, goes to a little bureau, pulls out a drawer and roots. 'Take one of these when you get home. You need to sleep properly.' She breaks out a couple of tablets from their blister pack and hands them over.

'What are they?' I'm wary.

'Dunno. All I know is that they gave them to me in case I can't sleep, sleep being the great healer and so on, and when I take one, I sleep like a baby.'

'I don't want to get addicted.'

'Oh dear!' She's derisive. 'How many have you there?'

'You're right. Thanks.' I put the tablets in the pocket already containing the phone.

'Call the cops! Dealer aware!'

'Mary! I get the message.'

'Don't forget, Maggie, tomorrow is another day!' she calls down the stairs after me as I clump down towards the front door.

There is the predictable sound of TV canned laughter in the house when I let myself in. There is also a smell of lasagne; Chloë has obviously fed herself. I don't have the energy to go into her, so just call, 'I'm beat, Chlo, going straight to bed, OK?' Not waiting for a reply, I pull my legs, one lead lump at a time, up the stairs.

In the bathroom, I allow my teeth just a glimpse of the toothbrush, pull off my jeans and jumper, then get into bed wearing only my bra and pants. I break one of Mary's sleepers in two, pop one of the pieces, close my eyes and know no more.

Until I'm pulled back to consciousness by the bedside phone ringing. Groggy and disoriented, I reach for it in the dark, knock it off its cradle and have to fumble for it on the floor, almost falling out of bed in the process. 'Hello?' I pull myself back from the brink, only to hear some sort of cacophony on the other end of the line, clanging and banging, men shouting. Still struggling with sleep, I turn on my lamp. The clock says it is just after eleven fifteen. Night or morning?

Still dark. Night. Had I slept for twenty-four hours?

'Hello?' I say again, more strongly, I hope.

'Is that you, Dumpy?'

Derek.

'Yes.' I breathe hard and shake my head, trying to clear it.

'You OK, Dumpy? You're not drunk, are you?'

I'm still too *trí na chéile* to take offence. 'I was asleep. What day is it?'

'It's Saturday night, Maggie. What's going on?'

'Nothing.' Bit by bit, my brain is coming back to life and I recognise that what I'm hearing in the background are kitchen sounds. Restaurant-kitchen sounds. 'I told you, I was asleep. Very tired.'

'I won't keep you. But I heard your dog is missing. I didn't even know you had a dog.'

'Who told you?' That jolts me sufficiently to bring me round.

'The head waiter here is from somewhere up Meath way. He was off yesterday and was visiting his mother. They heard you on the radio this morning before he left.'

'How did they know it was me? Or that I was connected to you?' There was silence, comparative silence, at the other end. 'Derek?'

'He's a friend,' he said. 'Do you remember Jimmy?'

'Big Jim? That one?' I do remember him, a country lad who started as a kitchen porter in one of Derek's first restaurants and who had moved up to make waiter.

'Yes. Well, he's still with me, head waiter now. I'd told him I'd met you. But that's not the point. He said you said on the radio that you were single.'

'So that's why you're calling me in the middle of the night? For Christ's sake! I'm hanging up, Derek. It was a figure of speech. You know the situation. You signed up to it. In every respect except legal, I am single.'

'No – hold on! Table Ten!' he yelled, then: 'Sorry about that. Look, can I ring you tomorrow? I'll help with finding the dog.'

'I'm out tomorrow. And Chloë's here.'

'Well, when, then?'

'I'll be in tomorrow night. Chloë will be back in Merrow from about five o'clock. Good night, Derek.' I hang up and fall back into the embrace of my pillows and my blessed narcotic miasma. My last waking thought is that even half of one of Mary's tablets is the real deal. I feel lovely. Weightless. Like one of her fairies drifting through a pink cloud …

When the phone shrills again, at eight on Sunday morning, I wake up, feeling fresh enough to answer coherently. But Mary gets in first: 'Rise and shine, darling. Sleep well?'

'I certainly did. Thanks. That stuff you gave me is dynamite, if that's the right expression.' I yawn and stretch my luxuriously softened muscles.

'Thought I'd better give you a bell in case you slept the day through. We're going to IKEA, remember?'

I hadn't, as it happened, but I did now. 'See you in about ninety minutes. OK?'

As I shower, I wait for the dread to descend but it doesn't, not at first, and I wonder whether that's a result of the pill itself or the effect of the long night's sleep it had engendered. I could see now how people could get habituated. Existence, while still not exactly peach-like, had had its corners knocked off, and I experience a little tingle of optimism that we will succeed in finding Flora.

Real life seeps in, however, when I get out of the shower and automatically seek her in her usual perch at the top of the stairs, waiting to take up escort duty. OK, I think, no weeping today. It's Mary's day. It's IKEA day!

Two hours or so later, as we pull into the almost full car park, Mary cannot get over the size of the place. Most of all, as we go up the first two escalators and she sees the scale of the restaurant where we're going to have breakfast, she becomes almost breathless with excitement. Overnight, it seems, Mary Guerin had turned into a consumer. I had warned her of the drawbacks – the heavy lifting, the need for a van or someone's large station wagon to accommodate the huge flatpacks, the perils and frustrations of self-assembly – but now she can't wait to get started. While my feet and legs still feel as though they're made of cotton wool, this new Duracell Bunny I have on my hands is bouncing around like a kid. For both of us, I think, drugs are doing their thing.

I'm sure I have no need to describe the next few hours. Any aficionado of the giant Swedish retailer – like half the country – will remember his or her first wide-eyed journey along its one-way systems and floor arrows, which are happily ignored by customers in IKEA's Dublin store. On Sundays, the place is a destination for family outings so buggy and trolley crashes are the order of the day. I believe there is no grey area here: like former Taoiseach Charlie Haughey, in Ireland at least, IKEA inspires either swooning devotion or outright fear and loathing.

Our Mary falls in love that day and, although we make no huge purchases, she manages to spend a hundred euro on— Well, you yourself have at some stage probably run the gauntlet of the primary-coloured cookware section and the aisles filled with handy-dandy storage thingies. She even buys a gorgeous little toolset in a bright orange box with a transparent lid. 'This could come in handy,' has become her cry. I am empathetic: I'd been that recruit. Still am. Which is why I've brought no credit card with me today and only enough cash to buy us breakfast.

We leave Ballymun at about two o'clock, each armed with a thick catalogue, long lists of potential purchases, and far too ambitious dreams of how to jazz up Mary's bedsitter. She has even become a holder of the store's loyalty card. 'What about the landlady?' We were in the car.

'A bit iffy, but she'll come round. I know she will.'

'Bed space?'

'Did you see the way they did that studio flat back there, Mags? Amazing. Like a camper van, with all that knacky storage, except much nicer. I've a high ceiling, as you know, and that'll be a great advantage. As soon as I get rid of all that big furniture, you won't know the space I'll have. Thanks for bringing me. I thought it would be just that blond plywood stuff. Beech veneer. Do you remember beech veneer, Maggie?' As she chats away and we start to inch forward, I notice in the back window of the car ahead of me the smiling head of a King Charles Spaniel, a real one, chin on the back of the seat. Every so often he turns his head, first to one side, then the other, bestowing kisses on the faces of a squad of children, then turns back to stare at us with dark, liquid eyes.

Flora.

All the gaiety of the previous few hours evaporates. It's not that she has been out of my mind while we were in the store, she hasn't. But she wasn't the entire focus. I could be frivolous back there because this was Mary's gig. I could be happy – for her.

I ferry her home and go straight back to my own house. Something is niggling at the back of my consciousness, something I'm supposed to do, or should do or didn't do. I know I have to get Chloë back to Merrow but what else? Something to do with Flora?

My brain will not co-operate.

My sister is packed and ready when I get into the house. 'That's great, Chlo. Sorry I've been out so much, but you understand?'

'Of course I do, Margaret.' This time she doesn't do the full-hug thing but again pats my shoulder. 'Don't worry. Flora will be fine. Everything will be fine. There was a message for you on the phone. I wrote it down.' She hands me a piece of junk mail advertising water softeners, on which she has written 'James' and a mobile phone number.

What can I do except say, 'Thank you'? And this triggers something, the piece of information that has been bothering me all day and that I couldn't quite bring to the forefront. Derek. I had been talking to Derek during my long night of narcotic-assisted sleep. He is to ring me tonight.

Dear God. How do I feel about that? I don't know. Pure and simple, I just don't know. 'You ready, honey?' I pick up Chloë's bag.

Concerning my sister: since she is so equable and so little trouble, why keep her at Merrow?

The reasons are simple. She's very settled and even contented with the two-home routine right now. That does change from time to time: she can get agitated and obstructive, as she did on St Stephen's Day, if she senses a change, even a good change, in this routine. Like, Christmas Day was on a Tuesday this year. She would prefer it to be the same every year. Doesn't make sense, I know, but her sense of what is safe or good is uniquely her own.

Second, I don't feel competent – I am not competent – to supervise her medication regime, which is responsible for her relatively good mental health at the moment. I am certainly not competent to recognise the danger signs if she deteriorates, as she has done once or twice, or, most specifically, decides not to take her tablets. I will never go through that again.

But the main reason is, of course, I won't live for ever. Chances are I will predecease her and, for my own sanity, I need to know that she will be safe and as happy as she can be in her circumstances. I'm repeating myself, I know, but, finding Flora notwithstanding, my sister is the number-one priority of my life.

The irony is that she is far happier at the moment than I am!

TWENTY-SIX

28 March 2013

When I wake up on the morning of Holy Thursday, the first thing I do, as usual, is reach out to switch on *Morning Ireland*, the radio news programme. I'm a little late this morning, just after, rather than before, seven o'clock and the newsreader is halfway through the bulletin, telling us that the Minister for Agriculture has announced he is introducing a new law by which all dogs, even old dogs, must be microchipped.

That news robs me of a few seconds of delicious drowsiness and brings the loss of Flora crashing again into my consciousness. She has been gone since 27 February. Almost a full calendar month. Four weeks and one day.

In the intervening time, there have been periods during which I think I'm getting over the rawness, but something always happens to bring it back into focus, some of it at my own hands, unfortunately. Two weeks ago, for instance, I had foolishly offered the *Sunday Business Post* a piece about dog-napping: 'The Heartbreak of the Dog Owner'. You can just imagine the feelings that brought up as I interviewed devastated families – the children seemed particularly affected – and wrote of my own experience, something quite new to me. The features editor seemed taken with the piece when I emailed it in. It had been due to be published on the Sunday after Easter but, with the possible change in the law, they might bump it up to Easter Sunday. Great fare to leaven the bunnies and the chocolate and the egg hunts, eh? I'm so sad this morning I couldn't care less what they do with the bloody article. I won't read it, as I usually do with my work; like picking at scabs, I go over the sentences and paragraphs, finding all the mistakes, the clunky writing, the sentiments I could have better expressed. I had offered it, not to cash in on poor Flora's disappearance, but in the forlorn hope that the publicity might help find her.

There have been false leads. I got two (phoney) demands for money in return for her, and a private shelter in Roscommon telephoned last week to say someone had brought in a dog of her description. She was microchipped but the chip was not attributable. I dashed up there but, unfortunately, no dice. The poor thing had looked hopefully at me through the mesh of her cage, had even given me a tentative wag, and I was tempted to take her, but in the end I didn't. For me, there is only one collie.

I lie in bed, looking at the ceiling, the rest of the news now a mere background hum. Even if Mary seems to have given up, I haven't. Not completely. To date, I have done everything I can think of – including a daily ring-around of the shelters. Every night I have been out around the neighbourhood, taking different routes, driving slowly, eyes peeled for movement in gardens or side alleys. I have got to know the highways and byways in the Phoenix Park in case she is lying injured in a ditch, rationalising that, even after all this time, she could have been in someone's backyard, fed and tethered, but managed to escape. After last night's fruitless search, however, I accepted that this hope was bordering on the insane and made a resolution that I wouldn't do it any more. It's too painful.

Mary has mined every source she could think of, but kept running into dead ends and is now concentrating on her refurbishment project, when she can. It has been watered down somewhat from our original wild imaginings in IKEA, but the landlady has given her blessing to the repainting and refreshing of the fixtures, and has agreed to supply a single bed. All the furniture and textiles currently in the flat are Mary's own.

I don't blame her for switching: she needs something positive to do because she has had some difficult times with reactions to the chemo, particularly after her sixth session. She had been dreading the seventh, three days ago, but so far so good with that one, and she's clinging to the fact that there is only one more to go, on 8 April.

So, it's been a rough ride for both of us this March, not least because the weather went mad, affecting most other aspects of life. We had floods, storm-force gales, snow in mid-month, and now, with Easter just a couple of days away, the north and north-east of our small island are covered with it. Not atmospheric like the charming, Fairyland enhancement of that white Christmas I keep talking about, the spring whiteout this year has killed innumerable early lambs, buried their mothers alive and left other livestock stranded and starving. There was a poor man on TV a couple of nights ago telling a news reporter that his career as a farmer was over.

So much for the tourist trade and the famous Gathering! I was in town yesterday and saw a few befuddled tourists, huddled together in the blizzard outside Burgerland; they were struggling to protect their cameras by shoving them into food bags.

Wearing her usual half-smile, one of the TV forecasters told us recently that the strong and freezing winds we are having these days are coming directly from Siberia. I love the way they do that. This being Ireland, they rarely have good news to impart, but they have obviously been trained: above all, look calm, sound as though this is news to you too, and don't forget to finish with a smile and even a reassuring twinkle. Let people see that, sure, isn't it all going through life? And aren't we all in this together?

Here's more of it now from the AA Roadwatch girl at the end of the radio news bulletin. She's warning us that it's still snowing in the east, but this is expected to ease off during the morning. Her words send me snuggling further under the duvet and, as has been my wont all through this prolonged March winter, I plan to stay there until I hear the central heating coming on downstairs.

I turn up the volume on the radio. Speculation about the Meath East by-election. I turn it down again. Who cares? Flora's gone. A light has gone out. And it's so quiet: no polite enquiries, no little nudges, no Collie Stares if she needs to go out and I'm not getting the message fast enough.

Oh, stop being such a masochist, Maggie Quinn. Think of something else.

OK. I try to think of something else.

Derek. Derek will do.

Derek, to be fair to him, held true to his offer of help with the search for her. He did ring me that Sunday night after I had come home from leaving Chloë in Merrow, and we had a conversation that was at least calm. Or became so.

He rang me on my mobile phone, a number I hadn't given him. I opened hostilities by asking him where he had got it.

'I went into the hospital after you'd stomped off. I told the cancer-patient services co-ordinator I was your husband. I left a note saying I needed your mobile urgently because my own had been stolen, and all my numbers with it.'

'You're good at notes.'

'Maggie, do you ever stop?'

'No. I can't. Not now. Anyway, I never got to have a proper row with you.'

Silence.

He broke it after a few seconds. 'What's this about your dog?'

'I have a dog. I had a dog. I don't have her any more. She was kidnapped. Dog-napped, if you like. There's a lot of it going about, the vet says. If you watch Crufts, half of that programme is taken up with interviews with people looking for lost or missing dogs.' I had watched the programme a few weeks ago, seen the T-shirts, heard the pleas, seen the 'missing dog' wall of photographs behind desperate owners.

'Was she microchipped?'

'Of course she was. I loved that dog.'

'What was her name?'

'Flora. *Is* her name.' I had burst into tears.

'That's it. Don't go anywhere, I'm coming over. I have a suggestion.' He hung up and there was nothing I could do. I was reminded of his first bloody note when, after a similarly interventionist tone on the phone, Mary came to my rescue. Well,

Derek needn't think I'd welcome him with open arms, I thought. The cheek of him – the hard neck! I had suffered too much hurt just to roll over and have a polite little tea party with him now.

But, at the same time, he had aroused my curiosity: he had said he had a suggestion concerning Flora. I was in no position to turn down any new idea, any offer of help.

He arrived with flowers, would you believe? 'I'm sorry you're going through a hard time,' he said, handing them over.

'Likewise. I was sorry to hear about your own trouble. I didn't really say that the last time.' I kept my tone curt as I took the professionally arranged bouquet, obviously from a florist. Where had he found a florist trading on a late Sunday afternoon?

The same place he had found a painting of a red rose ten years ago? So much for his spontaneous offer to come over when I had wept. This had been planned.

I kept my cool, however, ostentatiously dropping the flowers on to the bottom step of my newly carpeted stairs and ushering him into the sitting room, where I sat as far away from him as physically possible, not that far in such a small room. Carefully, non-verbally, we circled each other. I felt I had to be watchful: this man was probably homeless. There were practicalities involved. While he had long ago ceded the territory of this house, his name was on the deeds along with my own. I watched him closely: his mien was anything but cocky and not what I had expected. 'So, what are you doing here, Derek?'

'I wanted to see you,' he said bluntly. 'You ran off the last time, as you've just said. Also I wanted to offer my help with the dog. With Flora. Genuinely.'

'That's manipulation, Derek. Just like your flowers. Thank you for your offer but it's probably too late. We've done everything possible. What can you do? You're trying to worm your way back into my life. Not going to happen.'

'Dog, Maggie. Help with dog. And dinner. Have you thought about my invitation?'

'More games. Dinner has nothing to do with Flora.'

'Maybe you can't see it now but I can help.' He remained steady. 'I have more resources in that regard than you have.'

'What kind of resources?'

'I know the managers or owners of every restaurant in Ireland. I can have leaflets printed. I can have them fanned out beside every cash register in every restaurant in the country within twenty-four hours. Well, maybe forty-eight, if I'm being honest. We have an Eat Irish Foods promotion going for St Patrick's Day. I'm due to be interviewed on that new morning current affairs programme on RTÉ TV. I can use it to make a direct appeal. Those kind of resources, Maggie.'

There was a long pause. I had not put on the gas fire. I had not offered him a cup of tea. I was not going to ask him where he was living now. I was not going to break this silence.

I did. 'Would they let you do that? On the TV?'

'It's live. They can't stop me. Interested?'

'Of course I'm interested.'

'The payback for me? You let me take you to dinner in the restaurant of your choice.'

Briefly, I toyed with the idea of keeping the upper hand here by insisting on *me* taking *him* to McGarry's Fine Dining in Drumcattlin! But while that might have been well-deserved purgatory for him, I would have been indulging my childish side. 'To what end? What can a dinner achieve after all these years?'

'I don't know until I try.' In a way his openness was refreshing. I had no intention, however, if I went to dinner with him, of letting it go any further than the meal. 'Tell you what,' I said. 'I will go to dinner with you but only after I have Flora back here with me safe and sound. And if you can prove that you were the agent.'

'If it's possible, she will be.'

If she's not dead. It hung in the air, unspoken.

'Be honest, Derek. Why are you doing all this? It's not for Flora, is it? You don't even like dogs, as far as I know.' Oops. Present tense: 'As far as I remember, I mean,' I corrected myself.

'I have nothing against them.' Another breath. 'I miss you, Dumpy – sorry. I mean, I miss you, Maggie.' He flashed the Smile.

Mary was right, I thought. This whole palaver is because, deserter deserted, he is needy and lonely and feeling bad. Where was he during the long nights of no sleep I suffered? 'Well, I don't miss you,' I said shortly, 'not in the slightest,' but even as I said it, I was wondering if that was true. Before everything had gone pear-shaped between us, we had knocked a good few laughs out of our lives together.

No, no no, warned the little woman who lives at the back of my brain. I stood up. 'Thanks for the help with Flora. I accept that and I appreciate it. But it's time for you to go now, Derek.'

'You're the boss,' he said equably. 'I'll stay in touch. Let you know what progress I'm making.'

And from my perspective we parted not exactly on good terms but not on inimical ones either.

When I told Mary about it, she was initially annoyed. 'All that angst. All that listening, all the support, all the advice you asked for and got – and now you're going back to him?'

'I didn't say I'm going back to him. It's just a dinner, Mary, and it's on condition his intervention gets Flora back for me. That would be worth ten dinners. Twenty dinners. Anyway, it probably won't happen. It's been—'

'Look,' she threw up her hands, 'leave me out of it from now on. OK? I don't want to know. I mean it, Maggie.'

'I'm not asking for your blessing, Mary – I shouldn't have to anyway. It's my life.'

'Yes, it is.'

That spat blew over as we both knew it would, although she was as good as her word and refused from then on to hear a single word about Derek or what turned out to be his lack-of-progress reports in the search. Again, to be fair, the cul-de-sacs he encountered were not his fault. As he left my house that night I had given him one of the amateur leaflets I had made; he scanned and emailed me the proper version, as he saw it, and I have to say it was terrifically professional. And he did appeal, directly to camera, on *Morning Edition*, the TV programme. I saw him do it and, for that day at least, was fired up with hope.

But, like all the other initiatives, his fizzled out to nothing.

I hear the heat kicking in downstairs and, reluctantly, crawl out into the freezing open spaces of my bedroom. At least today there is something to look forward to: the Club is having its Easter meeting. For a couple of hours I will have something other than my own troubles on which to focus. In any case, Mary's and Lorna's make mine pale into insignificance, don't they?

We're meeting early because Jean, who is a convert to Catholicism and therefore devout, wants to do the rounds of the Seven Churches in Drogheda, a Holy Thursday tradition that in many parts of Ireland has not yet died out. The plan is to have a midday lunch in the Writer's Bar of the Gresham in O'Connell Street; I managed to reserve a table by the window where we can watch the world go by (and the pickpockets and petty drug dealers in action! Only kidding! O'Connell Street's reputation, at least in the daytime, is far more fearsome than the actuality). We had had great difficulty raising Dina for the event: her answering machine had eventually run out of space. Lorna was the one who had eventually captured her when Dina rang to enquire as to how she was doing.

The weather has let up a little by the time I'm heading for town: the blizzard has softened to sleet. I have decided not to take the car – the parking charges, even on-street, are becoming ridiculous, and with the extra heat and electricity bills due as a result of this awful winter, I'm having to be extra careful with money. I regret the decision as soon as I see the rear red lights of a bus vanishing into the white fog swirling beyond my bus stop, but grit my teeth and stick it out.

I arrive at the Gresham – bright lounge, comfortable seating, good art, cross-section of clients, both local and tourist – to find that Lorna, God love her, and Dina have got there before me. 'Hi there! Cold enough for you both?' I unwind the scarf from my mouth and neck and dump my gloves, bag and coat on the chair beside me.

'It's perishing.' Dina has, for now anyway, ditched the ditzy and looks fantastic in the type of outfit I never saw her wear before – a salmon-coloured biker jacket in soft leather, with quilted shoulders and an asymmetrical zip over a black T-shirt and black skinny jeans. She is nevertheless in complaining mode: 'What did we do to deserve this? Rain, rain, rain for weeks – and now this. We're all going to drown. St Patrick granted us the privilege of vanishing beneath a flood seven years before the rest of the world. Well, it looks as though this is year one.'

'Maybe you're right, Dina. You look fabulous, by the way. That colour really suits you. How are you, Lorna?' I take off one of the numerous woolly hats Jean has knitted for me over the years. 'I'm really sorry I seem to have neglected you lately.'

'Not at all, you haven't, Maggie.' Lorna, who has very obviously lost weight, is making a brave effort to sound cheery. 'You have enough on your plate!'

'And where the hell were you, Dina?' I turn to her. 'We've all been— Oh! Here's Mary!'

My best friend, fur-lined anorak hood pulled tightly over her bright yellow headscarf, is closely followed by Jean, who is muffled up like an Eskimo, with multiple snoods and jackets. After a bit of divestment, shifting of chairs and small-talk, we all settle down and pick up the menus. 'I recommend the Coronation Chicken, girls! I've had it here and it's really good.' I'm jovial and, although we'll split the bill, I'm in hostess mode because the Gresham had been my choice and I feel responsible. 'And, Dina, you can have your champagne by the glass!' She doesn't react. I had been teasing, of course, and had expected some comeback. 'You OK, Dina? Where did you disappear to? We were worrying about you.'

'I'm not a baby. I'm a grown woman. Time you got that into your head, Maggie,' she snaps, unzipping the biker jacket. 'Let's order. I'm starving.'

I can't believe this. Dina is languid, mischievous, provocative, scornful and all kinds of things, but she is never cranky. She's cranky today. I suppose we're all a bit grumpy: this weather would put years on a saint. I decide to take her words at face value. It's none of my business how she spends her time or where.

However, as unelected chair of the group, or so I feel, I'm duty-bound to keep things on an even keel and at present I decide Jean is the best prospect for communal good morale. 'How's Jerry, Jean?'

'Never better! I just can't get over it. I pinch myself when I wake up every morning. Who wants to wish on my ring?' Smiling fit to burst, she fluffs up her hair with her right hand while holding up her left. She notices that I'm looking at her other hand, to which she has transferred her plain gold wedding band. 'Ernest would approve! He would have wanted me to be happy!'

'Of course he would.' I'm embarrassed. It's none of my business anyhow. We all ooh and aah, then hand the little diamond solitaire around and put it on our own fingers to make a wish. Never mind my ring finger, it won't go beyond the top knuckle of the little one, but I make the wish in any case and there are no prizes for guessing what it is.

Our server, a tall young blonde I peg as Polish because of her accent, comes to take our order. 'Who's driving?' I look around. 'Will we have wine?'

Both Dina and Lorna had taken the Luas and the Dart respectively so the only car driver is Jean, who barely imbibes in any case. So we order G and Ts for Mary, Lorna and myself, a Dubonnet and soda for Dina and a Britvic pineapple juice for Jean to have as aperitifs, with a bottle of Sauvignon Blanc for the four public-transport users.

'And James, Lorna? What's happening there?' I give our lunch orders to the girl, hand back the menus and, continuing my role as self-appointed MC, turn to Lorna.

'He said you talked to him, Maggie.'

'I did. Twice. We exchanged numbers at Martin's funeral. He left a message with Chloë. I rang him back and we had a chat. He rang again about a week afterwards to tell me he was meeting you for lunch in Howth. He seemed very excited about it. Maybe I should have told you we were in contact but I really felt that it was up to him to get in touch with you without me acting as a go-between.'

'He did say you'd advised him and that you were being very nice.'

'Not really.' I didn't tell her that during our conversation it had occurred to me that, between Chloë, Mary, Lorna and now James, I should probably have been charging the HSE for social work. 'I just did what anyone would have done. I talked to him. So how did it go? Did you meet?'

'He wanted to know what Lennie was like,' she says tentatively. 'Where we met and all that. I suppose that to some degree he's entitled to know. It felt weird, though, brought a few things up that I didn't really want to think about. And the awful thing is that Lennie's dead now and there's no way I can have a go at him. None of this is James's fault, of course, so it wouldn't have been fair to take my husband's sins out on him. Then he wanted to know about his – his half-brother, what he was like … '

She spreads her hands and lowers her head, as though to examine the nails, and Jean, alert as always in the protective service of her friend, jumps in: 'You don't have to talk about this in front of all of us, Lorna. It's private. And it's too soon.' She glares at me, her little face screwed up, tight with warning.

'Thanks, Jean, but I don't mind.' Lorna looks up again. 'I trust you all. You've been great. It was very hard talking to James like that but in a way it was kind of good too. I don't know if you can understand how the two things can go together. He spent that whole Saturday with me. After the lunch – which he insisted on paying for – he came home with me and we went through all the photo albums and so on. When he left I was tired, but also sort of lighter, if you can understand that. He's my stepson, after all.'

Out of the corner of my eye, I can see Mary gearing up to comment on the precise nature of this relationship, but I hurry on: 'So what's to happen next?'

'He wants me to meet his adoptive parents.'

'Are you going to?' This from Dina.

'I suppose so. Do you think I shouldn't?' Lorna is uncertain now.

'Entirely up to you.'

'I told him I'll think about it. I suppose that's really a yes, isn't it?'

'As I said, it's your choice.'

'Dina, leave her alone!' Jean does her thing again.

'Only asking!' Dina bridles but doesn't pursue it.

If I didn't know better, I'd say she's sulking. What has got into her today?

Our drinks arrive and I pick mine up. 'Let's not bicker, ladies! Here's to us!' I raise my glass and we all clink, individually and collectively.

'What about you, Maggie?' Over her drink, Mary's eyes are challenging. 'You want to tell them about Derek?'

That got everyone's attention. 'Derek? Your husband, Derek?' Her ring safely back where it belongs, Jean's voice has escalated to the extent it can be classified as a squeak.

'Ex-husband, well, in all but name,' I respond lamely. Then, because I feel I have no option, I go into the saga of meeting Derek in the hospital, his revelation about being dumped by the popsy, the pressure to have dinner, the bouquet, the whole nine yards.

'So you're going to meet him again.' It wasn't a question. Jean, for whom happy endings are now top of the agenda, is wide-eyed and thrilled. 'Isn't life funny? Great but funny – after all, in a way he's responsible for us getting together in the Club, yeah?'

At that moment, the server arrives with the table settings and I'm saved from answering. Or so I think until she leaves again.

'Well, are you? Seeing him?' This, definitely a question, two of them, both querulous, from Dina.

'I haven't made up my mind.'

'All men are shits!' Pale with fury, Dina spits it, so loudly that the couple at the table beside ours look across sharply. We're astonished too.

'What's the matter?' I ask. We haven't yet seen even a morsel of our lunch. But with Lorna, Dina and me in play – we haven't got around to Mary and her news about the tendril of communication with Ramona and her 'long-lost' brother – there could be an interesting couple of hours ahead. 'Tell us the story, Dina.'

TWENTY-SEVEN

I'm safely home after our lunch in the Gresham Hotel.

We had splashed out on a second bottle of wine and this is possibly why, for the first time in more than a month, I wasn't listening for scrabbling paws when I opened my front door. I'm now resigned to Flora's absence, I think sadly.

Overtly at least, the others had been sympathetic when I had mentioned the lack of progress in finding her. But I could sense the feeling around the table that this was a lost cause and that it was time to let go and get on with my life: here she comes again, moaning about that bloody dog. Puh-lease! Next!

Obviously cognisant of this, Mary gave flesh to the communal wish: 'Not changing the subject or anything, I want us to set the date for our summer meeting here and now. Right away. If we don't, we'll get into a fuss. Jean will be gone by the end of July so we have to have a firm date and keep to it. No faffing around.'

Looking directly at Lorna, she added, 'We have to do that or let the whole group disperse, and you know what that means. We'll let it go for this year, our lives will move on and we probably won't get together again. That's why the next two meetings, summer and autumn, are crucial. Jean won't be here for either autumn or Christmas, and Christmas is looking iffy for you, Lorna.'

Caught on the hop, Lorna shook her head. 'I ... ' she glanced at me '... I don't really know. My situation is, well, fluid.'

'We know that, Lorna,' I said. 'And we understand, don't we, girls?' I flicked around. 'Of course we accept that, now you're getting the opportunity, you'll want to be with your grandchildren. Especially this first Christmas after Martin—'

Mary wouldn't let me go there: 'As I say, for the next few months we have to make the most of the time we have left together. I certainly need a date to look forward to.'

'It's a long way to Christmas, though.' Lorna didn't want to sound happy about abandoning us. 'Anything can happen. It means so much to you, Maggie.'

'Pish, tosh! Yes, it does. But it will still be Christmas, won't it? I'll still enjoy it, however or wherever it happens. So stop worrying about me and my stupid little obsessions and superfluities. Anyway, we're talking about the summer meeting now.' I've noticed this about women and diary dates. Mary's right: there is a lot of faffing around, as she calls it. A lot of cancelling and rearranging. 'I know!' Jean interrupts this train of thought. 'Let's make it a date to meet on Maggie's birthday! It can be a thank-you occasion for having had so many great Christmas dinners in her house, yes? Our treat.' She looks around the group. 'Jerry and I will be off the following week so it can be a double, to wish her a happy birthday and *bon voyage* to us. How's that?'

I was touched. I protested, of course, but they all brushed me aside. 'No presents, mind, it's not a big birthday, quite an ordinary one, and to be treated to lunch will be an "elegant sufficiency",' quoting one of my mother's frequent adages. 'I mean that.'

'Yeah, *carpe diem*, Maggie! We have no idea where any of us will be in two years' time.' Jean smiled happily, eyes shining and cheeks rosy. 'Anyway, this big-birthday obsession is stupid. Every birthday should be a celebration of being alive on the planet.' Lurve suited her, I thought.

'I second that, Jean!' Mary held up her hand. 'And, in my case, I have reason to know that every day counts.'

'Oh, Mary, of course you do and I do. We all do.' I could feel tears of gratitude clustering at the back of my eyes. Probably 11 or 12 per cent proof. The wine was strong.

'So. You heard it, ladies. Definitely no presents.' But Dina was winking at the others. Having got her story off her chest, during the telling of which she had topped our wine-drinking league, she was in far better form than she had been when we all came in, albeit, I supposed, temporarily. It was some adventure she'd had. I'll tell you about it presently. Believe me, it's worth your undivided attention.

In the meantime, I was secretly delighted about this new idea Jean had floated. My birthday had never been celebrated communally in adulthood, and my memories of the few attempts my parents had made to throw modest parties for me in childhood are overshadowed by more painful ones of Chloë's unguestlike behaviour. The stress of trying to gloss over this with friends present, not just Mary but my two Protestant chums from down the road, both of whom were extremely well behaved, was enormous. All of us, Mary included and even Dina, were in great form by the time we had finished the lunch. Jean rushed off first to attend her Holy Thursday devotions. And as the rest of us left the Gresham, going the rounds of hugging and air-kissing in enthusiastic farewell, we were once again, I think, newly grateful to have each other as friends. 'I'll wear my Alberta Ferretti to your birthday party, Maggie! Yiz can all throw sugar at it!' Dina made a grand, double-armed gesture as though describing a rainbow. 'And I'll wear my new muu-muu,' Mary called after her. 'Hides a multitude!' Dina responded by blowing her a kiss as she went out into O'Connell Street.

We went our separate ways then – Lorna to do some Easter-egg shopping, Mary to meet another friend for high tea, I to the bus stop. But as I walked through the sleet, I smouldered with an extra-warm, alcohol-fuelled sense of good cheer, which persisted all the way home.

In bed temporarily for a nap, I'm going through it all. We sure have a full house now, don't we? No one in the group has escaped a major life event. Only three months ago there we were, in flying form around my Christmas table – although, as we know now, three of us were keeping secrets, or attempting to. Four, if you include Dina, who was at the beginning of her Awfully Big Adventure.

Looking back, I'd say James McAlinden's presence and the distraction that that had caused acted almost like a gagging order because, especially if alcohol is involved, we're normally not behind the door in discussing our personal lives. That Christmas Day and evening should probably be consigned to our group's history as a sort of mass hysteria – think adolescent girls and boy bands, but with the 'girls' having bunions and spreading waistlines – but we all got sense about him pretty quickly. He's mentioned now only in connection with Lorna.

Under the duvet, staring up at the ceiling, I ticked the secrets off on my fingers.

Mary's cancer (and, in addition, the tentacle of communication with family).

For Lorna, it was poor Martin – but also James, the living manifestation of her husband's infidelity.

Jean had already found the man who is clearly the real love of her life. She has rarely, if ever, talked about the first husband, Ernest. To me he is a sort of shadow and I can't envisage him in any sense, personality, character, even what colour his hair was. But they had two children, so I suppose there had to have been something between them, particularly since she converted to marry him without hassle.

Now here's Dina joining the ranks of the affected.

And not one but two life-changing events for me. I lost Flora (small cheese I suppose in light of some of the other traumas, but very upsetting for me) and was contacted again by Derek.

Let's think about that. Am I, against my best friend's advice, plus the shrill warnings of my brain-resident little woman, on the verge of committing the cardinal error of allowing my yellow-bellied rat of a husband back into my life? Even for reasons of self-esteem, shouldn't I stop allowing him head room? Him and his bloody dinner invitation?

But do either of those issues, dog or Derek, register as a major life event? Nah.

Well, maybe Derek ...

After we had thoroughly thrashed out Dina's situation, it was love-chick Jean who started in on mine and they all got involved. I had been upstairs to the Ladies – quite a distance from the Writer's Bar – and was gone for maybe ten minutes.

When I got back, silence fell around the table: they had clearly been talking about me. 'So?' I looked at Mary, who was busily readjusting today's scarf, a beautiful shade of indigo with abstract patterning in a lighter blue. 'Is someone going to let me in on the conversation?'

'We were talking about you and Derek,' Jean responded brightly. 'We gather there's been a development.'

'I didn't say there'd been a "development", Jean,' Mary cut in. 'All I said was that she had met him accidentally, he's separated again and he's being persistent.'

'Well, I'd call that a development.' This was Dina.

'Me too,' Jean chimed back in. 'I think she should go to that dinner. It's exciting. Anyway, what's the harm?'

That notion is following me around, I thought irritably, but before I could say anything, Lorna gave her friend a dig in the ribs. 'Just because you're on cloud nine, don't be pushing her.'

Jean pucked her back. 'They have a history together, is all I'm saying, and—'

'I'm here!' I said loudly. 'I can hear you. I'm not deaf. Not yet anyway.'

To a woman, they all stared at me. 'Sorry, Maggie.'

But Jean neither looked nor sounded contrite. 'What are you going to do?'

'I haven't made up my mind,' I muttered.

'I think you have. I think you just don't want to admit it.' Mary wore her bolshy expression.

'I'll make up my own mind, thank you. I've been doing it for fifty-seven years. If anything of interest happens I'll send yiz all a telegram. All right?'

I was lying through my teeth. I had already met Derek for dinner the previous Monday. He doesn't open his place on Mondays so he's free.

I don't quite know how to characterise the occasion. Had it been covered by a tabloid newspaper, the front-page report would have gone something along the lines of:

Exclusive! HACK BACK WITH JACK?

Top Chef Derek Jackman and Ex, retired hackette, Maggie, were spotted deep in conversation (negotiations?) late Monday night and NOT in the cook's own restaurant. The pair, who split ten years ago, have never got divorced.
(Full Story, page 5)

The restaurant was the Trocadero, my choice. It's been there for ever. I've always loved the crimson, womb-like interior, with its retro candle-holders just short of old Chianti bottles, the velvety feel of the furnishings, its buzzy, theatrical clientele and, most particularly, no matter how long I've been absent, the wonderful welcome I get. You're always a prodigal at the Troc with its traditions, its steaks, its duck, its chicken-liver parfait, its house red – and Robert Doggett. Everyone loves Robert.

'Are you sure you want to go there?' As a chef and an inveterate foodie, Derek is always keen to size up the latest competition. 'You wouldn't like a bit of an adventure, push the boat out? Fade Street Social or somewhere like that?'

'No.' I stood firm and it felt good. When we were together, I had always deferred to Derek in the matter of cuisine.

When we got there, I had a shock. Gone was the red, the

snuggle. The place had been redecorated. Nice, but it would take me a while to get used to it.

There were other surprises in store: Mondays, I think, are, or were in my day, normally slack for restaurants but, in addition, last Monday had been the first day of Holy Week and, naturally, I had expected the Troc to be quiet and that we'd have no problem getting a table. But it was hopping. Robert worked his sleight of hand, though, and, after a short wait, managed to fit us in, even securing us a booth; he knows us of old but, being probably the most discreet restaurateur in Dublin, made no mention of seeing us together again.

It was awkward at the beginning, of course it was; and we both made quite a drama out of selecting from the menu. Diverting from my usual G and T, I plumped for a brandy and ginger aperitif, which seemed to settle me enough to behave as normally as a separated wife can when dining with her husband, who has been thrown out of his home by his popsy.

As for being 'deep in conversation', as in my imaginary tabloid piece, that implies words travelling both ways. Whatever the dynamic between us might have looked like to an observer, Derek was doing most of the talking while I, despite the brandy and a fair amount of wine, managed to remain on high alert for any kind of tricksiness. Wine talks to my libido and if that one-night, off-the-wall flirtation with a virtual James McAlinden had taught me anything, it was that while I had been celibate for a very long time, I wasn't yet dead to the heels.

At the same time I had to admit it felt good to be out for dinner in a nice restaurant, one to one with a man, even if the man was Derek.

By the time the main course came, we were halfway through a second bottle and I found myself watching Derek's hands. I had always liked his hands. They were in full descriptive mode as he recounted some of the funnier episodes of his kitchen reign. The popsy, I thought, had softened a few corners on him: his humour was far more self-deprecating than I remembered. He had really dressed up too: impeccable jacket and slacks, open-necked linen shirt in a shade I've always thought of as Virgin Mary blue, which brought out the blue of his eyes. And with the soft retro lighting, the infectious chatter and sheen of the young people, and the subtle scent of aftershave drifting towards me from the other side of the table, I was beginning to think that maybe Derek wasn't half bad after all— Oops! I had let my guard down. I was in danger of enjoying the man's company.

Get a grip, I scolded myself. This, after all, was no ordinary date. I had to remember I was dining with Derek the Rat. 'Tell me about the girls,' I interrupted the flow of his latest anecdote. 'How are they taking the break-up?' Innocently, I popped a forkful of lamb cutlet into my mouth.

The intervention worked as it had before. He shed the bonhomie and, for the next twenty minutes, I saw the real Derek, the one who didn't care that his pain was showing. Probably as half pissed as I was, I thought, glad that I had caught him, rather than the other way around. Take that, you swine. Now you know how it feels!

I sure can be a meanie! I was delighted with myself as he poured his heart out about how he missed Crystal, Marjorie and 'little Sunniva'.

Then I couldn't keep it up. The more he talked, the more wretched and shamefaced I felt. This was a real tragedy for him.

'I haven't seen them for six weeks now. She keeps making excuses and changing the arrangements, or insisting that I see them at times when she knows damn well I'm working.'

I did work hard to maintain my bitterness. I couldn't just let him get away with stuff, could I? 'Where are they now?'

'Dubai.' He was miserable. 'Easter holidays.'

Should I sympathise? Lady Wine came to help me, reversed her charms, showed her claws. 'And where are you living, Derek?'

'Short-term let. Ballsbridge, near the restaurant.'

'Nice, is it?'

'It'll do,' he said shortly. 'Functional. I try to be there as little as possible.'

We stared at each other, each knowing precisely what the other was thinking.

He: Is it lost? Or – could I push this now?

Me: Good enough for you. You'd better not say anything about coming home with me.

You're good at this, Maggie Quinn, I thought gleefully, boldly holding his eyes with my own as wine egged me on. It would have been so easy. But then, dammit, the whole nasty vibe suddenly backed off, denying me the killer blow. The claws were replaced with genuine sympathy. Always a perilous emotion for me in situations like this where the sensible thing to do is to maintain the upper hand.

Thank God for Robert, who, right at that moment, bustled over to our table for a chat, which meant that Derek instantly pulled on his public face. I excused myself and went downstairs to the Ladies.

Having used the facilities, I lingered, staring at myself in the mirror: face flushed, lipstick eroded, hair mussed, eye makeup smudged. Feck it, I thought, I'm not going to make repairs for him. Should I? I dithered. But then, 'When in doubt, leave it out!' The old journalistic adage rose to kick me in the backside and so, as used-looking as I had been when I'd left, I went back upstairs.

Walking towards the table, I saw that our waiter, having replaced Robert, was standing patiently while Derek, bill in front of him, rummaged through his wallet. The one I had given him the Christmas before he left. It was distinctive: tan leather with an emerald green seam. Don't think about it. Don't read anything into it. It's a fecking wallet. That's all.

'No discount for a fellow professional?' He grinned up at the young waiter as I arrived.

'I'm afraid not.' The kid smiled back.

'Not to worry – here you go, that's for yourself. Don't spend it all in the same shop.' He added a twenty- and a ten-euro note to the little pile of cash.

'Thank you.' The kid went off.

'Ready to go?' He looked up at me. Cautious now. Not knowing quite what to expect. 'Was it OK – did you enjoy yourself, Dumpy?'

'Yup!' I picked up my padded jacket and before he could reach me to help me into it – it can be tough getting out of those booths quickly – I had it on and zipped up.

He got the message. 'You have a hood, good,' he said. 'It's pouring again out there. Freezing too.'

And that was how we'd left it – except for his walking me to the taxi rank on Dame Street. 'I don't have a car,' he said, taking my arm at the traffic lights. 'I live so close to work I don't need it, sorry. Otherwise … '

'Of course.'

'And sorry about the dog. I did give it my best shot.'

'I know you did. Thank you.'

'It's awful to think that such a thing can happen. That even a dog isn't safe any more in its own garden.'

'Yes.'

He gave the taxi driver my address, then kissed my cheek while simultaneously trying to give me money for the fare. I wouldn't take it, climbed in and we drove off, leaving him standing. He had no coat. I forced myself not to look back through the rear window. I didn't want to start feeling sorry for him all over again, getting drenched, ruining the good jacket and trousers.

Now. Let's face it. Do you think I had anything concrete to tell my friends at our meeting in the Gresham today?

Thought so.

I'm feeling no pain right now, drifting off to sleep. Before I do, I set the alarm for eight p.m., remembering that there are a few housekeeping tasks to fulfil before Chloë comes tomorrow: I have to run the washing machine so I can dry her sheets in the dryer to remake her bed. The spares are still in the laundry basket. I haven't been the most efficient of housekeepers lately. The dishwasher is full, I've to run that too; and my bin collection is at the crack of dawn tomorrow. Both bins are overflowing and I can't miss it.

I'm up and about again in time for the nine o'clock news, then get caught into *The Takeover*. I mess about with the laundry and dishwasher, but then, of course, it's time for Vincent Browne on TV3: I can't look away from that in case I miss something.

It's midnight before I remember the bloody bins.

I tighten the belt of my dressing gown, pull the black bag out of the kitchen receptacle and, braving the frost in my slippers, go round the side of the house, dump the plastic bag into its wheelie bin and trundle the whole thing out to the front of the house.

As I open the front gate to pull the bin through, in the dim light cast by one of the streetlamps about five yards further down the road, I notice that someone has dumped a load of cardboard beside my wall. It's not the first time I've had to pick up someone else's detritus from this footpath and to see it again puts me in bad humour. Will I just leave it there for spite? But then, sighing, wishing I had my rubber gloves on but unwilling to spend the time further freezing my tail off to go in and get them, I march angrily towards the heap, wishing hell and damnation on the slob who left it there.

I'm bending over it to scoop it up with both hands when it moves.

Jesus! I take a step backwards. Is there a rat or a mouse or something in there?

I back off.

It moves again and, at the far end of the heap, I see a little white speck give a small twitch. Slowly, I approach it and, as I do, I hear a sound, very faint, but there's no wind tonight and it's very still on this early Good Friday morning. The sound was unmistakable. It was either the feeble cry of a baby or a dog's whimper. The front of the pile moves a little and I can see the outline of a dog's head.

'Oh, my God, Flora!' I kneel beside her and she attempts to raise her head, but she can't. She's too weak. She whimpers again, whether in pain or for joy at seeing me is unclear.

Tears running down my face, as gently as I can, I put my arms around her and pick her up. She is filthy, she smells like rotting fish, her fur is matted and the white markings on her face are black with dirt and mud, which is why I didn't distinguish it from the dark pile of what I had taken to be monochromatic wet cardboard.

As I walk in with her, she droops in my arms, making no

independent movement, but when I bring her into the sitting room and place her on the carpet, again I see that little white tip move. She's attempting to wag her tail.

Her eyes are sealed shut with mucus or some kind of infection. Under the fur, she is emaciated: I can see the line of her backbone, and her hipbone is sharp and angled. 'Oh, Flora! Flora!' I put my arms around her and lift her head, whispering into her neck, 'You're home safe now, darling. Stay with me. I'm going to get help.' As I put her down, a wide mat of hair falls away from her back, exposing a deep, open wound behind where her collar should be. Where her fucking microchip should be.

I run to the hall and ring the number for the emergency vet, taped to the banisters. The call is answered by the Spanish girl, Josepha. 'Please, please,' I jabber, then, somehow, manage to calm down enough to tell her what has happened.

She gets it right away. 'Can you come in? Or should I come to her?'

'I think she's too far gone. She's very weak … ' I describe Flora's condition.

'Give me your address,' she says.

While I'm waiting for her to arrive, I turn on the gas fire to warm Flora and dry her a little, then run upstairs and fetch a spare duvet from the hot press. I cover her with it, and then hare into the kitchen, fill her water bowl and carry it back to her but when I put it down in front of her, her nostrils move a little but she is too weak, it seems, to lift her head. So I crouch down beside her, wet my fingers and put them to her lips. That white tip on the tail moves again and her tongue comes out for an inch or so and, very tentatively, she licks the moisture from my hand.

I do it again and again until about a third of the water is gone from the bowl, most of it, unfortunately, wasted on the carpet. When she seems to want no more, or be too exhausted to continue, I dip a corner of the duvet into the bowl and being as gentle as I can, use it to bathe her eyes. Under the light of the sitting room, they are a shocking sight, encrusted with hardened, greenish-yellow pus. The wound on her back looks equally infected. The two pads I can see are swollen and cracked, the claws broken.

It's warm water I need. I'm lumbering to my feet to get it when I hear the car stopping outside.

Thank God. I race to the door and admit the vet. She is carrying a large bag.

I bring her into the sitting room. 'Oh, my God,' she says, kneeling down. 'This is terrible.' She takes the duvet off Flora, who reacts only with another twitch of her nose. She knows this vet and shouldn't be afraid. 'This is shocking. How long she be like this?'

'I rang you immediately. I don't know how long she was outside.'

'Much longer than this. Much longer.' She performs a quick examination, checking the pads, the wounds, parting the skin in various places. 'She is very thin. And I think that if you did not find her tonight she is dead.'

'Is it too late?' My heart starts to pound. 'Can she be saved?'

'I don' want you to think everything be automatically OK. Everything not OK. She need everything, nutrition, hydration, antibiotics, vitamins. She has walked a long way. She has had no food for long time, I think. She need a drip. I brought a stand, but she will need someone to sit with her all the night to watch. Can you do this? Or I can take her back to our place.'

'I'll do it,' I offer fervently. There's no way I'll agree to leave Flora's side.

'Her eyes?' Josepha continues. 'I don' know, let's see.' She delves into her bag and takes out a small bottle, shakes some of the contents on to a cotton pad and, expertly, applies it to the uppermost eye. Flora seems to recoil but barely. 'Don' worry.' The vet doesn't stop working. 'It stings a bit. Sorry, doggie,' she croons, picking up Flora's head. 'We try to make you better.'

Patiently, trying not to cause hurt, she continues to clean the eyes, first one, then the other, until, miracle of miracles, the first, then the second, opens and Flora and I look at each other.

I try to tell myself it was the cleaning solution but, honestly, I think she's crying.

I am.

TWENTY-EIGHT

As I mentioned, the newest and freshest news during our Gresham lunch had been Dina's, entirely unexpected – but, I suspect, not all that surprising to most of us, given what we know about her. I, for one, still cannot get my head around it.

As you know, she's an inveterate manhunter, and I don't mean that pejoratively. No moral judgements here. It takes all sorts, all God's children singing in the choir and so forth. Dina is just the way she is. She is single. She can do what she likes with her life, as she has pointed out to the rest of us in the Club many, many times.

To summarise her story, poor Dina met her Waterloo in the person of a half-Greek, half-Argentinian guy called – I hope I get the spelling right here – Manolo Kacoslodakis: something like that anyway. He was thirty-five years old, he told her, and enjoyed all the trappings of wealth, which, of course, meant that Dina didn't

389

need to be her usual suspicious self about his motives in wanting to get together with her. His father, he told her, ran a small but profitable yacht-chartering and brokerage business out of Turkey and he, as the only son, ran the company's UK agency, buying and selling boats while also organising small, exclusive (i.e. wealthy) groups on sailing trips through the western Mediterranean, the Aegean, the Black Sea and the Sea of Marmara.

Over our meal, she tells us that she had met this guy online, in a perfectly respectable chatroom, according to her. They started cybermeeting and flirting in a manner she found very flattering. The usual story. Older ingénue, young, virile aspirant. He had told her, in one of their getting-to-know-you cyberchats, that after a few tough years, this spring season had showed a renaissance in general business. Many of his European clients, including the Brits, had been through rough financial waters but now seemed to be emerging, if not intact, at least with renewed determination to survive. Better than that, from his company's point of view, many clients were eager to start 'living' again and were buying or upgrading to new boats and/or booking decent holidays.

Dina was adamant she had been careful during the initial getting-to-know-you stages. 'I asked all the right questions. Honestly I did, girls. We'd been communicating since the end of November, long before Christmas. So I did wait until I was absolutely sure he was on the level before agreeing to meet him. Three months should be more than enough, yeah?'

The deal, laid down by her, was that they would meet in London, in a public place. 'I told him it had to be in a busy café or restaurant and he came back with the Caffè Florian at Harrods. 'I Googled it and, girls, it looked fabulous! I'd been to Harrods before but never up there. It's a copy of the one in Venice. It might even be a branch, with frescos and gilded mirrors, the whole Italian vibe. It certainly serves the same food as the one in Venice and specialises in pastries. Luscious! Anyway, we agreed on that and he made a booking for three thirty in the afternoon.'

He also made a reservation for her at the five-star Montcalm Hotel near Marble Arch and insisted on paying for her air tickets. When she collected them, she found they were business class, and as she came out of Customs into Heathrow Arrivals, the first person she saw was a man in a dark uniform holding up her name on a piece of cardboard; her new friend had sent a limousine. On the back seat there was a bouquet of white roses, with a handwritten letter telling her he was sorry but now couldn't make Caffè Florian because of an unexpected but very important business appointment. He promised to make amends by taking her there during her stay.

If she couldn't wait for that, however, she was to go along by herself to Caffè Florian. He was a regular Harrods customer, was known in the restaurant, and had included his store card in the envelope so she could use it. He had left her name with the cash desk in case there was any suspicion. 'He knew I loved chocolate. It was one of the things I'd told him about me – we were swapping stuff like that. He told me his secret passion was pistachio ice cream. But, anyway, he said if I was willing to wait for us to go to Florian together, I could go to another café that specialises in exotic chocolate. He gave me its name and said the maître d' there was a personal friend of his. They came from the same town. He was so certain I'd like it that he had told his friend that if I went there I was to be looked after like royalty. He even enclosed a gift card for the place worth a hundred pounds. "Or," he said … '

Dina looked off into the distance '... "why not go to both cafés? What a lovely way to spend a spring afternoon!"

'So I did go to the chocolate one. Not just because of the chocolate but because I wanted to be treated like royalty, and in fairness I was. It was brilliant. The place offered all the desserts and drinks you could possibly expect but also main courses, like slow-cooked beef with a chocolate sauce. The friend, the maître d', couldn't have been nicer or more attentive. As for the patisserie – it was fantastic. I stuffed myself.'

There was some malfunction when she presented the gift card: Manolo's friend was full of apologies. 'He kept asking if I had kept it near my mobile phone and was wiping it on his sleeve and so on – and trying and retrying it, but in the end I told him not worry and used my own credit card. He was still full of apologies. He gave me a discount because of the inconvenience. Charged me only for the cakes, not for the coffee.

'Then, of course, because I was where I was, with time on my hands, I ended up shopping. I'm afraid I went a bit wild. I bought this ... ' she held up her wrist, from which dangled one of those chunky charm bracelets that have become fashionable lately '... and this.' She tapped the pink leather jacket. 'I got this in Harrods, but I didn't use his card. I used my own again. It's Balmain, the first designer item I've ever owned. Then, because I'd bought the jacket, I had to go looking in boutiques around the streets for something to go under it and ended up buying a really lovely black lace dress. That wasn't enough, though. I went back to Harrods and bought a pair of Jimmy Choo high heels. I really wanted to make a big impression on him that night. I spent an absolute fortune, so much so that after the Jimmy Choos I got a phone call from the credit card company telling me they had detected unusual activity in my account and asking me to confirm I was in London and making large purchases!'

She gave short shrift to the guy at the other end of the line, reminding him of the size of her bank balance and of the credit limit she enjoyed on her cards. Plural. 'And − I hate this −' she covered her face '− to cap it all, I also bought a really sexy sheer black nightdress and négligée.'

'Don't be embarrassed about that.' Jean, her little solitaire flashing under the lights, leaned over and patted her arm. 'We've all done things like that.'

'Jean!' Even Dina was astonished, dropping her hands. 'I wouldn't have thought—'

'So I was never young?' Jean's chin jutted aggressively.

'Of course we don't think you were never—' Lorna began, but Mary cut across her: 'Hush, everyone. Go on, Dina, what happened next?'

What happened was that this Manolo fellow wined and dined Dina that night, 'and he was the perfect gentleman, charming, funny, I had a great time. I wore the new outfit and the compliments were flying. He was really gorgeous-looking, sex on legs, much nicer than his photograph − imagine those polo players you see? I did my best,' she added ruefully, 'but there was no getting him into bed. He said it was too soon. That he wanted to make sure I was comfortable with him. He went on and on about this "surprise" he had in store for me the next day. He said he would collect me at half past nine and I was to come with my bag packed.'

On the dot, he collected her and her luggage, and before she knew where she was, she was being helped aboard a large motor yacht moored along the Thames by a guy in a white uniform. While Manolo briefly stayed on deck to chat to the guy, she climbed down

393

into the saloon where, on a table, there was a bottle of champagne in an ice bucket, two filled glasses bubbling beside it with a dish of chocolate-dipped strawberries between them. Then Manolo himself came down and told her they were off along the river on a jaunt. 'I asked him what had happened to the captain. "We are alone, darling Dina," he said, "and going on a lovely adventure." That boat was fabulous, girls,' Dina sounded rueful, 'the height of luxury. Cream-leather seating and shiny wood and brass in the sitting-room part and, I have to say it again, he couldn't have been more of a gentleman.' As he climbed the steps to the wheelhouse, she noticed that there was a suitcase, obviously his, on one of the banquettes. 'Are we going somewhere to stay?' she asked, when she joined him in the swing chair beside his as he moved the boat out into the river.

'Patience, Dina,' he said. 'You'll see!'

The weather, however, did not live up to the promise of the boat. When they had been travelling for half an hour or so, the wind got up, it started to lash, and although he brought the craft to rest, engine idling, at an empty mooring beside a set of steps, they were being thoroughly rocked about and Dina started to feel sick.

He was instantly concerned. 'This is terrible.' He cut the engine, went out on deck, threw a rope, went ashore after it, tied it and, drenched to the skin, came back down to where she now sat, green-faced, beside his bag on the banquette. He sat in beside her and put an arm around her. 'We shall have to get you to somewhere safe where you can rest. I had a great plan. But no worries, angel, we can do it tomorrow.'

Dina, who couldn't understand why she felt so sick — 'Never before, even going across the goddamned Irish Sea in the old mailboat' – nevertheless asked him what the plan would have been.

They were to take the boat along the river, sightseeing as they went, to where a limousine was waiting. There they would disembark, the car would take them and their bags to nearby London City Airport where they were booked on an early-afternoon flight to Nice. Another boat there, bigger, and with a crew, would take them to Monaco, which was only about twenty kilometres away. This would be their base while they visited, swam and attended the casino. 'Poor angel,' he had stroked her hair, 'you've been to Monaco, *non?*' He reached into his suitcase and showed her a picture of the palatial boat they were to have used.

Miserably, she had shaken her head.

'"Would you still like to go? When you get better?" he goes. And of course I could only nod. I was afraid to talk. I felt if I opened my mouth or made any sudden moves, like throw my arms around him to show him just how much I'd love to go to Monaco, I'd barf all over his cream leather and his priceless Turkish rugs. They looked priceless anyhow.'

She managed not to. He helped her up to the quayside, put her and her luggage into a passing cab, and then, having instructed the driver to take her back to the Montcalm, told her to get to bed and rest for a while. 'He kissed me then, girls, for the first time, and said he would come to the hotel as soon as he had dealt with the boat and the limousine and redone all the flight and boat arrangements on both sides of the Channel. 'I think we will take the cab all the way to the airport tomorrow, *non?* No nasty motor on the river! And the waters of the Mediterranean are calm. *Au revoir.*' He had handed the cabbie two twenty-pound notes and waved her off.

Although it was not yet eleven o'clock, the storm, added to the remnants of Friday rush hour, had created havoc with the traffic.

They crawled along and when Dina, still feeling awful, got back to the Montcalm, things got even worse. They had no booking for her. She checked in anyway, figuring she could sort it out with Manolo when he got there. 'He had really swept me off my feet, girls. I had no suspicions whatsoever. Not then.'

But when she woke up and looked at her watch, she had slept for two hours and it was just after two o'clock in the afternoon. She rang down to the front desk: no one asking for her, 'no messages, madam.'

And that was the last she saw of Mr Kacoslodakis, if that indeed had been his name. He had deleted himself from the chatroom, as she discovered when she used the hotel's WiFi facility.

It was not the last she had heard of him. Between leaving him and booking into the Montcalm, her credit card account showed three large purchases. A blonde, very well-dressed woman of approximately Dina's height and with the same kind of haircut had gone into three separate jewellery establishments in Bond Street, all reputable, within a single hour. Her face did not show on CCTV since, seeming to know where the cameras were, she had kept her head low over the jewellery counters. For £15,500, using the credit card, she had bought a man's watch, Patek Philippe, Calatrava series, 18-carat gold with black alligator strap; in the next place she chose a diamond tennis bracelet, 4.7 carats of gems set in white gold, for almost £22,000. Her third purchase was the most expensive, an emerald ring set on a bed of diamonds. All in all, the retail value of the items came to the sterling equivalent of approximately €72,000.

The police had no trace of anyone by the name Dina gave them.

His plan, they told her, had depended on the weather. Had she not seen last night's forecasts for storms over the south-east? The warnings of traffic chaos and so on?

She hadn't. But she did ask what, in their opinion, he would have done if the weather had not acted to plan.

'There's always a back-up,' the female officer told her. 'He wouldn't have used the boat, or the Monaco story. He might have talked about Paris by Eurostar or even the Highlands of Scotland via the sleeper train. He would probably have taken an urgent call and told you to go on without him, something like that, that he would fly or helicopter to join you. He might even have made the romantic gesture of throwing your mobile phone overboard in the Thames under the pretext that your romantic tryst should not be interrupted by intrusions from the outside world. Don't feel bad, Miss Coyne. It's also possible your champagne was spiked to make you feel ill. One way or another he would have got you. You're not the first and you won't be the last. They operate in groups. The boat was probably stolen from some yard or other – I'll check our records. All it cost this guy was the price of a dinner, an air ticket, a night in the hotel and a few odd pounds. You even paid for your own chocolate, right? He's good. He made a great return for such a small investment. He might keep the watch – they love flashy watches – but the other jewellery will be sold. That's realistically the best chance we have of catching him or his accomplices. We have perfect descriptions of the woman from the shops involved.'

'But where was the card skimmed? How did that woman know my pin to use in the shops?'

'When you used the card in the coffee shop, was anyone standing close to you?'

'Yes. That Maitre d'. He moved behind me. I thought he was

being respectful and not looking at what I was doing – was it him?'

'We're checking that. He's bound to have had his ducks in a row. Day off today and not at home. A legit employee, or so we're told. So far. Someone along the line was working with the gang. We're checking the false ID on the chatroom as well. Needle in a haystack. And you can be sure that whoever it was or wherever it happened, the equipment was dumped the minute it was used.'

'The more she talked, the worse I felt,' Dina said. 'The guy was probably not of Turkish or Argentinian parentage at all: false names are part of the deal and a lot of them are from Eastern Europe or some of the new places that used to be part of Russia.'

We all concentrated on our food. When the tension got too much for me, I pointed to the jacket: 'At least you have your lovely Balmain. That's something positive to pull out of the débâcle. You probably wouldn't have treated yourself otherwise.' I was thinking of the homemade *frou-frou* she wears to my Christmas dos.

'And my Jimmy Choos and my very expensive Alberta Ferretti cocktail dress,' she said sadly.

'How expensive is very expensive these days?' This was Mary.

'You don't want to know, Mary. Ah, to Hell.' She shrugged. 'Why wouldn't I tell you now? It's not in the same class as an emerald and diamond ring, I suppose. For that dress you wouldn't see change out of four thousand – and before you ask, the whole ensemble, including the shoes and the nightdress and this,' she rattled the relatively cheap charm bracelet, 'cost the guts of ten grand. And that's sterling.' She looked angrily at Mary, who stared her right back down. Sometimes, cancer or no cancer, Mary can be a pain in the arse. I could think of nothing further to console

Dina and there was a pause while again nothing was heard at our table except the sound of knives and forks and glasses being placed very carefully and precisely beside plates.

After a minute or two, Dina crumbled. 'I know. I know. I'm ridiculous. A laughing stock. You're right. All of you. And before you start denying what you're all thinking, don't bother. I can see it in your eyes. I made a great target, didn't I? That policewoman didn't say it out loud either but I could see it in her eyes: 'This foolish, foolish, ageing woman who fell for the flattery of a young handsome man.' Ten a penny for people like so-called Manolo or whatever his name really is.'

We chorused our denials and support and did the best we could to cheer her up. The alcohol helped (viz the second bottle of wine) and I think that by the end she was laughing at herself in a healthy way. Anyhow, she assured us she would not be on the breadline as a result of the escapade: 'But if it happened again, which it won't, I promise you, I can't guarantee that I won't be coming to yiz looking for handouts!

'And another thing: I'm retiring from sex. I'm letting my hair grow, all of it, everywhere, ladies. A relief, really, when you think of the amount of maintenance involved! The dress, by the way, has a boned bodice to keep everything in place. It's come to this! All for vanity – well, I'm through pulling everything in and propping everything up. It's droop, flop and bulge from now on. You'll see. Big lesson, girls. Well learned! Watch this space.'

TWENTY-NINE

22 July 2013

My Big Day! Happy birthday, Maggie!

It's been more than three and a half months since the last meeting of our Club that day in the Gresham, and sadly, in my opinion, it's possible that today's could be the last ever. The last full one anyway, I think, as I stare through the window from the comfort of my bed.

What's more, today's is no run-of-the-mill meeting. It has apparently morphed from a mere lunch into an Early Bird dinner in Chapter One at six o'clock. There's posh! Because it's my birthday and I'm being treated, I've been allowed no say in the matter, other than to confirm that this particular restaurant is OK for me. It is. I'm far enough away from memories of disputatious conversations with Derek in that place to be able to relax and enjoy it.

To add to the sense of occasion, Mary is picking me up in a taxi at half past five 'so you can have a few jars – and before you start getting all thrifty on me, absolutely no buses. It could be pouring and you'll be getting your hair done, so there'll be no standing out in the wind and rain. All part of the birthday service, Maggie!' I always get my hair done on my birthday. It started when I was with Derek because I knew his 'surprise' for me always involved going out for a meal. Since then I've just kept it up.

I absolutely love the feeling of someone fiddling with my hair. It's a genuine treat. I tried massage a few times but, probably because I was usually twice the size of the masseuse, was embarrassed about exposing myself. Having my hair done is far more relaxing and the results more obviously boosting.

Mary has had big news recently. Somehow, she has managed to find funding for the fairy project.

I know! I'm wondering too. This country is in recession, half the world is starving but some organisation – I keep forgetting what it's called but it has something to do with folklore – is willing to splash out on what is literally a fairy story. They've given her enough to pay a researcher for one day a week, or she can clump up the days, her choice. And there will be travel involved, particularly to Scandinavia and Germany. In the way such things tend to happen in our small village called Ireland, word has gone around and she has even been invited to participate in a TV documentary series called *Spooks, Spirits and Fairy Phenomena*. She's full of it, and after what she's been through, who would begrudge her?

She has asked if I would mind her coming to fetch me a little early this evening as she needs to look something up in the Writers Museum, which is beside the restaurant. 'It's so handy, Mags. I'll need only ten minutes, that's all. You can come in with me, do a bit of browsing while I find what I want.'

I reach for my coffee cup on the nightstand. Cold. Again. Got up half an hour ago, went downstairs, made coffee, brought it back up, put cup on nightstand, got into bed again, forgot to drink it. It's one of my least interesting quirks. I couldn't count how many cups of cold coffee I've poured down the sink. It used to drive Derek crazy when we were together. Unlike me, he always insisted on real coffee whereas I keep my cafetière for 'good'. Ignoring the ring of scum on the cup above the level of the coffee, I punish myself by drinking it. It still contains the same amount of caffeine, doesn't it?

Another few minutes here, I think – justifying my laziness by convincing myself that the water is probably not hot enough yet for the shower. I like a long, hot shower. Don't know what I'm going to do when they start charging us for water next year.

July, my birthday month, usually disappoints on the weather front. I have vivid memories of childhood holidays in Rush, north County Dublin. While our parents played cards in the comfort of the pub, Chloë and I were usually banished to the beach: 'Go outside and play!' As for protests that it was too cold or too wet: 'Put on a cardigan, then – and a bit of rain won't do you any harm, make your hair curly!' As a result, the two of us frequently found ourselves deafened by the sound of rain pelting on the 'roofs' of the plastic macs we held, tent-like, above our heads as we crouched on the cold, wet sand. Under hers, Chloë amused herself by making intricate X and O patterns in the sand; as for me, I would read, a difficult one-handed task when holding the mac over my head with the other. Sometimes I resorted to digging a large hole and folding myself into it with the mac as a complete cover. This only worked if there was no wind or if I could persuade Chloë to co-operate by using little rocks to peg down the garment around me.

These days, such treatment of children would probably result in them being taken into care by the HSE!

This year bucks the trend. July has been nothing short of spectacular. Ireland has opened up like an exotic flower under blue skies and warm sunshine. Wardrobes have been scoured for brightly coloured sundresses; young girls stroll the streets of Dublin as though they are boulevards. Long may it last.

Birthdays are supposed to afford time for reflection, yes? Another year over and what have I done? That kind of thing?

Let's see what boxes we can tick here.

No personal progress. No signing on for improving courses, not even for gym membership. No weight loss, no coruscating, earth-shattering novel begun, no brilliant new hairstyle to make me look like Sharon Stone. (Sharon and I share the height measurement but very little else.) Maybe I'll get a buzz cut. Might as well for all the attention my head gets me these days.

Nothing in the positive column, so?

Well, I did get Flora back but she should not have been taken in the first place so those two columns cancel each other out.

She definitely was taken, confirmation given by her vet. I'm so grateful to John Malone and his staff. I couldn't have asked for better care for her after she got home in such an appalling condition: they minded her night and day. Although I can still feel the scar, the wound on her back has healed, her pads too. While she continues happily to travel with me in the car and to go for walks with me, the most telling fallout from her ordeal is that I have now to go out with her to the back garden. If I don't, she simply stands at the open back door and collie-stares me until I give in.

It was touch and go for the first few days.

On the morning after I found her, John rang me at a quarter to seven to check on her; the subtext, of course, was to find out if she was still alive.

I had stayed with her all night. Josepha had shown me how to change the drip bags and we had gone through three when, at about four in the morning, I fancied I saw a definite improvement. Flora still could not raise her head, but the tiny indications of a tail wag each time I spoke to her had increased to the extent that they were now recognisable as such. She whimpered a little more too. I had been given little sponges on sticks, the type used in human hospitals after operations, to moisten her lips and swollen tongue. Bit by bit she was anticipating this.

By the time the vet arrived, shortly after eight o'clock, she had been able to open her mouth sufficiently for me to drip some water in via a small jug. She had slept a lot, but each time she woke, she fixed her eyes on me. I spoke constantly to her along the lines, 'I will never, ever let this happen to you again, dearest Flora. I promise you,' hugging her and trying to ignore the smell, stroking her fur.

Having examined her, John told me that she had been chained up somewhere. Two of her teeth, including an incisor, were broken: 'She's chewed her way out of captivity, no doubt about it, maybe a chain, maybe a metal kennel gate. A long way away too. They don't get pads like these after just a mile or two.' He picked one up and showed me the abrasions and swellings. 'It's a miracle she's here at all. We should take her in for a few days.'

'I can't bear to let her out of my sight.'

'She'll be OK. You can visit. But she really needs more care than you can offer, Maggie.'

'All right.'

I kept it together all the time he was disconnecting the drip and picking her up, as I followed him outside to his van, even when, very gently, he put her into a little carrying cage in the back. Before he shut the wire gate to enclose her, I reached in and patted her. 'I'll be in to see you this afternoon, Flora.' She made one small attempt to get out to me but was too weak and, eyes pleading, fell back. 'Try not to worry.' John closed the cage. 'I don't think there are any internal injuries but we'll need X-rays and so on. She's in good hands now.' Through the wire mesh door, he touched her nose gently. 'Home before you know it, girl.' Flora, still silently begging through the door of her cage, kept her eyes fixed on me. Apart from sitting beside Chloë in the speeding ambulance more than ten years ago, the hardest thing I have ever done was to turn away from her, leaving her in that cage. I couldn't look as they drove away.

I reach out now to touch her. She's there, safe and sound, in her old spot beside the bed, snoozing with her back against the base. 'Will we get up to face the day, Flora?'

She stands, stretches and, with one of those little licks on my bare arm, looks expectantly at me: I'm for that, Maggie. Let's go.

Boiling the kettle for a replacement coffee downstairs, I continue with my listings.

In the positive column, my little group of friends is still intact, up to today, anyhow. I'll miss 'little Jean', as I continue to think of her although it's a misnomer: she's as important to the group as any of the rest of us; we're interlaced like the five Olympic rings, interdependent like cogs of equal importance in a functioning machine. So much has happened to each of us in our communal world, especially in the last six months, that I think we have a good chance of remaining close, even if it is only via Skype from on board the Lady Jean.

Mary is going through a terrifically upbeat phase right now. Apart from securing her funding, she has come through all her treatments with flying colours. Medics are cautious with their predictions, of course, and it's still too early to say whether she's out of the woods for ever. She has been warned not to take anything for granted but so far so good. She found the radiotherapy even tougher than the chemo but, thank God, didn't need surgery. Her hair has started to grow back. Not hair as such, at present her head resembles a pale-ish coconut shell.

With my help, she completed her (far more modest than we originally envisaged) redecoration project in time for her niece's arrival at the beginning of this month. In the end it boiled down to wall paint, new curtains and carpet, a set of IKEA screens to divide the room at night, along with lots of throws, rugs and cushions, a few vases and other accessories. The flat is less like a souk now, more like a room from the IKEA catalogue. It's as welcoming as ever although in a different way. Less snuggle, more cheery bounce. And although she hasn't broached this yet, when Ramona has finished her summer course, Mary is thinking she might hire her for two months as a researcher. 'She's so intelligent and amenable, Mag. She's fantastic – and she's used to researching. Wouldn't it be great?'

Yes, Mary is at present over the moon about everything – including having renewed contact with her brother, who came for Ramona's first week. She is so busy now she has barely time to see me for the odd coffee. I haven't yet met the niece, who herself is busy with college.

No fresh news about Jean, who is packing, unpacking and packing again in view of the cramped quarters and skimpy storage she faces for the next year. She is not complaining. The lustre of her love affair shines brighter than ever.

Once again we have lost touch with Dina. None of us has been able to raise her for the past few weeks. But before she vanished, she did send us a flurry of mobile-phone messages, telling us she was 'going travelling' but to count her in for today. No need for psychology degrees or lengthy analysis here: we all agree that she was far more shaken by that adventure of hers than she let on at the time. After that day in the Gresham, we tried to gee her up, telephoning, individually meeting her for coffee and so on, but her confidence was shattered. No-brainer. My guess is that she has gone somewhere like the Seychelles for a decent holiday or even to a recuperative spa. Long term, I don't think Dina is destined for poverty, chastity and obedience!

Lorna is slowly coming to terms with her loss. I have met her quite a lot, as lately as yesterday when, after I left Chloë at Merrow House, I drove over to hers. James was there. No startling developments in that situation but he has been taken on full-time by the solicitor, who will fund his training as a legal clerk. 'And who knows how far he can go? He could be a solicitor himself some day.' We were in Lorna's kitchen and she smiled at him across the table where we were taking tea, as we the Irish think the English would say. 'Wouldn't that be grand? He's certainly clever enough!' She has met his adoptive family and, as far as I can judge, they're all coming to an accommodation, undramatic but, I think, incremental. I have to say James is still astonishingly attractive. You'd be proud to be his – auntie?

I mentioned Chloë there.

Well, I had a scare with her. It started in May, on 10 May to be precise, when I received the phone call from Merrow I had always dreaded. 'Would you like to come in for a bit of a chat, Mrs Jackman?' It was the director, the friend of Pauline (the Gimp) Dwyer.

I wouldn't, but of course I didn't say that. 'Is something wrong? Has something happened?'

'Best not to talk over the phone. You'll be collecting her later, but could you come in a little early and we can talk before you do?' It was a Friday.

'Of course.' My diary was not exactly bursting with entries, although that weekend I had a deadline for 500 words about a 'tri-autathon' on a local beach, a mass abseiling on a (lowish) cliff, followed by a wheelbarrow race and a communal paddle to raise funds for an autism charity. Cutting-edge Pulitzer Prize stuff. But, as I always say, it'll put a few buns on the table.

I won't bore you with the details of the meeting with Merrow's director, my trepidation, her calm unflappability. To my relief, however, the essence of the problem was the reverse of what I had feared: they weren't trying to get rid of Chloë, she wanted to get shut of them. 'It's up to you, and to Chloë herself, of course. We're not a prison, but I think her current routine suits her. She has the best of all possible worlds, split between home and here.'

The father of my sister's best friend Delphine was being re-located by his company, Apple, to headquarters in Cupertino, California, and of course his family were to move with him. 'Chloë is reacting badly – and again this is just an opinion – but I believe her reaction is impulsive. We think she'll settle down again after a few weeks, given the chance, but over the past days, she's been rather difficult.'

Understatement.

The goings-on over the next week would have tried the patience of Mahatma Gandhi. Suffice it to say there were tears, tantrums; for me there were daily attendances at Merrow. There were fruitless attempts at reasoning, not just by me but by the house psychologist, the carers and the director. At the end of it, the director and I came to an arrangement that, yes, I would take her home, but that her place would be held open for her for a month. Naturally that part was not conveyed to Chloë and she was elated when we lugged her belongings into the house and up the stairs to her room.

I did welcome her, genuinely. My most fervent wish for her had always been that she could develop a 'normal' life. But what I hadn't appreciated until she was with me full time was how institutionalised she had become, especially around food and mealtimes, which brought its own time problems. Mary was going through radiotherapy during that period and between driving her every morning, and helping her attend to the half-refurbished flat, it was hard to keep to a mealtime routine with Chloë, and I didn't want her stuffing herself with popcorn or chocolate. Flora, still fresh from her ordeal, had taken to following me around the house just an inch from my heels; she needed minding too. Then there were my bits and bobs of journalism. I was meeting myself coming back.

There was something else as well. Up to the time Chloë came home, I had been meeting Derek, almost in a clandestine manner. I felt as though I was having an affair, especially because I was lying to Mary, albeit by omission. Somehow it was like being unfaithful to her because she had been such a stalwart during the break-up and right up to the present. If Chloë had been responsible for the naming of our Club, Mary had initiated its formation in the first place.

So I told nobody and always insisted on eating in currently unfashionable restaurants where I hoped I would not run into anyone I knew. I was honest in explaining to Derek why I couldn't meet him openly for the present: 'I don't want anyone to jump to any false conclusions.' To my surprise, he went along without complaint.

Anyhow, as it transpired, these outings had now to stop immediately. I couldn't have kept them from Chloë without making an accomplice of her. 'It's only for a month, initially,' I said, when I rang him. 'Chloë needs my full attention for now.' I braced myself for an explosion along the lines of *here we go again*, but none came.

'I could come to the house?' he offered.

'Derek!' I was appalled at the suggestion. Talk about complications.

'All right, then, but you're saying this is to be reviewed in a month?'

'Yes, but it's up to her, mostly. I think she'll miss the companionship and the routine. It's a lovely place. But I want to emphasise, Derek, that at present I don't know which way she'll decide. It's not up to me.'

'OK,' he said, and down the wire I fancied I could hear a long-suffering vibe. But there was also something new. Could it have been a note of understanding? Understanding about Chloë? Maybe having children had been a catalyst for this new, softer Derek.

I hadn't realised until then how I would miss my nights of — what, apart from the food? Certainly not of passion. Of mischief? Childishly, I had enjoyed the sneaking around. It was like being a teenager again, simultaneously thrilled at your own daring and fearful of the consequences if your parents found out. Imagine! Fifty-eight today – what a dork!

Anyhow, the long and the short of it is that I've been seeing him. I would have been seeing him tonight, as it happens, because it's a Monday, but even before Mary had told me about changing lunch to dinner, he had cried off to facilitate some kind of special event, so important he thought it was worth opening the restaurant and paying the staff premium rates. 'It's for a conference group, forty-three of them. High net worth. I couldn't pass it up. Sorry. I'll make it up to you.'

'No need.' But I was disappointed – actually a little aggrieved. I had been looking forward to drifting from a celebratory lunch to dinner with Derek – and it had become quite nice being with him ...

Careful!

OK. I'll be careful. Anyhow, I reassured myself, I was the one who had taken charge of this ongoing 'whatever it is' between us; cancellations were up to me, not him. He had accepted the role of supplicant. Proper order.

In the meantime, the situation with Chloë resolved itself quite quickly. Two and a half weeks after she came home, it had dawned on her that I could not be at her beck and call every minute of every day, with meals on tap at regular hours and so on. With the other demands on my time, it was not physically possible so she was alone a lot. I came home from Mary's one afternoon to find she had packed her bags. So, now we're back to our old routine.

I look at my watch. Up and at 'em, time for my shower.

Afterwards, when I'm passing through the hall with Flora at my heels, I prop up my pathetic display of birthday cards – only three this year as of this morning's post delivery. However, I'm meeting my circle of friends later. That'll be at least four more. (What a dweeb I am, still counting at my age. But who'll know except myself?)

The first, obviously handmade at Merrow, is from Chloë; the second is from my lovely librarian friend – and the third, carefully anodyne with a picture of a lighthouse on the front, is from Derek, one of those LEFT BLANK FOR YOUR OWN MESSAGE. Inside he has written: *Happy Birthday, Derek.*

What's missing is the one I get annually from my photographer friend. I've kept a sheaf of them from over the years – he usually goes to a bit of trouble, sending me something personalised showcasing one of his own shots, usually connected with something or someone he knows I like.

Maybe he just missed the post – or maybe he forgot.

I'd hate that, actually …

Time passes pleasantly for the rest of the morning – I even watch a bit of daytime telly without a guilty conscience – and by half past two in the afternoon, with Flora walked and fed, and a piece filed for one of the provincial papers on the rash of mobile phone thefts in Dublin and other cities, I'm in the hairdresser's chair. Another treat. Katrina Kelly, the chatty woman with the Julia Roberts smile who owns K2, operates out of a salon on the Cabra Road not far from the house and, as far as I'm concerned, is a genius with fine, flyaway hair like mine. Whatever she does, she manages to make it seem full and glossy, even fashionable, so much so that when she's finished, even I like my lumpen self in the mirror. As I leave the salon to walk home, I'm in high good humour, especially as the rain has stopped. I've bought a new summer coat and nice sandals and my steps are light.

K2 is one of a little row of shops and just as I'm passing, my photographer friend, yes, that one, the one I've kept up with all these years and who FORGOT MY BIRTHDAY is coming out of the newsagent's. 'God,' he says. 'Mag! I hardly recognised you. You look terrific. What's your secret?'

'Good hairdresser.' I smile at him. 'And you're not looking so bad yourself, pretty swish, I have to say.' He was wearing chinos and a white T-shirt under one of those multi-pocketed photographers' jackets, shabby from use but somehow stylish. 'So what's up? Never go anywhere without that thing, do you?' I point at the camera swinging from his shoulder.

'Still gives me a living, and now that he's an Irishman, you'd never know when I'd run into Tom Cruise or even Wozzilroy – hang on!' Before I can react, gunslinger-like and just as fast, he has brought up the camera and snapped me.

'That's not fair! I didn't have time to arrange my face.'

'All right. Arrange it now.' He snaps again.

'Will you stop this?' I'm laughing – and he snaps a third time.

'Leave it, for God's sake!' I turn my head away and, when I'm sure I'm safe, look back at him. 'Great to see you, Tom. It's been too long this time. I've missed our lunches – when was the last one? Whose turn was it to ring?'

'Happy birthday, by the way, did you get my text? And it's your turn to ring me – I'm in the clear!' He grins, and I notice, not for the first time, that he has great teeth. Tom Cruise teeth, now that the star has been mentioned. He's actually very good-looking, this guy: I've often wondered how and/or why he never remarried. Touch of grey around the temples – must be in his late forties now, maybe even early fifties, I guess, but wearing exceptionally well, as do many men, quite unfairly.

While I rummage in my bag for my phone, he concentrates on replacing his lens cap. 'So what's up, Maggie?'

I pull out the phone. His text is there.

Tried to get u at home no joy. Hpy bday 2day. Talk mayb l8er 2day if u availbl 2 take call! T.

'Sorry, Tom, mustn't have heard it with the hairdryers.'

'No worries. So what's going on?'

'Loads as a matter of fact – tell you what, why don't I fill you in over a coffee? We can catch up – there's a place two doors up.'

'Unfortunately, I can't – I have to get these out to the client. Rush job!'

He's still fiddling with his lens cap and hadn't sounded as though he'd found it all that unfortunate that we can't get together. He's being a bit offhand, if you ask me. 'Oh, that's all right,' I'm careful to sound airy but, as in the case of the missing birthday card, I'm disappointed. Nice things are supposed to happen to you on your birthday. It would have been nice—

What age are you, Maggie Quinn? Cop on!

'Look,' he says then, with the lens cap still not seeming to catch properly, 'we'll definitely have a catch-up lunch soon. I'd love that, genuinely. It's just that I'm in a rush right now. So promise you'll ring me?'

The bloody cap clicks on at last and he looks back at me. A bit guarded – or is that just my imagination? The tone had sounded far more encouraging, though, and I smile at him. 'Of course. As early as tomorrow. What are you doing in this neck of the woods anyway?' I know he lives in Rathgar, on the south side.

'Papping you!' He laughs. 'No, I was shooting a few models in bikinis up at the bandstand in the Phoenix Park. Commercial gig. They had to hold giant bananas, would you believe. I'm on my way back home, just popped in here to get Panadol for a splitting headache. If any of these are halfway decent,' he indicates his camera, 'I'll send you a copy, OK?' Quickly, he kisses my cheek and draws away, walking a few steps backwards, smiling as he goes. 'Love the coat. You really do look great, Maggie. You're doing something right! Be in touch! I mean it – it's been way too long. I miss meeting you!'

'Same here.' But he has turned away, is hurrying off, and I don't know whether he heard me. I watch his retreating back but he doesn't turn again, and after a couple of seconds, I head for home in the opposite direction.

There was something different about him today. He was kind of jumpy but … I can't put my finger on it. Bikinis and giant bananas? Could he be a little hangdog about me having witnessed this lowering of standards?

But he's never made a big deal about what he does. He's freelance, and whether it's war zones, sunsets or bikini bananas, 'If it pays and makes good pictures, I'm there,' is his motto. Commercial stuff pays promptly, apparently, keeps food on the table. But maybe he's doing it as a nixer and didn't want anyone to know.

Anyhow, I'll find out when I ring him tomorrow and, in any event, meeting him on my birthday has to be a good omen. So, with his compliment ringing in my ears, Chloë's birthday card from Merrow – *mirabile dictu!* – in my handbag and the sun warming my face, I see nothing ahead this evening but blue skies, good food and great company.

THIRTY

Mary, who won't hear of any contribution from me, pays off the taxi. It's still intermittently cloudy but the sun has triumphed and the evening is warm. It's rush hour and, with the proliferation of diesel cars, the city air is dense with fumes. At least, it is where we are, having stopped in front of the old Coláiste Mhuire premises, empty now but destined, I hear, for great things if the City Council can find the wherewithal to fund the regeneration of this side of Parnell Square.

As I wait on the pavement, another taxi pulls up behind ours and Dina gets out of it. 'Fantastic.' I walk over to her. 'You're an early bird for the Early Bird, aren't you? Mary and I have to go into the Writers Museum for a few minutes. You heard about the funding for her project?'

She stares at me, puzzled. 'Funding?'

416

'Oh, you don't know?' I fill her in.

There's some hoo-hah going on with Mary and the taxi man: he can't change a fifty for her, apparently. I don't want to get involved. 'So,' I say to Dina, 'you look a million dollars. You're as good as your word – you're wearing your Alberta Ferretti!'

'Yeah.' She lets down her midnight blue pashmina to afford me the full effect. The dress is wonderful. One-shouldered with a full, asymmetrical skirt, it's fashioned from leaves of black lace over a nude lining. 'It's gorgeous, Dina. So where have you been? We were all wondering.'

'Tell you later. It's a long story.'

She seems distracted, glancing at Mary, who, thunder-faced, is now approaching. 'Idiot! This day and age, you'd think a taxi-man would have enough change, even if it is the beginning of his shift. Hi, Dina! You're a bit early.'

'Hi.' Dina sounds curt.

'I have to pop into the museum up here for a few minutes before the restaurant. Maggie's coming with me.' Mary sounds just as unfriendly. What's going on with these two? Maybe it would be best to separate them until we're all present. 'Hey,' I go, 'sorry, but here's an idea. Mary, why don't I go straight to the restaurant with Dina? It'll give you freedom to do your stuff without worrying about me being bored. We can wait in the bar – and maybe Lorna and Jean will be early too. Anyway,' I turn to Dina, 'I'm dying to hear all about your latest adventures.'

'Sure,' but Dina hesitates. 'Look,' she says then to Mary, 'maybe if she's going in with you, I could come too. Happy birthday, Maggie, by the way! Looking forward to it!' Then, to Mary: 'I've passed that museum tons of times, always wondered what it was like inside – we've plenty of time, so why don't we do that?'

417

'OK. Sure – come on,' Mary says, and moves off, leaving Dina and me to follow, me wondering if I've suddenly developed halitosis.

There is a short flight of stone steps leading to the doorway of the museum, and when we get inside, Mary goes straight to the woman sitting behind a desk in the small lobby and greets her by name. 'Are you taking the tour?' The woman smiles but then looks at her watch. 'We're closing in half an hour, and I think our guide has gone already, so I'll let you off the fee.' She must have said this thousands of times. She sounds as if she's learned it by rote.

'How much is it?' Dina asks, rather ostentatiously, I think.

Could some kind of money competition be going on between herself and Mary? Stay OUT of it, I warn myself.

'Seven euro fifty,' the woman says, 'but seriously, ladies, you'd need more time so you'll have to come back to us for the full tour. Just go on ahead for now.' She winks at Mary.

Dina and I follow Mary up a rather nice staircase. A hubbub coming from one of the rooms at the top gets louder as we approach. 'Must be a function,' Mary calls back to us. 'They rent out a couple of rooms up here for book launches and things like that. Could be some famous author – will we have a look?'

'It's probably by invitation …' but she ignores me and goes inside.

Making a face at Dina over my shoulder, I follow her in and, as I am wont to do every time I go into a new room, I look up. Don't know why, it's just a habit. This time I am well rewarded: although there is bright sunshine outside and the room boasts several large windows, there is a beautiful chandelier, fully lit, hanging from the ceiling. I'm admiring it when I'm aware that the hubbub has died, to be replaced by applause, scattered at first, then augmented by cheering.

Oddly, right under the chandelier, holding glasses of wine, are two colleagues from my newspaper days, sub-editors with whom I'm now merely at the Christmas card-exchanging stage. Over the cheering, I go across to say hello: 'Haven't see you for yonks. Are you here for the book laun—' Behind one of them, I spot Derek, arms in the air, applauding.

I look to my left. Lorna. Jean. Jerry.

Dina has passed me out and, grinning widely, is standing beside Mary's landlady, Mrs M, as she is known to all and sundry. Beside her is a really lovely blonde girl, tall, American teeth, well-fitting jeans. Has to be Ramona. Olive is beside them with her two children, who are dancing up and down with excitement. The little girl is wearing a dress adorned with gauzy angel wings.

For some reason, Katrina the hairdresser is there. Done up to the nines and, rivalling even Dina in the glamour stakes, she looks every inch the star attraction — is she launching a book about hairdressing? But how is she connected to all these people? As I stare at her, the woman from the desk downstairs comes in to stand beside me in the doorway. She, too, is smiling broadly now.

Then I see a blow-up photograph of myself. On an easel, festooned with fairy lights. It's the one taken this afternoon. The third one. The laughing one. Standing alongside it with my librarian friend is the man who took it. Grinning so widely you'd worry his face would split apart, he's still wearing the chinos but has changed into a shirt and a very nice sports jacket.

The seconds ping-ping as I recognise more and more people I know. If you have ever been the subject of a surprise party, you will understand that realisation is a slow burn. Shock. Paralysis. Disbelief. Jitters. Belief. Shock again and so on. As the clapping and cheering continue, I notice Jean's two sons and one of their wives with her two children. The dress of her little girl, too, bears a pair of angel wings.

And there's Chloë, standing beside the director of Merrow House. With them is the Gimp – sorry. I mean, there's Pauline Dwyer. And beside her, unmistakably recognisable despite her age and different hairdo, is Brainypants.

What?

And behind Derek, standing together, are Declan from Chapter One next door and Robert from the Troc; there's James McAlinden with Lorna – and, dear God, behind them is a fully decorated, artificial Christmas tree.

In July!

As I try to compute all of this, I see Mary signalling to one of Jean's sons, who goes towards a piano against one wall. He sits, plays a chord, waves like a conductor to the crowd and everyone breaks into a lusty chorus:

Happy birthday to you!
Happy birthday to you!
Happy birthday, dear Maggie,
Happy birthday to you!

While I'm still standing, stunned, just inside the room, they segue into 'For She's a Jolly Good Fellow'.

They finish that. Cheer again.

Mary, whose headscarf today is bright yellow with orange highlights, makes hushing gestures at them and they subside. She now walks to the piano, where Jean's son still sits.

'Ladies and gentlemen – and children, I'm no speechifier and we all know why we're here so I won't take up much of your time.

We decided, our Club and I, to do this for Maggie. Why her? Because she deserves it. I personally am living proof how much she deserves it.' Her voice cracks but she talks through it. 'We all do. And you all wouldn't be here if you didn't know it too. She's the Christmas genie who gives from the bottom of her big, generous heart, not only at Christmas but all year round. I'm going to call on Patricia, John, Carol and Martin Junior to come forward and to make this real for us.'

The four excited children, eyes dancing, march towards the piano and, with a little shoving and pushing, settle into a neat little row. Dazed, I join in the applause as one of the little girls reaches over carefully to straighten the wings on the back of the other. Then, given a note from the piano, they pipe up, sweetly but raggedly, to soft accompaniment:

Away in a manger,
No crib for a bed
The little Lord Jesus
Lays down His sweet head
The stars in the bright sky
Looked down where He lay
The little Lord Jesus
Asleep on the hay.

While they sing, I'm still trying to come to terms with all of this and look round the room at the fond expressions, at Chloë's, at Derek's, at everyone's as they move away from watching me to watching the children. Tears, from what source I can't tell you, rise to choke me when they get to the last verse.

Bless all the dear children
In Thy tender care
And take us to Heaven
To live with Thee there.

I'm barely holding it together. To the childless, the sweetness of unaffected childish voice reaches great depths.

But it's not yet over. Mary shushes us again and, reaching behind the piano, takes out her clarinet. 'First public performance, ladies and gentlemen. Be kind. I'm glad my teacher isn't here. He's been rehearsing me on this, but I'll have you know, this instrument is pretty unforgiving.

'For God's sake,' she waves down at me, 'would you ever come to the front, Maggie Quinn? We all worked our arses off for this! Show a little appreciation!' And when I take a few steps towards the front, she takes a few steps towards me. 'I know you hate this right now, Mags, but you'll appreciate it later. I promise you. Because this is a sincere "thank you" on behalf of us all, all your friends, past and present, for just being you, Mags. As for me, I can't thank you enough, my lifelong and best friend.'

Mary, stronger than I am, as always, clears her throat. She closes her eyes, takes a deep breath and, after a few hesitant notes, gets into her stride and, well in tune, slowly plays a verse of 'White Christmas'. During this, one by one, Jean, Dina and Lorna come to stand beside her, and when she gets to the second verse, they join in, singing. The piano follows, then, a few voices at a time, some humming, some singing, until everyone, even the woman from the desk below, is joining in, swaying, many holding hands, with the clarinet soaring over the lot.

Everyone, that is, except me. I can't. I'm crying too hard. I can see Derek looking at me. Chloë as well. I don't care. I'm lost. This is so – so poignant, so deep, so – I can't help thinking – so nakedly loving.

When the singing finishes, more applause, two girls carrying refills of red and white wine come in. People bear down on them but many divert to crowd around me; you could slice the delight in this room and serve it at a wedding.

'Were you really surprised?'

'You had no inkling, you weren't just pretending?'

'Here – here's a tissue. Are you just thrilled?'

'You so deserve this, Maggie. Wasn't Mary great to get so many people here?'

My responses are dazed as people pull at me and hug me and touch my shoulders from the back. 'Katrina! You're here,' I say to her. 'You were in on this too? And this afternoon … ' Then: 'Oh, my God,' to the two sub-editors, 'I can't believe you two are here after all these years – how are you?' Turning in response to a plucking at my sleeve: 'And you? You're here too? I can't believe it.' It's the director of Merrow House, who, with Chloë beside her, now gives me a bear hug. She's stocky but diminutive and has to reach up. 'Chloë!' I say, over her shoulder. 'Did you know about this?'

'No.' Chloë, possibly as overwhelmed as I am, is nevertheless smiling.

'We thought it better not to tell her until this afternoon. She got quite a land, didn't you, Chloë?'

'I sure did. You're my sister, Margaret, and you never said! Did you get my card?'

'I did.' I hug her tightly. 'As for this party, I didn't know – really I didn't. I suppose that's why they call them surprise parties.'

'We'll be off home now, if that's all right with you?' The director looks at Chloë. 'We have a date with a TV programme!'

'Sure.' I hug Chloë again. 'Thank you so much for coming,' I say to the director, and then, to Chloë: 'See you Wednesday, chicken. Love you!'

She does her little patting thing on my shoulder but backs off when we're interrupted by Robert and Declan, both of whom have to slip away to work. They hand envelopes to me (vouchers, I discover subsequently, for their respective restaurants) but before I can thank them properly I have to turn away to talk to others. Katrina has to dash off: she's doing a wedding rehearsal for a bridal party.

That kind of intercourse and more goes on for a good fifteen minutes, during which I can do nothing but repeat my thanks and appreciation. Derek, I see, is hanging back, and when I get free, I cross to him. 'You knew! That's why you cancelled.'

'Mary got me at the restaurant. She's good, you know. She told me about finding your school friends too. There's just one thing. I managed to get Fiona to agree that I could see the girls next Saturday. We're going either to Funtasia in Bettystown or to the zoo. I'd love you to meet them. Will you come with us?'

I'm taken aback, not just by the unexpected request but by his adoption of the winning little-boy expression I recognise from the past. Suddenly, from all around us, everything recedes and for a few milliseconds I experience a moment of luminous, almost filmic clarity, insulating Derek and me from all noise, glow and glitter leaving the two of us, spotlit, facing one another on a huge dark stage. Although we are approximately of an age chronologically, I am now so much older than him. Dealing intimately with the resilience and courage of my group of women friends in the face of trauma has taught me that mind games and the quests to be one step ahead of others' mood swings or reactions are destructive.

While still in learning mode, to my astonishment I find I have grown up. And this grown-up does not want to be used by Derek because, right now, he needs a mother, a nurse for himself or a nursemaid for his children.

Just as abruptly as it had arrived, the light insulating us is wicked away, letting in the celebrations of the throng. Derek, still waiting for my response, continues to wear 'that' expression. He hasn't noticed my brief mental absence and, in present circumstances, I can be neither rude nor harsh. It wouldn't be fair after that period of renewed contact. 'I can't tell you why, right now, Derek,' I say gently. 'It's not appropriate with all this going on here, but I don't think what you suggest would be a good idea.'

His reaction is of puzzlement, but before either of us can say any more, we're joined by Pauline Dwyer and Brainypants, whose name, to my horror, I cannot recall. 'You remember me?' she asks breathlessly. 'Isn't this great? And who's this very handsome creature?' She turns to Derek.

'Derek Jackman. I'm the husband of the star guest.' He is back in Public Derek mode, turning up the charm quotient. 'And you are?'

'Mairead McGovern,' she says. (Daeriam! Am I glad to see you right now!) She doesn't look like a Mairéad, more like a careless Penelope: hair, clearly self-coloured, all over the place, sequined denim gilet over a well-washed salmon-hued blouse. A little overweight but exuberantly so, the seams of her black pencil skirt holding, just, over wide hips and protruding belly. Obviously cares little about fashion or about what other women think. 'Just a housewife, I'm afraid,' she goes, then: 'Derek Jackman? Are you the famous chef?'

'"Famous" is a derogatory word in my profession but, yes, I'm a great chef, Mairéad. You must come to my restaurant some time. You'll be made welcome. And how do you do?' He's addressing Pauline.

'This is Pauline Dwyer,' I rush in, 'another school friend. Thanks so much for coming, both of you.'

'Well, here we are, all three together,' Brainypants trills. 'Isn't this gas, though, Maggie?' and then, explaining to Derek: 'Mary, Maggie and I were the three clever clogses in our primary-school class. Much good it did me, though.' She harrumphs.

'Don't mind her,' Pauline chips in. 'She's a happily married woman, very happily.'

'Children?'

'No, thank God.' The other woman is blithe. 'Can't stand the little buggers, although that was lovely, wasn't it?' She looks fondly across at where the children are now sitting, again in a row, sucking soft drinks through straws.

'Mairead's a champion bridge player,' Pauline says. 'Could make the Irish team if she was interested. I'm her partner. I should know.'

'Not interested.' The other woman harrumphs again. 'Who needs all that practice? Bridge should be a hobby.'

'And they own some of the best racehorses in Ireland. Meaning that they win races.'

'Which means I have to live in the sticks. In my opinion, they should knock down Tallaght and give us back the land!'

'Well, I'll leave you girls to reminisce. Work calls! I'll give you a shout, Maggie, and we'll talk again about Saturday.' Derek busses my cheek. 'Happy birthday!' For him, the job is oxo.

'Nice man.' Brainypants looks after him. 'Ye're divorced, are ye?'

'He's on the market, Mairéad! Good catch. Excuse me.'

I leave them, and the next twenty minutes or so are taken up with a whirlwind tour of the room, thanking people and continuing to express surprise. It's only as I'm walking around that I notice garlands of artificial holly, complete with berries, on every available surface. They've really worked at this, I think, in danger of tears again, but the atmosphere is so jolly, I manage to hold it together as, in ones, twos and threes, people leave, hugging and kissing me and making vows to bring me to lunch.

Tom Jennings, my photographer pal, is among the last to depart. 'You deceitful man!' He being as tall as myself, it's a pleasure to hug him. 'There were no models or bikinis, were there?' Still holding his arms, I draw back and stare at him. 'I shouldn't hug you, I should spank you!'

He blushes. 'Maybe you should! Will you forgive me?'

'Of course.' I hug him again. 'I'll ring you in the morning and we'll make arrangements, even though you don't deserve it.'

'I'll be good from now on. Promise.' He kisses my cheek. 'Talk tomorrow. And, Maggie ...' He hesitates. 'Here's my card.' He hands it to me.

'Yes?'

'Please don't forget to call, all right?' He's blushing harder.

'I won't.' Impulsively, I kiss him – the merest touch – on the mouth, and when I pull back, I delight in his evident shock. 'There you go! That was for being so devious – but so good! The airbrushing is great, by the way. We can discuss how you do that tomorrow! Bye now.' I turn away, tingling at what I've done. No time to analyse it. It was spontaneous and it was Maggie and I'm tickled pink as, almost dancing, I head across the room to join my women pals, who are beavering away, packing decorations and armloads of gifts into three boxes the museum woman has given them. Tomorrow will be fun, I tell myself, as, unnoticed for a few seconds, I hang back to steady myself. Then, while the other three go to sweep off the holly and untwine the fairy lights from around my portrait, I go over to Mary, who is alone. 'I could swing for you, you know. But I'm so grateful. How can I ever repay you for this?'

'I told them no presents,' she grumbles, stuffing yet another gift-wrapped package into a box. Then, gruffly: 'Joint effort. Jean's idea in the first place, remember? She was the one who said that our meeting should be on your birthday. Jerry brought the Christmas tree, already decorated, on one of his lorries – he's gone to fetch it so we can get it out of here again, Lorna got the kids together to teach them the song, Dina paid for the hall and the wine. All I did was make a few phone calls. Lisa wishes you a happy birthday. She says to tell you she's sorry she couldn't come.'

'Lisa who?'

'The Right Honourable Lisa. Monaco.'

'You tracked her down?'

'She would have come but she's hosting some charity do in Cannes tonight. Says she'll definitely visit us. And of course we're both invited to Monaco. I told her we had to get Lourdes over first.'

'Ramona is gorgeous but I got to say only a few words to her.'

'She's nice all right. She thinks Ireland is brilliant. Wouldn't be surprised if she stayed.'

'You don't sound too excited about that.' I frowned.

'It's nothing.'

'It has to be something. Up to this very moment you were thrilled with her.'

'I still am. It's just … '

'What?'

'Did you see the way herself and James took to each other?'

I shook my head. 'No, I didn't. They're two young people. The only two of that age here tonight. Of course they'd gravitate towards one another. Anyway, legally they're adults.'

'I'd never forgive myself – Jeffrey would never forgive me. He's trusting me!'

'Mary! Now who's worrying about ducks going barefoot? Stop it. Thanks to you, we've had a really lovely evening. Don't spoil it on me. It's going to take me weeks to digest all this.'

'It's not over yet. You hungry?'

'You mean the dinner wasn't just a ruse? We're having dinner as well as all this?'

'Derek's invited us for half past eight. He's gone to organise it. We've time for a drink. We could leave all this for Jerry and his truck.' She looks across the room to where the others have bundled everything neatly. 'He's to meet us at the restaurant.'

'I'll take the boxes of presents.' But I'm gobsmacked. We're the big-deal conference people for whom Derek is opening his restaurant tonight and paying his staff a premium. 'He's opening the restaurant just for the five of us?'

'James is coming, Olive and the kids, Jerry, of course, Jean's sons, their wives and kids. Two big tables, I gather. So,' she's looking expectantly at me, 'where'll we go for a jar in the meantime?'

'Half past eight?' I suddenly remember Flora. 'I expected to be done and dusted and home after the Early Bird. I have to feed my dog. Why don't we all go to my house? Just the five of us. The others know where to go.'

'Sure.'

'I have plenty of drink.' I always have, seldom drink it because I don't like drinking on my own. 'I think I might even have a bottle of champagne. You deserve it, Mary. By the way, how come you included Derek in this shindig?'

'D'you think I came down with the last shower, Mag?'

'I don't know what you mean.' But I feel telltale colour rising into my neck.

'Yes, you do. You've been sneaking around the city with him on Monday nights. If you didn't want word to spread you should at least have gone to Meath or Wicklow. But Derek is known in every restaurant in the country now.'

I stare at her. Why hadn't I thought of that? I was so concerned about hiding my own big, clodhopping self that it had never occurred to me Derek was the one everyone would recognise. 'Sorry.'

'Don't be. Just be careful. You're a big girl now, no pun intended.' She allows me the ghost of a smile. 'I'll support you no matter what you decide.'

'No need, as it happens, Mary.' I can see the other three have finished and are about to approach us from across the room. 'Tell you later tonight if I get a chance, but otherwise I'll give you a buzz tomorrow. OK? Don't worry,' I put a hand on her forearm, 'it's all good. I think you'll approve. Listen, quickly, before they get to us, what was going on earlier with you and Dina? You weren't exactly friendly to her when she arrived outside.'

She looks at me as though I have two heads. 'Get a grip! She nearly wrecked the surprise!'

You can read too much into any situation.

'Hi there!' I say to the others, who have now arrived. 'We're all going to my place and we're going to have champagne. OK? Real champagne.'

One great legacy of the weird Celtic Tiger days is the proliferation of taxis, and the five of us don't have to wait long until one of those people-carriers comes along, big enough to take all five of us and my boxes. As I get in, I feel as though holes have been punched in me to let light in and sorrow out. And maybe this new and exhilarating spirit of mine will fade but, right now, I doubt it. I truly have the sense that, like a snake, I have shed a skin.

I gaze lovingly at my friends as Mary gives my address to the driver.

Jean looks ten years younger than she did this time last year, and it's all happened since she met her Jerry. Since we last met, her hair has been cut boyishly short, the knitted twin sets and sensible skirts have given way to dresses, modest enough but flattering. Today's is a simple red sheath with cap sleeves. You'd feel like reaching out to play with her. As though she were Barbie.

Lorna's resilience is shining through. It's been, what, seven months now? The first year is the hardest, of course, but she's getting there. For this evening, for me, because she's so unselfish she's made an effort, she's had her hair styled and it's possible she's even had a professional makeup. Her outfit, a stiff dress and jacket in a kind of buff shade, is a little mother-of-the-bride, to tell you the truth, but it's the effort that counts, isn't it? Other than this, I haven't seen her in anything except black since Martin's funeral.

Dina, I've already told you about. She's the hibiscus among us, showy, and thereby seemingly shallow. She has a heart like butter, though, which, of course, is why she was so easily conned by that scumbag across the water.

And then there's Mary. What can I say about her? What can anyone say? I'm supposed to be the words expert, but for Mary, I can't find any that convey her depths, her intelligence, quirkiness, her downright Maryness. What she means to me. I love her to bits.

I am one lucky woman.

The trip to my house takes less than a quarter of an hour. Flora, of course, is enchanted by the influx. She still trusts people. That's quite a testament to her character.

I put down her bowl in the kitchen, give her fresh water and leave her to it, bringing glasses and the champagne into the sitting room, where my four friends are conversing quietly. 'Do you want to open your presents now?' Jean indicates the boxes.

'If it's OK with you all, I'd prefer to wait.' I'm embarrassed by such largesse, to tell you the truth.

I'm struggling with the miniature metal fence around the champagne cap when Dina speaks up: 'Wait a second, Maggie, will you? I have something more for you. Something for you all, actually, and I don't mind if you open them now or later. Maybe now is best because I should probably explain.' I put down the recalcitrant bottle while she opens her handbag and takes out four white envelopes. She gives one to each of us, marked with our names. 'They're not all the same, d'you see ...'

'What is it?' Jean, gazing at her envelope, is the first to ask. After the love-in and overheated gaiety at the museum, the atmosphere has turned abruptly sombre.

'You're probably going to fight me about this,' Dina begins, 'but please don't.' She has tightened her pashmina around her throat and is clutching it with both hands. Is it my imagination or are her hands trembling? 'What is it, Dina?' I'm staring at my own envelope, at my name written in her big, cursive scrawl. 'Please don't be shy. It's only us!' Why is she making such a big deal about what has to be vouchers?

'I'm not clever, I'm not charming, I'm not you, Maggie, with words at will – or you, Mary, with your ability to do everything. I'm just me.' She swallows hard. 'That fiasco in London was not that man's fault. It was my own. Why shouldn't he prey on someone as full of shit as I am? I've had a lot of time to think about this and I'm totally ashamed of what happened to me.'

'Dina—' Jean tries to interrupt but is hushed by Mary.

'Let her finish. This is really important to her.'

'Thanks, Mary.' Dina shoots her a grateful look. 'You know, I'm such a silly moo that if young James had been up for it I'd have gone to bed with him. Can you believe that?'

'We were all affected, Dina. It wasn't just you.' I look at the others. 'Isn't that right, girls?'

'But none of you would have gone through with it. I would have. That's the point. Dreaming and wondering is one thing, acting on those dreams is another. As I said, I've had a lot of time to think. I went away for a while – thank you for all your messages. I'm sorry I didn't answer any of them.

'Anyhow,' she drags out the word, 'I went to India. As a tourist, mind. I felt I needed something different, and I had the idea that I'd find some of the best healing spas there. Which, of course, I did. They were wonderful. I thoroughly enjoyed myself. The hotel was lovely and everything, and then, one day, I was walking along a shopping street in Mumbai and I saw the girl who had massaged me that morning. She was standing at a litter bin outside a McDonald's and beside one of the other big hotels. She had a tea towel spread over a small tin tray and she was sifting through fast-food cartons. And before you ask, yes, there are McDonald's outlets in India, but of course they don't have hamburgers, mostly vegetarian stuff. Anyway, this girl was taking cartons out of the litter bin and carefully scraping what was still inside onto the tea towel, little shards of lettuce and tomato and half bits of French fries. I dunno what happened to me but I kind of freaked. Not visibly, I didn't have a fit or anything. It just made me feel absolutely terrible. I didn't want her to see me watching so I turned and walked away.

'Anyway, next morning, she came to my room to give me a massage as usual but I told her I wanted to talk to her instead. To make a long story short, two of her brothers are dead. A sister is spastic. Her mother has cancer and her father can't find a job. She and her extended family, aunts, a grandmother, some orphaned cousins, live in a two-room shack near a rubbish dump. She is supporting eighteen people with what she earns in that hotel.

'There was no white light or amazing insight or anything like that. I was just disgusted with myself and the way I've been living. I gave her all the cash I had. I think it would have come, in euros, to just about a hundred. She refused to take it. Said she'd get into trouble and would lose her job because they'd accuse her of stealing it. But I insisted, said I was checking out that day. I eventually persuaded her, but she burst into tears. A hundred euro. I'd spend that on one meal for myself and a pal, no offence to Derek, Maggie – but in this country, in the West in general, we have no idea. None at all.

'To people like her, girls, I'm as rich as Bill Gates. And I *am* rich. But the point is, I didn't earn the bloody money, and given what happened to me in London, I don't deserve to have it. Don't worry, I'm not losing my marbles, I'm not giving it all away. I need to look after myself, but there's plenty of it.'

'How much?' Mary again. Leave it to her to ask what we've all wanted to know for years.

'My mother won six point eight million pounds in that Lotto. It came to me. After taxes and other costs and paying off my parents' mortgage and so on, the money came to five million plus. I was living in the house so no taxes on that. I got good advice and the share prices were flying at the time. I'm still getting good advice. Last time I checked, I had seven point six million. Thank you, Apple.'

You could feel the shock in the room. We had known, in a general kind of a way, about the Lotto and that she was comfortably off but not, obviously, by how much. She does splash the money around, but not remotely on this scale. And she has remained in her parents' house, which is big, but modest enough and quite shabby.

'What's in the envelopes, Dina?' Once again, Mary is the only one who has the courage to ask. The tension increases to the extent that the room seems now to throb.

'To each according to her needs,' Dina said quietly. Then: 'Jean, I want you to be able to have a good year with your lovely man. Stay in decent hotels now and then, have nice showers, swim in nice pools, eat nice meals, buy nice presents.

'Lorna, nothing can bring back Martin, but you've been through a terrible time and, although I don't know what your financial circumstances are, I have the sense that you could do with a bit of respite. Do what you like with the money.

'Mary, I didn't know until today that you'd got funding for your project. But there'll be other projects, won't there? There always are with you. And as soon as you're in the clear with the medics, you'll deserve a good break. Go to the Seychelles, trek through Alaska, whatever you want. And, forgive me for saying this, but your flat is a dump. In many ways, while Maggie is the body of our group, you're the core. The kind of engine. You're certainly the brains – begging all of your pardons! You deserve to have a place of your own. This should help.

'As for you, Maggie, I'm grateful to you most of all. You brought me into this priceless group – and kept me in it, no matter how silly I was or how badly behaved. I know you have this ongoing worry about your sister and what's going to happen to her after you pass on. I hope what's in that envelope will get that worry off your table.'

There ensues a long pause while we all attempt to take this in as she stands there, resplendent in her magnificent dress and lovely shoes.

'Would it be silly to ask for a group hug now?' Jean wonders, in a very, very small voice.

'Yes, it would!' The chorus from the rest of us is simultaneous. We're gobsmacked. None of us dares to open an envelope. I do notice, however, that none of us, including me, is protesting. I make a stab at it: 'Are you sure about this, Dina?'

'I'm sure. More than ever, I'm sure. And by the way, don't think I'm going to become Mother Teresa. This is a selfish act to make me feel better. I'll be doing something good for the world. At least for you lot first. That episode in London showed me what money really is. And don't be thanking me. I don't need it and I don't want it. If you thank me I'll cancel the cheques. I've been an idle bitch, able to doss around and live the high life, no thanks to my own efforts. That has to change. I don't know how, yet, but it will.'

After another communal pause, she turns away to look through the window into my garden. Again it's Jean, bless her, who breaks the tension: 'Maggie can write a book about us all. Why don't you do that, Maggie? You can change our names. We promise we won't sue, right, girls?'

'Thanks but no thanks,' I tell her fervently, as the doorbell rings and Flora pops her head around the sitting-room door: Will I answer that, Maggie, or will you?

I get up and respond to the summons. It's our people-carrier: we'd asked the driver to come back for us. I tell him to wait and go back to the sitting room where Mary, Jean and Lorna, still sitting, are clutching their sealed envelopes, Dina still with her back to them at the window. 'What about the champagne?' I ask the room, really for something to say. 'Will I send the taxi away for a while?'

But the sitting three stand up and Dina turns round from her vigil. 'Nah,' Mary says. 'Let's go. The others will be waiting in Derek's place and, anyway, I had no lunch.'

'Me neither,' Lorna says.

'I had only a sandwich. I'm starving.' This is Jean. We're all behaving as though life is proceeding, and will proceed, exactly as usual. That those white envelopes we hold are figments of our imagination.

Through the window, recently vacated by Dina, I can see that the sun is already losing height, but something flashes, way, way up in the sky. It has to be the space station. Up to the time he came back to earth in May, I had followed the daily tweets from the Canadian colonel, Chris Hadfield, revelling in his extraordinary and detailed photographs (Erris Peninsula? Dublin by night? Brazilian rivers curling like golden florists' ribbon through the dense carpet of bright green?), giving us earthlings a spaceman's view of our wonderful, enigmatic planet in all its beauty and savagery. Making a mental note to ask Tom tomorrow about how good the pictures were (taken, apparently, with a relatively simple camera), I go over and peer upwards. The station is there all right, reflecting the sun in tiny bursts of light: 'There's the space station passing by – I miss Colonel Hadfield.'

'Who's Colonel Hadfield?' This is Dina.

'Let's go.' I turn back to face the room. 'Don't want to keep Derek and the others waiting.'

'No,' says Mary drily, 'certainly mustn't keep Derek waiting. He'll be playing the Hugh Grant part in the miniseries of our book.'

I ignore her. Time enough to tell her tomorrow that, while her support is always welcome, it won't, after all, be necessary in this instance. In the meantime, I'm going to have fun. The food will be terrific – I'll never take away from Derek's genius in that department – and hopefully at some time in the future I'll be a welcome client in his restaurant.

Tonight, in different ways and to differing degrees, Maggie Quinn loves everyone. Everyone. I have the rest of my life to be serious, and tomorrow is another day, blah blah, but for tonight I'm one of Mary's fairies, a flitter. I'll flit, I'll flirt, I'll hover in the attention and bask in the lurve.

'Sorry about the champagne, girls,' I tell them now. 'Next time maybe we'll actually drink it. Come on. I'll tell you all about Colonel Hadfield in the cab on the way.'

ACKNOWLEDGEMENTS

As the number of books increases, my list of acknowledgements grows shorter – because that circle of friends who joined me during different phases of my life and who continue to walk with me have been thanked many times privately and publicly and they know who they are.

For this book, may I single out for particular gratitude Breda Purdue and my editor Ciara Considine from Hachette Books Ireland, to both of whom *The Winter Gathering* is dedicated – and my UK editor Charlotte Mendelson, and all at Headline. Hazel Orme, my copy-editor, has been with me through all my books from the very beginning and has saved me from embarrassment on many, many occasions

I am grateful to those who work so hard for these publishers on behalf of infant books, including mine, in their care. So, in

Ireland, thanks to Ruth, Siobhan, Edel, Joanna, Jim and all at HBI. Margaret Daly has retired now but she was a stalwart for many years and I would like to acknowledge publicly her help and faith. Gratitude to the novel's jacket designer Ami Smithson.

For their persistent encouragement, I owe a particular 'thank you' to Patricia Scanlan, Bernard Farrell and Dermot Bolger, and to Frances Fox, who 'gets' me more than most. Thanks to my agent, Clare Alexander, and of course I remain more than grateful to my loyal readers, without whom there would be no point to the endeavour, would there?

Finally, profound love to my immediate family: Kevin, Adrian, Simon, Catherine, Eve, Declan and Mary. I don't think I have adequately expressed how much each and all of you mean to me, and hope that now you know.

ABOUT THE AUTHOR

Deirdre Purcell was born and brought up in Dublin. She had an eclectic set of careers, including acting at the Abbey Theatre, before she became a journalist and writer, winning awards for her work on the *Sunday Tribune*. She has published twelve critically acclaimed novels, most recently *Tell Me Your Secret* and *Pearl*, all of which have been bestsellers in Ireland. She adapted *Falling for a Dancer* into a popular four-part television mini-series, while *Love Like Hate Adore* was shortlisted for the Orange Prize. Deirdre Purcell lives in County Meath with her husband. She has two adult sons.